I0769769

LADY DARING

LADIES LEAST LIKELY

MISTY URBAN

OLIVERHEBERBOOKS

All rights reserved.

No part of this publication may be sold, copied, distributed, reproduced or transmitted in any form or by any means, mechanical or digital, including photocopying and recording or by any information storage and retrieval system without the prior written permission of both the publisher, Oliver Heber Books and the author, Misty Urban, except in the case of brief quotations embodied in critical articles and reviews.

NO AI TRAINING: Without in any way limiting the author's [and publisher's] exclusive rights under copyright, any use of this publication to "train" generative artificial intelligence (AI) technologies and/or large language models to generate text, or any other medium, is expressly prohibited. The author reserves all rights to license uses of this work for the training and development of any generative AI and/or large language models.

PUBLISHER'S NOTE: This is a work of fiction. Names, characters, places, and incidents either are the product of the author's imagination or are used fictitiously. Any resemblance to actual persons, living or dead, business establishments, events, or locales is entirely coincidental.

Lady Daring Copyright 2025 © Misty Urban

Cover art by Dar Albert at Wicked Smart Designs

Published by Oliver-Heber Books

0 9 8 7 6 5 4 3 2 1

Most young ladies spent the morning before their court presentation preoccupied with their dress.

Henrietta Wardley-Hines was engaged in a kidnapping.

Rescue, she reminded herself as the carriage moved down Clifford Street, the clip of the horses' hooves muffled by the early morning fog. This was a rescue. And a test of her worthiness to enter the exalted ranks of the Minerva Society.

A test she was determined not to fail.

Only the night soil men and milkmaids were abroad at this hour, and they stepped aside for the smart phaeton and its stylish passenger. While Henrietta had dressed plainly for their covert operation, Lady Bessington's picture hat and her enormous muff of coppery fox fur proclaimed her an expensive lady likely returning home after a night of entertainments. A woman engaged in dashing activities, perhaps, but nothing nefarious.

Henrietta could afford to be neither dashing nor nefarious, given all that hinged on the success of the looming court presentation, etc.

But their abductee had agreed to be carried away. Perhaps

that would excuse them before the magistrate if the girl's master called the constable.

"I don't see her," Henrietta whispered, peering down the empty alley as her groom, riding the lead horse, turned into the mist-enclosed mews. "You don't suppose she changed her mind?"

"She'll come." Lady Bess stayed tucked beneath the calash hood pulled down against the chilly air. "I informed his lordship that I could find Nancy the service he requests. He's quite eager for it to be performed."

Henrietta's stomach turned, not alone from the ammonia scent of horse leavings and cesspools that lay behind the row of expensive town houses.

She agreed with her whole heart with the objects of the Minerva Society, dedicated to improving the lot of women of all ranks and means. But there were so *many* who needed assistance. So many a woman who, by wile or force or sheer bad luck, had been left with children she couldn't support, debts she couldn't repay, dreams she couldn't rebuild.

While so many men went along their way, unrepentant of the lies they told or the innocent hearts they'd broken.

A cold droplet worked its way down the collar of Henrietta's worn riding habit. Busy London, waking behind the looming fog, suddenly felt immense and lonely, a world apart from the quiet estate where she'd been born and raised.

"We're not returning Nancy to him, are we?" she asked.

Lady Bess gave a serene smile. "Not unless she wishes, and I very much doubt she will."

James slowed the glossy pair and grumbled from beneath the turned-up collar of his greatcoat. "Cavey business, Miss Hetty, gettin' in the way o' swells."

"Let me down here, James, and mind you don't spatter Lady Bess with mud."

"As if I would!" James retorted. "Fine steppers your Titans are, but gentle as lambs. Sir Jasper chose a cracking come-out gift."

Henrietta's heels smacked on the cobbles as she jumped down, and she whisked aside her wide hem before it fell in the muck. She wondered what her father would make of the use to which she was putting his extravagant gift.

She stood with the line drawn clear before her, and because she was the calculating sort, she knew full well what lay on either side.

Plain Henrietta Wardley-Hines, a northern mill owner's daughter, could racket about London attending debates and writing petitions and enjoying as much freedom as her family would allow, which admittedly was a great deal.

Henrietta Wardley-Hines, daughter of the newly knighted Sir Jasper, would have sharper eyes upon her once she made her curtsy to the Queen. She would enjoy a wider reach for her business interests and greater support for her causes, or so she hoped. But she would carry the weight of that rank and its dignities.

If she withdrew now, she could remain safe and above reproach. She would be accepted, mostly unobjectionable. The girls would grow up unshadowed, or only a little shadowed, by their eccentric half-sister, and neither Charley, nor Clarinda, would have grounds on which to lament or disapprove her behavior.

If she withdrew now, she might not lose Lady Bess's friendship, but her ladyship would certainly not sponsor Henrietta's invitation to the Minerva Society.

And she would still be Henrietta, inheriting the stubbornness of both her parents, unable to look away from injustice if she could right it. Meddling, Charley called it. Henrietta rather preferred to think of the Society and its patronesses as a formidable force for good. Precisely what Henrietta Wardley-Hines wished to be in the world.

She rapped on the bright blue door of the carriage house.

Her knock echoed down the narrow alley, along with the stamp of hooves as James turned the horses. But no one threw up the sash of a window to shout "Fire! Murder! Thief!"

The door cracked open, and a young woman in a drab muslin frock and large mob cap slipped through. "Nancy?"

A short, portly man appeared behind her, and Henrietta's heart sank. He wasn't supposed to be here.

The maid clutched a cloth bag and stared with wide eyes. The girl's fear roused Henrietta's protective instincts. Nancy might be her age, but what a world of difference in their stations. What a difference in what they could expect of life.

"I expect her back tonight, and you won't make a hash of the business."

His lordship had the flaccid, calculating face of a man who set his own pleasures above all, no matter the cost to others. The look he flicked over Henrietta's faded habit and unadorned bonnet held utter scorn.

His eyes narrowed as he took in the carriage. Henrietta guessed he identified its occupant despite the lowered hood and the fog. "And you'll keep quiet about it, too," he said.

Henrietta bit back a retort. Here was another man who thought of the women around him as objects provided for his comfort, convenience, and use. His property. But more tastes ran toward sweet than tart, her great-aunt Davinia always said, so Henrietta forced a brittle smile.

"I presume you've furnished Nancy with funds?"

The maid sucked in her breath. Henrietta would have laid odds that after this man had assailed his servant and left her with child, he expected her to pay to be rid of it. Most men of his station would turn the girl off without a character, setting her and her babe-to-be in the street. That he was here meant she could negotiate. She extended her hand, hoping that, in the dim light, he wouldn't see her trembling.

His lordship glared and fiddled beneath his coat, then thrust a small purse in Henrietta's direction. "Now be a good girl, Nan, and no fussing." His oily smile dripped with warning. "I'm the one taking care of you. Remember that."

Henrietta hefted the slight weight of the purse. It could hold only a few shillings. "Come now, milord!" she chided, mouth dry at her own audacity. "If you want her taken proper care of, you'll have to do better."

Nancy shrank as her master growled. Henrietta held in a sigh of relief as his lordship withdrew a handful of guineas and smacked them into her palm.

"There, and be gone with you," he snarled. "I'd best not see you again, you conniving wench."

"That you won't, sir!"

She should have made some attempt at disguise, Henrietta realized. Next time, she would. Euphoric and shaking, she led Nancy to the waiting phaeton, where Lady Bess pulled down the folding seat in welcome.

James watched with slitted eyes as his lordship slammed the blue door shut. "Best bite the gold, Miss Hetty, and make sure 'e 'asn't shaved the silver. Don't trust a flash cove with the gelt, I don't."

Henrietta hauled herself up the high step, kicking aside the heavy skirts of her habit. "Away, James, before he decides I've robbed him."

"Well done, Hetty." Lady Bess bestowed a kind smile on their guest, who looked as sick with fear and deliverance as Henrietta felt. "Now, my dear Nancy, where shall we take you?"

"His lordship said..." Nancy trailed off, her gaze falling.

"But he is not here to command us, is he?" Lady Bess tilted her chin. Her eyes shone beneath the brim of her hat as James urged the horses down the mews and back to fashionable Clifford Street.

Henrietta smiled as Nancy's mouth fell open. "Milady, you can't mean— His lordship thinks—"

"Oh, I know what he thinks," Lady Bess said. "I told him what he wanted to hear. But you may decide your own fate now. Are you acquainted with the Benevolence Hospital? The matron is prepared to take you."

The Benevolence Hospital for the Support of Orphans and Women in Distressed Circumstances, one of several philanthropic causes upheld by the Minerva Society, was currently full to the rafters with souls in need. But part of her test, Henrietta was sure, entailed not countering Lady Bess, much as argumentation might run in her nature.

Nancy shifted. "I-I'd like to go to me sister, mum. She's a widow now, and if I say I'm one too, we can set up together and no one'll talk." She placed a hand on her middle. "And me boy'll have cousins to play with."

Lady Bess nodded. "Do you wish me to tell him where you've gone?"

"Oh, no, mum. I don't want 'im to have a thing to do wit' us." Nancy's eyes flickered to Henrietta. "I know it's wrong, as e's got in a sinful way, but—"

"You did nothing wrong, Nancy," Henrietta said with firm conviction.

"I love 'im already," the girl whispered. "And I never 'ad a thing o' my own to love. Not really."

Henrietta's last hesitations whisked away with the parting fog. She had both feet in the pudding now, as her great-aunt Davinia would say, and she regretted nothing. This was her cause, and the Minerva Society her people. She had found them through the grace of her sainted mother, and she would do whatever it took to be accepted within those ranks.

They set Nancy and her bag down at the coaching inn that would convey her to her sister's. Henrietta slipped a few guineas of her own into his lordship's purse, and Lady Bess added to the weight. They accepted Nancy's tearful thanks and waved her off with good wishes.

Henrietta's sense of victory wobbled as James turned the carriage toward Lady Bess's townhome. That line was in stone, and there was no crossing back.

"I wonder what his lordship will do when Nancy doesn't return?"

Lady Bess stroked her muff. "I know him, and I know his circumstances. He can't touch Bessington, and if he wants to accuse me of anything, I'll make the full story known. That he asked me to relieve him of an unwanted child he'd forced upon a helpless girl in his employ."

Henrietta swallowed the taste of triumph turning sour. "Once I'm presented, I'll likely be recognized on these little escapades."

"We can find other uses for your talents, like leading debates." Lady Bess's keen eye turned soft. "This is a grand step for you, Hetty."

Henrietta tried to laugh. "A great leap from the daughter of a tradesman to the daughter of a knight, and a fair way to fall."

"Apollonia would be so proud of you, dear."

Henrietta sniffed away the sting of tears. Meetings and debates of the Minerva Society were open to all, but only a few comprised the elite inner circle, the Daughters of Minerva. Her mother had been a votary, and if Henrietta became one too, she would prove herself Apollonia Wardley's daughter at last.

"You'll sponsor me, then?"

James drew to a halt before stately Bessington House, in St.

James's Square, and Lady Bess gathered her skirts as a footman emerged to help her alight from the carriage. "You're well-liked, Hetty, and the others will approve of your helping me this morning. But remember, your Aunt Althea and Pell Mell have influence in places I don't. They move in different circles."

Henrietta nodded, swallowing hard. In the Minerva Society, she'd found a company of equals, a fit for her energies and convictions the likes of which she hadn't known since school at Miss Gregoire's. She dreaded being thrust into higher circles, but if a presentation at court could promote the causes dear to her heart—

"Very well," Henrietta said. "I'll go through with it."

Lady Bess squeezed Henrietta's gloved hand. "Courage, m'dear. A levee at St. James hasn't been the death of a British citizen in any number of years."

"Then why does it feel as if I'm St. Perpetua being thrown to the lions?" Henrietta muttered. Lady Bess laughed and waved her away as James urged the horses to walk on, carrying Henrietta back to Hines House to prepare for her afternoon on the rack.

HENRIETTA, having no head for fashion, didn't suspect her court gown was not quite the thing until she perceived her brother's expression as she approached the blue parlor, her broad and ancient skirts sweeping the floor like a soupy wave.

"Good Gad, Hetty! Everyone's going to be looking at you. Who put you in that awful rig?"

"Great-aunt Davinia sent her old court wardrobe for my use." Regarding the half-closed doorway of the parlor, Henrietta threw her elaborate train over one arm, clamped a hand to her towering headdress, crushed the panniers at her sides with her elbows, and launched herself through the doorframe. Once in the room, her train fell, her hoops exploded, and she twirled and weaved like a trained bear to keep her padded, powdered wig from toppling off her head.

"Aunt Althea said I would do. You don't agree?"

Sir Charleton Wardley-Hines snorted and lashed his leg with his decorative sword. Henrietta's elder by two years, he had come to London after university to be entered on the Official Roll as the 8th Baronet Wardley and had thereafter taken up with riotous circles. He made no secret of the burden he felt at being called upon to pause in his dissolutions to launch his unfashionable sister upon society.

"Aunt Althea don't want you to shine down Marsi," he grumbled. "I hope she hasn't given you notions about this Season. Best not put too fine a point upon it, old girl—you ain't likely to take."

Henrietta paused before a small gilded mirror and poked at the ostrich feather drooping over one eye.

Once, her goals had simply been to set her stepmother's household running smoothly and settle her brother down with a wife, then withdraw to her estate of Birch Vale to acquire her mills and experiment with reforms. Then her sister Fanny died, her father was granted a knighthood, and it was decided the family would remove to London for Jasper's investiture and to put her stepmother, Clarinda, back in spirits.

"I don't expect to *take*, Charley. Too old, for one thing." At five-and-twenty, she was well past the age for a society debut. "And for another—well." She pointed to her face. "The family resemblance works in your favor rather than mine."

On Henrietta, the bold Wardley nose was too big, the mouth too broad, the square jaw decidedly unfeminine, and the high, spare cheekbones too severe. Her eyes were flat gray, almost colorless, her hair a dusty, unremarkable red brown.

But she had a keen mind, many interests, and a voice that carried well in crowded lecture halls and debating rooms. Add to that, she had nice, strong, square teeth. Henrietta bared them at herself in the mirror.

"I think Hetty looks quite regal."

Miss Marsibel Pomeroy flowed into the room, a vision of silk and lace. Henrietta beamed at her. One of the benefits of London was finding her shy, mousy cousin had bloomed into an interesting, if rather reserved, young lady.

"You needn't be nervous," Marsi assured her. "'Tis a long, tedious wait, then over in a moment, and the Queen won't speak a word to you."

"Unless my costume comes apart, or I faint." Henrietta prodded the stiff panel lined with lurid green ribbons pinned to the front of her robe. "Anyone who claims women are the frailer sex has never spent a day in a stomacher."

Charley rolled his eyes. "Let me guess. Another favorite complaint of the Minerva Society is the style of female dress."

"I have been granted the honor of leading the next debate, and I may select the topic," Henrietta said with pride. "The papers say the great ladies of Paris have taken to garbing themselves like peasants in the republican cause. Imagine the liberty of movement!"

"Henrietta Wardley-Hines." Lady Althea Pomeroy sailed through the parlor door. "You will refrain from spouting Jacobin sentiments at the Queen's levee." She twirled a finger in the air. "Turn about."

"Olympe de Gouges wrote in her *Declaration* that female citizens of a new French republic should hold the same rights as men." Henrietta kicked at her heavy mass of skirts, submitting to her aunt's inspection.

"French sentiments, suitable for French subjects. I guessed that Clarinda would not trouble herself about your jewels, so I brought something for you." Aunt Althea held up an enormous collar of emeralds and diamonds.

Henrietta caught her breath as the cold, heavy necklace settled around her throat. "Another gift from Aunt Davinia? I would rather see it given to the Minerva Society's collection drive for the settlement in Sierra Leone. This collar could support any number of freed people in a new life."

"Henrietta Eglantine Wardley-Hines." Althea pressed a finger to the small frown that Henrietta often seemed to provoke. "It may have amused Aunt Davinia to send you to that eccentric girl's school, but you are in London now, where society is not as forgiving. People still say my sister Apollonia threw herself away on a mill owner, and that was three decades ago."

Charley slapped his leg with his sword again, and Henrietta smoothed away a scowl. Jasper Hines may have been born in a northern crofter's cottage, but by the time he came to court the eldest Wardley daughter, he could offer her five mills, a shipping business that brought his raw cotton in and ferried the finished cloth out, and a gracious estate in the Rossendale Fells in return for her hand and her ancient name, which he adopted.

"And your father may have reached even higher for his second marriage," Aunt Althea went on, guiding Henrietta to the mirror above the mantel so she might poke the drooping ostrich feathers back into Henrietta's wig. "But everyone knows he offered the Earl of Warrefield a fortune for Clarinda."

Henrietta choked beneath the necklace, the gown, these judgments she so loathed. Aunt Althea's society didn't care that the Wardley-Hines empire, which included canals, shipping interests, and textile mills, employed the inhabitants of five parishes and endowed almshouses, orphanages, and schools across two counties. They were involved in trade, and trade was demeaning.

"I suppose people will say that my father bought his knighthood as well," Henreitta said. For the Wardley-Hines income had also furnished a large loan to the Crown to support a militia protecting British interests in Mysore, and the conclusion of hostilities in March resulted in honors all around, including the Order of Knight Bachelor for Jasper Wardley-Hines.

"I cannot help what people say, Henrietta," Aunt Althea said. "I can only beg you to remember, for your brother's sake and mine, that the Wardley name still carries some dignity."

As Henrietta moved away from the mirror, the catastrophic sound of rending fabric filled the room. She slapped both hands to her mouth, holding back a giggle at her aunt's horrified expression.

"I fear that portends the state of my dignity, Aunt Althea!" Henrietta intoned, striking a theatrical pose which did not amuse her aunt in the least.

Marsibel, the peacemaker, rushed to her rescue, untangling Henrietta's skirts from the firedogs and fetching Lady Clarinda's sewing basket from the table. Henrietta spoke around the pins in her mouth as she repaired her hem.

"Miss Wollstonecraft writes in her *Vindication* that it is a disservice to teach young women only to concern themselves with appearance rather than equip them with practical skills. I wonder if that would be a fruitful topic for debate?"

"Miss Wollstonecraft would be a great deal more amiable if she would dispense with her endless complaints about women." Aunt Althea frowned at the white ribbon around Henrietta's sleeve. "Still, Hetty? It has been a year."

"Not quite. Lady Mama is wearing one too." Henrietta blinked back tears.

Charley scoffed. "Can't see why you're still mourning Fanny when Clarinda's adding to her nursery again. I suppose Jasper wants a boy this time?"

"Mama, do you suppose I—?" Marsibel indicated her own sleeve.

"No, my dear. The child was not your full cousin, only Henrietta's half-sister. Now, where is Sir Pelton? It is time we set out."

Sir Pelton Pomeroy strode into the parlor with his ceremonial sword swinging at his side, the badge of his order gleaming upon his chest, and his wig curled, powdered, and padded almost as high as the ladies'. Once a hot-headed MP from Devon known as Pell Mell, Sir Pelton had risen to a respected and crucial post in Prime Minister Pitt's cabinet, and no matter what the young dandies might think of him, he would wear his wig into his grave.

Sir Pelton bowed to his wife and daughter, then turned to his niece. "My dear Hetty. You look—"

"Like a dodo, or an emu," Henrietta confirmed. "A big, fluffy, flightless bird." She swept up her train and grimaced as she glimpsed an exposed pin.

"I think there's a portrait of your Aunt Davinia wearing that dress in one of the royal palaces," Sir Pelton said. "In fact, Her Majesty may recognize it."

"All to the good if she does," Henrietta said. "Then no one will inquire why the daughter of a man who made his fortune in cotton mills is wearing miles and miles of silk."

They filed out the door and commenced the complicated task of fitting three sets of hooped skirts and headdresses and the gentlemen's swords into the Pomeroy town coach, and Henrietta wondered briefly where Nancy was. Well on her way, or safely at her sister's already?

Henrietta envied her. Nancy was also embarking on a new stage of her life, but one of freedom and self-governance. The coachman cracked his whip over the set of six matched bays, and Henrietta's stomach jolted with nervousness as the coach rolled forward. She feared her new stage of life would mean fewer freedoms, not more.

Sir Pelton folded his hands over his middle and stretched out his legs. "Well, Hetty, what have you been up to this week?"

Henrietta's fingertips went cold with panic. Had her uncle heard of her exploits that morning?

"Making a cake of herself, as usual," Charley said. "Peddling pamphlets about the book rooms and tea shops, begging people for money."

"For good cause," Henrietta said. "One of the girls from the Benevolence Hospital opened her dress shop this week, and she's taken several girls on as apprentices. Tomorrow the St. Marylebone Ladies Auxiliary visits the parish workhouse." She sent her brother a lightly scolding look. "And tonight, Charley is escorting Marsi and me to Lord Ellesmere's to see his latest acquisitions."

"I advise you to tread lightly on the subject of your debate, puss," Sir Pelton said. "With the London Corresponding Society and Charles James Fox firing tempers with their radical talk, Pitt's on the hunt for any whiff of sedition. Marsi, my pet, when did you develop an interest in Greek marbles?"

"Lord Pinochle suggested he will attend this evening," Aunt Althea said.

"Surely we can do better than Pinochle for our Marsi," Sir Pelton said. "Hetty, you rely on Charley alone to keep the fortune hunters and rakehells away?"

"I am hardly a prize, with a small estate and no mill of my own yet," Henrietta said. "Even if Birch Vale does produce the best butter in the county."

"Nevertheless, there are some to be wary of," Sir Pelton said. "No flattering and fawning from a royal duke, for instance. They're cads, every last one."

"Married men of any rank," her brother joined in.

Henrietta rolled her eyes. "Do go on moralizing to me, Charley."

"Mr. Havering is often admired in the gossip columns," Marsibel said.

Her father frowned. "Heir to a viscount, but a jilt. Be polite but distant."

"Lord Alfred Highcastle?" Marsibel tried.

Charley shook his head. "Cool, very cool to him. Under the hatches, I've heard, which is why he went abroad."

Marsibel's eyes sparkled. "Lord Daring?"

Althea yelped as if stuck with a pin. "Wherever did you hear that name?"

"Oh, everybody's talking about him," said Henrietta. "And in the most scandalized tones, too. Though no one will say exactly what he has done."

"Something that ensures no proper hostess will receive him," her aunt said. "Marsibel, should he approach you—though I daresay he will not show his face in polite company—you are to cut him, do you hear me?"

"Mama!" Marsibel paled. Such rudeness flew in the face of everything she had been taught about being a young lady, pleasing, quiescent, demure.

Sir Pelton shook his head. "So much promise, that young man, but he's proved a scoundrel in the end. Pity. His father, Langford, is an excellent man to have in Lords. Can always be counted on to see sense."

"Charley," Henrietta whispered. "What is Lord Daring's crime?"

"He ruins young women," Charley retorted, ignoring his aunt's glare. "It's a sport to him. Any girl he talks to—anyone he *looks* at—unmarriageable on the spot. Yet they won't keep away! It's as if the man made a pact with the devil."

"But his latest peccadillo is despoiling the Duke of Highcastle's daughter," Sir Pelton said. "The girl refuses to marry him, not even to give her child a name. Highcastle has her mewed up in the townhouse and intends to send her abroad."

Henrietta sat back, eyes wide. The beau monde considered many shocking behaviors routine, including adultery. This Lord Daring must be truly wicked. "What will happen to the babe?"

"None of your concern. I warn you, stay away from him, Hetty," Charley said. "Daring ruins everything he touches. It's high time someone ruined *him*."

Henrietta thought again of Nancy, how her eyes had widened at the thought of determining her own future. Duke's daughter or chambermaid, they were alike when it came to the ease with which a powerful man could destroy them.

It was an intolerable injustice. Mary Wollstonecraft had the right of it: being taught nothing but to be decorative and please others, who could blame a girl for being easily led into vice? But Lady Bess was right too. Being a knight's daughter would give Henrietta a different kind of power, power that might do real good.

The coach reached the end of the long line of carriages waiting before St. James, and the others disembarked to join Sir Jasper and Lady Clarinda in one of the withdrawing rooms. Althea paused in the coach, her face set in lines of worry.

"Henrietta." Her mouth held an uncharacteristic tremor. "What your mother would have given to see you presented."

Henrietta blinked away the sudden sting of tears. "I hope to be a credit to her when I am accepted into the Minerva Society."

Her aunt's mouth hardened into a line. "Do not be the fool that my sister was, child. She gave up a great deal to marry your father. I have done what I can to make up the lack in your training, which Clarinda has sadly neglected, but I cannot think it is enough. I only hope you will do nothing to sink our name."

She exited in a swish of ruffled silk, leaving Henrietta shaken.

She felt eight years old again, motherless and washed up on Aunt Davinia's doorstep in Bath, sent away by a father lost in grief. Why should it be a shame if her mother had loved her father and enjoyed every moment of their time together? But the Pomeroys moved in a world defined by wealth and status and display. It was the world Clarinda inhabited, the world that Charley and now her father had entered, the world her half-sisters were born to.

Henrietta would lose them if she went her own way. And if she proved an embarrassment, or worse, if her escapades with Lady Bess were discovered, they might choose to send her away again. She would not be able to bear that.

But if it would please those she loved to see her bow before the Queen in an outrageous costume with an entire bird balanced upon her head, why, she would do it, and paste a smile on her face the entire time.

CHAPTER TWO

─────────

"You've done it now, you insolent puppy!" The Marquess of Langford threw the last broadside upon the pile on his desk and glared across the room at his son. "Cast yourself beyond the pale, once and for all. What should I do? Scratch your name from the family Bible?"

Darien affected a careless shrug. "If it will make you feel better, sir, I'll furnish the pen and ink."

It took all his effort not to stand to attention under his father's wrath, but Darien forced himself to lounge against the expensive marble mantelpiece that lined one wall of the comfortable library. He flicked a hand over the smart blue waistcoat gleaming with silver braid, knowing the insolence of appearing in his riding coat, buckskin breeches, and high boots would be noted.

He didn't need to glance at the portrait on the wall above him to see how much he resembled his father in his youth. Except at the age Darien was now, Cassius Bales had sole charge of an extensive estate and all its debts and incomes, while Darien wasted his youth and his advantages racketing about, seducing damsels, designing impractical machines, and generally exhibiting no shred of the sense his father had tried beating into him. He could read this lecture to himself and spare his sire the trouble.

"If I disown you, my estates go to your cousin," the marquess grumbled. "My brother's insolent, grasping whelp. Bad enough he's running Bellamy to rack and ruin, when *you* ought to have charge of it."

"You suggested, in light of my many failings, that Ratty was better suited to administer Horace's estate." Darien poked a finger at the scrolls piled on one side of his father's desk. "You haven't looked at any of my designs. My improvements could increase Bellamy's profits by—"

"Bellamy doesn't need profits!" the marquess shouted. "It needs a proper executor who can sign contracts and stand up in court. Do you know how many suits of action are backed up by now?" He glared at the pile of blueprints. "All you could teach Ratty is how to be a libertine."

It spoke to his sire's vexation that he used the cruel nickname his three strapping, rowdy boys had given their less hardy cousin Rathbone when the marquess had always tried to set an example as a gentleman.

The marquess rested his elbows on the heavy oak desk that had stood in the library of Langford House for over a hundred years, as old as the building. He had put aside his wig for this interview, and Darien saw with a start, as his father buried his head in his hands, that the griefs of the past years had streaked the steel-gray locks with white. White hair belonged to old men.

Three strapping, boisterous boys the marquess had sired, and now he was down to one. Two years ago, Horace, the sturdy eldest and by courtesy the Earl of Aldthorpe, collapsed of heart failure at the bottom of the stairs of Bellamy Hall, the estate his wife had brought to their marriage. That loss alone would have flattened a man.

But then word reached Darien, while he was drowning his sorrows in the arms of a lovely Venetian courtesan, that Horace's son, the heir, had taken a sudden fever. Darien returned in time to walk in the family procession behind the small black coffin, holding up his brother's grieving widow with one arm and his white-faced, silent niece with the other as they laid Lucretius to rest next to his father in the Bales family tomb. The memory of that awful day made Darien itch for a drink, but he knew his father would never countenance liquor at this hour of the afternoon.

The marquess spoke through the cradle of his hands. "I can't take legal control of Bellamy. It's Horace's estate, and he left it in trust for his children, with your brother Lucien as their guardian. He never would have imagined—"

His father's voice broke as he looked up to one of the newer portraits in the room, the portrait of a handsome, coal-haired young man wearing a scarlet coat and a cocky grin, his plumed hat under one arm. Seven years ago, Lucien, the marquess's second son, had taken his commission and his plumed hat and his vibrant sense of life to India to fight in the Mysore Wars. He hadn't been heard from since.

Darien braced his shoulders against the tide of old anger and grief. He had no right to still feel betrayed that Lucien, his playmate, his brother, his closest friend, had bought his colors and left for war. Certainly, he'd never meant to disappear. Doubtful he even knew of the bloody bad fortune that had felled their noble Horse and then Lucretius, the scion and hope of their house.

"Bellamy Hall needs an overseer, Darien. And I need an heir."

Darien stood by the fireplace as if carved in stone. "You have an heir," he said. "Lucien, Earl of Aldthorpe."

A tense silence followed. Darien studied the elaborate design on the rug to avoid his father's burning stare.

"He's been gone seven years, Darien. That's grounds to declare him deceased. And then you can take Bellamy in hand and look after Horatia."

Darien clenched his jaw. "He's merely traveling, as I've done across the Continent so many times. You can't—" He couldn't speak the word. Not when there had been so much death already. "You can't simply remove him. I won't support it."

"And I won't have *this*!" The marquess thumped a fist on the pile of gossip sheets. "This is not behavior I would condone from a schoolboy." He shook one paper at his son. "Have you no thought of this family? Of the name?"

"Truthfully?" Darien affected the insouciance he knew his father hated. His father angry was better than his father broken, bowed by defeat. "I was not thinking of our name while I was with Celeste."

In fact, not thinking had been the goal of his many escapades over the last several years. Not thinking about his failures, his losses, his many ghosts.

The marquess regarded the sketch in his hand. "Randy puppy."

"I look far more like a wolf in that one." Darien leaned over the desk. "And I daresay the artist has overemphasized Celeste's...charms."

The sketch exaggerated Darien's bold features with the addition of canine fangs, hair, and ears, his hands outstretched like claws and his mouth salivating. A young woman was trying to flee as her fashionable robe parted from her. The nipple of one plump, bared breast was fixed in the mouth of a canine-toothed infant, its smile as wolfish as its sire's. The caption read "My baby! My baby! Lord Daring will devour us too!"

"Lord Daring, is it? And you say she won't have you." The marquess shook his head. "Could make Highcastle force her, you know."

"Let Celeste decide for herself." Darien caught himself before he snapped at his sire. He couldn't show weakness or his father would pounce.

Darien had reason to suspect he wasn't the only candidate who could claim paternity of Celeste's babe. But the news was unlikely to sway his father or stem the tide of gossip. Darien had been the one associated with her, and public knowledge of her several affairs would hurt Celeste more than it would hurt him.

The marquess swept the papers to the floor. "All those innocents pointing their fingers—how can you have ruined so *many* of them? And not care for a single one? Your mother would hang her head in shame."

His father leaned against the hard back of his chair and rested his elbows on the carved arms. This time, his gaze went to an older oil portrait of a beautiful woman clad in vaguely Roman dress. A sheer veil floated around powdered gray hair, and a knowing smile curved her poppy-red lips. Giuseppina had been the sprig of an Italian royal family with only nominal claims to its ancient seat, but quite a prize for the sober Cassius Bales, then Earl of Aldthorpe. Everyone who knew her had loved her and called her Princess Pip.

Darien had no more than hazy memories of a soft woman who laughed uproariously, smelled of strawberries, and always had a book in her pocket. Princess Pip had not lived long enough for her hair to go white.

Darien groped for a chair beside the fireplace and sat down. His father wouldn't forgive his reputation even if he knew the truth behind it. It was status that mattered to the marquess, the respect due his title and name. It wasn't the lives of his sons he cared about, or he would show the slightest interest in Darien's designs. He would turn over heaven and earth to find Lucien.

Instead, he'd decided to move on to the next available son, the third and least, the disappointment. The marquessate and all its lesser titles, all the houses and estates, were entailed upon heirs male. The lot of it, including the mines and canals, the annuities, and the pensions and duties and debts would devolve upon Darien if his brother were declared dead in absentia.

It was not the responsibility that terrified him.

"Horace, gone." His father dropped his head again, his voice muffled. "Lucretius, gone. And God alone knows where Lucien is. If you don't marry and bear a son, everything goes to Rathbone. And you won't be received now. My line will die out. They'll lock up their daughters against you."

"They never have before." Darien's voice sounded hollow to his ears.

For all his reckless acts, real or fabricated, the marquess had never suggested Darien had sullied the name. The accusation shook him to the core. Whatever else he was or did not want to be, he was a Bales, one of the Langford Bales. The Saxon manor of Langeforde had been given to Jehan de Bailles at the Conquest, and by luck and cunning, the estate and the lineage had survived intact for the next seven hundred years.

Darien made his voice steady. "I'll still be received. You'll see. It will take more than ruining a duke's daughter to shut doors to a Bales."

The marquess shook his head. "The Queen won't have you at court, and George thinks you're worse than his sons."

"No one is worse than George's sons," Darien said, shocked. "Prinny has bastards all over the place, not to mention a certain Mrs. Fitzherbert."

"He is the Prince of Wales," the marquess said. "You are not."

"There's a levee this afternoon, some stuffy function," Darien said. "I'll go. Queen Charlotte will acknowledge me—I'll wager you anything."

His father's sad smile pained him more than anything else that had transpired in the last hour. "Not a betting man, you know. Too much bad luck."

Darien was glad he was sitting or he would have buckled at this glimpse into his father's grief. His own losses were still too much to bear. First had been their beloved Princess Pip, taken by tuberculosis while Darien was up at school. Then Lucien abandoned him, trading their childish tricks for war. Horace, gone in an instant. Lucretius, lingering in agony.

The 4th Marquess of Langford had borne the losses nobly. Darien, regrettably, had not.

"I shamed you, and Celeste's family as well." Darien drew to his feet, back straight, hands at his sides. "I ask your forgiveness for that. But I beg you, sir." He took a deep breath and met his father's gaze. "Do not bring this suit. Lucien will come back."

A light of calculation entered his father's eye. The marquess plucked the wig from his desk and placed it on his head, as if the attire of judges, court goers, and the Lords assembled in the House made theirs an official transaction.

"Very well. If you will see fit to keep this house and my name out of further scandals, I will refrain from bringing a suit this year. You can play about with your drawings and your hey-go-mad friends, and Ratty—Rathbone can continue at Bellamy Hall. But you have till the end of this session of Parliament, no later," the marquess said. "Be received. Become respectable. Better yet, find some well-bred woman to wed and bed. I won't consider any of your foolish improvement projects, but I will give you time to come to a sense of your duty."

He waved a hand in dismissal. "And pray every night, as I

do, that Lucien will come back to us, wherever in God's name he is."

"I already do." Darien bowed.

"A rich bride," his father called as he left the room. "Good family, fertile stock. Stop this business of ruining good girls for other men."

"Enough that you've ordered my reform, sir," Darien said with a grimace. "Don't press me into the parson's mousetrap as well."

"No more scandals," the marquess repeated, "or I won't wait till next Season. I'll bring my suit before the King's Bench this year, and you'll have to hope your wretched cousin hasn't reduced Bellamy to sticks and dirt."

DARIEN DECIDED to walk to his house in Jermyn Street and tossed ha'pennies to the sweepers who cleared the streets for him. He wished it were as easy to clear his head. The conversation with his father had left him gutted.

The marquess thought it another insult that Darien didn't live at Langford House, but the family townhouse held too many memories. Winters in town while his father took his seat in Lords. Romping with his brothers about various pranks while their mother attended to her meetings and projects. Later, when Horace brought down his family for the Season, the house echoed with new laughter as Lucretius and Darien bowled in the ballroom or, playing pirates, tied Horatia to the grand stair.

Darien didn't dare sleep under the same roof as those ghosts. He'd bought premises of his own from a friend he bailed out of the River Tick and filled the place with his own things, books and drawings, odds and ends from his travels, assorted friends who were as reckless and unattached as he.

Voices drifted from his library, but there were fewer old friends calling since he'd returned from his last trip abroad. Some had married; some could not keep up with Lord Daring's lifestyle. It was possible a good many shared his father's belief that his latest scandal had put him beyond the pale.

Well. Looking into the library, Darien saw there were at least two men left who would acknowledge him, possibly because they had him to thank for the roof over their heads. One was his old schoolmate, Peregrine Empson, at loose ends because his uncle refused to buy his colors so he could join the regiment as an officer. The other was his weedy cousin, Rutherford Bales, Rathbone's younger brother, who had been ordained into the priesthood but had no living and no prospects.

"What! Still have your head attached, I see." Perry slouched in an armchair next to a decanter of brandy. "Disinherited at last?"

"Not yet, though he considered it." Darien accepted the glass Perry handed him. "He threatened to have Highcastle force Celeste to take me."

Perry choked on his liquor. "Tenant for life? With that baggage?"

"Can't see how she refuses me, prize that I am," Darien drawled. "Jilting Havering, that I can understand."

"Pestilent harpy," Perry grunted. "Know yet whose babe she carries?"

"Not Havering's, and it may not be mine." Darien swept up the brandy decanter. "I'd very much like to know who else she had on the line."

"They say the duke is threatening to send Lady Celeste to a nunnery if she won't name the father." Rutherford spoke from behind the afternoon paper.

"Rufie, please tell me that my valet was not responsible for that atrocity around your neck. Also, tell me how you manage to hear gossip about Celeste when you live in my library."

Rutherford cast a self-conscious eye over his attire. "I beg your pardon. You said your servants were at my disposal. Lady Celeste is under discussion in all the coffee shops, when they're not talking about France, that is. Or you." He fussed with his cravat, crumpling it terribly.

"Perry, remind me when I get up to deal Rufie a facer," Darien said. "By the by, cousin, his lordship wants me to take over Bellamy. In fact, he wants to have Lucien declared dead and have me made heir."

Rutherford lowered his paper. A dreadful silence filled the room.

"It has been seven years, Darien," Rutherford said finally. "It is not out of bounds for him to do so."

Darien stared into his drink. "He could be rotting in some Hindoo hovel. He could be chained in a galley plying the coast, carrying silk and spices." His fingers whitened around the glass. "He could be in some sultan's prison, blinded and trapped, not knowing his own name." They'd sent inquiry after inquiry, with no result. Perhaps it was time Darien went himself, now that the latest war in Mysore had ended.

"It's a simple process," Rutherford said. "A death certificate from the coroner, and it's done."

"Not with the estate involved." Darien topped off his drink. "It will entail legal action. My father came to town to start hunting up support for his cause."

Again, that terrible silence. Perry avoided Darien's gaze. Rutherford, called by his pastoral profession, made an effort.

"Your father is concerned—"

Darien held up a hand. "Stow it, Rufie. Perry, what's to do this evening?"

Rutherford had suffered their family losses with dignified

solemnity. He had come pious and black-garbed when they laid Horace to rest in the tomb at Bellamy. It wasn't Rufie who lost the brother he loved, their solid, respectable Horse, whom his younger brothers led around by the nose and blamed when they were caught out in a mischief. Rufie came again to officiate when they ferried Horace's son to the family tomb, laying that slender, laughing, mischievous boy beside his father. Rufie had his studies and the cold promise of his faith to console him.

Darien, with no such recourse, tried to escape his sorrows with travel abroad and, when that didn't work, returned to his London townhouse and commenced drowning himself in the clubs and theaters, pleasure gardens and gaming hells, trying to obliterate the sense that he had failed his brother and his brother's son.

Waiting for the family curse to cut him down too.

"To do tonight?" Perry yawned. "The usual, I suppose. Card party at Sharp's, or we might take our mutton at the club and see what's playing at the theater. Isn't there an opera dancer you'd like to visit?" He waggled his brows.

"She's moved on," Darien said from the bottom of his glass. "What invitations have we gotten?"

"Your man put them there." Perry pointed to the mantel, where a small silver tray sat next to the clock.

There were three envelopes. Darien could usually expect a mound of invitations during the height of the Season. He read them aloud. "Dinner at Grafton's—not to be borne. Musical evening with the Snellings—hideous. And a conversazione at Ellesmere House. Fitz must have purloined some new marbles that he wants everybody to admire."

"Show your face in a drawing room? Are you loose in your top hatches? No—you're out to curry favor with the marquess." A look of horror crossed Perry's face. "*Can* he make you marry the shrew?"

"He wants me married. That much was clear." Darien grimaced.

"Well, find some unsuitable gel, then! Put his lordship's nose out of joint."

"And how is my cousin to conduct a courtship," Rutherford asked, fumbling with his neckcloth, "when any young woman he addresses at a social function is considered ruined on the spot?"

Perry took refuge in his glass. "An ugly girl! Questionable family, or a Long Meg. We'll know you won't make an offer, but his lordship won't."

Rutherford looked down his nose at the other man. "Or perhaps Darien would prefer to pursue connections that will restore dignity to the name of Bales, which, if you will allow me to point out the obvious, I share."

The words came too close to his father's chastisement. Darien advanced, and Rutherford drew back, no doubt recalling the earlier promise of a facer.

"I've had my father rattle me off already," Darien said. "Now come here."

He yanked Rufie's neckcloth out of its knot and rearranged it with a few elegant tucks. "Stop fussing and it will last the night."

Rutherford looked surprised. "I didn't know—"

"That I could dress myself?" Darien smiled without humor. "I'd be ruined if I let my man have the dressing of me. He's a poor lad from my estate who wanted to try his luck in the city, but he can't get a post without a character, and he can't establish character without having a post."

Rutherford met his cousin's eyes but said nothing. The two men had never been close, and not just due to their difference in age. Rutherford resembled Lucien, tall, rangy, with oil-black hair and the same noble, well-shaped features. Horatia, Horace's surviving daughter, had the same striking coloring.

But Rufie's shoulders bore a noticeable stoop, the Bales blue eyes were disguised behind eyeglasses, and he had none of Lucien's deadpan humor or ready, contagious laugh. Really, a man could put up with only so much from a cousin born of a second son, and one who had gone into the priesthood to boot.

Darien picked up the decanter. "Wish me well. I'm off to prostrate myself before the Queen and beg for redemption."

"St. James!" Perry exclaimed. "That bad?"

"My father thinks so." Darien drained the second glass—or was it his third? "If I'm banished, where should we go this time? Rome again? Greece? The fighting is over in Turkey."

Perry's eyes slid away, and Darien sensed that, for the first time, his friend would not merrily go to hell in a handbasket with him, though Perry had been, since Lucien had left, the instigator for most of their madcap schemes. Perhaps Perry, like the marquess, felt that in blundering about shackled in misery, Darien was sinking everyone else with him.

"Very well." Darien put down the glass. "I hope that miserable valet of mine can find my court costume."

"Would it be so bad, Darien? Taking over Bellamy?" Rufie asked. "You've been a good steward for The Revels, but that's a tiny farm in comparison. It would ease your father's mind to know you can oversee the marquessate when the time comes."

"Bellamy is not mine to administer," Darien snapped. "Langford and the marquessate will go to Lucien, and I will not take a pebble that is his. Whatever my faults—and I'm aware there are many—I do not steal from my kin."

He downed the last of the liquid in his glass. "Now, to our more pressing matter. Anyone want to lay odds that the Queen will call for my head?"

CHAPTER THREE

Henrietta paused too long. Aunt Althea, no doubt thinking her niece right behind her, disappeared into a clump of visitors entering St. James Palace.

Her entire family was here to see her presented, and Henrietta had no idea where to go.

For a wild moment, she contemplated telling the coachman to drive on. She could circle St. James Park until the levee was over, sparing herself an afternoon of agony.

But such a desertion would humiliate her family. Clarinda was so pleased with her husband's elevation and Henrietta's entrance into society. Aunt Althea would never forgive her, and Sir Pelton would look a fool. Whatever Henrietta Wardley-Hines might lack in grace or delicacy, she did not lack in mettle. Taking a deep breath, she flung open the coach door and pushed through, headdress, hoops, and all.

She ducked far enough that she managed not to dislodge her wig, but her attention toward the upper extremities neglected the lower. As she descended the steps, she planted a foot on her enormous train and alighted on the paving stones to the distinct sound of rending fabric. Henrietta Wardley-Hines, gentleman's daughter, uttered an exclamation that ought never be voiced in polite company, and never, ever before the palace of the King.

"That, if I am not mistaken, is the sentiment of a lady in distress," a deep, very amused, very masculine voice said.

Henrietta looked up from the wreckage of her gown to the splendid figure of a man with lean hips and broad shoulders, then up further still to prominent cheekbones, a wide jaw, and insolent, wickedly blue eyes. He was the most elegantly attired, arrestingly handsome man she had ever seen, and he was quite clearly trying not to laugh at her.

"Someone will have to tell Aunt Davinia that my presentation gown never made it to my presentation." Henrietta sighed at the sight of her poor abused train.

There was no escape. The broad avenue before the palace was crammed with all manner of chairs, vehicles, horses, and pedestrians. She could flee down St. James Street, or duck into a shop on Pall Mall, but any number of people she knew might see her with a gaping hole in her hem. But to go inside and be seen in such a state by everyone coming to attend the Queen—it was not to be thought of.

Her last hope of refuge rolled away, the coachman obliged to remove the carriage by the threatening shouts of those behind in the queue. Her one hope of deliverance was for the street to open and swallow her.

Which it did not.

Her only recourse was to brave her way into the palace. Henrietta regarded the red-brick façade with its octagonal towers and massive one-handed clock.

"I don't suppose you know where I might find a retiring room," she addressed the amused man.

He held out his elbow, clad in a gorgeous silk coat embroidered with silver thread along the long formal tails, which draped in the most attractive fashion over a set of knee-buckled breeches. Henrietta tried not to stare at his very shapely male legs.

"If you dare be seen with me, I can find you a spot, and Aunt Davinia need not be disappointed." His mouth curved with a hint of mischief.

Why shouldn't she be seen with him? Because they had not been introduced, or because he was expensive-looking and therefore undoubtedly of higher rank? Henrietta couldn't afford to quibble. She gathered up her skirts, hiding the tatters as best she could, and laid her hand on his arm.

He was firm and strong, and the material beneath her gloves felt warm. Her cheeks heated as she walked beside him through the archway, past the red-coated guards. They stared straight ahead, as if wooden dolls, but she swore one of them surveyed her companion with a raised brow. Had she just fallen into the clutches of a royal duke?

She hadn't a choice. She stuck close as he strolled into the crush of people milling about a large quadrangle. He appeared unconcerned with the throng, but the assortment of vibrant colors, lustrous gowns, and dazzling headgear made Henrietta feel faintly dizzy.

"The Colour Court," her escort said, as if giving her a tour. He had a fine, resonant voice. "And through there is the Chair Court, which the royals use, and where the mad needlewoman tried to assassinate the King."

He drew her through a plain wooden door into a wood-paneled room, oblong in design, with organ pipes set high into the wall and a colored wash of light falling through clerestory windows set with stained glass. They'd stepped into a jeweled secret, and they were quite alone.

"The Chapel Royal?" Henrietta looked about with a thrill of wonder.

"Quite empty, except on Sundays," her escort confirmed.

He pointed to the enclosed box of a pew. "Not a proper retiring room, but private enough."

"Brilliant." Henrietta rewarded him with a grateful smile. Her squire positioned himself at the door, and she closeted herself in the pew.

Finding the new tear was an easy task; locating the pins among the yards of silk and lace and repositioning them was less so. The fabric was heavy yet fragile with age, and she feared the repairs would show. Charley had scorned her gown; with a self-consciousness new to her, Henrietta wondered what her handsome, elegant rescuer thought.

"No wonder grand court ladies employed ladies in waiting to carry their trains," she remarked. "They are a nuisance, if not an outright danger. I do believe most female fashion is designed to keep us helpless and thus in subjugation."

She glanced his way and met a raised brow, amused but not condescending.

"I wouldn't call male fashions accommodating by any stretch," he said.

She regarded his. The tight coat outlined a broad chest and shoulders, and his breeches were as beautifully embroidered as his coat, the satin clinging to his thighs and the white silk stockings revealing a muscular curve of calf. A strange flutter moved through her belly, and when a slant of mockery shaded his features, she realized she was staring. He must be very accustomed to female admiration. Still, good tailoring and clever padding could achieve that exceptional silhouette.

She pointed to his heeled shoes with two large rubies set in the buckles. "I cannot imagine those are any more comfortable than mine."

"I'll wish my feet cut off before the afternoon is over," he agreed.

The trace of smugness disappeared into a genuine smile.

Henrietta felt as if she were floating above the ground, a strange, new awareness lifting her. She was alone with a man—an attractive man. She busied herself with repairs.

"And why should court functions require such antiquated dress?" She spoke around the extra pin between her teeth. "It's risky as well as unwieldly. Why, I could smuggle any number of royal treasures out of the palace beneath these skirts."

"Do you have plans to do so?"

"Of course I don't *mean* to. But I could." Wonderful. Now she was not simply a shambles, but a vaguely treasonous shambles. What a marvelous impression she was making her first time at court.

"Margaret Nicholson, the needlewoman, smuggled in a dessert knife," her rescuer said. "Assassination attempt. She managed to nick His Majesty's waistcoat."

"If His Majesty's coat has as many layers as my stomacher, there's no hope of a knife cutting through." Henrietta stabbed at her hem.

He studied her ensemble over the shield of the pew. His bright blue gaze touched the headdress, which she feared was in sad disarray, the fussy cascade of ruffles over her undergown, the glaring gold trim on her robe of jade green silk.

His gaze lingered on the enormous emerald collar at her décolletage, and his eyes darkened. Her breath hitched.

"You oughtn't be here alone with me," he said. "There will be any number of yeoman guards about you can ask for direction to the Presence Chamber."

His voice echoed in the wooden room, emphasizing their isolation. He had the most thrilling voice, the match for his perfect face. Motes swirled in the shafts of light like the remnants of dreams or fairy dust.

"I haven't the faintest idea where to go," Henrietta said, her heart pounding. Nervousness, no doubt. "Please don't leave me."

That small, peculiar smile showed again, amusement and something else. He had an expressive mouth to match the bold nose and square, solid-looking jaw. He wore no wig but had pulled his hair back in a simple queue. Not a macaroni, then, for all his elegance.

"I'll stay," he said, and it was absurd how pleased she felt about that.

Striking men did not often offer Henrietta escort. The few who had paid her court at home were neighbors in Rossendale who had an eye on her father's fortune, or neighbors in Bamford hoping to take possession of Birch Vale. When their suits were rebuffed, several of these gentlemen had taken pains to illuminate Henrietta as to the failings they had been so kind to overlook. The enumerations did not make her repent her decision, but they did leave her well aware she was not a woman to inspire admiration.

"Unless, of course, you have someone waiting for you." The light, floating sensation vanished. A man this rich-looking and well-formed would have an equally rich and handsome wife and half a dozen offspring stowed somewhere.

"There is no one," he said, a hard edge to his tone, his eyes tightening as if he were bracing himself against this confession. A small thread pulled tight in her chest.

She fastened the last of her pins and stepped out of the pew. "This is my first time in St. James," she said. "Rather plain for a chapel, isn't it? I read this is where Charles I spent the night praying before his execution."

"This is the original chapel from the medieval hospital of St. James," her companion said. "Henry III evicted the community of leprous women so he could have the site. George still comes here for services, though Charlotte finds it too cold in the winter months." He pointed overhead. "The ceiling by Holbein is quite unique."

Her eyes caught on the firm, strong neck that showed above his neckcloth as he tilted back his head. His look of concentration as he regarded the ceiling pulled another small, sharp twinge from her chest.

"Oh, my word. That is exquisite." Holding her wig in place, Henrietta marveled at the intricate pattern of crosses and hexagons, all composed of tiny painted squares. When she lowered her chin, she found her rescuer regarding her with a strange expression, one that held self-mockery and appeal at the same time.

That self-consciousness stabbed her again. She gathered her train and draped it over one arm as Aunt Althea had taught her. "I suppose you can detect the pins."

"Not if you hold it this way." He stepped forward and rearranged the heavy green silk. "But your feather—if you will permit me?"

She inclined her head toward him, the errant ostrich feather dangling before her eye. He pushed the slender stalk into her wig, and a thrill of awareness moved through her at his nearness, his touch. The faint citrus tang of eau de cologne washed over her senses, cool as a breeze in summer. She sighed with relief and something else as he stepped back—disappointment, as if she had wanted him to move closer, rather than away. How absurd.

"You mustn't be seen with me," he reminded her. "Your reputation."

"I suppose so," she said, fearing to move her head by nodding in agreement. In the north, it would not be a matter of concern for an unknown gentleman to provide assistance. But the manners of the London *haut ton* were nicer and more obscure, at least where a knight's daughter was concerned. She could not give her family more reason to be distressed with her, not when they already forgave her so much.

"I don't know how to thank you." She gazed up into his face and blinked. "In fact, I don't know your name."

"That's for the best." He stepped away with a small bow, his sword swinging. "Go back through the Colour Court and take the grand staircase to the guard room. You'll know it by the display of weapons. The Queen's levee chamber is the third room in. Give your card to the attendant and he will unite you with your party."

She held out her hand, sorry to leave him. She liked this quiet interlude, now that her immediate distress had been remedied. "I am very grateful, Mr.—"

"And here!" A gorgeously gowned lady surged into the room, a trio of meek girls in her wake. "This," she proclaimed, "is the Chapel Royal, where King George and Queen Charlotte were married in— Oh, heavens. It's got a ghost." She gave Henrietta a stare that made her very conscious that her train was barely holding together, her ostrich feather did not want to behave, and nothing in between could be helped.

"We were just leaving," Henrietta said.

"We?" The dowager arched one artificially dark brow.

How such a tall, striking man could make himself invisible, Henrietta couldn't guess, but her rescuer was nowhere to be seen.

He'd stepped in like a knight of old, saved her from disaster on this most important day of her presentation, and then vanished before she could properly thank him.

The afternoon was bound to hold further disappointments, but the greatest, Henrietta already knew, was that she was unlikely ever to see her gallant, interesting rescuer again.

CHAPTER FOUR

His neckcloth itched, his breeches were too tight at the knee, the full skirts of his heavy coat were cumbersome, and the ceremonial sword knocked against his leg. Darien would rather be fighting a duel or wrangling with his father than stuck here attending Queen Charlotte at her levee.

But if he waited, the damsel he'd rescued would eventually appear, and he might learn who she was.

A second chair of state sat next to the queen's throne under its canopy of crimson velvet and gold lace. Murmurs passed through the crowd as the door to the Royal Closet opened and his household guard escorted King George III into the room. Darien had heard George was being circulated now and again, brought out from his new residence at Buckingham House to prove to detractors and Jacobin sympathizers that the head of the British monarchy was yet in possession of his faculties.

Florid and breathing heavily, the monarch took his chair next to his queen. Darien fell in with the rest to make his bows, and as the son of one of the older marquessates in the realm, he was among the first.

"Langford's son!" George barked. "What am I to call you now?"

Darien's guts dropped straight into his heeled shoes. Did the sovereign think his father had disowned him? Would he demand it?

"They call him Daring," the Queen replied. She studied Darien as he executed his bow. Darien had long ceased to find satisfaction in the power that his appearance had over others; his looks wrought more mischief than good. But he responded to the appreciation in the Queen's eye with the same swagger he'd shown the girl in the Chapel Royal when she'd looked him over. He leaned back on one leg, rested his hand on the hilt of his sword, and gave her an insolent grin.

But his damsel hadn't fluttered or blushed or become coy as most damsels did. Her gaze had been curious, direct. And then she'd made that remark about smuggling things under her skirts. He suspected she hadn't actually been trying to direct his thoughts to what lay beneath her gown; she'd seemed innocent of any innuendo. Anyway it was impossible to tell what lay beneath that enormous horror of a dress, which left everything to his imagination.

Queen Charlotte's tone was cool as she held out her hand to be kissed. "Lord Darien. I hear yet another flower of a noble house has fallen to your...scythe. I would not think even you would cast off a duke's daughter."

Darien's chest clenched. "The lady informed me that she has directed her hopes elsewhere. I did not think it wise to press my suit."

The Queen looked through the door to the mill of people awaiting their moment before her. "It seems time you met a girl whose affections are not otherwise engaged. Perhaps someone here today will catch your eye."

Darien suppressed a groan. It was as much as his father had

done, ordering him to marry. Perry's suggestion to find someone inappropriate had merit, should he wish to spike his lordship's wheels.

Darien knew precisely how the afternoon would unfold. The debutantes would troop in with train over arm, all looking the same. They would curtsy to the Queen as their names were announced, say nothing, and back out of the sovereign's presence like crabs.

These gently reared, very young girls weren't raised to be interesting. They were trained *not* to have interests, to be blank slates for the man they would marry. They expected to address their husband as "milord" and have little interaction beyond polite exchanges across the dinner table and greetings as they crossed paths in the hall on their way to their respective entertainments.

Such a wife would expect pin money every quarter and five hundred pounds a year for gowns, in return for which she would permit him occasional access to her bedroom for activities conducted in silence, in the dark. She would produce an heir, keep her own coach, and be discreet about taking a lover.

As dismal as his prospects had felt of late, the vision of such a barren future made Darien want to run howling mad.

"I will take your advice under consideration, madam," Darien answered the Queen, then moved to the window where he could gaze outside at the garden as the endless presentation line began. And throw himself over the sill, if need be.

He did not object to marriage in principle. The Bales men enjoyed rare fortune in their spouses. The marquess had been utterly devoted to his pretty Princess Pip. Horace, allowed by a secure fortune to marry where he wished, chose Nell Bellamy, the gentleman's daughter next door, and never looked at another woman for the rest of his life. Even Rathbone seemed happy with the heiress he'd chosen, though the rest of the family thought her a viper.

It confounded everyone when, mere weeks after the death of her son, Nell picked up and left for the Continent with a portrait painter, leaving her home, her jointure, and her remaining child, Horatia. Darien could only suppose she'd gone a bit mad with grief. He felt much the same.

But the marquess was clearly uneasy about Ratty's steward-ship of Horace's estate and daughter, and that old sense of unworthiness, ancient and familiar, itched under Darien's skin. Horse had been the responsible brother, Lucifer the one who broke boundaries and made his own way. Daring, third and inconsequential, was at liberty to pursue his pleasures without responsibility.

Which was why everyone, including his father, so easily accepted his reputation as a notorious rakehell. Darien sensed the covert stares and bold whispers among the Queen's atten-dants. But to tell the truth would betray the secrets of several young ladies and was unlikely to change his father's opinion of him anyway. Even when Darien had designed a drainage system for his estate, turning acres of fens into arable land, the marquess took no notice.

His father might threaten to bequeath Darien the marques-sate, but he would never view him as worthy of it. The brothers had been assigned their roles at birth, and their sire would never see them as anything else.

Then *she* appeared in the doorway, and the storm cloud of Darien's thoughts broke apart.

"Sir Jasper Wardley-Hines and Lady Clarinda Wardley-Hines," the Queen's herald announced. "Sir Charleton Ward-ley-Hines, 8th Baronet Wardley. Miss Henrietta Wardley-Hines, daughter of Sir Jasper and the late Apollonia Wardley-Hines. Their Majesties will remember that Sir Jasper was recently invested as Knight Bachelor, by the Grace of His Majesty, for services to the Crown."

"Cits collecting honors now, are they?" muttered a voice beside Darien.

"When they own most of Lancashire and half Cheshire besides," a second voice drawled. "Can you blame George if he wants to tap those coffers?"

Sir Jasper looked like a man of business, his eye sweeping the room and summing up every man there. His lady was nobility to her fingertips. The young baronet was the swaggering youth who had adopted the opera dancer Darien left behind when he went abroad.

Miss Henrietta Wardley-Hines. What a mouthful of a name. Her dress, a bilious shade of green, did not improve upon acquaintance, but she had successfully disguised the tear. Despite his ministrations, one of the two ostrich plumes that signaled her maidenhood drooped over her eye. She had none of the dimpled freshness or wispy grace of the others; this girl had steel in her backbone.

Any other girl who found herself before St. James in a ruined court gown would have screamed, wept, or run away. His damsel had marched through the gatehouse with him, chin high, and now she marched up to the Queen as though she were a soldier charged with a duty.

She stopped so quickly that her skirts swayed, and she clamped a hand on her panniers to steady them. As she curtsied, her headdress tilted and the ostrich plume brushed Her Majesty's nose, while her train slid down her gloved arm. Darien nearly started forward to save her before the entire arrangement—gown, girl, wig, and train—toppled into a heap. She looked for all the world like a green pudding trembling in its casing, with two sad feathers sticking out on top.

Inside that wreckage, though, he perceived beauty, intelligence, and courage. In a humiliating situation, she'd taken refuge and sensibly pinned up her dress, though from whence the pins had come, he couldn't imagine. She'd studied Holbein's ceiling with a clear appreciation for the craftsmanship. Those absurd statements about her aunt and stealing royal treasures showed a disposition toward humor.

And though the ghastly dress hid everything else of interest, above that grotesquely huge emerald choker, she possessed a lovely neck. Her shoulders were square instead of the soft, yielding slope that was fashionable, and her jaw was equally square, her strong features set with determination.

Finally he saw the white armband, and a blazing red bolt fell through Darien's head, riveting him to the floor. His damsel had lost someone too.

"Sir Pelton Pomeroy," intoned the herald, "Knight Commander of the Most Honorable Order of the Bath. Lady Althea Pomeroy, and their daughter, Miss Marsibel Pomeroy."

Another group came forward, made their bows, and joined his damsel's family. The hooped skirts of Henrietta's green pudding dress quivered.

"I remember Apollonia," the Queen said with a soft smile. She studied Lady Pomeroy and her small powdered wig topped with three impeccable ostrich feathers, her expression that of a woman who habitually drank vinegar. "Your sister, I believe? I wanted her for my lady-in-waiting, but she was betrothed so soon after her debut. You have been fortunate in your marriages, Sir Jasper."

"Most fortunate," Sir Jasper agreed. His languorous wife rested a hand on her middle with a small, satisfied smile.

"Lady Clarinda is Warrefield's youngest," the Queen whispered to the King, who was watching the pudding dress as if waiting for something gruesome to erupt from its depths.

"Warrefield!" George sat up, his gaze focusing. "With the

library. Heard he had an excellent catalogue done. Want to hire the man myself."

"That was Henrietta's work," Sir Jasper said proudly. His daughter, radiating delight, swept into a deep curtsy that inclined her wig to a dangerous angle.

A learned woman. Darien should have guessed.

"You?" The King eyed her with fresh alarm.

"Yes, Your Majesty. What an honor that my catalogue should have come to Your Majesty's notice." He liked that clear, strong, confident voice of hers. A shame she had such a tragic sense of style.

"Need a catalogue if I'm to leave my library to the nation," George said. "M' grandfather did, you know."

She nodded. "I've looked through the Royal Library. Adding to it would be a magnificent gift, Your Majesty. Though of course we all hope," she added hastily, as gasps traveled through the room, "that will be many, many years in the future." One did not discuss the sovereign's death, especially not with him.

"Like my museum, do you?" The King beamed.

"Oh, yes, Your Majesty. I am particularly fond of Hamilton's Greek vases." She beamed back.

"Well," said the King, a competitive gleam in his eye. "Suppose I could arrange for you to poke around in my books. Have one of my secretaries give you a tour. See what I have that Warrefield don't."

At this invitation, which on Darien's list of enjoyable activities would rank between getting blood let and having a tooth drawn, Miss Henrietta Wardley-Hines looked like she had been handed the moon. Her face showed every thought of her quick mind.

At a nudge from her aunt, she swept into another curtsy, but as she thrust her leg back, her hoops tipped up, exposing a length of white clocked stocking that ended in a buckled shoe. The defeated ostrich feather released its purchase in her hair and swirled in resignation to the floor. Her stepmother smoothly lifted her, and Darien glanced about, hoping no one else had observed his damsel's slim, fine-boned ankle and dainty feet.

The Queen's gaze fell on the white armband. "But you are observing mourning." White was the color reserved for members of the royal family and children. "Forgive me, Clarinda, one of yours?"

Henrietta blinked rapidly, and Darien sent her a silent reminder of courage. Her presentation teetered already on the brink of disaster; she could not exit in tears. "Frances, Your Majesty. She was seven."

"Our condolences, of course," the Queen murmured. It was a rare woman who lived to see all her children grow to adulthood. Charlotte herself had lost two little princes, and it was said that in his madness the King had babbled conversations with them.

Lucretius should have turned eleven this year. How he missed that bold, laughing, beautiful boy. Darien felt the old axe of grief shear his heart, leaving cold air to rush in.

Sir Jasper's group prepared to depart, and Darien held his breath as Henrietta backed away, one hand on her errant headdress and one on her shuddering skirts. Near the door, it happened—her train slipped free, and her heel came down hard on the mended hem. Her expression said she'd just driven a pin into her foot. She gave the ruffled mass a valiant kick, made a final curtsy without letting her wig fall to the floor, and scooted out of the room, bottom first.

Another girl would rush straight out of the palace and throw herself under the nearest passing carriage, but Darien had the sense that Henrietta Wardley-Hines would march out of St. James as determinedly as she'd entered.

As the herald announced the next group, Darien stepped forward. Without quite knowing why, he plucked the crushed ostrich feather from the carpet and tucked it inside his waistcoat.

An eternity later the drawing room broke up, and Darien headed for the door. He longed to get home and out of his court dress and into breeches and boots, and to find some remedy for the ache in his chest as soon as possible. He wondered how his damsel would deal with the debacle that had been her presentation.

As he pushed his way through the knots of people waiting for their carriages, he spotted her, a head above the other women, that single feather waving like a forlorn flag. Her family stood clumped around her, laughing at some cocky joke from the cit. Then the young baronet pushed past him, and Darien put a hand over the ostrich feather in his waistcoat so it wouldn't fall out.

He'd been right to warn her not to be seen with him. He couldn't have her tainted with the scandals that cloaked him.

"Finally!" she said to her brother. "Now we can leave, thank heavens."

"Well, Hetty, you were an utter goosecap and no mistake."

"Was I ever." She sighed. "I am glad Aunt Davinia was not here. She threatened to come see me presented, and you know she never leaves Bath."

"I think you were a triumph, Hetty," said the small brunette beside her. "The King offered you a tour of his library!"

Henrietta laughed with delight. "How soon might I have it? Tomorrow?"

"I should not put too much weight on such an invitation, Henrietta," said the vinegar-faced aunt. "You shall have to make an appointment with the King's secretary, and Sir Pelton can tell you that will take a while."

"So the whole kingdom knows my sister is a bluestocking," said the sprig. "Famous! I'll be drinking on that all night."

"Charley," Henrietta cried, "you promised us the Ellesmere marbles. You *promised!*"

Darien drifted down St. James Street to the line of hacks waiting for hire. It was good to have his evening plans determined upon. He, too, would be seeing Lord Ellesmere's new acquisitions this evening.

Despite Perry's suggestion, he would not sink the Bales name by wooing the daughter of a tradesman. However, standing beside Henrietta Wardley-Hines was one of the most powerful men in the prime minister's cabinet, a man who could influence the court of the King's Bench or rally the House of Lords. Sir Pelton Pomeroy could single-handedly defeat an action to declare dead a ranking marquess's long-lost son and heir.

His father had promised Darien the Season to reform himself, but when that effort failed, as it was destined to do, it would behoove Darien to count Sir Pelton among his allies. Indeed, he might know of a recourse Darien hadn't thought of yet.

Besides, ostrich feathers were dear and must mean something even to the daughters of rich merchants who owned half of Cheshire. He ought to return Henrietta's just to see whether her eyes, before they filled with tears, really were the same deep green shade as the emeralds at her throat.

His damsel's undisguised vulnerability had pierced him to the heart. And nothing had pierced the thick fog surrounding the heart of Lord Darien Bales in a very, very long time.

CHAPTER FIVE

She'd survived her presentation, barely. Now, if she were to cultivate connections that could be of use once she was admitted into the Minerva Society, Henrietta must survive the gauntlet of social events that came after.

The family villa at Salford was grand, their spacious estate in the Rossendale Fells even grander, but Henrietta was still awed by the opulence of London's buildings and parks and the magnificent neoclassical façades springing up along the north and west boundaries of town. As they bumped among the line of carriages thronging Cavendish Square, Henrietta felt like the country mouse of the fable, the one overwhelmed by the bustling city so unlike her plain, quiet home.

Inside the cavernous entrance hall of Ellesmere House, while they waited in line for the butler to announce them, Henrietta held her wig and tipped back her head to examine the ceiling. Frescoed Olympian gods cavorted without shame, many of them in nude splendor. Zeus sported the wide shoulders and solid arms she had detected on her rescuer earlier that day.

Aristocrats were impressed by personal attractiveness and fashionable display, Henrietta reminded herself. Character or respectability mattered little, and approval could be swiftly withdrawn. One could be the queen of her circle one day and disgraced and exiled the next, like the Duchess of Devonshire.

Henrietta did not want to be the Duchess of Devonshire.

"I wonder if anyone has asked Lady Ellesmere to help support the settlement in Sierra Leone?" she remarked to Charley. "I shall have to ask where she stands on the subject of abolition."

"God's teeth, Hetty, can you leave off your peddling for one night?" Charley muttered. "The evening bodes to be a crashing bore already."

Henrietta shifted under the weight of panniers, several petticoats, and an open robe thick with embroidery. In furnishing the wardrobe that had made her the beau monde's darling forty years ago, Aunt Davinia had saved Henrietta hours at the mantua-maker, but these costumes weighed a stone or more.

"Poor Charley. I suppose you would rather be with your opera dancer."

"Hetty! You ain't to know of such things. Now, stay close to Althea and try not to be a goose. Ellesmere must have a card room somewhere." The moment they were announced, Charley peeled off, his duty as escort discharged.

"I am hopeless at these conversational evenings," Marsibel said. "The talk will be of war, or art, or philosophy, or politics." Marsibel took politics at home with all her meals plus tea.

"But so are discussions in the debate societies, and tea rooms, and in Elizabeth Montagu's salons," Henrietta offered. These were the places she spent what time was not devoted to looking after her family. "The insurrections in the West Indies. What the National Assembly is up to in France."

While Marsibel was being reared in papered rooms, learning music and drawing and dancing, Henrietta had been at

Miss Gregoire's Academy for Girls, studying classical languages, natural philosophy, and the sciences. Debate was her métier.

Marsibel heaved a sigh. "How I wish there were dancing."

"Henrietta, have a care whom you speak to." Aunt Althea adjusted her gloves and surveyed the glittering crowd like a general plotting a campaign. "The Ellesmeres are mushrooms who will receive just about anyone."

"The Daughters of Minerva, I hope. Lady Bess said she would be here."

Aunt Althea pinched her lips together. The Countess of Bessington was one of the leading Whig hostesses and a fixture of Mrs. Montagu's salons, known as the Blue Stocking circle. Aunt Althea tended to collect staunch Tories around her table, though Sir Pelton belonged to both clubs.

"It will perhaps serve you best to remain silent," her aunt said with a pointed look, "and follow Marsibel's lead."

Henrietta took the hint. She was here as companion to Marsibel, even if she meant to use the time to identify patrons she could approach for support of the Minerva Society and her various petitions. Obediently she followed her aunt and Marsibel through the gaily garbed press of people, speaking when spoken to, murmuring niceties about the weather. She was not looking out for any particular person, she told herself, not when town entertainments included several different events every night.

But there he was, standing near a plaster pillar bearing a bust of Mars. Compared to his companion, a dark-haired man in black, he was the epitome of elegance. His dark plum tailcoat was embroidered with roses, gold lace fell from his neck and cuffs, and the dazzling embroidery continued on his matching waistcoat and bronze breeches. He'd exchanged the ruby-buckled shoes for a copper set dusted with diamonds. Every inch of him gleamed.

She would expect a man that mesmerizing to draw everyone into his orbit, but a peculiar space held around him. As Henrietta watched, the Duchess of Argyll steered her lovely daughter in a wide berth, and the Duchess of Buccleuch dragged her daughter in the opposite direction. When the Countess of Clarendon turned to find him lounging behind her, as graceful and careless as a cat, she yelped and spilled her punch in the effort to shove her daughter, Barbara, behind a potted fern.

This must be the cut direct, the keenest weapon that Polite Society had to punish one of their own. And what had her gallant rescuer done? Probably nothing more than violate some obscure point of etiquette, like wear a morning coat in the evening or decline to get his head shot off in a foolish duel.

"Aunt Althea, who is—?"

Henrietta stopped as a short, bilious-looking gentleman sidled up to them.

"Lord Pinochle!" Aunt Althea fluttered her fan. "I hoped you would find us in this sad crush. Marsibel longs to see some of Lord Ellesmere's objets d'art. I don't suppose you would give her a tour?"

Henrietta froze. Pinochle was his lordship from that morning. The man whose unwanted advances had left Nancy swollen with child and who had arranged with Lady Bess to see, as he thought, to ridding her of it.

"I am sure he is on the to-avoid list," Henrietta hissed to Marsibel.

"Mama says to encourage him." Marsibel edged closer to Henrietta for support. "Milord, have you met my cousin, Miss Henrietta Wardley-Hines?"

Henrietta stood rooted to the spot as Pinochle regarded her with a smirk. She knew her garish robe of burnt umber made her resemble an ambulatory pumpkin, a far cry from the plain riding habit of that morning, but the game would be up if he recognized her face.

Pinochle, however, didn't glance at her face. His eyes returned to the costly string of pearls wreathing Marsibel's neck. "I would be delighted to escort your lovely daughter, Lady Pomeroy." His stiff bow suggested he was wearing a corset beneath his evening coat.

"I am perishingly fond of classical things," Henrietta announced, sliding an arm about Marsibel's waist.

"You shall only be in the way, Henrietta," Aunt Althea said.

"Nonsense! I am agog to see what treasures Lord Ellesmere has ransacked from the Italian peninsula. Lead the way, Lord Pinochle," Henrietta cried, planting herself like a shield between him and Marsi. If he made the slightest feint at her cousin—if he so much as glanced at her bosom again—she would kick him in his padded calves, peer or not.

The long, narrow gallery of Ellesmere House occupied the first floor of an entire wing of the house. Doors on one side opened to a series of spacious, symmetrical rooms, while the set of windows that lined the opposite wall overlooked a set of gardens landscaped to geometrical perfection. Lord Ellesmere's collection was fast-growing and undiscriminating, Henrietta observed. She stuck like a burr to Marsibel as Pinochle lectured his way down the hall.

"And this one is Psyche fleeing Cupid," Pinochle intoned before one excellent piece. "The story goes that, she being the most beautiful woman alive, the god of love desired her for his wife."

Marsibel's cheeks grew pink as she gazed at the bared, sculpted chest of the pursuing male.

"But when Psyche broke her promise not to try to see him during the night, Cupid left *her*," Henrietta said. "I think this must be Daphne fleeing Apollo. Look at her feet. She is already turning into the laurel."

"Foliage," Pinochle said. "I am sure it is a Psyche." He cleared his throat and moved to the next statue. "This is the acquisition Lord Ellesmere invited us to see. A copy of the Diana of Gabii recently discovered in Rome."

The women gathered around him with a collective *aah*.

Diana was a bold beauty, slender and strong, one shapely foot stepping forward in confidence. A soft smile curved her lips, but she held her head at a proud angle, cool-headed, self-possessed. She was a woman who took pleasure in her strength and freedom, who would acknowledge an equal but never a master, secure in her sound mind, her worth and abilities. A goddess, Henrietta thought, who met the world without flinching.

All the same time, it was easier to meet the world when one had such a perfectly symmetrical face.

"How old is the Diana of Gabii?" Henrietta asked. "The detail is exquisite, even if she is a copy."

Pinochle shrugged. "First or second century, perhaps."

"Fourth century BC," said a new voice. "The Diana of Gabii is by Praxiteles, who is also responsible for the Aphrodite of Knidos."

He was here. With his sculpted features and lean height, he looked of a piece with the statuary around them. Delight curled through Henrietta's belly. They needed deliverance from Pinochle, and again, her rescuer had appeared.

"Is the Psyche by the same artist?" Henrietta asked him.

"That is Daphne," he said with a hint of laughter in his eye, "and she is a copy of the Bernini owned by Prince Borghese. One of the masterpieces of Renaissance art." He returned her admiring stare with a frank, open grin, and the curl of delight fanned out through her body.

Pinochle scowled and stepped nearer to Marsibel. "Surprised to see you here, Lord Darien," he said curtly. "Care to identify this one, if you are the expert?" He pointed to a statue of an entirely naked man.

"Oh, my." Marsibel stared at the figure's perfect proportions, a blush rising to her cheek.

"Hercules," her rescuer said. He had such a lovely, rich voice, deep and confident. "Gathering apples from the golden tree in the Hesperides."

Lord Darien. She didn't recognize the name. Why had he not been pointed out to her before? Aunt Althea made certain to identify anyone of importance. She could not have overlooked someone so noticeable.

"He could be the prince from the legend of Atalanta," Henrietta said. "He dropped the golden apples to distract her so that he would win the footrace and thereby her hand. The suitors who lost to her, if I recall, were executed."

His eyes were a startling hue, even bluer outside the dim light of the Chapel Royal. "You know your classical myths, Miss—"

He waited for Pinochle to do the honors, and when the dratted Pinochle did not oblige, Henrietta considered being so bold as to identify herself. Would he kiss her hand if she held it out to him? She shivered at the thought.

Marsibel shook her head. "Those legends are all so gory. If he wishes to marry her, why not just ask?"

"But why should she simply accept any handsome prince who comes along? Atalanta had talents of her own, you know. If she had to submit to a man, she wanted to ensure he was a match for her." Henrietta glared at Pinochle, who stood closer to Marsi than she liked. "After all, men acquire much more than a bride—they gain a dowry, family connections, a housekeeper and hostess and nurse. And women, in return, give up every freedom."

"For the protection of a man's name," Pinochle tutted. "A home of her own, a loyal guardian who will devote himself to her comfort, honor her as the mother of his children." He glanced at Marsibel to judge her reaction.

Henrietta set her teeth. That Pinochle should pretend to gallantry when he had set his pregnant housemaid in the street with a few shillings! "In the best of circumstances, perhaps," she said.

"How does the story end?" Marsibel asked. "Does the prince win?"

"He does indeed," Lord Darien said. "The golden apples fascinate Atalanta and delay her enough that he wins the race. But I like to think that they were happy together." He watched Henrietta as he had in the Chapel, as if she were an unusual artifact whose provenance he could not place.

"A romantic notion, sir—er, milord." Who *was* this interesting man?

"There you are!" A young woman appeared beside her rescuer, tucking her hands around the elbow of his expensive, handsome coat. "My dear Daring, I see you received my note to meet me in the gallery." She gave the other women a challenging glance. "You have not invited company to our rendezvous, I hope?"

"Good evening, Miss Pennyroyal," Marsibel said with the air of one determined to be civil. "Have you met my cousin, Miss Wardley-Hines? Henrietta, this is Miss Forsythia Pennyroyal, daughter of the late Colonel Pennyroyal, a hero of the Seven Years' War."

Henrietta noticed that Marsibel did not address her rescuer, but then, perhaps she was waiting for Pinochle to introduce them. Pinochle continued to disoblige.

The new girl tittered behind her hand. "Miss Wardley-Hines, I must say I admire your courage. I heard of your disastrous presentation! I don't know how I would have been able to hold my head up, and yet here you are, as if nothing had happened." She made a long, pointed perusal of Henrietta's gown. "I do applaud your fearlessness in keeping alive the fashions of decades ago. I would never have the courage, myself."

Henrietta considered her gown, a far cry from Miss Pennyroyal's exquisite royal blue silk, with the blue feathers in her hair dyed to match, or Marsibel's elegant cream silk robe with its brown overdress. Althea had insisted Henrietta would do, but Henrietta wondered if Charley was right and Aunt Althea meant for her to look a provincial, far behind town fashion.

"The King himself invited Miss Wardley-Hines to examine his royal library," her rescuer said. "It seems he may ask her to catalogue it."

Henrietta sent him a look of gratitude and surprise. She had not noticed him at the Queen's levee, so intent had she been on not tripping on her gown. That he had taken note of her made the pleasure unfurl further.

"A rather tedious task, I should think," murmured Miss Pennyroyal. "Miss Pomeroy, those pearl eardrops! I am sure I saw you wearing them at a dinner party at Grafton House last week? I noted how darling they were. I am sure I would wear them all the time, myself."

Marsibel colored but did not acknowledge the hit. She had been bred from birth to stand against girls of her class and not be found wanting. Henrietta, however, felt her temper flare.

"Miss Pennyroyal," she said, "what an astonishing memory. Only think if you were to turn those powers of observation to worthy causes, like the plight of the poor, or the consequences of the Enclosure Acts. May I invite you to attend the next debate of the Minerva Society? I intend to discuss Miss Wollstonecraft's argument that stifling the female mind leads to fool-ishness and vice."

"Vice, you say?" Miss Pennyroyal nestled close to her companion. At the contact, the delighted grin he'd directed at Henrietta—amused by her cattiness, was he?—vanished.

"Alas, I have been discovered with the infamous Lord Daring!" Miss Pennyroyal preened. "My reputation shall be ruined, I don't doubt."

"Other reputations have," the stranger said, a grim set to his mouth.

"Lord *Daring*?" Henrietta exclaimed. "*The* Lord Daring?"

"La, Miss Wardley-Hines, the very one!" Miss Pennyroyal giggled. "He is more handsome than the cartoons portray him, is he not?"

This was the moment, Henrietta realized, to snap open a fan and hide behind it. She didn't know where hers was in this vast expanse of gown. "I confess I have been interested to see what sort of man went with the...ah, colorful reputation."

"And what sort of man do you see, Miss Wardley-Hines?" A muscle ticked in his square jaw as he met her gaze, a challenge in his eyes.

The pleasure she'd felt at his approach twisted and soured. The man who had so gallantly come to her aid at the palace was the man her uncle, aunt, and brother had all warned her was a ruinous influence. She had to get Marsibel away.

"I see a man of clay, as are the best of us," Henrietta said, turning away as disappointment washed through her. "Marsi? Shall we move on to the Etruscan pieces?"

"*Daring*." Pinochle mocked him with a surly smile. "Servant."

Lord Daring bowed. "I was moving in that direction myself." His tone shifted to freezing condescension. "I would not wish your reputation to suffer a stain, Miss Pennyroyal, by asking you to accompany me."

"Oh, but I must," she cooed, fluttering blackened eyelashes. "You might expire of boredom while everyone proses on about a lot of old broken pottery."

Henrietta abandoned the courtesies. She couldn't look at him, so fascinating, so forbidden. She took Marsibel's elbow and marched them down the gallery, her antique panniers asway. She fled the notorious Lord Daring as Daphne did her Apollo, and unlike Daphne, she did not look back.

CHAPTER SIX

"Lord Daring!" Marsibel located her fan and applied it as she and Henrietta sought refuge in the expansive drawing room where the Ellesmeres' guests chatted brightly among the ruins of ancient civilizations. "He *is* more handsome in person." Her voice dropped. "Do you suppose he has ruined Forsythia Pennyroyal?"

"My dear Miss Pomeroy, how fortunate that you had me as your escort," Pinochle said. "I alone stood between you and the dreadful Lord Daring!"

Henrietta glared at him. Given the choice between Pinochle, the man who kept his depredations secret, and Lord Daring, whose were broadcast across town, she would choose the man who at least owned his faults. She cast about the room for recourse and spotted Lady Bess conversing with a group of elegant women. The countess spotted Pinochle, and her eyebrows rose.

"Miss Pomeroy." Bess appeared beside them a moment later. "I was hoping to catch you. You won't mind, Pinochle, if I steal this darling girl away?"

Pinochle turned brick red. He knew what else Lady Bess

had stolen from him. Henrietta stopped breathing, fearful of what he might do.

But Bess was right; her influence, and her secret knowledge, cowed his lordship into silence. As she drew Marsibel away, she muttered to Henrietta, "Pinochle? Surely your aunt would not condone him."

"I'm afraid every unmarried lord is in consideration at this point," Henrietta muttered back.

"Never mind," the countess said. "Come, Miss Pomeroy, let me introduce you to some friends of mine. Hetty will handle your suitor."

Pinochle, relinquishing his prize with ill grace, stalked off without an acknowledgement to Henrietta. She wondered whether he had detected her gawping at the very elegant Lord Daring. Aunt Althea would have a thing or two to say about that. At least no one knew—yet—of their interlude in the Chapel Royal. Who could say what the consequences would be if Lord Daring chose to advertise *that* event?

Henrietta had nerves of steel, but the gossip apparently had her being a complete ninny at court, and she was wearing another outmoded, disastrous gown. If there were any Daughters of Minerva here tonight, they were not seeing her at her best. And if they were to judge her as Forsythia Pennyroyal had—

Marsibel safe with Lady Bess and a circle of important-looking women, Henrietta dawdled among the artifacts, taking the chance to compose herself. So she lacked style and countenance. She was intelligent and—intelligent. And she had cast her lot this morning, starting the work she meant to continue. If Pinochle exposed her, she would have far more to bear than ridicule for her dress.

She stood regarding an elaborate funerary run when a deep voice sounded at her shoulder. "Everyone speaks of Roman influence, but I think the Etruscans drew more from the Greeks."

She tossed up her head and met his smile of greeting, but his face held a shadow of caution, as if he were unsure how he might be received.

She had no wish to repulse him. He was the most fascinating man she had ever met, and he had done her a great kindness that morning. Furthermore, they stood in the middle of a crowded room. Surely her reputation could not be destroyed by a civil conversation.

She tilted her head, noting that her heart rate ticked up in his presence. Interesting. "Greek influence, you say?"

"The Romans were ravishing the Sabine women while the Etruscans were inventing the dome. A rather sophisticated architectural technique."

"I've heard their circular designs were unique," she replied, her ears warm. The scandalous Lord Daring was speaking to her of ravishment, with the Daughters of Minerva watching! She could not cut him, not after what he had done for her earlier. But she did possess one weapon guaranteed to rout a man: the aforementioned intellect.

"Herodotus suggests the Etruscans were not native but migrated to the peninsula," Henrietta said. "Perhaps they learned their pottery techniques alongside the Greek vase makers. Though I thought this black pottery was distinctive?"

Daring stepped forward. Her fingertips tingled. He was tall, but leaning to peer at the piece brought his face close enough that she could detect the bronze tone of his skin, the wheat-gold streaks in his hair and sideburns, the rather perfect shape of his lips and jaw. Her stomach knotted.

"Bucchero," he said, glancing at her. "They also worked in bronze, but that glossy black finish is the mark of Etruscan work.

One sees it all about the Mediterranean, including Greece and Rome."

He wasn't taking flight. She shouldn't feel pleased about that.

"This is not bronze," she challenged him, moving to a small figure of a man with a blank, nearly featureless face but a body carved with strong detail very like the shape of the man beside her. Daring's broad shoulders could be due to padding and the flat, narrow stomach achieved by a corset. However, there was no mistaking the curvature of muscled male thigh in his close-fitting breeches.

"Terracotta," Daring said. He brushed her skirts as he stepped close, and the sway of her panniers sent a bolt of awareness from her hips up her spine. "Apollo or Hercules is my guess."

"But those are Greek deities. Did they worship the same pantheon?"

He fairly vibrated with masculine energy, much like the statue. It was rare that a man could make Henrietta feel delicate.

His smile reached his eyes. "Once we can decipher Etruscan writing, we might know. Have you read Herodotus, or are you teasing me?"

It took her breath away to think this man suspected her of flirting with him. "The Earl of Warrefield has a copy of the *Histories* printed at Venice in 1502 for the doge. One of the earliest print editions, bound in calf gilt. An exquisite book."

He tilted his head. She needed to stop staring at his lips.

"I'll assume that edition is in Greek?"

"Yes," she confirmed. Now he would go away, and she would be safe. A woman could succeed as an eccentric only if she were well-born, preferably titled, with heaps of money and leisure for salons and philosophical talk. Scholarly women, *femmes savants*, were detested like the pox.

"Tell me what you think of this tomb painting," he said.

Curiosity warring with prudence, Henrietta followed him to a fragmented piece of tile pieced together on a cloth of dark velvet. "But that is Minerva," she exclaimed with delight. The brown paint was faded, and some of the tiles were chipped, but the outline could be discerned. "Do you suppose they borrowed her from the Greeks as well?"

"It is possible, but difficult to know." He shrugged. "The Romans stole what they wished from the Etruscans, and when the Republic rose in power, they crushed them. They obliterated their language, their literature, their history, their religion—everything."

There was nothing sly or seductive in his manner, warning her to guard her virtue. He didn't behave like a gazetted rake. There was nothing of the macaroni about him either; he had not once lisped, or taken snuff, or held up a quizzing glass, or played with the fobs strung across his coat. He stood at ease as if waiting for her response. As if he were interested to hear it.

She turned back to the display. "Perhaps the Etruscans had their own Minerva. How exciting if they did."

"You seem certain of the identification," Daring murmured.

"I know Minerva when I see her," Henrietta said, pointing. "She has the helm, the chiton, the breastplate, and the spear. And that is her aegis, the head of Medusa on her shield."

He bent over her shoulder to look at the long-faded traces of paint, and Henrietta panicked. She stepped back, collided with a firm obstacle—his chest or shoulder—and trod on his foot. As she lurched away, the toe of her slipper caught the hoop of her skirts and pulled her off balance. Before she could topple, he caught her upper arms, keeping her on her feet.

"I beg your pardon," he said. "I was crowding you."

"No, I must beg yours," Henrietta gasped. "I am exceedingly clumsy."

His gloved hands were as strong and masculine as the rest of him, the fingers long and shapely. The heat of shame and something else soared through her arms and chest. There was nothing to do but flee to the next funerary inscription, displayed in pieces on a plaster pillar.

He followed.

"The Greeks were great sailors," he remarked. "No doubt they traded heavily with the Etruscans, with the influence going both ways. From these fragments, it seems possible the Etruscans borrowed from the Greek alphabet as well."

Henrietta peeked at him from the corner of her eye. His tone was neither flirtatious nor condescending. Clearly, he was prepared to behave as if she had not tripped and practically fallen into his arms. As, legend had it, a hundred other young women had done before her.

She was arming herself for battle, and he was pursuing a conversation, not her virtue. She felt both grateful and annoyed.

"The characters do resemble the Greek far more than Latin," she agreed. "But I thought the Greeks borrowed their alphabet from the Phoenicians?"

"It's also possible the Etruscans had a fully literate society before any Greek influence," Daring said. "The burial customs, too, are quite different."

"You know a great deal about them," Henrietta observed with surprise. Surely gazetted rakes were not also intelligent and charming. Something about the mindless pursuit of pleasure dulled a man. Mary Wollstonecraft said so.

"As a dilettante only, not a scholar. My interests are principally architectural, so if you would like to discuss Roman or Greek building practices, I might wax much more eloquent on the subject."

He looked directly at her, holding her gaze. How rare it was for a person to do that. Most people's eyes slid away after a second or two of contact, usually to see if there were someone else in the vicinity they might wish to talk to. Small lines fanned about his eyes, and his skin was tanned from the sun, contrary to the pallor that was so fashionable for ladies as well as gentlemen.

"Your eyes are the most astonishing color." The remark slid out before she could catch it.

He drew back. "I have sometimes been told that, thank you," he said. "I believe blue eyes are quite common, however."

"Not in such a pure shade." She peered into his face. "Most blue eyes have streaks of gold, or green, or something else. Yours are the lapis lazuli of a medieval illumination. It was quite a prized pigment, you know—very valuable and difficult to procure. Found only in Afghanistan."

The creases around his eyes deepened and grooves appeared at the sides of his mouth, warming his austere expression. He did not resemble a classical sculpture as much as Forsythia Pennyroyal had claimed. His features had a touch of ruggedness, the nose a bit large, his jaw broad and square, but altogether it was a pleasing countenance. Too pleasing, if his reputation were to be believed.

He leaned toward her. The bottom dropped out of her stomach, but he was only subjecting her eyes to the same examination she had given him. Her lungs gulped for air. His eau de cologne brought to mind summer meadows and spicy earth, damson fruit fresh from the tree, humid dusks thick with shadows, and her mother's elderberry wine as soft on her tongue as a bolt of patterned silk.

She must *not* be a goose around London's most notorious seducer.

He straightened. "Gray," he pronounced. "Rather unusual."

"Flat gray," she managed. "Quite unremarkable."

"On the contrary, all the great ladies of courtly literature have gray eyes. Arthur's Guinevere. Petrarch's Laura. They were thought the epitome of beauty."

Now that was laughable, that Henrietta might possess any feature that came close to the appellation of beauty. "But only when paired with blonde hair, a dainty manner, and a white—"

She almost said "bosom," but one did not discuss bosoms with a gentleman, particularly not a dissolute roué who must have seen thousands of them. Suddenly overconscious of her own deficiencies in that area, Henrietta moved on to the next display, a death mask.

He would tire of the exchange soon; he had nothing to gain by ruining her. She was not in possession of great beauty, nor great wit, nor great wealth. Whether or not he was as dreadful as portrayed, she still could not be seen as the target of seduction.

His eyes flared. He knew exactly what she had been about to say.

"I have told you my interest. Now you must tell me yours. Art? History? You knew something of the chapel when we met earlier."

When he had offered her assistance for which she had not yet properly thanked him. She could not be boorish when he had saved her from disgracing herself and her entire family before the Queen. Her foot still smarted from stepping on a pin in the hem of her train.

"I too am a mere dilettante, sad to say."

"I suppose you shall try to convince me your accomplishments are no more than the average young lady's. Music, drawing, a smattering of French?"

"French, German, Italian, Latin, and Greek," she could not resist saying. "Well, a little Greek. I am slow at reading."

"Italian?"

"So I might read Dante in the original." Charley had promised that discussing books would send potential suitors running, but here he still stood, Lord Daring in the flesh. Strong, masculine flesh.

"The *Commedia?* How did that go?"

"Slowly. I bogged down in the *Paradiso* and never finished. Beatrice is so very...virtuous."

He laughed. It was a deep, splendid sound, pure and unfettered, and several heads in the room turned in their direction. Panic unfurled along with the bloom of pleasure in her chest at the sound of that laugh. She was speaking with him! Alone! She had been warned not to encourage him. Would the Daughters of Minerva think her ruined already?

"Every woman alive wants to be Beatrice, or at least have her power over a man," he said, his expression amused and—of course not intrigued. Not by her. "You are a very unusual woman, Miss Wardley-Hines. From, it seems, a rather interesting family."

His eyes drifted across the room to Marsibel, and Henrietta's suspicions flared. She had not rescued Marsi from Pinochle to deliver her to a different debaucher.

"Lord Daring—" She caught herself. That was not his name. She gripped her skirts to pull herself together. "Lord Darien. You rendered me a service this afternoon for which I am deeply grateful. But I will be in the basket if my brother catches me conversing with a man who is a stranger to us. I'm afraid I must bid you good day."

Fool! It was far too late to wish someone good day. Further proof he had addled her wits.

"Of course. I should have realized." He gave her a stiff, formal bow. "Allow me to hope we will meet again. Perhaps I shall see you and your cousin riding in the park tomorrow."

It was what all the fashionable young ladies did, and Marsibel had tried once or twice to take them on an airing. But Marsibel was not a strong rider, and if Henrietta were to be in a carriage, she preferred driving herself to a specific destination. "No," she said, "I am visiting the parish workhouse tomorrow."

Dark brows drew down over those magnificent eyes. "The workhouse is hardly the place for a young lady."

"It is hardly the place for anyone, and yet far more people find themselves there than should be," Henrietta replied, stung. She had forgotten that Lord Daring was an aristocrat. He might be the most elegant, amusing, intelligent, well-looking man she had ever met, but he was also born to privilege and the aristocrat's belief that anyone in poverty had brought it upon themselves through laziness or weakness of character. The reminder was a refreshing dash of cold water.

"Good *evening*, Lord Darien," she said politely and compressed her panniers so she did not knock over any displays, nor trip and pitch into his arms again. Once was enough.

"Before you leave, Miss Wardley-Hines...I have something of yours I feel obliged to return to you."

He slid one of those strong, firm-fingered hands inside his coat, pushing aside his impeccably tied cravat, and held something out to her.

It was an ostrich feather, white, broken at the tip. The soft down waved gently in the air.

"How did you come by this?" she whispered.

"It parted ways with your headdress at the Queen's levee. I took the liberty of retrieving it."

She balanced the delicate item in her gloved hand, hefting its weight, which was nothing. "But how can you be sure it was mine? Every girl there was wearing ostrich feathers."

"I noted this." He touched the white silk band around her arm.

There were layers of fabric between them: his gloves, the thick silk of her dress, the thin satin of the mourning emblem and, added to that, the cascades of ruffles at her elbows that served as sleeves. Yet the warm pressure of his finger left a print on her arm.

Something bleak and pained in his eyes tugged at her even as the familiar hurt ripped through her chest. She had forgotten, while talking to Lord Daring, the wound that lay beneath everything. She was forgetting Fanny more and more these days.

She felt an odd prickle on the back of her neck and turned her head to find Pinochle staring at them. More to the point, he was staring at her hand held out in a gesture he had seen her make just that morning as she'd hefted his purse of coins in her palm. His gaze dragged to her face, and cold horror splashed through Henrietta.

He knew.

"Sorry to interrupt, *dearest* sister." Charley, seizing her arm, shook Henrietta out of her trance. "Time to gather your wrap. Aunt has taken a headache and wants to go, and Uncle Pell won't budge an inch until he's argued Fox into the ground, so I must squire you and Marsi home. Servant, Daring," he snapped, scowling.

"Same," Daring said coolly. Henrietta watched his face shut down at the interruption. He had relaxed with her, but now his reserve reasserted, the skin around his mouth tightening, a shadow dimming the intense blue of his eyes. His shoulders straightened. His height had not seemed intimidating before—he was taller than Charley, even—but it did now.

"Have a care at the workhouse, Miss Wardley-Hines," Daring said. "It's not a drawing room, you know. There are desperate men there."

"And also women, and children, and entire families who have no means to support themselves." Lord Daring, concerned with her welfare? Hadn't he led dozens of women into desperate situations? "I enjoyed our discussion, sir," she said politely, surprised to find that was true. "Do you ever decipher the Etruscan alphabet, I hope you will share your findings."

Good heavens, that sounded like she was casting out lures, which she must on no account do.

"Hetty, you goose. You oughtn't have stood so long talking with him," Charley hissed as he hauled her to safety. "Everyone noticed. They'll all think you're his next conquest."

"I tried to repel him." Henrietta clutched the ostrich feather to her breast, feeling Pinochle watching her as closely as Lord Daring was. "I told him about my languages. And that I read Herodotus."

Charley paused, a hand on her arm. "And what did he do?"

"He wanted to know what edition. You know, I'm always told men can't stand such talk, but Lord Daring actually taught me something."

Her brother gaped at her. "Good Gad, Hetty! What could you possibly learn from that rakehell?"

"Bucchero," she said, and Charley set his mouth in a grim line.

"That tears it. I'm calling him out."

"Charley!" She shook her arm free of his grip. "It's a pottery finish, you clodpate. We were discussing the artifacts! And standing in plain view. What could he possibly do?"

Besides, she had worse things to worry about now that Pinochle had identified her. He feared Lady Bess, but what might he do to Miss Henrietta Wardley-Hines?

"Oh, any number of things," Charley muttered. "If Aunt Althea hears of this, she'll fly up in the boughs for certain. You'd best hope your face isn't on a broadside plastered all over town tomorrow either. Lud, Hetty, all that schooling is meant to fright the fribbles and fortune hunters away, not lure them in!"

"Another salient argument for educating females," Henrietta snapped. "I shall incorporate it into my debate."

Across the room, Lord Daring joined his dark-haired companion with a remark that made the other man light with interest and glance their way. The full force of what she'd done crashed in on her.

She'd fallen under the spell of a man known to have no discretion and great seductive power. He crooked a finger and impressionable girls followed where he led, be they Miss Forsythia Pennyroyals or duke's daughters.

It was easy to say she was not such a wet goose as to land herself in the same situation as Lady Celeste, ruined, outcast, a babe in her belly, and a virtual prisoner in her family home. But Lord Daring did not work by bold flirtations or empty flattery. No, he had subtler, more powerful means.

Intelligence and an ease of manner to go with his potent charm. Keeping a lady's token and carrying it next to his heart. Giving it to her while it still held heat from his body, a gesture as intimate as a kiss.

If this was how he wooed and won susceptible lasses, he was devastating. Fortunate she had been warned.

She let Charley clap her hat on her head and shove her into the Pomeroy carriage. No need to protest she was unlikely to encounter Lord Daring again. It was for the best. Whether or not Pinochle made a public accusation over her mischief of that morning, Henrietta could not risk her standing with the Minerva Society, or Aunt Althea, any further.

Still, she understood now why so many girls had traded their reputations and risked their hearts for the chance to stand in the light of Lord Daring's piercing blue eyes and incandescent smile.

CHAPTER SEVEN

The new St. Marylebone parish workhouse sat on a generous plot of land donated by the Duke of Portland. Beside it stood a freshly built chapel and a tidy rising square of bricks meant for the new infirmary. Unlike the gloom and privation that attended London's houses of correction, the Marylebone workhouse was well-kept and well-ordered. The ladies of the Auxiliary kept up a lively chatter over the sounds of the construction workers banging hammers and hauling wagons and the steady, racketing hum from the workrooms where able-bodied residents sat spinning.

Henrietta had been overpowered in the foyer of Hines House by the combined forces of Jasper, Lady Clarinda, and their butler, Dearbody, all insisting that while she might be accustomed to tramping at her liberty around their estates in the north, the wilds of London demanded more caution. She had not seen her name touted in the morning gossip columns as Lord Daring's latest ruin, nor had any denouncement come from Lord Pinochle, but nonetheless, Henrietta thought it wise to concede.

So, while other ladies stepped down from worn family

carriages with a maid beside them, Henrietta bowled up in a spanking new coach with the newly designed Wardley-Hines coat of arms in fresh paint on the door, a coachman driving, her groom beside, and two tall footmen of matching height hanging off the back.

"I see that some of us bring all our servants on missions of mercy," Mrs. Spickey, a deacon's wife, loudly observed to her daughter.

Henrietta pretended not to hear. She had initially been welcomed by the Ladies Auxiliary of St. Marylebone's, but then her father was knighted and Henrietta took that precarious step from the rising bourgeoisie to the ranks of lesser gentility. What before had been dismissed as the free manners of a tradesman's daughter or a northerner were now marks of her unfitness for the ranks of the gently born. The judgments stung, whether or not she heeded them.

Poor Constance Spickey, one of those proper girls taught from birth that she existed to serve men, stood in silent agony while the workers paused to whistle at and offer crude evaluations of the gathering females. Henrietta decided to show Constance her trick. Never mind it hadn't worked to drive Lord Daring from her side the previous evening; the principle stood that one must take a firm hand with bold men.

She marched up to one of the worst offenders, who leaned on the handles of his wheelbarrow. "I say, is that Bath stone you are using?"

The man straightened and snatched off his cap in an ingrained gesture of respect. "Nay, miss, Portland stone, it is," he said in the lilt of a Cornishman.

"Ah! That is what Wren used on St. Paul's, I believe?"

The man nodded and showed Henrietta the contents of his wheelbarrow. "Aye, miss. Can ye conscience the yards o' stone in that pile? Portland's the best ye can build in."

"Is it? I like Hopton Wood stone myself. Such a lovely color, and there are quarries near my house in Derbyshire."

"Aight, but there's a stone for the inside, mum," a second man said with the rolling r's of Yorkshire. "Duchess o' Devonshire 'as it all over Chatsworth. I cut that rock meself, sure enough."

"Well! I shall consider your advice when I refurbish the mill I am hoping to acquire. And how well the infirmary looks already."

Henrietta beamed at them. The men returned to their labor, their heckling turned on one another, and she joined the queue at the door.

Mrs. Spickey scolded, "Miss Wardley-Hines, you oughtn't speak with them. Such men are beneath you."

"Beneath me?" Henrietta said as the porter opened the workhouse. "I only wish I possessed such a useful skill as masonry."

"Sapskulls," said James, her groom, following close at her side. "Fashes me why you gentle morts come 'ere anyway. Naught but anglers, bunters, and the merry begotten. Might as well fling your coppers into the Thames."

"They're not criminals, James," Henrietta said. "Just people who don't have a home."

Peter, one of the two footmen, looked about. "I've an uncle in 'ere," he said. "Got turned off without a character. Ain't seen 'im in an age."

"Buzz man?" James asked with interest. "Filched from the wrong mort?"

"Blue ruin," Peter responded, and James shook his head with a *tsk*.

Blue ruin, Henrietta had learned, meant gin. "You must find this uncle and ask what we might do for him." She handed Peter a thick woolen blanket, worsted stockings, and a pair of mittens.

"Aye, saw off, ye big gollumpus." James shooed him away. "I'll see to Miss Hetty." He immediately began an argument with the remaining footman, John, over who would hold the pile of things Peter had carried.

"I will hold the packages," said another male voice, and a pair of gloved hands, attached to arms clothed in a glossy superfine, reached for the footman's load. Henrietta looked up with surprise into the face of Lord Darien.

"You!"

Excitement, apprehension, curiosity, and a deep, bright pleasure surged through her at the sight of him, polished, elegant, and entirely out of place. His light brown hair was unpowdered and drawn back into a neat queue, his neckcloth was expertly tied, and everything about him exuded health and strength. Henrietta peered into his eyes. He didn't look like a man who had spent his night in riotous dissolution.

"Miss Wardley-Hines." He gave a brief bow, watching her warily, those perfect lips quirked in a smile. "Good morn."

Apprehension won out. She glanced about, wondering who here might know him. If she were spotted with him today after their conversation last night, she was sunk for certain. A lack of marriageability wouldn't matter much to her, but to lose Aunt Althea's grudging goodwill, endanger her election to the Minerva Society, cast a cloud upon Lady Mama and Marsibel and the girls—there was too much at stake.

Add to that, her northern neighbor would never sell his mill to a woman of loose morals, no matter how many ciphers she added to the offer.

"Lord Darien. I cannot begin to guess what business brings you here."

"I was interested in your mission of mercy. I thought that while your friends are imparting Christian consolations, I might offer the wisdom of the Stoics, or some others of the ancient Greeks."

He nodded toward the Spickeys, who distributed moral pamphlets along with shawls and stockings. Mrs. Spickey would have an apoplectic fit if she recognized the infamous Lord Daring.

Henrietta narrowed her eyes at him. As pleasurable as his company might be, she must make him go away. "And now you are a philosopher too? You are a man of many talents, Lord Darien."

"Kind of you to notice, Miss Wardley-Hines. Are you unaccompanied?"

"My father sent three men with me, and the coachman is outside."

Darien surveyed her companions. John looked respectful, but James eyeballed him from a cocksure stance, chest thrust out like a bantam.

"I see a running footman and a dwarf," Darien drawled. "Do you also lead a young African boy about on a golden chain?"

"James is not an accessory," Henrietta snapped. "He is my groom." She reached for her packages. "You'd best leave, Lord Darien. I cannot look after them, attend to my mission, and keep an eye on you as well." Good heavens, what if someone offended his lordly sensibilities or, worse, committed indignities upon his person? She could not be responsible for that.

Darien studied her from head to toe, marking her sensible German riding habit, at least five years out of fashion, and sturdy boots. "Keep an eye on me? And here I labored under the assumption that I had come to look after you."

"On yer guard, Miss Hetty," James advised, glaring at Darien. "The gentry coves don't let this fine swell in their drawing rooms no more, an 'e's on the hunt for a ladybird. Well, long shanks, Miss Hetty is no looby, and she ain't laced mutton neither! So ye best cut your sticks afore we cut 'em for ye."

"James, mind your tongue," Henrietta scolded as Darien's face shuttered behind the mask of the bored aristocrat. The reminder of his reputation, that he seduced women for sport, stung him. But why, if he had earned it?

He held her gaze, and her pile of supplies. "I shall leave if you have concern for your reputation," he said quietly.

Here was the man she recognized, her rescuer who had found her in tatters on the street before St. James and swept her into the chapel for repairs. The man who had chatted with her over Etruscan antiquities and returned her ostrich feather, which, though she would never tell him this, Henrietta had kept under her pillow while she slept.

"John," Henrietta addressed the remaining footman, "if this gentleman proves impertinent, I hope you will...box his ears."

"Miss!" said John, his eyes wide.

Darien laughed, and the mask dissolved. "Really, Miss Wardley-Hines? You instruct a man in your employ to lay hands upon the son of a peer?"

"Oh, very well," Henrietta said. "If you take liberties, I will box your ears myself. Now, to the business at hand." She caught the eye of the ward nurse, a tired-looking woman in a neat apron. "I wish to visit the infirmary ward."

The nurse beckoned. "This way."

Mrs. Spickey sidled close. "Miss Wardley-Hines, surely you did not arrange for Lord Daring to meet you here?"

"Indeed not, Mrs. Spickey. I met Lord Darien last evening at Lady Ellesmere's conversazione and mentioned we were visiting the workhouse today. It seems he felt moved to contribute to our efforts."

Mrs. Spickey's pinched expression reminded her of Aunt Althea's. Mrs. Spickey would never be invited into the drawing rooms of the upper class. "Lord Daring at a conversational evening," she said. "And now visiting the parish workhouse? I did not think either of those activities in his usual style."

"Perhaps there is more to Lord Darien than we have been given to believe," Henrietta said.

"I will not allow Constance to talk to him," Mrs. Spickey decided. "And you must not encourage him, Henrietta."

"So I have been informed by my brother and Sir Pelton," Henrietta said firmly. "Several times."

Constance trailed behind her mother, her hair primly tucked into a straw bonnet, lace mittens covering her hands. She was a darling, biddable girl, and she could not be trusted out of her mother's sight because she had never been taught to use her own mind. Henrietta thanked her lucky stars and Aunt Davinia for Miss Gregoire's Academy for Girls. She only hoped she would not have to guard Constance from Lord Darien, in addition to everything else.

The infirmary ward for women and children was occupied past capacity, with rows of cots bracketing the walls. Light and air being considered unhealthful and possibly carrying disease, the few high windows were shuttered, and tallow candles sputtered smoke. The air stank with illness, medicinal herbs, and the chamber pot in the corner behind a sheet, its contents emptied outside the one open window as needed. Henrietta looked around and wondered where to begin.

"Ooh, 'ere's a rum mort," squealed a woman in a ragged gray cloak, long unwashed. "Draw your bung for ye, shall I? Fancy there's some gelt in that nugging dress!" She reached for Henrietta's skirts.

Henrietta clamped a hand over her pocket. The woman's breath held the stink of rotten teeth, and her face was scarred from smallpox.

"I haven't any coin," she said, it having been emphasized by the Auxiliary matrons that any money they distributed would at once be extorted or traded for gin. "Would you like one of these?"

The woman seized a knitted shawl and turned to Darien. "Yer Jemmy fellow, then?" She tugged down her bodice to expose a pair of heavy round breasts. It was only her face and hands that were worn, Henrietta realized; she was, in all likelihood, young.

"'Ere, ye great gorger," she cooed at Darien. "Tip me a hog and I'll tickle your rod! Blow your pipe for a kick!"

Darien tried and failed to tear his eyes away from the woman's bared bosom and the dark, prominent nipples pointing straight up. How like a man to be knocked senseless by the sight of a woman's bosoms, Henrietta thought as Darien sent her a stricken look. She pulled the shawl firmly about the woman's shoulders, tying her up in a tidy bow.

"Do you require stockings as well?" she asked.

"Not the drawers you got, gawkey!" The woman laughed and moved away to proposition the porter.

"Shift yer bob, ye draggletail!" James cried after her. "An' quit sportin' the dairy."

"I needs me one o' them shawls," piped a woman sitting on the floor.

Henrietta offered her one, noting the dirt and scars on the woman's face, the tangles in her hair, the shabby, threadbare state of her dress. The Sisters of Benevolence would never allow their tenants to remain unwashed or thinly clad. The woman rose and hiked up her skirt, pulled the shawl between her legs, wrapped and tied it around her waist, and then dropped her skirt back into place. It was fair to say she was wearing neither drawers nor stockings.

"It's thanking you I am," she said, patting the bulge at her hips. "Ran out of small clothes, I did, and bleedin' like a stuck pig all o'er the place."

Henrietta tried to stand her ground as other women surged forward and plucked at the items in her boxes, fighting over the ones they wanted, throwing those useless to them on the floor. This was not at all like her missions to the hospitals and workhouses of the north. There, she bent over cots and tucked soft blankets around the shoulders of shivering women, swaddled babies, exchanged words of hope and encouragement in quiet, soulful murmurs. Here, faces swirled before her while handkerchiefs, blankets, and stockings flew through the air and her arms were pulled this way and that.

"Please," Henrietta said as one woman wrenched a small blanket out of her arms. "That's for a baby."

"It's fer me now, ain't it!" the woman cried. "Stiff rump! Dog's wife!"

"Sauce box!" James yelled back.

The woman turned and spat. Henrietta clamped her teeth together and fought the impulse to throw the box at them and run away, shrieking.

All of a sudden Darien was before her, one strong arm sweeping the crowd of women away. "Stand back, all of you," he said in a commanding voice. He took one of her boxes and stepped forward, shielding Henrietta from the horde. "Do not pull Miss Wardley-Hines about. Sit down," he said over his shoulder, without looking back.

"Where?" Henrietta asked with a shaky breath, looking around.

In a corner of the room, a young girl lay on a cot under a thin blanket, an infant at her side. The poor child squirmed and kicked weakly. The girl stretched out a hand to soothe it but did not lift her head.

Henrietta laid an extra blanket over the girl's legs. "Look at you," she cooed at the baby. "Is this your brother? Sister?"

"Brother?" The girl had a thin, freckled face, but her eyes were unfocused. She was either under the influence of opiates or exhausted. "'E's mine."

Henrietta blinked. "Oh. I did not think you old enough to be a mother."

"Hush, ye great roarer." The girl patted the wailing infant with a thin hand. "'E's sick as a horse," she told Henrietta. "Nothing settles 'im. Can't eat, can't sleep. An' never stops crying."

"He may need his breeches changed," Henrietta said, detecting a distinctive smell.

"I run out of cloths for him," the girl said. "Wash day's Friday."

Henrietta gagged when she opened the swaddling clothes. There was a bucket in the corner that appeared to be the sole water supply; she poured some onto a cloth and carefully cleaned the baby. He stopped squalling and watched her with a resigned squint, as if he already knew the world he had been brought into was a cold, cruel place.

"How old is he?" Henrietta asked.

"Six months," the girl said with a tired smile. "A fine banging boy, aye?"

"He's lovely," Henrietta murmured. She'd had a hand in the care of all five of her half-sisters, so she managed a fair swaddle in a fresh cloth and blanket. The poor mite poked a fist into his mouth and watched her with hopeful eyes.

"I believe he's hungry."

"I barely got milk," the girl said, her lashes drifting closed. "And what grub I give 'im, 'e shoots up."

And how could she nourish a baby, being malnourished herself? Henrietta looked around and saw a small dish of something clotted and brownish gray not far from the girl's head. She poured a little water into the dish to make a thin paste of the gruel. Then she took off her gloves, scooped gruel onto her finger, and slid it into the baby's mouth. He mewled and turned away, giving that thin, hoarse wail.

"What's his name?" Henrietta asked. The noise of the room had faded. It was just her, the baby, and this frail girl, at sea on a frayed blanket.

"I named 'im Elijah." The girl watched her son with a small, sweet smile. "The one so special that God took 'im straight up to Heaven, aye?"

"Yes," Henrietta said past the lump in her throat. "Yes, I believe he was."

"'E won't make it if 'e don't eat," the girl said with a weary sigh.

Henrietta's stomach clenched. All those days and weeks she had sat at Fanny's bedside, able to do nothing. She knew that helplessness. It was part of what drove her to assist Lady Bess with her rescues. Now, given that Pinochle had recognized her, she'd be thwarted in her role of assisting rescues. Lady Bessington might be immune to gossip or criminal charges. Henrietta Wardley-Hines was not.

But there were other ways she could help.

"I am Henrietta Wardley-Hines," she announced. "What is your name, dear?"

"Mary Ann Dowdy. Named after both me grandmothers, I am." The girl heaved herself up and held out a hand. "Pleased to meet you."

Henrietta smiled at her manners. "How long have you been here, Mary Ann?"

"Two days. I can stay, but they want to send Elijah to a baby farm." She blinked away tears. "I don't want 'im to go, but we got nowhere else."

The London workhouses frequently sent infants out of town to be nursed and raised, it being thought they had a better survival rate in the country. This also left their parents free to work. "Your home?" Henrietta asked, knowing Mary Ann would not be in the parish workhouse if she had other options.

"Rushy Green." Mary Ann clenched her jaw. "An' if I go back, my da'll just trade me to another man to pay his debts. I left to get away from 'im."

Henrietta swallowed the bile rising in her throat. Such great, undeserved fortune she'd had, born the daughter of Jasper Wardley-Hines, a man who would never abuse those in his care.

"E'ryone said there's work in London." Mary Ann's voice was a thin thread. The baby cried silently as he worked his face against Henrietta's arm. "I said I'd do anything. Scullery maid. Sweep stables. But no one'll take me with a belly full." Mary Ann tried to keep her expression hard, but Henrietta saw fresh tears gathering in her eyes.

"I tole'm what'd happen to me if I go back, but it's policy to send folk to their home parishes. The master said 'e don't care where I get off the cart, so long as I don't put a burden on their poor rolls. But there ain't work in the other villages, not from those who know me. I dunno what I'm to do."

Henrietta drew a handkerchief from her box and handed it to Mary Ann, then withdrew a packet of thick, creamy calling cards. "Here's what we will do. Have you heard of this place?"

The girl looked at the card with polite interest. "Can't read, mum."

"Oh. Well, it is a hospital for women and children in distressed circumstances, run by the Sisters of Benevolence. I will take you there. We will find you a bed and food and proper clothing, and Elijah will stay with you."

Mary Ann looked with wide eyes from Henrietta's face to the infant in her arms. "But why would they help me, mum?"

"Because you are in need of it," Henrietta said. "Take Elijah and gather your things, Mary Ann. I will tell the nurse we are leaving."

As Mary Ann took the infant, he stiffened, arched in her arms, and then puked down the front of his mother's soiled dress. The girl sighed and dabbed at the thin line of undigested gruel with the handkerchief Henrietta had given her. The baby gave a soft, mewling wail.

Darien leaned against the far wall, empty boxes at his feet. John and James diced with a set of bones, but Darien watched her. Even across the room, Henrietta felt his gaze as she would a touch.

She put up her chin and marched to the ward nurse, exhilarated at the thought that, finally, she could do more than offer a blanket or a carriage. She could do something to alter the course of this girl's life, and that of her child.

But this workhouse was not in any of the northern places where the Wardley-Hines name held cachet. The porter summoned the master, and the master held adamant that it was against the rules for Mary Ann to leave anywhere but back to her home parish. He was eager for her to cease being a burden on Marylebone, but he had to account to a commission for anyone in his care, and private citizens could not liberate workhouse residents at their whim.

"Why should it matter where she goes as long as she is leaving?" Henrietta argued. "You will have one less person to deal with. Two, actually."

But no mere woman was going to budge the master from his duty. He and the porter seemed immune to the name Sir Jasper Wardley-Hines. At the name Sir Pelton Pomeroy, the master gave a gravelly, condescending laugh. She was about to invoke the Earl of Warrefield when Lord Darien unfolded himself from the wall and crossed the room.

He looked the elegant, bored aristocrat from the top of his sleek head to the heels of his polished boots. He stood next to her as though he had every right to be there, as if Henrietta belonged at his side.

"Miss Wardley-Hines," he drawled in a careless tone, "let us have a word here, man to man."

The porter nodded with respect, and the master swiftly reconsidered his stance. Lord Daring couldn't be bothered with such things as rules and policies. Henrietta collected her boxes, seething. She would go to Hines House and speak with Jasper, then call on Sir Pelton and explain the situation to him, and then—

"Gather your kit," Darien said, strolling up a short minute later. "We are leaving."

"I cannot leave Mary Ann here," Henrietta said. "If I cannot bring her with me, then—"

"We are *all* leaving," said the bored aristocrat. "Now. You, Long John," he called to the footman, "go find your mate. And you, Jack o' Legs," he addressed James, who glowered back at him, "find the coach. I do not care to spend another minute in this hellhole. The stench will never come out of my coat."

Henrietta's jaw dropped. "But he told me—"

"Yes," Darien said, a hard edge to his tone. "But he had a different answer for the son of the Marquess of Langford. Does that surprise you?"

She snapped her mouth shut and turned to her task. Lord Darien had achieved her purpose, not because her cause was just, but because he was a high-born man. It didn't matter that she was the daughter of a knight, sister of a baronet, step-granddaughter to the Earl of Warrefield, niece to Sir Pelton, or subscriber to the Minerva Society. She was a woman, and her wishes mattered only if a male chose to humor them.

Outside, the carriage bowled toward them, and James

scrambled up beside the coachman. "All your cards are trumps now," he called to Mary Ann. "Miss Hetty collects strays where'er she goes. Got me out of the Fleet, she did."

Darien's gaze swung to Henrietta. "You found your groom in prison?"

"In for debt," James snapped. "Not thievin'."

Henrietta took the baby as Mary Ann struggled up the carriage step. Seeing the expensive equipage, a crowd of peddlers formed, eager to display their wares. Henrietta gripped the baby as the sudden horde jostled her.

"Tag-rag and bobtail," James shouted. "Fall back, ye bung nippers, or I'll thump ye on the jolly nob! Miss Hetty, mind they don't file your pockets."

Henrietta struggled to free herself from the tugging hands. Not once in all her forays in Rossendale, Bath, or Bamford, the small village on her estate, had she ever had reason to fear for her purse or her person.

Suddenly, the jostling stopped. A warm, firm heat enveloped her back and bore her like a strong wave up into the carriage. Before Henrietta knew quite what had happened, she was seated on one of the plush benches of the Wardley-Hines carriage, and Lord Darien crowded next to her as he slammed shut the door. The coach dipped as the footmen leapt to their posts in the back, and the conveyance jerked forward at a shout from James.

"I'll go with you for a way, if you don't mind," Darien said. "You may set me down anywhere you like."

"Lord Daring, in my coach," Henrietta observed. "I suppose this ensures my name will be all over the scandal papers. What will the Daughters of Minerva think of me now?" She ought to feel despair at her certain ruination, but instead she felt soothed by his competence, his calm strength.

"Do you not have a maid to accompany you?" Darien's glance took in the new leather and velvet curtains of the coach.

"Oh, do you mean, do I pay a young person to follow me about and hold my packages?" Henrietta held the baby close to her breast. His tiny eyelashes fluttered, and the little lips made sucking motions. "Not when their time could be better spent. Do you know, if I had a signature on my petition for every person who follows your daily activities in the gossip sheets, Parliament would abolish slavery on the instant."

"That ought to redeem my name in the historical record," Darien said. "What is the direction of this place?"

"Are ye certain they'll take me, miss?" Mary Ann said anxiously, her thin hand bunching her dirty skirt. "I've no coin to pay for me and Elijah, but I'm willing to work, I am."

"That matter can be settled once you and the baby are well," Henrietta said. She had not forgotten that the Benevolence Hospital was overflowing, but she could not leave Mary Ann and her babe at the workhouse. "The Sisters will take you and see you both back to health. Once you find work, they may collect a placement fee, but they will ask no payment nor charge a surety for—" She bit her lip. Most hospitals required a commitment in advance that someone would pay for burial fees.

"A private hospital?" Darien inquired.

"A charitable institution supported by the Minerva Society," Henrietta replied, "and staffed by a lay order, the Sisters of Benevolence. One of several they run in London and nearby. You might consider offering your support, milord, if you are interested in the cause of mercy."

She held the swaddled baby against her chest, wondering how many women and their babes, in his career, he had bundled off to such circumstances. She must hope no one who saw them would cast their mission in such a light. What a relief that Henrietta was impervious to his charm.

Mary Ann's eyes widened as they arrived at the large, gracious façade of the hospital. She dabbed at tears when they were turned over to the matron with promises that she and her babe would be fed, clothed, and comfortably settled wherever room could be found. The girl looked as if she could not quite trust she had actually found refuge, and her lip trembled as she faced Henrietta.

"Mum, I don't know what to say. What you've done—you're an angel, you are."

"Far from it," Henrietta said, stroking Elijah on the forehead as he squirmed and mewled. "It is the Sisters who are angels. I shall check on you tomorrow and hope to find you comfortably established, and Elijah feasting."

And, she decided, she would bring a large purse for the Sisters. She was saving up to buy an old mill near her estate, but this expense she could spare.

Her heart was still aching from Mary Ann and Elijah's plight when she stepped out to the street to find the infamous Lord Daring lounging against her coach. He looked as if he had just come fresh from the hands of his valet, not as if he had spent the morning in the workhouse.

The realization nearly lifted her straight off her feet. She had accomplished a rescue of her very own today. With his help.

"I owe you thanks, Lord Darien." She released a shaky breath. "Whatever it took to bribe the master, I will repay you."

"The Langford title is better than gold." Darien straightened from his indolent pose. "Why this girl and her poor sickly brat? When there are dozens, if not hundreds of women and children in the workhouse?"

"They would have taken Elijah from her. He'd never survive at a baby farm. At least here he has a chance." Henrietta's heart twisted as she thought of that too-small, too-quiet baby.

Fanny had been small for her age too, tough in her temperament but not her constitution, which was one reason the fever had ravaged her while leaving her siblings untouched.

Daring's eyes followed her movement as she touched the white armband on her sleeve. "But you are not responsible for the girl or her condition." He sounded puzzled.

"Is it so inconceivable I would be touched by her plight? Besides, you assisted as well." She crossed her arms over her chest, wondering at the sudden antagonism that rose within her. Because he, like so many men, could afford not to care about the reams of women and children left to support themselves in a friendless world?

"The Benevolence Hospital," she said, pointing to the building behind her, "specializes in assisting women and children in distressed circumstances. Unless I am in error, any woman you make your acquaintance would do well to know about this place. They would take in even a duke's daughter if she asked."

His face turned to granite as he opened the coach door. "If you will allow me to see you home, Miss Wardley-Hines, I should like to take you into my confidence about something."

Ask her, she assumed, how to make arrangements for said duke's daughter.

Henrietta's heart sank as she realized she could not leave him here. Seeing she had brought him to Knightsbridge, it would be rude not to offer him transport. At least she was well accompanied. James and the coachman were there with their twitching ears, the two footmen still behind.

Still, the open hood of the landau would expose them to every curious onlooker. They would be seen and remarked upon, even if his intentions toward her were not untoward.

She had oft been warned her meddling would lead her into

trouble, but curiosity was her fatal flaw. Henrietta very much wanted to know what would happen to Lady Celeste.

And, the more dangerous confession—she did not wish to be free of Lord Daring. Not just yet.

Though she was perfectly capable of hauling herself into her father's carriage, she gave him her hand as she ascended the steps. His fingers clasped hers, strong and warm. Then his lithe form dropped into the seat beside her, his thigh brushing hers, and a slow flush crawled through Henrietta's belly.

What a flat-out bouncer she was telling herself, thinking she was impervious. She was far from immune to him.

Lord Daring did not ruin young women against their will. They came to him willingly, in droves.

And no doubt enjoyed their debauching whole-heartedly. Every single time.

CHAPTER EIGHT

H e had her alone, at last, but he could see she was reserved
and wary. As well she should be. It was another mark of
her insight.

"Lady Mama was very interested to hear that I conversed
with you last night at Ellesmere House," Henrietta remarked as
John Coachman clicked to the horses and the Hines carriage
rolled into the street.

Darien drew a blank for a moment. "Lady Clarinda, your
stepmother? Daughter to the Earl of Warrefield?"

"Yes, my father reached very high for his second marriage,"
she answered calmly. "Some say he went too far above himself,
in fact."

"Are the two of you on good terms?" To Darien's knowledge,
the marquess had never thought to remarry after his wife died.
No one could replace Princess Pip.

"She is the most darling creature," Henrietta said. "Quite
tender-hearted, a touch helpless, and a wonderful mother. Sir
Jasper and I dote upon her."

She said this without a trace of guile. Darien had thought
that, behind her indolence and plump beauty, Lady Clarinda

was rather shrewd. But perhaps she was one of those women who were shrewd only about, and around, men.

"I beg your pardon." Henrietta looked around. "Did you tell my coachman to drive us through Hyde Park?"

"You need something to lift your spirits," Darien said. "You've a very sad droop to your mouth."

It was a mistake to look at her mouth. She tried setting it in a prim line, which did nothing to detract from its distinct shape, the marked bow-like curve to her upper lip and the full curve of the bottom. He'd made a study of that lovely mouth all morning, watching it tremble when she was set upon by the women at the workhouse, turn firm as she spoke with the girl and her baby, then bare her teeth at the master as she argued for the girl's release.

"Lord Darien, I do not wish to appear rude, but I am sure you are aware of the speculation that will attach to your being seen with me. I assume that is why you abandoned me in the Chapel Royal."

Their first interlude together. Darien thought fondly on it. Not knowing who he was, she had dealt with him innocently, forthrightly, with clear interest in her eyes. It was a mistake also to look at her eyes. Her lashes were a coffee color, several shades darker than her hair, and they were heavy and thick. Her eyes were large for her face and wide set, greenish-gold in the outdoor light.

So she had lovely eyes as well. It was not to the point. Darien moved his gaze away from her searching, straightforward one. It would not do to play his hand too soon, but neither could he afford to woo her at his leisure. The marquess was not a patient man, and whatever he had said about waiting out the Season, Darien had no doubt he was already visiting friends, testing the waters for support for his case.

"Your dwarf was bragging about the matched set your father

bought you, and I wanted to see how they go. Do you fear for your reputation?"

"His name is James," Henrietta said. "I should think you, as the son of a marquess, have an entire stable full of prime goers. And I am not interested in marriage, even if I were marriageable. My father's money is tied up in investments, the jointure for Lady Mama, and settlements for the girls, leaving my portion rather small."

Now, who had put it into her head that a man would want her only for her father's money? How could she think that, with those eyes and that mouth?

He suspected her new acquaintances underestimated Henrietta Wardley-Hines. He would take care not to fall into the same error.

"Perhaps I am not trying to ruin your reputation but repair mine," Darien said. "You seem a person who interests herself in reform."

Henrietta looked out at the double row of walnut trees lining the road. "If you refer to the Duke of Highcastle's daughter, I should think the way to repair that situation is marriage."

He found her directness a relief. Henrietta Wardley-Hines was not soft, plush, and coy like so many wealthy girls. It amused him that she so clearly thought herself unsusceptible to him. He considered educating her on this point; the thought of awakening her had a strange appeal.

But she would go on to use her new knowledge on another man, and that left a dry taste in his mouth.

The mention of Celeste roused a familiar twist of guilt in his belly. She carried a babe. Possibly his babe. This had meant nothing to him, viscerally, until he stood against the wall in the St. Marylebone parish workhouse and watched Henrietta try to spoon gruel into the mouth of a starving infant.

"I offered to marry Celeste," Darien said. "I did not realize at the time of our—involvement—that she was hoping I would help her escape a betrothal."

More fool he. It was the chief reason women approached him, Lord Daring, breaker of troths. But he'd made the mistake of attending his friend's house party when Lucretius was barely in the ground. He'd been a raw nerve, wild with grief, and Celeste had been so warm and sympathetic.

Darien understood now why people in mourning weren't to be set loose in public. Grief had its own unfathomable logic and the ability to set one's customary mental faculties out of train.

"What happened?" Henrietta watched his face without judgment.

"She used her liaison with me to break that engagement, but when her jilted fiancé challenged me to a duel, in the course of inspecting our swords on the field of honor, we discovered a third man had been enjoying Celeste's many charms. She pursued me to make this mystery man jealous, but it seems he did not appreciate the game, for he has not stepped forward to claim her or the babe. And so she is eating herself into a fine fury at Highcastle House, from everything I hear."

"Is the babe yours?" Henrietta asked.

"I can't be sure. She won't name the father."

"Do you wish to marry her?"

"No." Darien shuddered at the thought. Marriage to Celeste would guarantee a life of misery. "She declined my offer in no uncertain terms. And she refuses my solicitor's every offer to make arrangements for the babe."

"At least you are offering," she muttered, looking away.

Darien felt the smuts and dust of this dirty city penetrating to his skin. The story made him look despicable. Havering, Celeste's fiancé, was a friend of his. Darien hadn't known of the betrothal when Celeste had snuck into his room last fall, though he could have discovered it in an instant if he'd asked. He ought to have asked. He'd been a blind fool not to see what she was about.

"What will you do now?"

"I haven't a notion," Darien said. "But I do wish I knew what she plans."

Silence fell between them, quiet and comfortable. He wondered that she continued to converse with him, rather than heaping scorn upon his head.

A pair of ladies in a high-perch phaeton passed them, openly staring, and Henrietta stiffened.

"You have twice done me a kindness, Lord Darien, but I fail to see how I might repay you. I am hardly likely to repair your reputation, for being seen in my company might lead people to question your taste." She looked at him with dancing eyes. "Charley tells me I am developing a reputation as an eccentric."

She confessed this with complete candor. Miss Wardley-Hines certainly did not run in the usual style.

"I could make you fashionable," Darien said. "It is largely a matter of conduct, and only partly a matter of dress."

The instant he said it, he wanted to. He could transform her. In dress, he had an eye for what flattered a figure, male as well as female. In conduct, she would require little coaching. He rather liked her forthright, uncomplicated manner; it made her refreshing and unusual among a class of females trained to be coquettes. In addition to the regal shape of her head and those masses of cinnamon-brown hair, she had that lovely throat. He could make do with that.

"I see little point," she said, "unless it gains me signatures for my petition, or draws attention to the upcoming debate of the Minerva Society. Your character, sir, might be improved upon, but I fear that my lack of style cannot."

"I could make you a diamond of the first water, if you wished."

"I should have to be beautiful for that."

In another woman, this would be an invitation for flattery, but he could see that Henrietta thought she stated an accepted fact. A pity she couldn't see her own profile. The nose that looked prominent from the front had a nice straight line to the side, and her square jaw was elegance itself. And those eyes—out of doors, they were the green of a mysterious forest, dark and cool.

"Besides, I am not suited for a life of leisure," she said, gesturing at the fashionable people and vehicles mincing along the drive. "Promenading through the park and talking about—what? Which party to attend? What color ribbon to wear with my new hat? When there are so many troubles all around us."

"It is not a crime to take pleasure in an airing in the park or conversation with friends, Miss Wardley-Hines," he said sternly. "Perhaps these young ladies you see have, like you, spent their days dedicated to various causes and are now taking a moment to relax and enjoy a warm afternoon."

"Perhaps. Or perhaps they do not concern themselves with the plight of the lesser, so long as they may remain untouched by their miseries." She turned to him, the spark in her eyes sharpening. "But what is the difference between Mary Ann, a mother in the workhouse at fifteen, and this young girl riding in her mother's curricle? Birth alone. And the wealth that comes with it."

She choked on her words and stared ahead at the circular reservoir that stood in the drive before them. "Would you like to guess who fathered Mary Ann's child? That tiny, helpless being?"

"A heartless cad such as myself, I suppose," Darien said heavily.

"Not a husband. Not a lover. Not a man she chose of her own free will." Henrietta leaned over and spat on the ground like any fishwife in the streets. Darien looked around to see if anyone he knew had seen the gesture.

"Her *father*, the man who is supposed to protect, nurture, guide, and shelter her, traded her to a friend to pay a debt. As if she were nothing more than coin." She curled her hands into fists on her lap.

Darien wished he could soothe away that unhappy frown, but he didn't dare touch her. The footmen would see it. They were not on the fashionable Ring, where those who knew him were airing themselves and their costly attire, but he guessed from the many stares in their direction that he had been recognized. And he was quite sure her half-sized groom would leap from his seat and sink teeth into him if Darien laid hands on his mistress.

"Perhaps that should be the topic for my debate," she said in a broken voice. "The duty of men toward their dependents."

He felt this as a spear through his insides. She did not condemn him to his face, but she lumped him part and parcel with the lot of dishonorable men. He might deserve it. Even his father felt he had stained the Bales name.

"Henrietta," he said quietly. "That is not how a man ought to behave, but too many men behave in such fashion. We cannot save all their victims."

"We can try." She swiped at her cheek, unashamed to cry in public, given they were tears of righteous fury. "Might I go home, please? I have had quite enough of being fashionable for one day."

She sat wrapped in her own thoughts until they reached Manchester Square. It was a new experience to have his companion preoccupied with something other than him. Darien found he did not like it.

He leapt down from the carriage and held her hand to help her descend, curling his fingers around hers. "There is a way you might oblige me, if you feel I have been of assistance to you in any way." He took great care to sound offhand. "Your uncle has a place in the prime minister's cabinet, does he not?"

She dropped his hand. She had such slender hands and a firm grip, another unfeminine quality he found interesting.

"Marsibel is not for you," she said in a cool tone.

He almost smiled at her prickling like an adorable hedgehog. Instead, he shrugged. "I have no designs on your cousin. There is a legal matter I thought your uncle might advise me on. That is all."

She raked him with that level gaze, her eyes back to the gray-green of a cloudy pond. "You had best approach Sir Pelton yourself in that case. I have no influence with him, and I make it a practice not to bring supplicants."

Thus she destroyed in a moment the careful offensive he had spent hours building. He'd wasted the morning combing through the city's many workhouses in search of her so he might play the noble rescuer. He should have guessed that Henrietta Wardley-Hines would upset all his plans.

"It is not pressing," he lied.

But Lord Darien Bales was not a man to go down easily in defeat. Ignoring her protest that Charley would not like it, Darien allowed the butler to show him into a lovely parlor furnished in blue and gold, where Lady Clarinda sat like Venus in her shell of pearl.

The lady could not hide her delight at finding Henrietta in the company of an eligible male. She welcomed him in, sent for tea, and in five minutes had reacquainted herself with the entire Bales family history.

Darien sensed Henrietta hanging on every bit of information, though she tried to appear disinterested. When Lady Clarinda conveyed her condolences on the loss of his nephew,

Henrietta shot him a shrewd glance, guessing why he had marked her white armband.

Darien let Lady Clarinda lead the conversation, knowing she would reach his desired end if he merely sat through a review of the Wardley, Hines, and Warrefield family tree. Mentioning Rutherford's scholarly bent put the seal on things. The polite fifteen minutes concluded, Darien stepped into the street in possession of an invitation to dine at the Wardley-Hines table the next night, with Lady Clarinda promising to send to Lady Pomeroy to make up a small family party.

Henrietta saw him out with a frown. "I intended to spend tomorrow evening preparing for my debate, and now I must plan a dinner," she grumbled. "I expect there will be no end of talk. Why on earth would Lord Daring join the Wardley-Hines for a very dull evening at home?"

"It will smooth over any damage to your reputation for being seen with me. Dining with your family will assure the gossips that they condone our association."

Perry would congratulate himself that Darien was taking his advice to rile his father by dangling after unsuitable females. Darien would bear Perry's derision with cheer if the night gave him access to Sir Pelton.

Still, his male pride was nettled that Henrietta could take so little notice of him. While he'd chatted with Lady Clarinda, she'd busied herself with sorting through her correspondence. Now she fretted about what to feed him and where to place him at table.

She was determined to ignore the attraction that hummed between them, and Darien knew he should allow her the deceit. But that pride of his reared again. She felt the hum; he'd known it the moment she tripped in the Ellesmere gallery and he caught her. The spark had singed him through his gloves, and she hadn't been able to hide the blush that rose to her skin.

Still, exasperating woman, she snorted and looked him in the eye.

"Let us be clear. Lady Mama might condone an association with you. Charley is going to have kittens."

She kept pretending she was immune to him. He wanted her to admit that she was not.

He stepped close and bent over her hand, pitching his voice low. "I shall make good on my promise and help you decide what to wear."

They both looked down at her plain, worn riding habit. He was beginning to find that frown adorable, the one that indicated irritation with him.

"I can do that myself, thank you," she said.

He gave her a smile he had not yet given any woman, one meant to remind her he was a notorious rake and she ought to be on guard for her virtue. "But wouldn't you like someone to *dress* you?"

She snatched her hand away. "Good day, Lord Darien."

He watched as she ascended the steps with a furious swish of skirts. She was supposed to shiver and melt at the blatant innuendo that he was thinking not about dressing, but rather undressing her. Instead she was miffed that he had insulted her frock.

Darien told himself to focus on his goal. He ought not divert himself with provoking Henrietta Wardley-Hines. It would take far more than flirtatious hints and seductive charm to win her over. Providing assistance was a start, but Henrietta had a knack, it seemed, for roping people into her causes. He had to find a way to make her need him. Trust him.

He looked forward to the challenge.

It was well he had moved at once to approach Sir Pelton. Visiting his club the next day for a midday cold collation and a drink, Darien learned the marquess had been seen consulting with the Duke of Devonshire, the Duke of Ancaster, and the Marquess of Buckingham. His father, too, was setting the board. And his allies were far more powerful than Darien's.

"Took my advice, I see." Perry, chuckling, brought the broadsides to his study that afternoon as Darien worked on a design. "A tradesman's daughter! That'll send his lordship round the bend. Told you a Long Meg was the way to go."

The cold cuts turned in his stomach as Darien saw that London's prolific and remorseless satirists had gotten Henrietta in their sights. One cartoon lampooned her presentation, showing her in an awkward curtsy with an idiotic smile on her face as she extended a paper entitled "Petition" while burying the Queen's face in an enormous ostrich feather.

Beside them, another man, a knight's badge prominent on his chest, slipped a bag full of coins to a greedy King George. The caption contained some doggerel verse about Sir Grasping presenting his daughter, a Miss Hop-Higher, while the girl in her enormous, dilapidated gown resembled nothing so much as a fatuous stork.

The second was worse. It depicted Daring with wolfish fangs, paws hanging from the sleeves of his evening coat, facing the stork girl among the pillared displays of Ellesmere House. A banner of speech extended from his mouth: "Miss Hop-Higher! Do you suppose your father might buy some good graces for my poor self?"

In answer, a fatuous Miss Hop-Higher, in another odious dress, proclaimed, "Lord Daring! I fear your excesses are beyond even the scope of my infamous talents for reform!"

He'd made her a target, without wishing to. More than the wrath that her family might display over the ridicule, he feared how Henrietta might receive the cruel taunts. She had seemed to take pride in being thought eccentric, but no woman would appreciate being made to look a fool.

Darien's dark mood had his valet sweating as the poor man dressed him for dinner, and it took five tries before Darien was satisfied with the way his neckcloth was tied.

His ire deepened as he drove into Manchester Square, Rufie beside him, to find a knot of people on the sidewalk before Hines House. Two men in the working man's fustian leaned against the iron rail that led to the kitchen steps, but as Darien pulled up in his dashing whisky and handed the ribbons to a waiting boy, one of the men straightened and tossed his cheroot onto the pavement.

"Statement for the press!" he called. "What can you tell us about the fire? Do you agree that the topic the Minerva Society proposes is treasonous?"

The second man elbowed his friend in the ribs. "I say, you're no cit! That's Lord Daring, you sapskull." Both took out small notebooks and started scribbling, the first man glancing up as he drew a quick sketch.

Darien resisted the urge to throw the man's notebook into the street. Manchester Square being new and expensive, street sweepers kept it free of dung and filth, but the gesture would be satisfying.

"Lord Daring nobbing with cits now?" the first man inquired.

"Or Sir Jasper's handing out loans to the nobles," the second said around his cheroot. "Buying a title for the reform girl, is he? Did as much for himself."

It was too bad swords were out of fashion everywhere but at court; Darien wished he had his on hand. "You'd best move along," he told the men.

The front door burst open, and the two footmen who had accompanied Henrietta to the workhouse hurtled down the steps. They formed a guard around Darien and Rufie while the butler shouted.

"There is no news, you ruffians! There is nothing remotely treasonous in the topic Miss Wardley-Hines has proposed for the upcoming debate of the Minerva Society. You will permit the family's guests to enter the house!"

"What recourse falls to the dependent when those in power fail to protect those they govern?" one of the reporters asked, chortling. "That don't reek o' treason? What'd be your answer in that debate, milord Daring?"

Despite an elbow to the stomach from one of the footmen, the newsman broached the top step to lean into the butler's face. "What'd be *your* reaction, pops?"

"You will please disperse!" the butler shouted and slammed the door.

Shouts followed. "Open up! Send someone out! The press has a right to know!" Small stones pattered against the door, and the butler shook his head.

"That'll need repainting," he said. "Rude lot."

The entry hall blossomed with flowers. Bouquets lined the occasional tables and spilled onto the floor. Darien looked around in surprise as the butler took their hats and coats. It seemed an excessive display for a small family party.

Henrietta came to the top of the stairs, draped in a mountain of feathers. "You survived the gauntlet, I see. None the worse for wear?"

The pleasure he felt at her welcoming smile was absurd. Darien tamped it down. "No worse than Brooks's at the dinner rush," he said. "The greater trick will be wading through all these flowers. Are you starting a conservatory?"

"Yes, they're outrageous, aren't they?" She led them to a large, lofty drawing room adorned with neoclassical frescoes, warmed by oil lamps and rich fabrics. Her tiny cousin perched like a sparrow on a settee fresh from the Chippendale showroom. There was no one else.

"The flowers have been coming all day," the sparrow said shyly. "And the spectators, too. Hetty's advert announcing her debate for the Minerva Society appeared in all the papers this morning."

Darien hoped neither girl, nor her family, had seen the ha'penny broadsides featuring the adventures of Miss Hop-Higher. His suit with Sir Pelton would not speed if Darien made his family figures of public ridicule, but more than that, Darien didn't want to see what either of the men with the notebooks would make of Henrietta's current costume.

Henrietta made the introductions. "Marsi, you will remember Lord Darien from the Ellesmere gathering. This is his cousin, Mr. Rutherford Bales, in orders. Lord Darien, Mr. Bales, my cousin, Miss Marsibel Pomeroy."

Henrietta held out her hand and shook Rufie's with a frank smile. "You are the scholar of the family, I hear. Well and good.

Lord Darien and Marsi can talk fashion, and you can tell me about your studies."

Annoyance made Darien bridle. Both of the girls left unchaperoned when expecting a notorious rake for dinner? And how could she possibly find Rufie more interesting than him?

"Do the Wardley-Hines generally have newsmen clustered at their door?"

"Would you like a drink while we wait for Lady Mama to come down? Sir Jasper is in the study finishing up with our man of business. Marsi is having sherry, and I am having a nip of Canary wine. It is my Aunt Davinia's favorite, and she likes her liqueurs to stand on their own, if you know what I mean." Henrietta distributed glasses, then raised her own like a barmaid in the public house. "To new friends!"

"There was mention of a fire," Darien prodded.

"Yes." Henrietta took a sip of Canary wine. "Someone burned down the mill at Bamford that I'm trying to buy."

Darien stared at her. Fires at textile mills were epic disasters, with so many flammables at hand—fabrics, thread, wooden equipment, people. And Henrietta, who had wept over a sickly infant in the workhouse, was drinking wine and flirting with Rufie. Was she a trifle disguised?

"How unfortunate," he said flatly.

"No, it's wonderful. I'm certain Steppenfield set it after I outbid him. He did me a favor, really." Seeing Rufie's horrified look, she explained. "It was an old corn mill, long abandoned, and he likely fired it so Hodge would come down on the price. But I intend to hold firm on my offer, and if Hodge sells to me, I can rebuild with iron framing. Papa's done so in several of his mills, and it reduces the risk of fire considerably."

She noisily sipped her wine. "I've any number of improvements I want to experiment with, but I need a mill of my own. I want to try the new style of looms, with one of Newcomen's steam engines to power them."

Darien sniffed his glass. The smell was potent. "Does this fire account for all the floral arrangements in the hall?"

"No." She flushed a pretty shade of rose. "Those are from friends and supporters of the Minerva Society." She glanced at her cousin on the settee, as delicate as a china ornament. "What can be taking Lady Mama so long?"

Darien set his glass on a mahogany table. "Miss Pomeroy," he said, "who approved your cousin's ensemble for this evening?"

Henrietta looked down at herself. Instantly the pleased chatterbox fell away. "I *beg* your pardon."

"You cannot wear a day gown into dinner," Darien said. "Just what impression is this meant to achieve? To make you a stork in truth?"

Miss Pomeroy smiled, mischief in her eyes. "Miss Wollstonecraft believes that the efforts women spend on self-adornment are better devoted to cultivating their minds and rational interests."

"Miss Pomeroy, I promised to give your cousin the benefit of my advice on matters of dress. Would you think it very wrong of me to do so now?"

"I should think Hetty might benefit from your instruction." The sparrow's brown eyes danced with amusement. "If Duprix is with you?"

"I do not see how my dress is any of his concern," Henrietta snapped.

"It is an offense to taste, and moreover, looking at it will put me off my feed. Come," Darien prompted, holding out his hand in command.

He waited as her face reflected her inward struggle—indignation, distrust, and a flicker of—could he hope that was a flicker of interest? Women threw themselves at Lord Daring en masse; he couldn't remember the last time he'd had to woo one. When she stepped toward him, consenting, his breath released in a painful rush. She would come to him.

Frowning. "I know I oughtn't leave Marsi alone with *you*," she said, "but is it altogether proper to abandon her to your cousin?"

"Oh, good heavens. He's a priest," Darien said as he hauled Henrietta out of the room. "Moreover, he's Rufie. He wouldn't insult a gentleman's daughter even if he knew how."

THE LADY'S maid proved a ready ally once Darien marched Henrietta to her dressing room and announced his quest. "Surely Miss Wardley-Hines has an acceptable dinner gown? This Brunswick is three decades out of fashion."

"She 'as evening gowns, my lord," the Frenchwoman responded, "but I cannot call them acceptable." She opened a massive mahogany wardrobe.

"Duprix!" Henrietta protested. "These gowns are Aunt Davinia's, and she was the toast of court in her day."

"I doubt your aunt expected you to wear them," Darien said. "More like she sent you the dresses to take apart for the fabrics."

"That is what I told ma'mselle," Duprix cried. "*Bien sûr!*"

"This one seems the least offensive." Darien lifted an ivory silk *robe à la française* covered in ruffles. "Go behind the screen and try it on."

"I most certainly will not remove my gown. A man in my dressing room, and a rogue at that?"

"I shall be in your sitting room, next door," Darien said, "and you shall not set foot from this room until you are properly attired. Now hurry. It won't do to delay dinner."

She stepped behind the screen, muttering, and Darien could not resist teasing her. "It was once the done thing for a lady's admirers to attend her *toilette*. They would choose her gown and accessories. Am I correct, Duprix?"

"Ma'mselle has proven herself sadly indifferent to matters of fashion. And entertainment," Duprix replied, whisking the feathered horror out of sight.

Her sitting room, as Darien had hoped, revealed a great deal about Miss Henrietta Wardley-Hines. A tumble of books, colored rocks, and dried flowers lined the mantel above the fireplace, and several amateur watercolors lined the walls. Atop the escritoire stood a stack of foolscap, bottles of ink, a chipped Wedgewood teacup holding a bristle of quills, and a list of debate topics for the Minerva Society, all but the last crossed and blotted.

A pile of books on a small table beside bloomed with silk ribbon bookmarks. He detected the complete volumes of Catherine Macaulay's *History* and, atop them, Elizabeth Carter's translation of the Stoic philosopher Epictetus. He smiled.

Squeezed between Mrs. Montagu's writings on Shakespeare, Olaudah Equiano's autobiography, and Helena Maria Williams's *Letters from France*, Darien detected, was a novel, *Cecilia*, by Fanny Burney. So Miss Wardley-Hines had a trace of romantic sensibility after all.

Darien picked up the top volume, his eye drawn to the marked passages. *True dignity and human happiness consist of strength of mind and body,* he read. An appropriate Stoic sentiment. *The character of every man is in some degree formed by his profession.* Now, that was the belief of the professional class. One passage was heavily underlined: *An air of fashion, which is but a badge of slavishness, proves that the soul has not a strong individual character.*

That hit home. Worse were the arrows pointing to a sentence following: *Idle superficial young men, whose occupation is gallantry, and whose polished manners render vice more dangerous, conceal its deformity under gay ornamental drapery.* An exclamation point heralded this discovery.

The cover of the book confirmed his suspicions: *A Vindication of the Rights of Woman, with Strictures on Political and Moral Subjects,* by Mary Wollstonecraft. He dropped the volume as if it were a serpent about to strike.

Henrietta emerged from behind the screen, still grumbling. "If you are so interested in my dress, Lord Darien, you might recommend suitable attire for my debate. I must be presentable and persuasive, but not too fine."

Darien stared at the new gown, which was no more flattering. "I shall be happy to advise you." He walked around her, flicking a finger at the items he named. "Duprix. Take in the sack back, here, to give her more shape. Remove this ruffle around the neck and take these flounces off the shoulder as well. When you have time, sew them into a nice fall of lace at the cuff, but tonight she shall do without. And take off these feathered overskirts. She looks like a goose pulled through a hedge backwards."

"Another bird." Henrietta sighed.

"But a moment's work, my lord," the maid said with a gleam in her eye, and in short order she had the dress off her mistress. Henrietta stepped from the screen with a worried expression and the ugliest wrapper he had ever seen.

"Charley is going to read me a lecture," she fretted. "And what would Lady Bess say about Lord Daring in my chamber, telling me how to dress?"

There would be talk enough once her friends saw those cartoons, Darien knew. But if he made her stylish, she could better bear the gossip and snickers. She didn't know Polite Society well enough to know how much fashion ruled.

Darien pulled out the chair before the dressing table. "Now your hair. Take off that deplorable cap. You are not a milkmaid."

"I was meeting with my man of business about my mill," Henrietta reminded him, "and did not have time to dress my hair. What progress have you made with your own business which we discussed?"

He took a moment to sort through their conversation from yesterday morning. She didn't know of his father's intentions, so she must be hinting at something to do with the women's hospital.

"Celeste turned my solicitor away again." Darien consulted the boxes and bottles on the table. "Do you not know red powder is out of fashion? You might try blue."

"That is m'amselle's natural shade, monsieur," said Duprix from the chair where she sat ripping out stitches with lightning precision. "I give her a weekly lemon rinse to keep the shine."

"You might ask a woman to approach Lady Celeste." Henrietta took the set of pearl pins he held, looking up at him with wide, concerned eyes. "Perhaps a fellow creature can gain her confidence."

"Catch up these curls at the sides and add these." He handed her a string of pearls. "Whom can I ask? The ladies of her rank are locking up their daughters against me. I understand why, of course."

She arranged her hair and jewels as he bid, biting her lip. "You seem on good terms with Forsythia Pennyroyal."

"She is not one for such a task. I cannot rely on her discretion." He shrugged his shoulders in frustration. "If I had family, perhaps, but the only Bales girl left is my niece, Horatia, and she is barely fourteen."

"Poor little orphan," Henrietta murmured. "Lady Celeste has no sisters?"

"None of age, and no friends. She dislikes the company of women. I suppose I might try Freddy. He's her favorite of her rattle-pate brothers, and back from abroad."

Henrietta's mouth fell open as she stared into her glass. The classical look was simple and softened her features.

"I look agreeable," she said in surprise.

Darien cleared his throat to free a sudden tightness. "You should never hide your neck or bosom," he said. "Show them everywhere, and often. Now, go to Duprix. She is ready with your robe."

"It feels lighter," he heard Henrietta comment, then a whisper of silken fabric. "Oh, that is better. Far less ostrich, and more—"

"Swan."

Darien made no attempt to hide his satisfaction. With the excess pared away, the gown turned Henrietta's figure to advantage. She was slenderer than the fashion, but the gleaming fabric swirled and clung to her form in a way that made her deficiencies seem less pitiful and more...fascinating.

"What have you done to the bodice? You are meant to wear it—" He gestured. Duprix, with an efficient yank, lowered the neckline by two full inches.

"Good heavens, no," Henrietta said. "I shall catch my death of cold."

"M'sieur is correct. It is the accepted look for evening." Duprix shook out a pair of silk evening gloves and rolled them up Henrietta's arms. "You must have a set of bosom friends. I will make some for you."

"We will not discuss this with him in the room," Henrietta said, mortified.

Darien grinned. "You ought to show your shoulders more often too. Do you not wear stays?"

"Of course I do." Henrietta flushed. "Oh, very well. If you must know, I gave my old set to the housemaids and have not had time to go shopping."

"You might try some for evening, to elevate the bosom. Well, Duprix, this is an improvement."

"*Oui*, monsieur," Duprix allowed. "I will cut down the back and put in a fall of lace. Ma'mselle has a lovely back but no derriere to speak of."

"Excellent idea," Darien approved. "She does need a bit of a curve there."

"Would you like to check my teeth as well?" said an acidic Henrietta. "Or my hooves?"

"Speaking of hooves," Darien said, "nothing but silk slippers for evening. And gad, Henrietta, those stockings—they might as well be blue worsted." He shook his head at the maid. "Make sure she gets some nice silk ones next time she is out."

"Ma'mselle rarely visits the shops, milord. She has too many other demands on her time, so she says."

"No wonder her clothes are ten years out of date." Darien circled her again. "This fan. And this shawl, draped so. There— you are quite fetching."

Henrietta scowled. "I suppose now I must apply rouge, or patches, or something equally ridiculous."

"Why should you? You are only dining en famille. If you are endeavoring to captivate me, I prefer a simpler look," Darien answered.

"Captivate!" Henrietta gaped. "As if I—!" He grinned and ducked out of the room before she could throw a pot of something at his head.

Outside the chamber, Darien paused for a deep, calming breath. He had undressed more women than he could remember, but dressing this one was strangely more affecting. He had certainly not expected to find that Henrietta's badly fitting and outmoded gowns concealed such an elegant shape.

Darien smoothed the front of his suit to ensure everything was in order, then adopted the most casual air he could achieve as he strolled back to the drawing room. Henrietta, with her stubborn cleverness, might very well find a solution to his tangle with Celeste. Moreover, he had the satisfaction of knowing that Miss Wardley-Hines, however unconventional in other respects, was not completely unaffected when she saw him appraising her breasts.

CHAPTER TEN

In the drawing room, Sir Charleton, wearing a waistcoat similar in color and pattern to the one Darien had worn to the Ellesmere soiree, broke off his conversation with Marsibel to give Darien a fierce glower. Lady Clarinda held out her hand with a serene smile, glowing in an emerald satin *robe à l'anglaise.*

"Why, Hetty," she exclaimed as her stepdaughter entered the room. "That gown becomes you! My dear, you are quite transformed."

"We must never let Duprix return to France," Henrietta said, kissing her stepmother on the cheek. "I heard Dearbody showing Mr. Stokes to the door, so I suppose Papa will join us soon?"

On the word, the man of the house appeared. Darien steeled himself for the next test of the evening. But there was barely time for Sir Jasper to greet Darien before the front door opened again and a female cry of dismay floated up the stairs.

"An abomination, I tell you, sir! A vulgarity not to be borne! Oh, *where* is my niece? I have a thing or two I must say to her!"

Marsibel sent her cousin an apprehensive look. "Hetty, I meant to warn you, but I forgot—"

"Never mind that," Henrietta said, straightening her shoulders. Darien's eyes dipped to the interesting effect this had on her bosom. She faced the door as Lady Pomeroy entered with an anguished cry, shaking a folded newspaper in the air.

"Henrietta Eglantine Wardley-Hines! How *could* you?"

Her ladyship checked her tirade, gaze hardening as she recognized the infamous Lord Daring, then darting to Marsibel, who looked lovely and angelic. Clarinda made the introductions, and then, though anyone could see that Lady Pomeroy wished for her dramatic entrance to be forgotten, inquired, "But what has upset you, dear Althea? I do hope it is nothing too bad. Hetty, my love, do try to remember all that we owe Althea for taking you in hand and launching you on your first Season. We are a great deal indebted to her."

"This," Lady Pomeroy said, crumpling the paper in her gloved fist. "This...advert. Jasper! Did you know anything of this?"

"I'm sorry to say I've been in meetings all day," Jasper said in a genial tone. "What have you done now, Hetty?"

"My debate topic was printed today," Henrietta said, her chin set in a familiar way.

"And she's been receiving flowers in the dozens because of it." Clarinda beamed. "Surely you must have noticed, my love?"

Lady Pomeroy smoothed the paper and read, "To be discussed at the next meeting of the Minerva Society: *What is the appropriate response of dependents when those charged to protect them fail in their duty?*"

Darien stiffened. Was this an accusation toward him about Celeste?

"Oh, I say." Jasper grinned at his daughter. "You're bound to set up some backs with that, pet."

"Jasper! I wish you would not encourage her! What can she be thinking? What will Pitt say? Or the King? We will be thought Jacobins, all of us!" Lady Pomeroy cried.

Jasper turned to his brother-in-law. "What do you think, Pell? Will my daughter be hauled off in chains?" Darien sensed a serene lack of distress in the inquiry.

Sir Pelton cleared his throat. "Pitt's in a fury at France for declaring war on the Holy Roman Empire. I imagine he'll take notice if he senses a challenge to the King's authority. That incident of the closet has everyone on eggshells, though it finally got Pitt's mind off Russia."

"Incident of the closet?" Jasper asked, pouring drinks. Darien accepted one, though Rufie did not. Rufie, silent beside Marsibel, looked flushed and dazed, but Darien had greater things to worry about than his cousin's inadequacy in fine company. He had to make a strong impression on Sir Pelton.

"You didn't hear?" Pelton took the glass of sherry his host offered. "Some guards found a set of breeches in a closet in the House of Parliament. They'd been set afire, a sure effort to try to burn the place down, and everyone in it. Pitt's calling it treason and trying to blame it on Charles James Fox and his crowd. I'm bound he'll be monitoring all the assemblies very closely now."

"Good Lord. Burning breeches?" Charleton turned on his sister. "Hetty, you know Pitt's got his eye on that Corresponding Society. Bunch of rowdy cobblers and blacksmiths who ought to stick to their trades. Best have nothing to do with them."

"My debate is hosted by the Minerva Society, and there will be nothing seditious in it," Henrietta said with a stubbornness Darien was beginning to recognize. "My points are taken mostly from Miss Wollstonecraft. Mr. Pitt will see that, should he choose to attend. Perhaps a ticket might be provided for him."

"Well, my girl, should you get dragged off by the constable, I'll post bail," Jasper promised and topped off Sir Pelton's drink.

Darien hid his smile behind his glass. Yes, Sir Jasper seemed quite accustomed to his lively daughter getting up scrapes.

"Jasper," Lady Pomeroy cried again. "You cannot take this so lightly. Think of the scandal! How it could reflect on our name."

Henrietta bit her lip. "Lady Bess thinks my topic will draw a splendid crowd."

Darien raked his mind. Lady Bess must be the Countess Bessington, a famed London hostess, confirmed friend of the Blue Stocking circle, and well known as the ruling force behind several reforming organizations. He was not surprised Henrietta had been caught up in her orbit.

Jasper shrugged. "Bess set a store on your mother, so I doubt she'll steer you astray. Pell! Have you heard what happened to Hetty's mill? We suspect Steppenfield set the fire, the skunk."

This drew the menfolk off in conversation, leaving Lady Pomeroy to confront the unexpected guests. Darien stiffened his back as her icy glare fixed on him.

"Lord Darien," she said. "What a surprise to find you here. I trust..." She trailed off, at a loss for safe conversational ground.

"I escorted Miss Wardley-Hines home from the workhouse yesterday, and Lady Clarinda kindly invited me to dinner." Darien gave her a polished bow. "I hope I am not intruding."

Lady Pomeroy's eyes widened as she finally examined Henrietta, noting the pearls at her hair and throat, the delicate expanse of shoulder set off by the red of her India shawl. Her ladyship shot a jealous glance toward her daughter, as if reassuring herself that Marsibel still had the advantage.

A woman like Althea Pomeroy had no inkling of how Marsibel's girlish pinks and glossy browns were overshadowed by Henrietta's statuesque auburn and ivory, the bold cut of her collarbones, the enchanting arch of her neck. A man would see it, certainly.

The butler announced dinner, and Lady Clarinda quietly arranged the procession. With a light touch she drew Darien to her side; Charleton took in his aunt; Sir Pelton offered his arm to Henrietta; and Rutherford escorted Marsibel. Sir Jasper strolled in and seated himself at the head of his table with a lack of self-consciousness that made the whole show of precedence look silly.

"I admit our numbers are uneven," Lady Clarinda said to Darien, "but I was not certain that Charley would be joining us. He often dines at the club with his friends, though we are very glad to have him." Her eyes twinkled. "And any young lady he might wish to invite, in due time."

"Which club?" Darien inquired.

"The Eccentrics," Charley grumbled. "Don't have a recommendation to Brooks's, stiff-rumped lot."

"I could put in a word for you," Darien offered, wondering why on earth he did so. He did not need the sprig's approval to succeed with Pell Mell.

"Would have thought you a White's man," Sir Pelton said, settling himself beside Henrietta.

"White's is my father's club," Darien replied.

"Don't have much use for clubs myself." Jasper smoothed his serviette over his lap. "Do enjoy the coffee shops, though."

Darien tamped down a grin at Charley's answering mutter, but he felt along with it the old, dull ache. He had not dined with his own family, whole and complete, since he went down to school. He dimly remembered his father sitting large and imposing at the head of the table and his regal mother keeping her sons in line with no more than her soft voice and a few quelling looks from her magnificent dark eyes.

The pang deepened. Horace had known their mother, and Lucien had spoken of her often. Darien had only vague recollections of her scent—rose water, a touch of hartshorn for her nerves, talc powder, and the smell of oak gall ink when she was writing.

Jasper grinned at Darien. "Hetty warned me you would find our manners shabby. The infamous Lord Daring under my roof! I suppose I shall turn up in a broadside tomorrow?"

Darien blanched, wondering what Sir Jasper had seen of himself already. He glanced across the table at Henrietta. She glowed like a classical statue in her ivory gown, a Diana come to life. The candlelight flickered over the warm golden tones of her skin.

In other circumstances, he would indeed have considered the casual manners of the Wardley-Hines table shabby, at least in comparison to the high *ton* adhered to at a Bales dinner. But Henrietta's assumption made him immediately decide that the tradesman's table had its own convivial charm.

There was no fault to be found in the fare. The family dined in the old style, affably serving one another. Lady Pomeroy was too prim to request a dish beyond her reach, but the others freely interrupted conversation to make sure all the cook's tasty dishes came within their circuits. Darien gathered that Lady Clarinda had not engaged an expensive French chef but brought down their plain cook from Lancashire, who knew how to produce all of Sir Jasper's favorite dishes exactly as he liked them.

His first problem was finding someone to drink with. Sir Jasper and Sir Pelton drank with one another at a pace far too slow to suit Darien. Rufie was all but abstinent. Charley was the only one Darien could depend on to meet his eye and take wine with him, and so a glowering truce developed between the two men as they went glass for glass in a discreet, unnoticed competition to see who could best hold his drink.

The conversation was certainly lively and unrestrained. The mill fire and its ramifications were hashed out in full.

Henrietta's trip to the workhouse, the rescue of Mary Ann and her child, and Darien's part in it were fully elaborated. Jasper and Henrietta argued with Sir Pelton over the proposed Libel Act, with counterpoints provided by Charley, who had not left off the lace at his sleeves in sympathy with the French radicals as some of his set had done.

Even Marsibel was ribbed about Lord Pinochle, who had taken her driving in the park that afternoon. Darien wondered if he ought to mention that Pinochle was under the hatches and on the hunt for a bride to restore his credit.

Rutherford was pressed to speak of his studies, and then, as he had anticipated it would, the scrutiny turned to Darien. The covers had been removed and the dessert trays placed on the table, along with several bottles of port, when Jasper Wardley-Hines lit upon his notorious guest.

"So. Lord Daring. Do you mind the nickname?"

"It seems to amuse people," Darien allowed.

"And what sort of prospects await you? How does the lesser son of a marquess amuse himself? No estates of your own, I take it."

"You wouldn't have heard the news, sir," Charley said with a savage edge to his voice. "Daring won an estate from its proper owner some years ago in deep play. Stripped the man of everything he had. Word is the former owner blew out his brains the next day, leaving a destitute widow and children."

Conversation halted. Their expressions were a blur to Darien save for Rufie's look of horror. His cousin had been at Eton and knew none of the details. Darien never spoke of how he'd obtained The Revels, but he'd been warned by Perry that many held him responsible for the previous owner's death.

Jasper diplomatically moved on. "What else do you do with your time? Or are you fashionably idle, like our Charley here?"

Henrietta watched him with a curious, level look. Confound her for not being coy and flirtatious like other girls.

"Sir Charleton's behavior can at least be said to be above reproach," Lady Pomeroy remarked.

"I'd spend more time at my estate," Charley said, "had you not hired such an excellent steward, sir. But I find there is little for me to contribute."

"Your presence, son," Jasper said mildly. "A good manager keeps an eye on his business. Take Hetty's example."

"Lord Darien," Henrietta said, apropos of nothing, "is an expert on early Mediterranean art."

"He is also an amateur engineer," Rutherford volunteered. "He spent much of his time on the Continent documenting the building practices of the ancients and the Renaissance greats. His library is full of drafts and sketches for various sorts of machines and improvements for his and his father's estates."

Everyone at the table looked at Darien with expressions that ranged from polite interest to incredulity. Lady Pomeroy seemed dubious that he had ever had a thought in his head beyond what waistcoat to wear and which woman to seduce next, which made all his contrary impulses rise to the surface.

"An inventor, are you?" said Jasper. "Care to design me a loom that will improve on Arkwright's? The wretch patented his mechanism."

"My scribbles are nothing so useful, I'm afraid. Most of them have to do with drainage. My land is in Huntingdonshire, near the fens, and I need to address the flooding if I expect to grow anything other than moss."

"Hetty," said Sir Jasper, "are you taking heed? Our guest might be able to help you with some of your schemes."

"I was thinking the same thing," Henrietta answered, with that cool, shrewd look that so annoyed him.

It had been a fatal mistake to fix her frock. He was having a difficult time looking away from her. Every glance revealed a detail he had not hitherto noticed: the delicate shape of her ear, the deep hollow between her collarbones, the dainty bones of her wrist as she sipped her glass of expensive port. The candlelight turned her hair a deep, lustrous auburn. In a society ballroom, looking like this, she would draw every eye.

Darien forced a smile. He'd expected Jasper would pitch Henrietta at him. Perry had warned him that the bourgeois wouldn't hide their daughters; on the contrary, his rank would outweigh his reputation for those eager to advance their status. It would give the marquess apoplexy, though, to think a cit, a man who made his living by trade, would presume to consider a Bales a match for his family.

"Miss Wardley-Hines seems to be involved in many schemes," Darien said.

Henrietta put her chin on her fist. "I should like to hear more of your estate, Lord Darien. What are your feelings about enclosure?"

Darien went on the alert. He was not accustomed to discussing politics with women at the table. So far, he had passed muster on his attitudes toward slavery—could not condone—and the revolution in France—optimistic that Louis XVI would institute the reforms for which the National Assembly was calling. He had avoided commenting on Britain's next moves in India, a place he could only think of with red rage. For his usual circles, a repertoire of witty remarks was all that was required for conversation.

"I have not thought of enclosing my own lands," Darien replied, "though my brother Horace tried it at his estate of Bellamy. But The Revels has done well enough since we introduced crop rotation, and we only pasture the animals the farm can use. Are you in the market for wool sources, Sir Jasper?"

"Our mills are cotton," his host said. "Which I can't buy

from the Americas any longer, since Hetty won't let me support the slave trade. Won't even take sugar with her tea if she suspects it comes from the West Indies."

"I should like to see these designs of yours," Henrietta said, business-like. "I am interested in ways to improve land."

Jasper smiled, confirming Darien's suspicion that her father played a large role in encouraging Henrietta's unladylike endeavors, allowing her greater liberties than most unmarried girls could claim. Her elegant but languid stepmother saw no need to exercise corrections, and Lady Pomeroy's exertions to refine her niece, while heroic, had no effect.

The footmen cleared the table, and Sir Jasper rose. "Lord Darien, Mr. Bales, we do not observe the postprandial segregation of the sexes in this household. If you have eyes and but look on my lady, you will understand why. Dearbody will bring our port through, and we can quiz Hetty on her debate topic for the rest of the evening, eh?"

"Perhaps Marsibel will favor us with a piece or two at the pianoforte," Lady Pomeroy suggested as the party adjourned to the formal drawing room.

This attempt to elevate the tone of the evening met with little success. Henrietta made a beeline for Rutherford and cornered him in conversation on the desperately dry subject of library catalogues. She sat next to him on a low settee, her knees nearly touching his, that graceful body bent toward him as she hung upon his every word. Light from the whale oil lamps cast lovely bronze shadows over her fair skin and cinnamon hair.

Darien's pointed stare went ignored. It was insulting enough that she should be fascinated by Rufie, the dullest stick in the room, when she ought to be fascinated with Darien. They were both supposed to be allies in his crusade but, having ensconced themselves in scholarly conversation, they left him on his own.

Very well, then. Once Sir Jasper wandered off to flirt with his wife, who sat behind the tea tray, Darien bolted a glass of brandy for courage and made his opening move.

"Sir Pelton. I wonder if you might advise me on a small matter."

Pelton, leaning on the Italian marble mantelpiece framing the fire, lifted his gray eyebrows. "Not sure I know a whit of the subjects that interest you, lad."

Darien tamped down a flare of irritation at the barb. "Legal issue," he averred. "Concerning a man whose son and heir has been missing for seven years. His men of business think he should have the son presumed dead so the succession can be fixed on the next in line."

He felt a burning ball in his throat and swallowed past it. The fare at table had not been of so inferior a quality as to cause dyspepsia. "Others of the family, however, feel he should be making a better effort to find the current heir."

"Who's next in line?" Pelton watched him shrewdly. He knew exactly what situation Darien referred to. He'd wager Sir Pelton knew every family listed in *The New Peerage*; it made him potent in forming alliances.

"A worthless younger son," Darien said. "Rather a rakehell, I'm told. No substitute for the missing son, who's a soldier and a fine man." That burning lump grew larger, pressing on his windpipe. God, how he missed Lucien. He should be here, sparing Darien all this.

"Where'd the heir go missing?" Pelton asked.

Darien swallowed hard. "Mysore. During the second war."

"Ah." Pelton shook his salt-and-pepper head. "I'm sorry, lad, indeed I am." Sympathy shone in his eyes. "But that's not the Antipodes. A man would have made it back to civilization by now, were he able."

"So the coroner can declare him dead? With no evidence?"

"If there's a peerage involved, the suit must be brought before the King's Bench. Might go before the House of Lords, depending on the judge."

"What's to stop such a suit?" Darien asked desperately.

The other man shrugged. "Besides producing the missing son?"

"But if the heir presumptive were thought unfit?"

Pelton narrowed his eyes. "He'd have to be a felon or non compos mentis to be removed from succession. Too many in Lords would favor having the line of inheritance clear. And the King's men would have the same interest, unless, of course, there were some chance of it going to the Crown."

Properties of peers reverted to the Crown only if the line was extinguished or forfeited for treason. Darien's hopes puddled into his boots. His cravat, tied so expertly, pinched his windpipe. He didn't want to destroy his father's legacy; he wanted it whole and intact and waiting for Lucien when he finally came home.

He cast his mind about. What caused a man to be thrown out of Polite Society? His scandal with Celeste had made his father determined to tie him down as his heir, rather than disown him.

"Too much debt?" he wondered aloud. "Threat of imprisonment, or transportation?" But he didn't care to commit the kind of crime that would merit that penalty. Nor did he wish to get himself killed on the field of honor, as enlivening as the challenge from Havering had been.

But Nell, Horace's widow, running off to Italy with a portrait painter and leaving her last child behind, had stunned them all and also forfeited any claims to her husband's estate. "An unsuitable marriage?" he suggested.

Pelton's face froze, and his eyes went beyond Darien's shoulder to where his daughter sat on the settee. "Wouldn't advise that, lad," he said in a low voice. "A man can come back from ruin. A woman can't."

"I didn't mean—" Darien stopped himself, appalled. And now Sir Pelton, along with Charley and Henrietta, would be watching with drawn swords every move he made around Miss Pomeroy.

Henrietta paused in her conversation and looked up. Her eyes were mossy gray in the candlelight and her lips red-stained and glistening from the strawberry comfits she had eaten for dessert. When she rose and walked toward him, Darien couldn't stop staring at the way the silk caressed her legs as she walked. His mouth went dry where before his throat had been burning. Just what kind of spice had their cook put in the food?

Henrietta regarded him with a complete lack of flirtatiousness, as if he were a puzzle she was bent on solving. Darien straightened his spine.

"Lord Darien. Mr. Bales has been describing your designs for a water wheel to me."

Now this was taking her meddling too far. Did she pretend to be an engineer too, the way she pretended to have a stake in her father's mills? He resolved to be polite, at least until he could leave Hines House and this parlor and this maddening company and howl out his frustrations elsewhere.

"I'm afraid they are only conjectures at the moment," Darien said. "I haven't found a landowner who will let me build a model on his property."

"Try it on Hetty's," said Sir Jasper, strolling up to them with a dish of tea he had teased out of his lady. "She's got a swamp at Birch Vale she don't know what to do with. The men keep digging it out, and it keeps filling. I say she should cover the whole thing over, but she wants to create a stream."

"If I fill it in as you say, Papa, it won't create more arable land," Henrietta said. "The best a bog could provide is furze and firewood, and we've plenty of that already. What I need is to improve the irrigation of the Lower Hundred, and if I put in a water wheel, I'd have power into the bargain."

"Birch Vale is where?" Darien asked, diverted for the moment by the land-owning talk. He never got enough of it. Most of his friends didn't own lands, the men he knew who did were interested only in their income, not the administration, and good landowners, like his father, never took Darien seriously.

"Hetty's got a little estate near Bamford, in Derbyshire," Jasper said. "Three thousand acres. Surprised she didn't mention it. She's always going on about how her butter is the best in the county."

Darien did some quick math. A well-run estate could yield an annual profit of a pound an acre. Miss Henrietta Wardley-Hines had a comfortable income of around three thousand a year.

"But if I can find a pump that works at the Vale, we might adapt the design for a cotton mill," Henrietta said. "The drop in the river at Bamford isn't steep, and the corn mill used horses for power." Her face brightened. "Do you suppose it would be possible to build a water conveyance system throughout the building? Think of how useful that would be in the case of fire."

"I am sure such a thing could be designed." Darien caught his mind before it darted away into thinking how to pull off such an invention. "I am surprised to find you a landowner, Miss Wardley-Hines. In addition to your charitable interests."

Jasper gave his daughter an indulgent smile. "Hetty's a businesswoman, didn't you know? She's tried her experiments on my estates, then Charley's, and then she inherited Birch Vale from her mother's dowry and started saving up to invest in mills of her own. I believe she plans to compete with me and steal my business."

"You own an estate *and* a mill," Darien clarified.

"Only if Hodge sells to me." She shrugged. "And only if I do not marry. If I do, by law, every property I possess becomes my husband's."

Darien looked at her with new attention. "Why haven't you found any engineers before this to help you with your ideas about your land?"

She made a quick, sweeping motion that drew a line in the air from her head to her hips. "Woman," she said.

Was she ever. He was very aware of her breasts, the tops of which showed clearly in the low-cut gown. The sight sent his thoughts scrambling.

"Miss Wardley-Hines," he said, "you told me you were not rich."

"Not compared to my father, or yours," she said. He managed to drag his gaze away from her bosom, and she narrowed her eyes at him.

"She'll have a settlement at marriage," Jasper said, "but I won't sell her to the highest bidder. Hetty needs a man who knows her value."

"We'll be beating the fortune hunters away once her holdings become known," Darien said to Sir Jasper. His use of "we" escaped him until he saw Jasper's smile turn speculative.

Henrietta shrugged again. Darien was determined not to track the movement of her breasts at this gesture. "I've had fortune hunters test the waters before," she said.

"But you are launched now," Darien reminded her. "There will be plenty more cads who hope you will tow them out of the River Tick."

"Hetty's no fool, and she has a family to look out for her," Jasper said. "But perhaps you can give her a hint about the worst of them, eh? I expect you'll know who they are."

Darien stiffened as he perceived which way the wind was

blowing. Jasper was not throwing Henrietta at Darien's head; he thought Darien no more worthy of her than Rutherford. A businessman to the bone, and a shrewd one, Jasper wanted the best for his daughter. He was socializing with Darien to indulge his wife, who came from high circles, but to this owner of his own empire, Darien was like every other useless nobleman with little to recommend him beyond his handsome face and the cut of his coat.

The snarling cur inside of him, too close to the surface these days, had already taken a blow from Sir Pelton's rebuff. Now it wanted to snap. Did everyone here think him nothing more than the caricature made of him in the papers?

Henrietta clucked her tongue against her teeth. "I know a scoundrel when I see one, Papa, and if I don't, Charley will tell me."

She didn't see him as the slightest threat either. There she stood, all gleaming innocence, as smooth and untouchable as the Diana in the Ellesmere gallery. Miss Henrietta Wardley-Hines needed to be put on her guard, or she would fall prey to the first rascal who saw those creamy shoulders and slender neck, whether or not he knew of her income.

"Miss Wardley-Hines," Darien said, "would you care to show me the gardens? It is a most pleasant evening."

"Oh, certainly," she said, and gathered up her shawl. "They're quite lovely. Papa, do you mind?"

Her sire shrugged, casting his daughter all unwitting into the jaws of the wolf, and moved to the settee where Rutherford and Marsibel sat. "Go right ahead, pet," he said. "I want to ask Mr. Bales if he thinks I should enroll my new son in Eton or Harrow."

CHAPTER ELEVEN

D arien marveled at how easy it was. In the ballrooms of the elite, the daughters were hedged off by glowering mamas, and he couldn't go on a ride without seeing parasols of the upper crust raised in guard. Here in Hines House, he was a fox set loose in the henhouse.

He had no sooner stepped with Henrietta out the door from the library to the quiet walk behind the house than he stopped and turned so she ran into his body. She gasped and fell back, and when he moved toward her, she stumbled back again, plastering herself against the low stone wall. He held her pinned there, his chest an inch away from hers.

"Rule number one," he said. "Never, *never* let a rake get you alone. It only takes a moment to be compromised."

Her eyes flared, and then her brows shot together. "You're not—"

"Oh, yes, I am," he said, leaning in so the lapels of his double-breasted coat brushed her breasts. A warm burst of air touched his neck as she exhaled in surprise. "I could do anything I wanted to you right now."

There were several things he wanted to do to her right now. He was so close that the silk of her gown slid over his breeches when she shifted. All he had to do was move forward an inch, and—

"I could poke you in the eye with a pearl hairpin." She pushed at his chest.

He smiled and stepped away. The tartness of her response showed her complete innocence, and her strong defenses. She was a woman well worth the wooing.

"Point to me," he said, and his entire body warmed with pleasure as the light of battle entered those bottomless dark-gray eyes. She wouldn't be easy to conquer, and no man would ever break that fierce, bright spirit. He'd never met a woman like her, a burning flame who fed everyone around her with warmth and light.

She wrapped her shawl around her shoulders with a huff of disapproval. "I wouldn't expect such behavior from a guest in my father's home."

"You should," he said. "You need be on your guard at all times in the company of a rake."

They walked side by side through the warm enclosed garden, drenched in moonlight. Vegetable beds and herb borders alternated with carefully pruned shrubbery and fruit trees, while vines climbed the wall in several places. It was a lovely refuge, and the night air fell on his skin with a cool touch. Here and there, Henrietta paused to inspect a branch or a young fruit.

"You look like a Grecian nymph wandering the forest," he said. "Tending the things you have brought to life."

Something hard and uncomfortable clenched in his gut at the pristine beauty of her. Unlike every other woman of his acquaintance, interested only in her own success, Henrietta focused outward, using her gifts to rescue others, right wrongs, and improve the world about her.

She paused before a vine studded with flowers as white and delicate as she was. "The moonflowers are blooming," she said. She touched her fingertips to her red lips, then placed them gently on a blossom.

"Fanny's favorite," she explained, her eyes glossy with tears.

That old, familiar bolt of loss sheared through his chest, leaving cold air to rush in. He craved for her to touch him with such tenderness. He could not ruin her by association with him, and he could not have her; she was far, so far above his touch.

"Tell me, Lord Darien," she said, walking on, "why you are interesting yourself with a tradesman's family when your usual diversions, so I've heard, are to entertain female...admirers."

The world applauded Lord Daring for his string of conquests, the many virginal females who had passed through his arms and, supposedly, his bed. Henrietta made the whole game feel tawdry.

Dairen debated how much to reveal. He didn't wish her to know he had designs on her uncle. She had no notion of her own attractions, which he found absurdly endearing.

And he wanted her to know the truth behind his salacious reputation. She was the one person who could understand.

His voice sounded low and hoarse in the dusky light. "My brother and I were hellions. We were known for it even as boys."

"Lord Daring?"

She drew her India shawl about her and walked beside him. He felt her listening with her whole body. It was rather alarming to be seen by her. Everyone else, man or woman, looked at him calculating how to get what they wanted. Henrietta watched him as if she wanted to learn who he was.

"And my brother Lucien was Lucifer. Horace, the eldest, was the steady one. We called him Horse."

His throat tightened, and they walked in silence for a while. He pushed aside the occasional drooping branch so it would not tangle in her hair. The night air, thick with fragrance, calmed him.

"But my...reputation, shall we call it, began in university. My first conquest was Clothilde Canderley. A friend's elder sister, forced into a betrothal she didn't want. She was complaining of this one day, and I suggested she do something scandalous. Compromise herself, so her groom would cry off."

Henrietta's brow lifted. "And she chose you to ruin her?"

He nodded. "It was easy to arrange a damning tableau. My wildness helped. Lucien had a thought for his future, but I—didn't." He paused. "Clothilde was sent away in disgrace, but eventually she was allowed to marry the man she did want, a penniless clerk whom she helped win a diplomatic post, then a barony. She now enjoys wealth, comfort, and much envy as a hostess of *ton*."

Henrietta's gray-green eyes widened. "Lady Ellesmere. My aunt wondered how you had secured an invitation."

"Clothilde told her secret to a friend in similar circumstances, and demand for my services grew. You'd be surprised how many clever young women wish to escape marriages or want a reason to be pressed into one."

"And now," she said, shaking her head, "all you need do is pause with a girl on the street—take her for a turn on a balcony during a ball—" Her brow furrowed. "Forsythia Pennyroyal?"

He winced. "There is still the occasional ambitious maiden who would like to set her cap for the son of a marquess."

"But you have not taken advantage of her."

He turned to face her. "My character as a rakehell is exaggerated, but not undeserved."

"So Lady Celeste—"

"That, I'm afraid, is entirely deserved."

He'd erred gravely with Celeste. He'd thought her among the experienced women who regularly propositioned him, women who were confident and discreet. Dumb with grief over the death of Lucretius, wallowing in misery, he hadn't realized she was using him to make Havering cry off. He'd had no idea of her designs until he came home from the Continent to encounter a challenge from Havering and learned that Celeste had been hiding a pregnancy, jilting her fiancé, and refusing to name the father of her babe.

In the moonlight, Henrietta's skin looked as smooth as polished marble. The curve of her brow, her throat, her bosom beckoned for his touch. Darien took a deep, bracing breath of the chill night air and moved to a path on the opposite side of a flower bed.

"It's a rather sad story, isn't it?" she whispered.

He clenched his jaw. "Celeste's?"

"Yours." She faced him, her puzzled frown drawing his attention to the lush line of her mouth. "You have helped any number of independent young women arrange their own futures, poking convention in the eye. And yet your name is drawn through the mud, to the point where mothers fall over themselves to remove their daughters from your path."

He shrugged. "I have no need of society's approval."

She bit her lip. "But to let yourself be so judged, and never speak the truth? To allow yourself to be so used?"

"Henrietta." He took the path that brought him around the flower bed, close to her. "I am no paragon."

She blinked. "It seems to me that you have been reviled for doing someone a kindness, for preventing a wrong. I know a little something of what that is like."

She stood facing him, so self-reliant, so utterly composed, and showing not the slightest sensual awareness of him. He couldn't bear it when his every sense was so full of her that it nearly brought him to his knees.

Her coolness was a taunt, a defiance. He wanted to awaken her. He wanted her to know desire, that hot, liquid tide. He wanted her to feel that pull to *him*.

"Henrietta." His voice was a low growl. "You have clearly never been kissed."

"I, sir, am kissed daily. I have more than my fair share of kisses."

"Not from children, you wet goose. The kiss of a man."

"Oh, that. There was a boy who worked for Miss Gregoire who was always trying to kiss us. He made a game of it, whomever he could catch."

"I said, the kiss of a *man*." He moved closer, and she stepped away, giving him a wary look. Her skin had the same luster as her pearls.

"Of what possible interest could this subject be to you?" Her voice wavered.

"Now that you will have suitors, you should know how to kiss."

"I do not intend to go about kissing my suitors." She batted at the branch of a fruit tree that tangled in her hair as she backed into it.

"Ah, but they will try to kiss *you*. And you will want to kiss the man of your choice."

"It cannot be all that difficult." She went perfectly still as he reached up to free the budding branch from the pearls in her hair. Her breathing came fast and shallow. He smelled moon-flowers, her.

"On the contrary, it takes some practice to kiss properly." His hands itched to draw her to him. But he knew enough of seduction to know that she had to close that last inch. He wanted not just her mouth but her surrender.

She regarded him with a suspicious pinch to her lovely full lips. "And you are so gallantly offering to teach me."

He lifted his shoulders. He was aware of the fine fabric against his chest, the cling of the pantaloons to his thighs. His skin had come alive with sensation. "I am in proximity and suited to the task. I have some experience."

He could do this. He was good at it, expert. She would fall into his trap, yield to him, let him touch her. And then she could breathe some of her light and purity into him.

"I can only imagine that you do." She tapped her finger against her lips, thinking. He watched the movement, entranced.

"I suppose I should know something of the skill," she said after a while. "I would not wish for my husband to think me clumsy, should I have one."

Her husband would wish to be the first and only man to kiss her. Any man would want to be the first to awaken Miss Henrietta Wardley-Hines. To fix her complete attention upon himself and bask in the radiance of her desire.

Darien nodded as his throat closed. "Yes."

"Very well." She stepped close and lifted her chin. "You may show me how it is done, then. I prefer to learn from a skilled teacher."

He looked down at her face, turned up to him like a flower blossom. Her dark lashes feathered over the elegant curve of her cheeks. A few locks of hair curled delicately at her temple. From this vantage the slope of her nose looked graceful, and below that the broad mouth with its soft, inviting lips.

Darien took a firm grip on his instincts. If he kissed Henrietta with everything in him, he would go up in flames, and that would not do. He did not intend to lose his head over the girl, merely teach her a lesson.

He gathered every errant emotion and shoved the lot to the

bottom of his mind. This was a maneuver he had practiced a great deal. Cool, calculated distance—that was the goal. He throttled any excitement at the thought of kissing Henrietta Wardley-Hines and instead made his mind cold and empty. Now he was in a position to instruct.

He bent his head and placed his lips on her warm, pliant ones. He brushed his mouth across hers, once, twice, like a painter preparing a canvas. He paused a moment, and she waited, lips slightly parted, her whole body still. He nudged her lips apart with his own, and she complied. He repeated the gesture, pushing her lips open, and she dutifully followed suit.

Her mouth was warm and delicious, and the scent of her fogged his brain, but she was not yielding. He ran his tongue along her teeth, pressed his lips against hers in one last caress, and lifted his head, his breath ragged. His self-control held by the slenderest thread.

She blinked, then focused on him. Her eyes were deep and entirely clear, her brows divided by a small, furrowed line. She twisted her strawberry lips into a small grimace.

"Is that it?"

"That is the general idea, yes." His voice felt two octaves lower than normal, gravel in his chest.

She sighed. "And that makes a woman want to..." The implication hung in the air.

He stared at her, flattened, gutted with surprise. "Typically, yes."

She nodded. "You are indeed very practiced," she said. "Like a set of fencing moves. It's obvious you've done this dozens of times."

Hundreds, you chit, he nearly blurted.

"I suppose there is something lacking in me. I suspected as much." She held out her hand to shake. "Thank you for the lesson, Lord Daring."

Darien didn't shake her hand. He couldn't move. He simply stood there, rooted to the spot, about to go up in flames of mortification and rage. Blithely, as if she had not just been kissed by the most practiced rakehell in the kingdom, Miss Henrietta Wardley-Hines rearranged her shawl, nodded politely, and strolled back into her house.

CHAPTER TWELVE

Henrietta sat in her study, staring at the sheet of foolscap before her. Yesterday her themes had seemed so orderly, her points well-made, but now her chicken scratches seemed substanceless and stupid. And what did an intellectual debate matter, anyway, when there was so much staggering sorrow and injustice in the world?

Sometimes she wished the angels would descend with swords and fire to smite all the wicked. But then who would be left?

She pulled a fresh paper toward her and took a small knife and quill from the escritoire. The letter required only two lines, but her tears blurred the ink. She sanded the page and let it dry while she hunted for her seal, a small soapstone with the profile of Minerva carved into it, a gift from her former schoolmistress. Henrietta folded the letter, dripped the hot wax to seal, and addressed it.

The notes for her debate stared up at her. She put her face in her hands.

"Caller for you, Miss Hetty," the butler said from the doorway.

"I am not receiving today, Dearbody," she said through her fingers.

The butler cleared his throat. "Lord Darien Bales, miss."

Henrietta wiped her tears with her hands, wishing she could as easily push away the flutter in her belly. There he stood, taller than she remembered, in a burgundy coat that brought attention to how very wide his shoulders were and breeches that left nothing to wonder about the length and strength of his legs. He was like the big cats explorers had discovered in faraway lands, huge, supple, lithe, predatory, walking the earth as if they owned it.

"Lady Clarinda sent me up," he said, an apologetic note in his voice. "She said you might be in need of company."

"In fact, I am just leaving on an errand," Henrietta murmured. She was glad to have tasks to distract her, a reason to avoid Darien's unsettling company.

He was calling only because it was proper to call at a home where one had been a guest. Lord Darien had exquisite manners when he chose to exercise them.

He had pinned her to the garden wall, given her a long, practiced, mechanical kiss, and held rigid and cold and distant the entire time. She could not name all the emotions that had swirled through her then and rose again at the sight of him now, but she would do her best to hide them. Some new awareness swept through her body at his nearness, but she was alone in it; he was the tutor, instructing, correcting, unaffected. She would not let him see how he affected her.

She rose. "Dearbody, would you ask Sir Pelton to frank this letter for me? The family will not be able to pay the post."

Dearbody withdrew but gave Darien a hesitant look. Henrietta rarely received male callers.

"What is the matter?" Darien asked. He had black lashes

around his very blue eyes—one reason the color seemed so intense, his gaze so riveting.

She reached for her sodden handkerchief. "Mary Ann," she choked.

"The girl from the workhouse?"

She nodded, surprised he remembered, even more surprised when the truth came pouring out. "The one we took to the Sisters of Benevolence." She curled her hand into fists. "Her son is dead."

"Oh, that poor girl." His face softened with pity. "You found out today?"

"It happened this morning," she said, chest heaving. "He... he died while I was with them."

She covered her face again. She had been strong for Mary Ann, held the girl and comforted her, commiserated with her loss, promised she would write her family. She'd had no one to comfort *her*.

She was surprised to feel Darien's warm, firm hands on her shoulders. She had thought he would bolt from the room. What man could endure a woman's tears?

"That poor child," he said. "Both of them. You did all you could."

"Not enough," she sobbed. "If I'd called another doctor— found a wet nurse— If we could have found a way to make him eat—"

To her utter astonishment, Darien put his arms around her and drew her against his chest. "I'm going to ruin your cravat," she muttered.

"Good," he said. "My man needs practice tying them."

She learned against his solid warmth and let the storm of grief toss her. He smelled lovely, like leather and tobacco and warm, pungent pine. His embrace was a safe, strong shield.

After a while, she drew a calming breath and laid her cheek

on his shoulder. Her lips were close to his neck. His skin looked soft, with the barest hint of stubble.

Darien stood very still. His arms felt strong and delightfully heavy around her. A warm curl unfolded in her middle, telling her she wanted more of this, more from him.

She ignored it. He offered comfort only, a friendly gesture of support. A favor, like improving her gown.

And why he should offer friendship to her, when he had ruined swaths of girls, she could not fathom. She smoothed his wrinkled cravat and stepped away. His arms opened as if the muscles had frozen.

"Thank you," she said, trying to wipe her nose on her handkerchief in the most discreet and ladylike manner possible. "I'm afraid I really am not at home today. I told Mary Ann I would arrange for services and have Elijah buried in our parish. She won't need cards, and she doesn't want mourners, but I need to find him a coffin, and clothes to be buried in, and mourning dress for her."

She scrubbed the tear tracks from her face. "Then I mean to find a small locket for her, like the kind Lady Mama had made for Fanny, and after the undertaker, I shall need to talk to the vicar. And then I need to prepare for my debate."

"Shall I go with you?"

"Why?" She gave up and blew her nose, loudly. "Don't you have duties of your own today?"

"Frankly, no. And I regret what that says about me."

She stared, catching the bleak expression that passed through his eyes. He was garbed for showing himself in the fashionable walks and promenades, as suited to his class. She, on the other hand, had things to do.

"I cannot think you should wish to be seen with me." She gave him a watery smile. "I understand the satirists are howling with delight that you condescended to dine at a tradesman's table." What a relief the lampoons did not know how the evening had ended, with that kiss.

A trace of dull red touched his sculpted cheekbones, as if he were recalling that kiss too. "I suppose your family is furious at the ridicule. Lady Pomeroy seems a high stickler."

Henrietta hunted about for a fresh handkerchief to tuck into her pocket. "On the contrary, Lady Mama had a round dozen callers this morning, all dying to know why she had entertained the notorious Lord Daring. Ten of them pledged support for the Sisters of Benevolence, and five signed my petition to Parliament calling for full abolition."

She collected her shawl and gloves. "In addition, several of the gossip sheets mentioned my debate, which, if it is well attended, will guarantee my admittance to the Minerva Society. So you see, your infamy works to my advantage." She tied on the enormous picture hat that Lady Mama had gifted her. "I must go."

He regarded her German habit, shaking his head. "Did you learn nothing from my lesson?"

She had learned she was terrible at kissing. That he was bossy and high-handed with her but unmoved by desire. Heat singed her cheeks.

"This habit is excessively comfortable and allows me a free range of motion. I'm surprised women don't wear them for all occasions."

"That muddy color is appalling, and there is entirely too much fabric." He followed her down the stairs. "You ought to accent your shape, not hide it."

"I live in the north," Henrietta said. "I like being warm."

"You are in London for the Season," he reminded her, "and no one says that learned females cannot be à la mode. We will run your errands, and then I will introduce you to a modiste I know. Fear not, Duprix will— Hey now, Jack o' Legs!" They reached the street to find James stroking Darien's matched blacks, whispering nonsensical words into their ears. "Don't you be fashing my high-steppers. They're nervy enough."

"Drive you, milord?" James offered. The sweep boy Darien had employed held the ribbons, resentful to give over his post or his promised pay.

"If you could bring my gig around, James," Henrietta said.

"Nonsense," Darien said. "I will drive you. Since you do not have a maid to hold your packages, clearly the duty falls to me."

He clamped those warm, strong hands to her waist and lifted her to the high step of the whisky as if she weighed no more than the yards of fabric in her habit. All the breath left Henrietta's body.

Their embrace in her sitting room had scattered her wits if she thought it was safe to be seen about town with him. Or wise to sit so close to the big, splendid heat of him, hear his low rumbling voice near her ear, enjoy the attention of that dizzying blue gaze. Lord Daring broke hearts as casually as he destroyed reputations.

She was no Forsythia Pennyroyal, foolish enough to set her cap for him, but being with him was a danger to her reputation and her sensibilities, no matter what credit he thought he might gain with Sir Pelton by running her errands.

Darien swung himself easily into the whisky and shook out the ribbons, tossing a coin to the sweep. "I drive myself, imp," he said to James, "but you may ride behind as my tiger."

With a broad grin, James scrambled to the perch, puffing out his chest. "Miss Hetty needs friends around her," he said. "It's been a lowerin' morn. She's taking the lad's loss deep."

"I know something about funeral arrangements for young boys," Darien said in a low, rough voice, and Henrietta's throat clamped shut as he glanced at the white armband on her sleeve. She tucked her hands and feet close to her body, on dangerous ground. She could shake off a careless roué who wanted to take advantage of her, but she could not deny a fellow creature in pain.

To her surprise, Darien proved more than helpful. He possessed taste for more than just his coats. He selected a modest coffin, burial clothes for Elijah, and mourning dress for Mary Ann. He found a lovely memorial locket to hold the tiny curl of baby hair. And when he spoke of his nephew, Lucretius, Henrietta wanted to weep and take him into her arms. He wore the expression of a man who had taken a knife to the belly, astonished by the pain and outraged at the injustice.

At St. Marylebone Church, he did little but lean against a stone wall, examining his watch on its gold chain jingling with seals. He then took out an enameled toothpick case and proceeded to clean his teeth. But Henrietta suspected that the expensive look of him induced Reverend Dingley to agree to bury a baby not of his parish. When the Reverend led them through the cemetery to show her the tiny plot of land reserved for paupers' graves, Darien took her arm, and Henrietta leaned gratefully on him. It was indeed useful to have an expensive, well-born man about.

"And now, the modiste," Darien said when they emerged from the church. He gave himself a shake, throwing off the gloom of their business. "I have someone to recommend."

"I have my own modiste," Henrietta replied.

He folded his arms. "Madame Beaudoin dresses the most fashionable ladies in London."

"And so has no need of my custom," Henrietta retorted. "Alywen grew up at the Benevolence Hospital and was apprenticed to a dressmaker. She needs clients to make a success of her new shop."

The small smile playing about those sinfully well-shaped lips of his told her he wasn't accustomed to opposition from women. Well, she didn't intend to let him command her. She'd sensed his awareness of her body after he had redesigned her gown at dinner, leaving her practically naked. She might still be tingling from that kiss, but she wasn't going to risk her acceptance into the Minerva Society, no matter how delicious or warm or intimidating Lord Darien Bales could be.

Nevertheless, Lord Daring caused a sensation when he stepped into the small shop on Holles Street. Henrietta had helped Alywen find and refurbish her premises, so all the girls, even those in the back, hurried out to welcome her but also, Henrietta suspected, get a look at her notorious escort.

"Have you come for a visit, Miss Hetty?" Alywen was working to hide her Welsh accent under a French one. "Or are you finally going to let me make you some new gowns?"

"Can you provide her with an entirely new wardrobe?" Darien inquired. "It's as though she didn't prepare for her Season at all."

He took possession of a pattern book as if he visited dress shops every day. Perhaps he did, Henrietta thought, to clothe all his mistresses. In a moment, Darien was deep in discussion with Alywen over styles and silhouettes, while the girls unrolled bolts of luscious, gleaming fabrics and began swooping about Henrietta with tapes and trims.

"I was too busy with other preparations to consider gowns," Henrietta said. "And I see no need to bother now."

Darien overrode her protests with a wave of his hand. "You are in desperate need of an update. Or do you wish for the likes of Forsythia Pennyroyal to continue to make sport of you?"

That stung. "Forsythia Pennyroyal may concern herself with matters of dress, but I have other matters to attend to. Like my debate."

"I have just the gown for that." Alywen held up a handful of filmy white ruffles. "Marie Antoinette made the *chemise de reine* all the craze across Paris. The Duchess of Devonshire was painted in hers."

It was for Alywen, not Darien, that she tried on the dress, Henrietta told herself. But the look in Darien's eyes when she emerged from the dressing chamber wearing the delicate muslin sent tingles to every extremity. He'd worn that heated, appreciative look in the garden, and like a ninny she'd let him kiss her, only to find he was merely amusing himself. A Henrietta Wardley-Hines did not fascinate an experienced rakehell like Lord Darien Bales.

Uncaring of this fact, butterflies flitted about her middle. "I look like an opera dancer," Henrietta said, gaping at herself in the full-length glass. That couldn't be *her*, that graceful, long-limbed creature with glowing cheeks and bright eyes.

"You wish to make an impression, do you not?" said Darien, a man who could not help but make an impression.

"With my ideas, sir, not my appearance! No one will credit me with any seriousness in this gown."

"She'll take it," Darien told Alywen. He flipped through the pattern book and pointed to a plate. "And this for the Bicclesfield ball. It is her first Season, so nothing too bold yet, though she could carry it off with that hair. The robe in that buttery duchesse satin, with the petticoat in that lavender taffeta and a matching stomacher trimmed with a few gauze ruffles. Mind you, only a few."

"I am not attending the Bicclesfield ball," Henrietta said, then signed with her hands as she addressed the little seamstress crawling about her hem. "No, Peony, you didn't stick me, only my shoe. You're doing a fine job, dear."

Peony blew a sigh of relief around the pins in her mouth. She had been left deaf due to a childhood illness, and for her sake, the Sisters of Benevolence had developed a signing language based on that developed by Abbé Charles-Michael de l'Epée in France. Henrietta was slowly becoming fluent.

"Of course you are going to the ball," Darien said. "Clarinda wants to show off her new Sir Jasper, and your aunt and uncle are attending. I shall reserve a dance."

A streak of perversity Henrietta would have sworn was not in her character suddenly reared its head. She was risking her reputation, becoming a subject of lampoons, all because he wanted to be close to Sir Pelton. Not her.

"Are you endeavoring to put me in your debt so I might approach Lady Celeste on your behalf?" He'd admitted he had no one to ask. "Because I cannot see what influence I would have." Henrietta waved away little Mary, approaching with a bolt of violet silk. "Shall I quiz her on her intentions? Ask her to name the father?"

Darien maintained a stony face, turning pages in the pattern book, but a muscle in his cheek flickered. Remorse filled Henrietta. She was being unutterably cruel, all because she did not want to be thought his mistress.

He glanced at the shop girls, who watched them avidly. Even Peony looked fascinated. "I don't see what more I could do," Darien finally said. "I cannot force Celeste to see my solicitor about arrangements. She can simply claim the child is not mine. I'm not likely to ever know the truth, either way."

Henrietta glanced about at the wide-eyed girls. All of them had survived to adulthood thanks to the charity of the Minerva Society. "Did you tell your solicitor about the Sisters of Benevolence?"

"I won't have a child of mine raised in an orphanage," Darien snapped. "If it is indeed mine, I will provide for it as I see fit."

"Yes, I suppose you haven't much faith in the Hospital, after what happened to Mary Ann's child." Guilt and grief slammed into Henrietta's chest. She'd forgotten the weight of the morning, mincing about Alywen's shop thinking of dresses. As if there weren't graver matters pressing for her attention.

"Henrietta," Darien said, his voice changing, "I did not mean—"

"Never mind." She turned away to hide tears. "Alywen, my dear, I shall take all these gowns. Send the bill to Hines House along with a list of whatever else you may need for your shop, and I will see it delivered." She fled into the tiny changing room.

Darien drove them back to Hines House in a strained silence, foregoing Hyde Park and its fashionable Ring. She was glad of it. Enough people stared as it was.

"I suppose you will not believe that I am not trying to ingratiate myself for return favors. That I might simply enjoy your company," he said as he turned the whisky into Manchester Square.

"You've made it clear you are accustomed to much more fashionable companions." Henrietta rubbed her burning eyes. "Is that what you wanted to ask my uncle about? What to do with Lady Celeste?"

"My conversation with your uncle is no business of yours, Henrietta. I told you about Celeste because you asked. I did not give you leave to meddle."

"Meddle!" Henrietta said. She welcomed the sharpness in his tone. Better he be put out with her than trying to seduce her.

All the same, when she tried to climb down from the vehicle, he was there to catch her about the waist and swing her to the ground. She fought the jolt that went all through her at his touch.

His eyes searched hers, that vivid, disconcerting blue. "Not quite so sad," he said in a quiet voice.

"Of course I'm sad," she snapped. "A child died in my arms today."

"I meant me." A small, crooked smile touched his mouth as he stepped back, releasing her. "Mind you save me a dance at the Bicclesfield ball. I am fond of the gavotte, though I like a good galop too."

Henrietta entered the house with a heavy step, shaking her head to clear it. She had causes to uphold, households and a farm to manage, a mill to purchase, souls who depended upon her. It was well the infamous Lord Daring had no designs on her reputation; the Daughters of Minerva would drop her like a hot stone.

A thoughtless, reckless rake hadn't the power to cut up her peace. But Darien Bales, the beautiful, exasperating, perplexing man veiled behind a sensual swagger and bored reserve—that man had the power to destroy her peace completely.

She only hoped some new fancy would catch his attention before the Bicclesfield ball. If he simply forgot about and moved on from plain Henrietta Wardley-Hines, it would be the best possible outcome to guard any further damage to her heart.

CHAPTER THIRTEEN

The morning of Elijah's funeral was, cruelly enough, warm and bright. A fresh wind wafted away the smells of burning coal and other industry, leaving the churchyard smelling like turned earth, hellebore, and the massive yew cradling its branches over one corner of the cemetery. With no one else to mourn the infant, his mother and Henrietta were allowed to attend the short graveside service.

At Fanny's funeral in their home parish of Rossendale, mourners had come from three counties to help the Wardley-Hines bury their dead. Elijah returned to his Maker as briefly and quietly as he had come.

Henrietta drove Mary Ann back to the hospital, thinking sadly that her first solo rescue had not been very successful. In the old guildhall, under the airy space of the high arched ceilings with their hand-carved beams and the light falling through the leaded windows, the residents sat in neat rows at trestle tables, taking their midday meal.

Henrietta was proud to be part of this place, so tidy and serene. Small sprigs of anemone and spring snowflake from the herb beds brightened the room. The women and children looked well-dressed, fed, and healthy. Many of the maids in their white and gray muslin uniforms had come as foundlings or destitute women and stayed for employment, finding their first stable home.

The voices were friendly but subdued, and white armbands had been distributed. Though the Sisters could boast of many supplicants who had come in despair through those heavy doors and left in health and optimism, white and black armbands had their own boxes in the linen closet and saw regular use.

Henrietta walked Mary Ann back to her small, shared room. All six of the beds were neatly made, straw pillows flush against the wall, the chamber pot tucked beneath a washstand, and a small press held clothes. Relieved of her chores for the day, Mary Ann slipped off her shoes and lay down on the bed. Her face looked older, weary with grief.

"What will you do now?" Henrietta asked softly. "You cannot go back to Rushy Green."

"I thought I might find a place here? I know I'm clumsy, but I'm not afraid of hard work."

"Of course," Henrietta said. "The Sisters have put many girls in good positions. One became dresser to a countess. Others marry, and—" She paused as Mary Ann winced and put a hand to her breast. "Are you still— I thought your milk had dried up?"

"Not yet. They feed me good here."

"Then you could stay as a nurse. You are young, strong, and healthy."

The girl's eyes gleamed with tears. "What if I kill someone else's baby?"

"Oh, child," Henrietta said. "It was not your doing. God decides these things, not us." It was no less than what Reverend Dingley had said in his short remarks, but the words sounded hollow, lacking comfort.

Mary Ann sat up and rubbed her face. "I'd best go talk to the matron, then. Nothing gets done by lying about, as my gran says."

"My Aunt Davinia has a similar motto." Henrietta nodded, touched by the girl's resolution.

She wished she could bring Mary Ann to Hines House, but while Clarinda let Henrietta have her head in household management, she would want to choose the wet nurse for her own little stranger, due to arrive soon.

Henrietta, though, knew someone else who might require the services of a wet nurse.

She had resolved she would not press Darien about his situation, not after he had accused her of meddling, but Mary Ann's weary, baffled face haunted her. James leapt to his feet, straightening his striped coat as Henrietta marched out of the hospital.

"Home then, miss, or a turn through the park for an airing?" he asked, tossing his dice to the sweep boy. James loved when Henrietta tooled through Hyde Park. It was very dashing for a woman to drive her own gig and have a tiger in livery perched behind, and James liked to show off.

"James, I do not wish to ring a peal over you, but isn't it gambling that put you in the Fleet in the first place?"

"Just throwing the bones, miss. No stakes, eh, my lad?"

"You owe me thruppence!" the boy shouted. "Miserable dwarf!"

"Cheating tallboy!" James shouted back. "Big people," he muttered as he swung into his seat. "How'd he do in a world made for *my* size, I'd like to know."

"Wouldn't last a day," Henrietta soothed.

The Duke of Highcastle's enormous house occupied one entire side of Portman Square. Henrietta had walked past it on her way to Elizabeth Montagu's bluestocking salons. She tossed the ribbons to James as she hopped down from the vehicle.

"Don't go far. I expect to be tossed out on my ear with a flea in it." She held out her card to the stone-faced butler who opened the door. "Lady Celeste, please."

The man gave Henrietta a cold, measuring look. She wished she had worn something smarter than her riding habit to the funeral services, but she had not anticipated she would be visiting a duke's household today.

Or had she? Her heart had been tugging her toward this child since she'd first heard of its plight. And Darien had asked for her help, hadn't he? In a way?

"Lady Celeste," the butler said, pushing the door shut, "is not at home."

Henrietta stuck the toe of her half-boot in the threshold. "Then may I speak with someone who attends Lady Celeste?" She presented a second card, and the butler's dark brows drew together.

"Turn her off, Hemsworth," came a commanding voice.

"I am in the process of doing so, Your Grace," said the butler. He glared pointedly at Henrietta's shoe.

The duchess appeared. She was just the sort of woman, elegant and intimidating, who made Henrietta's knees quake with envy. Her hooped train swept across the polished parquet floor, she wore a full panoply of jewels, and her towering wig bristled with fruit and feathers.

"My daughter," the duchess said with cold hauteur, "is not at home."

"My card, Your Grace." Henrietta held it out. "If you please."

The duchess's thin nostrils narrowed. "We have had *quite* enough of your kind making rude inquiries," she hissed. "You're like jackals! You can't wait to profit from our misfortune."

"I do not wish to profit, Your Grace," Henrietta said. Hemsworth pushed at the door without appearing to do so. She put her elbow in the closing gap. "I only wished to make you aware of this establishment—*oof*—in the event that someone—ouch—in your household—really!—might be in need of such accommodations."

"I cannot imagine why you think *anyone* in my household would stand in need of such accommodations," the duchess snapped. "Good *day*. Hemsworth!"

The portal swung toward her nose, and Henrietta found herself routed, an unusual outcome for her. She fell back against the unexpected form of a person. An arm in a fancy embroidered sleeve with a fall of lace at the cuff shot out and caught the door.

"I say, Hemsworth!" said a male voice. "This how my mother receives callers now?"

The door opened to the butler's livid gaze. "Alfred," said the duchess, glaring at her son with black eyes, "Hemsworth was dispatching a peddler. I don't know why they don't use the tradesmen's entrance in the back."

"Tradesman!" said the astonished young man, who was not, despite her first befuddled thought, Darien. He set Henrietta on her feet and indicated for her to precede him through the door. "This is Charley's sister. Sir Charleton Wardley-Hines now," he added, as if the title would sway his mother. "Was in the Bullingdon Club with me up at Oxford."

Having set foot in the grand marbled foyer, Henrietta faced him with a quizzical look. Lord Alfred Highcastle had no business knowing who she was. The young man gave her an abashed grin.

"Asked the dwarf out there whose the sweet goers were," he confessed. "Don't suppose you'd be interested in selling?"

"Lord Alfred. I am here to call on your sister," Henrietta said with a curtsy, hoping this enterprise wouldn't cost her the Titans. She'd come to adore her father's gift, and it would crush

James to lose them. Especially to one of Charley's rackety companions, of whom Henrietta had heard a great deal.

The duchess glared. "Celeste is indisposed."

The young man's face darkened with wrath. He was handsome and well-dressed, though on him, the touches that Darien carried off with style looked a touch overdone.

"Indisposed! I'll say." Freddy grabbed Henrietta's hand in a grip firm enough to be painful. "You come talk to her. Maybe she'll tell the truth to another woman. Haven't been able to get a word out of her m'self."

"Me! Why should I— That is, I am not certain Lady Celeste will confide in me," Henrietta said, struggling with the sweeping skirts of her habit as Freddy dragged her up the stairs. "When she has refused Lord Darien—"

"Daring!" Freddy barked. "He's the villain, then?"

The stairs went on, floor after floor, until finally they reached the top of the vast mansion. Freddy tugged Henrietta into a small bedroom where a young woman sat in a chair beneath a window that had been covered over with a dark curtain. She wore a dainty, ruffled nightgown in rose pink and sewed a baby cap, a seraphic expression on her face.

"Lady Celeste." Henrietta curtsied.

"What do you want?" came a sharp voice from the other side of the room. "Who are you?"

Henrietta's face bloomed with color as another young woman rose from the chamber pot and moved toward them. A tight belly, low and ripe, preceded her across the room.

Henrietta gulped down a sense of panic. She'd circulated at her ease among her father's powerful friends of the north, and titles held by various Daughters of Minerva held no awe for her. But this was her first encounter with a ducal household, and she was aware it was going badly.

"Milady. I am on the board for the Sisters of Benevolence

Hospital for Distressed Women and Foundlings," she stammered as the duke's daughter surveyed her with a look of scorn. "It is the mission of the Sisters to minister to children and their mothers in...er, displaced circumstances."

"I'm hardly *displaced*, am I?" Celeste hissed. She pointed at the maid sitting beneath the window. "A prisoner, more like! Trapped here by my parents, may they rot in hell. And you." She turned on her brother.

"You know what you need to do," Freddy barked, his face stormy. "Give us a name, so I can call out the knave and drop him in his tracks."

Henrietta's stomach clenched. "I beg your pardon?"

"The blackguard who put this in her!" Freddy gestured. "Wasn't the *Honorable* Havering, who won't have her now. Who's the man, Celeste?"

"It doesn't matter." Celeste made a choking sound, half sob, half screech. "My dear, dear darling—he's said nothing. He means to abandon me here!"

She stumbled toward the bed, made up for a lying-in. The anger in the room, the lack of fresh air, and the stench from the chamber pot turned Henrietta's stomach. She saw no books, papers, magazines, or news sheets anywhere. Very different from her own rooms.

She could not help examining Lady Celeste. This was the woman Darien had taken to his bed, taken pleasure in, even if there had been no love in it. She had pretty brown hair and bold, strong features. The loose slammerkin showed generous breasts and a plump bottom. So Darien liked his women fleshy and soft. Small wonder he hadn't shown the slightest interest in Henrietta.

"Darien wishes to provide for the babe," she said quietly. "And you."

"And what would you know about it?" Celeste rubbed the

side of her belly and pierced Henrietta with a scathing look. "You're not anyone."

"Wardley-Hines." Freddy nodded. "Charley's bluestocking sister. The one everyone makes fun of."

"I know a responsible wet nurse," Henrietta said, her face warming with mortification. Charley had warned her against appearing eccentric; now she saw how it might work against her cause. "She's a clean, healthy girl from the country. You can send the babe to the Sisters of Benevolence. They will see to its care."

Celeste's eyes, a cool, powdery blue, widened suddenly. "So you're Daring's new whore. He went from me to *you*?"

She advanced, and Henrietta fell backward. She could not take her eyes off that turgid belly.

"You mistake the nature of our relationship," Henrietta said on a gasp.

"Tell him I hate him!" Celeste screamed. "Tell him I hope he goes to hell, the rotter. I'll never forgive him for ruining me."

Freddy clasped his arms around her, and his sister struggled in his grip. "Daring, is it?" Freddy exclaimed. "I knew it! He'll be hearing from my seconds."

"No," Henrietta whispered, feeling the blood leave her face. "Can you not simply let him arrange for the babe? He is willing to mend things—"

"*How*, you little fool?" Freddy snarled. "Look at her! She's mad as a cat. Utterly ruined. No decent man'll have her, no matter what m'father pays him. Daring should pay too, with his blood."

"I want his heart," Celeste wailed, sagging in her brother's arms. "I want to rip it out and *eat* it! My dear darling would have me if not for Daring's brat."

For once, Henrietta did the prudent thing. She made a quick curtsy, hoisted her skirts, and raced out of the room. Her heels clattered on the grand staircase as shrieks floated down from above. The butler glided to the door, his face blank and furious at the same time, and Henrietta barely swept her rumpled skirts out the door before Hemsworth slammed it shut.

"Well?" James called, guiding the horses to the curb. "Tied it all up in a bow, have ye?"

"Not quite." Henrietta nearly tripped hurrying down the broad steps. "Her Grace tried to eat me alive, then Lady Celeste tried to eat me alive, and now Lord Alfred is going to call Lord Darien out in a duel. We must warn him."

James clucked his tongue in disapproval. "Your cicisbeo's after all, then?"

"He is not my escort, or my follower, or any other such thing," Henrietta flared as James helped her into the phaeton.

"Why didn't he slap a shackle on the nob's daughter, then? Would've hitched myself to that honey wagon, I would've."

"Darien said she was using him to incite the jealousy of another man," Henrietta said. "Not the one she was affianced to, from the sound of things."

"Gentry morts," James scoffed. "Like he's a Domine Do Little, or a bob tail, an' that's why she rattled off. When ye want to play the blanket hornpipe, miss, I hope ye pick a rum bluffer."

Henrietta's ears burned as she recalled, once again, Darien's confusing, masterly kiss. His broad chest against hers, his arms tight about her back, the heat, the strange contrast of his skin feeling soft and smooth while his body was firm and hard. His eyes had been full of dusk and shadows as he'd learned toward her, but his kiss had been so aloof, analytical, as if he'd been conducting a scientific experiment.

Frogs jumped about in her belly. She did not want to repeat the experiment, and yet she did.

She urged her horses to a trot as they turned from Portman Square onto Seymour Street, which was clogged with traffic.

"James, I am about to do something very unadvisable. There will be consequences if anyone finds out."

"Like I'd cry rope on you," James cried. "Rather ye box my ears and give me a powder and turn me off without a character. Ey, now, Miss Hetty, that van driver don't see you! Mind you don't catch 'is wheels or you'll turn us into the gutter, and I don't care to get my calf-clingers muddy."

CHAPTER FOURTEEN

"You're in the basket if word gets round that you're toddling up to a gentry cove ken," James remarked as Henrietta drew her phaeton to a stop before Darien's house.

"I don't have much choice, do I? Am I to send over a note saying nice knowing you, but Celeste named you the father of her child, and now her brother is going to call you out? Forgive me if I'm not entirely certain how these things are done. If you're concerned, you may be my chaperone."

"And leave the Titans for the sharks and snafflers?" James eyed the crowd of small children who thronged the high wheels of the vehicle, hoping for a job and the bit of copper that would go with it. "If 'e does tup ye, all I'll say is I told ye so!" he called as she ascended the steps and banged the knocker.

The steps to Darien's house had not been whitewashed that day, just another way in which a bachelor residence differed from a ducal palace, and her own. It had not escaped Henrietta that, as spacious and rich as the Highcastle abode was, Hines House was inferior only in size.

Her father's wealth, the result of hard work and shrewd investments, rivaled that of the ages-old propertied class.

Little wonder the King used honors and titles to ensure that wealth kept bedfellow with status, and the rest of the unwashed could lie in the gutter, a hierarchy that God and king had perpetuated for centuries. It was so unjust. Perhaps a further topic for a Minerva Society debate, if her first were a success.

A young man in a golden frock coat and white periwig opened the door. "What a clutter yer makin'," he griped.

Henrietta handed him her card. "Lord Darien, please."

The lad scowled at the creamy card embossed with swirls and lace. "What do I do with this, then?"

Henrietta rolled her eyes. "You are a country lad, aren't you? Give it to Lord Darien and announce me. Trot along now! It's rather urgent."

"You'd best come wit' me then." The boy turned and walked down a narrow hallway. At the back of the house, he went to a door and announced, "A girl 'ere what wants ye, an' she gimme a card." He thrust out the object as if the imprint of Henrietta's female hand had soiled it.

Darien sat behind a large desk, papers tumbling about him, quill in hand. His hair was unpowdered and pulled back in a simple queue. He wore no neckcloth and only a waistcoat over his shirt.

"Good heavens," Henrietta said, "you aren't even dressed! What is the matter with your butler, bringing me to you like this?"

Darien gave her the strangest look, studying her as if he had not seen her in ages and was reminding himself of her features. Then he rose and put down the quill.

"He is my valet, and a useless know-nothing," he said. "Quinby, I ought to turn you off this second. Don't you know you are not to bring an unaccompanied female in to see me? *Ever?*"

Henrietta raised her brows. "I thought unaccompanied females visited you all the time."

"Not here," Darien said, taking her arm and steering her away from the window. "Henry, you pea goose, didn't you bring a chaperone? Don't you know what this could do to your reputation?"

"James is outside," Henrietta said, lifting her chin, "and I didn't have time to swing round for a maid. This is a matter of life and death, Darien!" The familiar address slipped out, but she did not beg his pardon. Had he just called her *Henry*?

"A matter of *your* life and death if your father thinks he must force you to marry me." Darien turned to find his sullen servant had slunk away. "Rufie!" he called in a thunderous summons. "Perry, you worthless sot! Why aren't either of you in the library for once? I need you."

Henrietta grabbed the ruffles of his shirt and tugged. "There isn't time," she said in a rush. "You must listen to me. I was just at—"

"Rufie!" Darien bellowed again, then focused on Henrietta. "What is the matter? Is someone hurt?"

"You're going to be hurt!" she exclaimed, pushing his chest. This expanse was very firm, very broad, very warm beneath her hands. "You must leave at once! Your estate—one of your father's homes—perhaps the Continent— Oh, Rutherford—that is, Mr. Bales. Hello."

Rutherford rushed into the room, buttoning a black coat. Henrietta blushed and tried stepping away, but Darien kept hold of her arm.

"I regret to say that your cousin is about to be called out in a duel," she said, knowing Rufie at least would take proper measure of the situation. "You must help him get away before this awful event can transpire. He could be killed, or worse."

"Or worse?" Darien said, lifting a brow.

"Yes, worse," Henrietta cried, turning toward him. "Do not give me that supercilious look of yours. I have just been at Highcastle House to see Lady Celeste, and she told Lord Alfred that you are the father of her baby, and he means to call you out and...and *shoot* you." She put her hands over her mouth as a sob welled up. This was unlike her. She was not at all prone to vapors.

Darien pulled her into an embrace as Henrietta fought down her emotion. "You must leave town," she sniffled. "I don't want you to die."

At last, he had an appropriate response. She felt the tremor run through his shoulders. Then, as she lifted her head to hunt for her handkerchief, she saw that he was holding in laughter.

Another man strolled into the room, in a shabby suit with his hair uncombed. "Who wants to shoot Daring this time?" he inquired.

"*This* time?" Henrietta echoed. "This is no laughing matter, *Daring*! How can you be amused by this, you exasperating man?"

"Henry, do not put yourself into such a taking," Darien replied. "I am in no danger from Freddy. He couldn't hit me with a pistol if he were standing where Perry is, and he won't be idiot enough to choose swords. In fact I doubt very much he'll have the liver to call me out at all. He'll want to settle it with fisticuffs, and I'm rather handy with my fives."

Henrietta stared. "You aren't at all afraid he'll kill you?"

"Not in the least." His lips twitched. "But I appreciate your concern."

Henrietta sank into a chair. "Well, I did not expect this," she said. "And here I thought duels were a matter of some gravity."

"I've had my share of them and always escaped," Darien informed her. "Does Freddy know about the third man? He's the one he ought to set his sights on. From what I understand, he's the reason Celeste staged her whole Cheltenham tragedy in the first place."

A clatter came from a side table as Perry knocked over a vase. "Beg pardon?" he stuttered. "A third man, you say?"

"She said quite clearly you had ruined her," Henrietta said. "We all heard."

"But what did she say about the babe? Will she accept my arrangements for it?" Darien pressed.

"We did not exactly have the opportunity for a thoughtful discussion, due to the threats of vengeance and blood," Henrietta retorted. "But I believe she said her darling would have her but for...er, your progeny."

"She said that?" Perry bumped against a cushioned chair and then sat down in it. Rufie frowned at him, and Henrietta wondered whether the man was foxed.

"Have you two met?" Darien said. "Henry, my schoolmate and hanger-on, the disreputable Mr. Peregrine Empson. Perry, Miss Henrietta Wardley-Hines, reformer." He went to a small shelf filled with bottles, above and below it rows of books. "Drink, anyone?"

"Heavens, no, Darien," Rufie said. "It's not even noon."

"God, yes," Perry said. "A tall draught of whatever you've got."

"Cognac," Darien said, lifting a decanter. "Henry?"

"Yes, I believe I could use a nip." She accepted the glass, frowning as his fingers slid over hers. "Why are you calling me that?"

"Henry?" he said, smiling at her with that beautiful mouth. "Henrietta takes too long to pronounce."

Her brow furrowed. "It's not proper."

"Neither is it proper for you to be here in my library, drinking with three gentlemen."

"Gentlemen." She snorted. "I suppose it is rather fast of me.

Well. Circumstances warrant." She sniffed the liquid in her glass, swirled it, and tipped the contents into her mouth in one neat gulp. Then she drew in a long breath, placed the glass on the table beside her, and straightened. "I suppose, since I have no other news to report, I should be going."

Darien stared. "Are you rather accustomed to spirits, Henry?"

"What?" She blinked. "Oh, that. Not ladylike? Shame. Am I meant to take a sip, and simper, and protest I am not used to strong liquor?"

"You may do exactly as you like in my house," Darien answered, "but I am surprised that did not go straight to your head."

"Of course it did." She rose, wobbled a bit, and smiled. "Feels wonderful. Oh, Darien— Are these your drawings?"

She moved to a table covered with scrolls full of engineering designs. She saw Darien make a sweeping gesture to his companions in the direction of the door. She rolled her shoulders in the thick riding habit. Glory, but she'd needed a strong drink. She was no longer concerned about Darien's imminent death. She was no longer concerned about anything.

She looked around to see that the other two men had obeyed. "Alone, are we?" she inquired.

He set his glass to the side and approached her. "Do you want to be?"

"Of course not. I've a meeting with the London Committee for Abolition tomorrow and my debate for the Minerva Society coming soon. It's trial enough to be taken seriously as a woman. No one would listen to me for a moment were it known I'd succumbed to a rake."

"What if it were not known?" Darien said in a silky voice.

She wrinkled her nose at him. "Oh, who am I fooling? I

could run about shouting like the watchman and no one would believe you'd touched me."

"Why wouldn't they?" He moved closer.

She indicated her disheveled attire, her wild hair under the enormous hat, her lumpy and unfashionable habit. "Do you require spectacles, sir?"

He tilted his head slightly. "I've done more than touch you, you awful girl. I *kissed* you."

"You did? Oh, that. A demonstration only." She shook her head. "Is this for a mill? Would a wheel that size generate enough power?"

He turned her to face him. She glanced at his hands covering her shoulders. He had such strong, lean hands. The nails were neatly manicured and his fingers lightly callused, as if he did hard work without gloves. She imagined those hands moving over Celeste's curved body and hunched her shoulders.

"Henry," he said, and his voice had that low, husky quality she'd heard in the garden. His eyes were a smoky blue and his lids lowered, as if he were sleepy. "I think perhaps you *should* be concerned that I might ruin you."

"I'm not concerned in the least," she said. "I've seen what kind of women you fancy."

His hands fell away, and the smoky look disappeared. He reeled as if she had slapped him in the face.

"Besides which," she said, turning once more to the drawing board, "you aren't the sort of man I fancy either."

"Indeed?" he said in a voice that approached a growl. "What sort of man is worthy of Miss Henrietta Wardley-Hines?"

"I like men of industry, like my father. Men who have a passion, and a talent, and work hard at employing it for the betterment of others." She turned a paper to examine the sketch from a different angle. "Men who are called to serve, who feel a higher purpose." She put the drawing aside and looked up. "Scholars are my weakness, if you must know. Men like your cousin, actually."

He looked thunderstruck, his voice rising in volume. "*Rufie?*"

She drew back, embarrassed. "Not—that is— I meant men *like* him," she hurried to say. "I would not presume— Unless— Do you think he might—?"

Darien's eyes looked almost violet with passion. His hands came to her shoulders again, but not, this time, in a caress. He yanked her to him and she stumbled, treading on his toe. "You are not," he muttered through his teeth, "going to throw yourself at *Rufie.*" And before she could think to avert her mouth, he ground his down upon it.

She waited, part of her curious. It was not a scientific experiment this time; he was trying to exert his will. His mouth moved in that calculated way, demanding something. A small thread of tension curled low in her belly. He was being masterful again, trying to master *her.* She drew back, and his mouth followed, insistent. The thread of tension grew.

She stood on the edge of something—of tumbling into the abyss that had swallowed all the other scores of women who'd been kissed by Lord Daring. Not the ones for whom ruination had been fabricated, but the many for whom his reputation was in part deserved. She ground the heel of her boot into his toe.

He lifted his head. He was breathing hard, but so was she. Some emotion that she couldn't read swam over his face. His fingers dug into her back, and it seemed he meant to draw her to him again when they heard a sound. Slowly, cold with horror, Henrietta looked toward the doorway.

Rutherford cleared his throat. "Did you...call me?" he croaked.

"Go away, Rufie," Darien said in a freezing voice.

Henrietta clasped her hands over her mouth, her eyes stretched wide with shock. "Am I...am I *compromised*?"

Darien glared at her. "Rufie will say nothing," he snapped. "Henry, I *said* you oughtn't be here."

"I'm not." And for the second time that day, Henrietta bolted for the door, fleeing the mess she'd created.

James was lying relaxed on his seat in the phaeton, flipping a coin with one hand and holding the ribbons in the other while he chatted with the street boys.

"I hope that was honestly earned and not won," Henrietta snapped, hauling herself up the high step.

"Ey, now." James sat up. "If yer goin' to comb my head, I'll know the reason. All dished up, are ye?"

"No rake alive has the power to ruin *me*," Henrietta said, fighting her way into the vehicle. "Move over, James. I'm driving home."

He caught a whiff of her breath and his eyes widened. "Not for a minute," her loyal groom cried, refusing to surrender the reins. "As if I'd put these prime articles in the hands of a girl who's *bosky*!"

CHAPTER FIFTEEN

She'd begun a fight with Darien in Alywen's shop so she might not appear fascinated. She'd teased him that she preferred scholarly men like his cousin, provoking that furious, most unsettling kiss.

And he had not called in the days since, leaving Henrietta with a strange, restless ache under her skin that she didn't know how to soothe.

It would be best if she had no more to do with him, Henrietta told herself. All that should concern her about Darien was the welfare of Lady Celeste's child.

"You're home!" Marsibel smiled with eagerness as Henrietta entered the blue parlor of Hines House. "Just in time to dress for the Bicclesfield ball."

Oh, that dratted ball. Darien had instructed her to save him a dance. Did he remember? Would he make good on his promise? The thought of being held by him made Henrietta's heart skitter.

"Er. I've had a rather busy day, dear. The Minerva Society shipped off our crates of shoes and clothing for the settlers in Sierra Leone. A new donor sent an extremely generous donation to the Benevolence Hospital, so I've been buying supplies. The Sons of Africa have reviewed and endorsed our petition to Parliament calling for full abolition. *And* Lady Bess approved my notes for my debate. I thought I might spend a quiet evening with my sisters, reading about Etruscan art."

"Your gowns arrived from the dressmaker's today," Marsibel said with a mischievous twinkle in her eye. "Don't you want to see them?"

Part of her didn't. The broadsides and cartoons had already linked her name with Darien's in the most mortifying fashion. Some supposed Lord Daring was pursuing Miss Hop-Higher for a loan from Sir Grasping. Others predicted that London's reigning rake, having ravished all the gently born daughters within reach, was moving on to the rising bourgeoisie.

Miss Hop-Higher, in all these depictions, was a feather-brained ninny, flattered by Lord Daring's avaricious suit and unaware that the elegant libertine had lowered his sights considerably. And in all of them, she wore the most appalling gowns.

Clarinda and Aunt Althea stood arguing in Henrietta's dressing room while Duprix opened boxes with the reverence of a priestess performing sacred rites.

"You must allow that he has the most exquisite taste, Althea." Clarinda ran a hand over piles of fine muslins and silks.

"But to allow a man to purchase her clothing? It isn't done!" Althea cried.

"Of course I had the bill sent to me, Aunt Althea," Henrietta said. "Lord Darien only had a hand in the selection."

"You may leave the matter of ma'mselle's clothing to me, *mesdames*," Duprix said. She hustled Henrietta behind the dressing screen to extract her from the worn round gown she had worn to her meetings that day.

"All this fuss about gowns simply illustrates Miss Wollstonecraft's point about vanity," Henrietta grumbled as Duprix tied a rump pad around her waist.

"Ma'mselle will not sulk when she is in something that becomes her." Duprix tied on a lilac petticoat, then held open a pool of yellow silk for Henrietta to step into. With a few deft pins the maid fastened the bodice to the open robe, then tied up the short train. She fluffed the tiny ruffle that lined the bodice and peeked out at the sleeves, then stepped back to study the graceful retroussé effect in the back.

"Hetty," Marsibel breathed.

Duprix clapped her hands together. "Finally! How clever M'seiur Daring is."

Henrietta moved to the glass, and the dress swam gracefully with her. "I look exactly like the fashion plate."

"The corsage requires something." Duprix advanced with two half-moon pads and tucked them into the bodice of the gown. Henrietta, for the first time in her life, had a bosom.

Duprix smiled. "I think M'sieur Daring will like the effect, *n'est ce pas?*"

"You look divine." Clarinda touched her fingers to her lips. "The colors suit you perfectly. Hetty, dear, I wish I had said something long before this."

"She looks like Covent Garden wares," Aunt Althea yelped.

Henrietta stared at the transformation. Beneath the beautiful gown, she was her plain old self, but she felt alive with new possibilities.

Darien had flattered and paid court to her because he wanted access to her uncle. She knew that now. But the woman in her glass wasn't a silly Miss Hop-Higher, taken in by blandishments. She looked like a woman of means and influence.

She looked like a woman who might be welcomed if not into Polite Society, then at least by the Daughters of Minerva.

"I predict our Hetty will be a smashing success," Clarinda

sang as she led the women downstairs, where they meant to dine before the ball.

"I do not wish to be a success," Henrietta protested. "I wish for my debate to be well-attended, and for Hodge to sell me his mill, and for—"

"No business tonight, Hetty." Marsibel entwined their arms as they went into the parlor where Sir Pelton and Sir Jasper were waiting. "Tonight, you will be light and gay and dance with every young man who asks you. Not even Miss Wollstonecraft can think it a crime to be young and merry."

HENRIETTA'S CONFIDENCE ebbed as they waited in a long line of carriages before the rows of stately homes that lined Grosvenor Square. It ebbed further as they entered a vast marbled foyer that reminded her of the Ellesmere home and waited at the top of an enormous staircase to be announced.

Jasper, with patient resignation, shifted on his heeled shoes while Clarinda, her hair powdered gray and dotted with small bows in the fashion of Marie Antoinette, waited with a seraphic smile on her face. She had chosen an open robe with a pinned bodice and crossed sash designed to flaunt, in the most fetching manner, that she was in the family way.

Henrietta clung to Charley, who blew loud sighs and tapped the tip of his walking stick on the parquet floor.

At last, the footman announced their names, and the whispers rose around them like the rustlings of her expensive silk dress as Charley dragged her gracelessly down the stairs.

"Yellow!"

"Very French—"

"Her hair—"

"Did you hear Lord Daring—?"

"With a *bluestocking?* No!"

Oh, *why* had she ever consented to a Season? This wasn't her place. There would be some new and damning cartoon tomorrow, ridiculing her dress or her manner or her reform efforts, making it all the more difficult to rally support for her causes. She ought to have stayed home reading to her sisters and working on her debate. Though the ballroom was already crowded, despite the high ceiling with its frescoes of frolicking Olympians, Henrietta felt every eye directed toward her.

"Don't leave me," she muttered to Charley through a clenched smile. Even she could feel the disgrace of being a wall-flower at her first and possibly only ball.

"You've got Clarinda, and Marsi's right behind us," Charley said. "I'll be in the card room when you're ready to leave. I hope they *have* a card room. Try not to be too much of a goose."

Henrietta looked around for reinforcements as her brother melted away. Clarinda maneuvered her husband to a group of society matrons and began introductions, ignoring their displea-sure at making the acquaintance of a mill owner. So the wall of resistance extended to Jasper, too, her hard-working father who never turned away a soul in need. Henrietta, gnashing her teeth as she waited for Marsi, startled when she heard a deep, familiar voice at her elbow.

"Shall we join the first dance? The lines will be forming soon."

A shiver of pure delight ran down her back, oblivious to all her attempts to stifle it.

"Darien! You're not shot yet."

"And won't be, if I have my way. I nearly sent a note telling you to wear the yellow and violet, but I trusted your maid to know her work." His eyes moved with approval over her décol-letage, and a wash of heat followed the shiver. She wished she had not left her stole in the cloakroom.

"I thought you detested these functions," she said.

"You promised me a dance." He placed her hand on his arm and walked her about the room. "Is Sir Pelton with you?"

"Yes, there on the stairs." He wanted something from her uncle; that was the reason for his attentions. She must not lose her head, even if his nearness wreaked havoc on her senses. How could he be so calm, so aloof, when he kissed her the way he had in his study?

Because he kissed women all the time. Kisses meant nothing to him. It was only she who still felt his lips on hers. She could think of little else.

"Ought you be here? What if Lord Alfred finds you?"

"Not even a hothead like Freddy would issue a challenge in a crowded ballroom," Darien said. "Why did you tell Celeste to give my child to the Benevolence Hospital?"

Eyes followed them on their promenade, and confusion clouded the heat blooming through her. Darien was beautifully turned out in deep purple satin and an amber waistcoat, as though he had designed his dress to echo hers.

"You said she wouldn't see your solicitor. And Mary Ann means to stay on as a wet nurse. The babe would be safe there, well provided for."

"I told you I didn't want any child of mine raised in an orphanage."

His voice, though low, was a whip, and his fingers clenched painfully over hers. Henrietta set her teeth so she did not wince and betray anything to the eyes watching them. She was sure she detected the sallow face and avaricious eyes of Lord Pinochle among them. She had quite forgotten his grudge against her among all the competing distractions.

"Raised as a pauper?" He was truly furious with her. "My solicitor will arrange for a family to take it in. A good family."

His accusing tone set Henrietta's back up. She had been

trying to help! "You have met this family? You approve of them?" The leaping muscle in his jaw betrayed him, and she pressed her point. "Where is the babe to stay while this family is found?"

His brows drew together in a scowl. "It is not your business."

"You expect me to simply shrug and turn away when a child's life is at stake?" Pinochle stood in her periphery, an oily black shadow. "Perhaps men have the luxury of ignoring the welfare of infants. Women do not."

She held his challenging stare, chin up. He looked away first, and she exhaled, shaken by his anger. Better that than his playing at seduction, she told herself, trying to soothe her rattled nerves. She was accustomed to scorn.

"Miss Pennyroyal," Darien greeted the girl with a stoic calm. Forsythia was dressed head to toe in a blushing pink, but her eyes were sharp.

"Daring," she cooed. "So the cartoons are true. You have been cast so far out of Polite Society that you are obliged to associate with tradesmen and bluestockings." Her look turned to surprise as she surveyed Henrietta's dress. "My word, Miss Wardley-Hines. This is quite a change in your style."

"I gave her some hints," Darien said. "She was wise enough to take them."

"My modiste persuaded me to try something new." Henrietta gritted her teeth. So this was to be the tenor of the night, raked down by one and all. Polite Society was a sea of sharks, worse than a town council meeting at Salford when one was trying to obtain permits for rebuilding. She glared at Darien, who had adopted his impassive face.

"Next she will turn you out in public in a nightgown." Miss Pennyroyal snickered. "Daring, my dear, I think perhaps you should not take the advice of your friend Mr. Empson. Miss

Wardley-Hines may not have the power to repair your reputation as you wish."

"I don't know what you're talking about." Darien looked about as if seeking escape and beckoned to a nearby group of gentlemen who were watching their discussion with great interest. One of them strolled over, raising a quizzing glass.

"But I saw Mr. Empson in the park just today, and he told me all about your little scheme," Miss Pennyroyal pressed on. "I do not think you need stoop to granting your attentions to unsuitable females to annoy your father, however! Turn to the Pennyroyals, milord, if you wish to redeem yourself in the polite world. For we at least have some claim to breeding and are not sullied by trade."

Henrietta tried to step away. She didn't need to stand here, a target for Miss Pennyroyal's barbs. But Darien clamped his hand over hers as she tried to withdraw.

"Miss Pennyroyal," Darien said. "May I introduce to you the Honorable Mr. Lionel Havering, heir to the Viscount Bourchier, unless he gets himself killed in a duel before he can claim his coronet. Havering, Miss Forsythia Pennyroyal. Her father was the late Colonel Pennyroyal, distinguished for his service in the Seven Years' War."

"I gave you your chance to run me through, Daring," Havering drawled. "Gone through all the duke's daughters, have you, and reduced to preying on the orphans of our national heroes? I've told you before I won't take your cast-offs."

Havering raked Henrietta with an insolent gaze that turned to interest and then, as his eyes traveled back to her face, approval. "This one, now," he said, his drawl deepening, "you may introduce to me. She can't be seen next to you, wearing that frock. I have a weakness for damsels in need of rescue."

Henrietta felt a furious blush spread down her neck to her décolletage. She recognized him as Lady Celeste's former fiancé. Darien said Celeste had jilted the man, but Henrietta wasn't sure. "I know a duke's daughter in need of rescue, Mr. Havering."

Havering chuckled at her challenge. "That horse has fled the barn, I'm afraid. Come, Miss Wardley-Hines, take refuge with me. You are too interesting to fall prey to Daring's version of sport."

Miss Pennyroyal narrowed her eyes. "As am I," she huffed. "Nor am I Daring's *cast-off*. What tales are you spreading, sir?"

Darien held his arm before Henrietta as if Havering meant to steal her. "I warned you about being seen too much in my company, Forsythia."

The girl went still. "Daring! All those visits to our house, though my mother and grandmother hate you. Your attention, your gifts— What did they mean, if not—?"

Darien shook his head, saying nothing, and Forsythia's eyes filled with tears. She whirled and ran away, pushing ball-goers out of her path.

Darien steered Henrietta to the middle of the floor, where sets were being made up.

"That was cruel," Henrietta said. She should not be surprised that he was capable of it. What man gave regard to a woman's tender feelings? But it was disappointing to realize he was just another self-interested roué after all.

"She ought not go on thinking I am courting her when I have no such intentions."

And what were his intentions toward *her*? Henrietta wondered. Oh, yes: advice from her uncle, and her help managing Lady Celeste, though he didn't like the offer she had extended. Kissing her had meant nothing to him, a demonstration only. She pushed the lowering thought away.

"Of course. You break betrothals, not hearts." She made her

curtsy as the dance began. "But why should Forsythia think you were courting her if you were not?"

He placed his hand against hers as they circled one another, and she hoped he did not feel her fingers trembling. "Do you recall what your brother said over dinner, about how I gained my estate at cards?"

"Yes," Henrietta said, sick at the memory. "And how the owner took his life thereafter."

"I went the next day to his hotel suite to return the deed and settle our debt some other way," Darien said. They switched hands, circling in the other direction. His face was like marble, his eyes bright and hard. "I found the body there, unattended. His man had robbed him and left. The landlord nearly had apoplexy when he saw the gore. He left a wife and three daughters with no idea that he had plunged the estate into debt and mortgaged their futures."

"The Pennyroyals," Henrietta guessed, completing her turn.

"The pension from the Royal Army is next to nothing." Darien grasped her arms and lifted her in a circle. He was warm and firm. She tried not to flush at the heat, the strength of his body.

"He made some terrible investments, then tried to retrieve them with worse gambles. His bailiff told me that his wife had been raising the children in London to be close to her ailing mother, so she never knew what things had come to. Because, of course, a proud husband would try to protect her with ignorance."

"So what has kept Miss Pennyroyal in the manner which she feels her due?" Henrietta asked as they circled one another again, palms pressed together.

"With some correction and investment, the estate has been restored and continues to yield income." He kept his voice low, aware that the dancers around them were very interested in their conversation. Pinochle in particular never took his eyes from them. "Part of the profits are conveyed to Mrs. Pennyroyal through her late husband's solicitor. She thinks it is a trust he left her. I retain part for myself, to keep me out of my father's pocket."

"And you visit the family to be sure they are not in want." This was altogether unexpected, overturning her assumption—the assumption shared by everyone—that he was a heartless cad. Miss Pennyroyal clearly had no notion that Darien was her family's benefactor. "Yet you let people like my brother believe that you drove the Colonel to suicide."

"I doubt I could have stopped him even if I hadn't been nursing a thick head that morning," Darien said. "A man who is set on self-destruction will find a way. Never mind who he leaves behind. Or how many other good men are taken from their lives when they would have given much to keep them."

She saw the white lines come out around his mouth and guessed he was thinking of his brother, fighting the savage tide of grief. She understood that blinding pain, how in the threat of that enveloping blackness one might use anything—or anyone—as a shield. He'd hinted that he hadn't had his head on straight with Celeste. But he was doing his best to repair the damage now.

"And you let all those high sticklers think you are an indiscriminating seducer," she said quietly. His hands were so warm, his grip on her sure and commanding.

"The truth would not serve. If her family knew a young lady were plotting to avoid an undesirable marriage, she'd be pressed to it all the faster. Far more expedient to have her ruined and left to her own devices after. A gentleman keeps a lady's secrets."

He drew his hand slowly along her bare arm as they reached

the end of the line and parted. Henrietta held his eyes over their joined palms as they met again at the top.

"But the truth could repair your reputation far more than I could. Forsythia is right. Associating with me will gain you ridicule from more than just the marquess."

His eyes turned wary. "Perry took some maggot in his head that I should pay court to unsuitable females to foil my father's demands that I marry. Pay him no mind. No one else does."

Henrietta forced a shrug. "The cartoons seem to have paid him some mind. But the thought is indeed silly. A tradesman's daughter, and a bluestocking at that? Hardly a prize for the infamous Daring."

He pressed those beautiful, mobile lips together. "I hoped you would not see those cartoons. They are cruel, and inaccurate."

"I find them highly amusing," Henrietta lied. "If only they knew your real interest in the Wardley-Hines lay with Uncle Pelton. How disappointed the scandalmongers would be."

He studied her, and his eyelids lowered into a sleepy, seductive look. Her toes curled in her silk slippers.

"Havering was right," he said, his voice deepening. "No one will care you are a bluestocking in that gown. You look utterly delectable."

She floundered a moment in the pleasure she took in that declaration. He was a practiced seducer. That was one of his lines.

"Wonderful. I hope the attention shall gain more signatures for my petition." Henrietta tugged her hand free of his and made her turn. "Save your skills for worthier targets, *Daring*. I have no betrothal to break."

He closed his fingers about her wrist. She felt the warm strength of his hand through her gloves, and an answering warmth stole through her belly. His eyes darkened to violet as, quite deliberately, holding her eyes the whole time, he pulled her up against his body and lifted her in a turn.

Heat radiated from him. At the end of the turn he set her on her feet, sliding her slowly down the front of his body. Even through the layers of muslin and silk, she felt the hard planes of his stomach and thighs. A thick gush of heat splashed from her throat to her belly, and when he withdrew to his place in line, she nearly toppled.

He had been attempting, since that first night in the Ellesmere gallery, to provoke a reaction from her. To arouse her—there was no other word for it. Her last shred of dignity lay in not letting him know he had succeeded. Henrietta cleared her face and skipped to her place in line, attempting insouciance.

"You'd best behave yourself with me if you want my uncle's help," she said when their palms met again. He stepped too close, his leg brushing her skirts. "Though for my part, I should think if you don't wish the responsibilities of your inheritance, you might simply ask your father to break the entail."

"I already—" He bit off the words, bristling with anger. "Interfering female. I broached a private matter with your uncle. How dare he share a confidence?"

"Private?" She laughed. "Nothing you do is private. Every deed of yours shows up in the broadsides. Every person you have a word with. Including me."

"I thought you planned to take advantage of the attention," he said in a sharp tone, his eyes dark. "More signatures for your causes, etcetera."

He understood her even less than she understood him. "Oh, naturally. And I couldn't care a whit if the attention is bought at the cost of respect for my family. How amusing to see us lampooned in the street, to have my brother twitted because he inherited by special remainder, my uncle mocked because he won his title for service, my father ridiculed for supporting the King. As if one is more worthy for being born to an inheritance rather than earning one's gains by hard work."

"That is the way of the world, Henry. You can't change it."

She tore her hand from his and stood glaring at him. "But it's unfair. My father, whom your class thinks nothing but a vaunting tradesman, helped fund an army so the British might make peace in Mysore. He helped bring the rule of law to an unsettled land."

Darien halted in his tracks, and the blankness in his eyes cut off her tirade. "Mysore," he repeated. "Jasper paid for the wars in Mysore?"

Henrietta curled her hands into fists at her sides. The rest of the dancers stumbled to a halt to watch their exchange, but she paid them no heed. "My father made a loan to the King, and the King used the funds as he wished."

"To bring good men to their deaths." Darien's voice rose. "So that he can have cotton for his infernal mills, and Lady Clarinda might have her tea! How can you be proud of them?" He stepped close, looming over her. "Does your father have any notion how much blood is on his hands, thanks to those wars?"

Henrietta stood her ground. "I regret the costs of war as much as anyone, but sometimes a price must be paid for peace."

"Enough." He flung out a hand as if to push her away. Every head in the room turned in their direction. "Look at you, trying to pull children out of the gutter while your family hands over the blunt that sends gallant men to suffer and die in some hellish land, making orphans. How can you bear the hypocrisy?"

Her face burned with humiliation, and not because people were staring. Her entire body was frozen in shock. She knew people died in war, horribly, senselessly. The overseer on her estate was a man scarred by war. But no one had ever accused Jasper of being culpable, blaming his money for the deaths of men and innocent others.

"My father has devoted himself to improving the lives of the less fortunate," she stammered. "And so have I. We at least make an effort, which is a better use of our time than many alternatives."

"You may think me reprehensible," Darien said softly, "but you're a fool, Henry." And without a bow or a word of parting, he turned and walked away.

The crowd parted before him like the Red Sea. With his face so set and forbidding, his shoulders broad and taut with anger barely leashed, no one stepped forward to ask him what the matter was. He stalked from the ballroom, the most elegant and fascinating of men, and he was entirely alone.

"Hetty. My dear."

Marsibel touched her arm, her face troubled. "Are you quite well?"

Henrietta summoned a smile. It felt small and bedraggled, a pitiful effort. "I suppose I've made a complete spectacle of myself." She couldn't bear to look around the room and meet the avid eyes. "Can I hope the Bicclesfields have a trapdoor that might swallow me, like some theatre device?"

Aunt Althea joined them, her face lit with an astonished smile. "My word, Henrietta. You've done it! Everyone saw Lord Daring set on you, try to seduce you, and you sent him off with a flea in his ear!"

"We had a terrible row." Henrietta put a hand to her ribs. Her stomacher was pinned too tightly. "I said some very unfeeling things, and he...he..."

He made her body flame from scalp to sole, and she pushed

him away in a blind panic at what that meant. How it made her weak, all too susceptible.

He was the secret benefactor of the Pennyroyals.

He was, in essence, the benefactor of any number of young women whom he had helped free from unwanted marriages, though to the rest of the town, he looked to be cutting a ruinous swath.

He had put her in dresses that, for the first time in her life, made her feel graceful and lovely. He had helped her bring Mary Ann to the Sisters of Benevolence and arranged Elijah's funeral.

He had, as a matter of fact, signed every one of her petitions.

And she had accused him of acting irresponsibly when he was trying to set things right with Celeste. She ought to have asked him why he didn't wish to become his father's heir, rather than calling him to account for it.

"He saw you are immune to his tricks, as any Wardley must be," Aunt Althea said. "Despite that gown! Henrietta Eglantine, I am very proud of you. Whatever else happens tonight, you are already a success."

This proved a prediction true beyond even Lady Clarinda's fondest hopes. Gossip shot through the ballroom with the speed of flame. The infamous Lord Daring had assayed the virtue of Miss Henrietta Wardley-Hines, and the knight's daughter routed him, boot and bayonet, sending the villain to heel with a long list of his faults in hand.

Matrons with tender daughters thronged her for advice. Young tulips who competed for the fashionable debutantes saw a girl not easily won and wanted her at once. Everyone who had interested themselves in gossip over the scandalous Lord Daring wanted an introduction to the girl who had vanquished him.

Miss Henrietta Wardley-Hines, knight's daughter, was the undeniable toast of the Bicclesfield ball.

She danced every dance, laughed at every compliment and flirtation, and drank every glass of champagne that interested suitors brought her. But the champagne was as bitter as used tea leaves, and the sweets turned to dust in her mouth. She saw no further sign of Forsythia Pennyroyal, though she wanted to talk to the girl.

Lord Pinochle, however, watched her closely, and when partners changed during a country dance, she could not avoid touching her hand to his clammy one without risking notice. She was glad for her kid gloves.

"I see you are becoming much talked about, Miss Wardley-Hines," Pinochle said with an unctuous smile. "But I thought your cause was to tear unwitting girls from their safe homes, rather than reform known rakehells."

"Safe homes?" Henrietta nearly spat on the highly polished floor. "Do you not rather mean a home where her goodwill was taken advantage of, her virtue destroyed, her character shamed in being forced to submit to attentions she did not welcome? I call it fortunate if a girl might escape those circumstances."

His answer was a savage sneer. "You had best watch your step, girl. You will not be sheltered for always beneath the wing of your Lady Bess. You're treading on dangerous ground with your meddling, and taking up with Daring too."

A chill slithered down Henrietta's spine. She looked to the end of the line of dancers where, mercifully, their promenade would end so she could return to her partner, Mr. Lionel Havering, who had promised to sign the Minerva Society's petition calling for the full abolition of slavery.

"I am leading a debate for the Minerva Society in a few days, milord, on a topic that might interest you. What is owed to dependents when their protectors prove unworthy." She gave him the barest curtsy, as the dance dictated, and was astonished at her own audacity. This gown was making her bold. "Perhaps you might attend."

"I rather think I shall." Pinochle glared as he rose from his bow. "But I do not think I will support your theme."

That taunt troubled Henrietta as she jostled home with Clarinda and Althea gushing about her success and about the invitations she was sure to receive. But once Duprix had peeled the silk robe off her and she fell into bed, sore from head to foot, the deeper hurt she had tried to push away surfaced into the quiet dark.

She had not repulsed the rake. She had craved his look of approval, reveled in it. She had clung to his arm with all the shallow pride Miss Wollstonecraft condemned, knowing the entire ballroom saw that Lord Darien Bales chose to dance with her, Henrietta Wardley-Hines, tradesman's daughter.

When he lifted her against his body, she had reveled in the shameless desire that flooded her, in understanding, at last, what drove young women to lose their heads over a man. It was powerful. Intoxicating. Even now, the memory of that contact thrilled along every nerve, rousing her body with a nearly painful awareness.

She was not immune. Not to his potent allure, and not to the look of bewildered shock and horror on his face when she spoke of the wars in Mysore. The hollow grief that had entered his eyes made her heart crack open.

It served her right to have her vanity thwarted, to know she, in her new gown, held no appeal for a seasoned seducer. A Henrietta Wardley-Hines did not have what it took to fascinate a man the likes of Lord Darien Bales.

But to lose the slim thread that had begun to develop between them, among their confidences, their adventures, their racketing about town together—that loss she regretted deeply. It went far deeper than the blow to her feminine pride. He was a man she wanted to know more of, and she had cut off any possibility for trust, for friendship, for any deeper connection, with one fell and terrible confession.

If Henrietta's pillow and the ostrich feather beneath it grew damp with tears in the smallest hours of the night, no one save Henrietta, the pillow, and the feather knew.

CHAPTER SIXTEEN

In the thin gray light before dawn, the chambermaid stole into Henrietta's room with a summons.

"James said to fetch ye, miss. The babe's arrived," she whispered.

"Lady Mama?" Henrietta tossed the covers aside.

"Nay, miss, it's a good two months to 'er time yet, an 'er ladyship's in 'er bed. Whose babe does 'e mean, then?"

"My German habit, Hazel, and a fresh chemise. I must go, quickly."

"That duke's mort and 'er by-blow," James reported when Henrietta arrived in the kitchen. He crouched near the door to the scullery, glaring at the cook, who glared back, her wooden spoon raised in warning. "I 'ad a lad keepin' his peepers on the place. The midwife left in the wee hours, a babe with her."

Henrietta's sleepiness fell away in a rush. "Where did she go?"

"Owm I to know?" James demanded.

Henrietta's heart rose in her throat as she steered her phaeton through the waking streets, around carts, wagons, carters hauling refuse, and housemaids throwing night soil into the street. Celeste had birthed her baby and sent it away. But where?

At Highcastle House, James slipped into the mews, winning the argument that the daughter of Sir Jasper Wardley-Hines could not be seen at the servant's door. Henrietta muttered to herself as she trotted her chestnuts around Portman Square. As the daughter of a tradesman, she had free range of the Rossendale Fells along with the family villa at Salford, and she and the girls of Miss Gregoire's ran tame through Bath.

But as the daughter of a knight, she exchanged status for freedom. Any gossip about her would go straight to the ears of Aunt Althea and the Daughters of Minerva. Only the highest-born could behave with utter disregard for propriety, and sooner or later, even they achieved censure—the Duchess of Devonshire and Lady Celeste herself were proof of that.

That wasn't at all the world she wanted to be in. Why was she trying?

James emerged shaking his head. "Peery scrape, the whole of it. The mort said to spirit it off and not mouse to anyone, an' that's all. Sounds a bit like me own mum, don't that?" He spat in the street, then leapt to his perch in the phaeton, as light as a cat.

"Oh, James." Henrietta tasted acid, though her mouth was dry. "Do you think she sent it to the Foundling Hospital? Where should we start searching?"

"The workhouses, and the alleys, and the baby farms," James said with a grim face, and Henrietta shivered.

"I pray not." There would be little chance of finding it if the child were sent out of the city. The children of workhouses, when they survived, were sold to apprenticeships as soon as could be. She had seen plenty of children sent to work in the mills, where their small bodies could dart beneath the heavy machines. They were fed and housed, and in parishes like hers attended Sunday school, but not all mill owners shared Jasper's concern that children should not be overworked or endangered.

Oh, why hadn't she begged Lady Celeste to see Darien's solicitor? If she couldn't locate the babe and some ill befell it, she would never be able to forgive herself.

The day passed in a blur. The midwife, when they called at her lodgings, was attending another childbed. Henrietta left her card. Though she knew most of the charitable institutions in town, without James she would have become hopelessly lost in London. Narrow passageways twisted between buildings that had been split to accommodate more tenants, then split again. There was no order or plan whatsoever, just rickety structures that leaned atop one another, shoddy and hastily made. Her wheels flattened refuse left in the middle of the street, and the smells of the markets made her gag.

How she missed Salford and their sweet Mersey River, which provided fresh water at one end of town and collected its refuse at the other. Here in London, which was girdled by the Thames, one drew from the river what another had just put into it. The constant noise was astonishing, worse than the relentless grind of the machines at a mill. Over everything hung the smoky haze of burning coal, the fuel for the noisy, tireless engines of industry.

She stopped at a tavern, chafing at the lost time, when James informed her that if she didn't fill his breadbasket, he would chew off her stumps. Leaning against the rough piece of lumber that served as the counter for the small shop, she ate a pasty filled with some chewy meat she didn't care to identify and wiped greasy fingers on her habit. James used his uniform for the same office and finished her untouched pint of ale, and they returned to the phaeton for more fruitless searching.

Finally, as the coal smoke blended with approaching dusk, Henrietta called a halt from sheer exhaustion. She wanted to cry from frustration and fear. She was rubbish at rescues. She'd earned Pinochle's enmity by helping his maid escape. She'd not been able to save Elijah. And what could she say to Darien, as it was her fault the child had disappeared?

For solace she stopped by the Sisters of Benevolence Hospital to see the one girl whose life she had at least managed to improve. In a pool of warm, quiet light, Mary Ann sat rocking in the matron's sitting room, a newborn at her breast.

Henrietta's heart skipped several beats.

"Came at the crack of dawn, poor wee one," Mary Ann said. "Mother said I might feed her."

Henrietta swallowed the ash in her throat. "Was there a note?"

Mary Ann drew a small card from her apron, one engraved with the name and direction of the home. On the back was a crooked scrawl. *You asked for the brat, so take her. Tell Daring to rot in hell.*

"What's it say?" Mary Ann asked innocently.

"It says the mother has surrendered all claim. A girl, is it?" Henrietta sank to the small stool by the fire. The child was here, safe. She might sob with relief. "Are you— Is she feeding?"

"Like a farmhand," Mary Ann whispered. "And I've milk enough, mum, more's the wonder. I tole you they were plumping me up."

The matron entered with a pile of swaddling fresh from the laundry. "Ye've met our new one, Miss Hetty? The midwife said she's sound, so that's a blessing, but my word, that's the fifth this week."

"D'ye want to hold her? Mind ye keep her upright and get the bubble out." Mary Ann pulled up her bodice with one hand and held out the infant with calm expertise.

Henrietta stared at the tiny creature. She had fed, changed, and burped each of her younger half-sisters, and this felt oddly the same, as if the child belonged to her somehow. Thick black hair mossed the baby's head, and dark strands traced her brows and the lids of her eyes. A web of tiny red veins spread over her round cheeks and chin, with dark pink patches on her eyelids and one in the center of her forehead, an angel's kiss.

This might be Darien's child. Henrietta took the baby as if she were made of glass and rubbed the swaddled back.

"Five, Mother? All newborns?"

"And seven last week, one for each blessed day." The matron handed a pile of cloths to Mary Ann to help fold. "I can't think where we're to put them all. We'll be stacked to the rafters soon."

"Are there enough nurses?" The wee mite pressed one fist to the side of her face, her lips still sucking in the rhythm she had just learned. Henrietta's lungs closed at the thought of any harm coming to her.

"Aye, nurses enough, all too many." The matron sighed. "It's a needful care we provide, Miss Hetty, and I don't begrudge a one of them. But the Good Lord keeps giving, at least unto us."

The words emerged before the thought had finished forming. "I'll take her," Henrietta said. "Home with me. And Mary Ann too, if you can spare her."

The matron paused and raised her eyebrows. Henrietta had never been able to guess her age, nor did she know her hair color, but the matron's eyebrows were a thick and startling black.

Mary Ann's eyes grew equally wide, and Henrietta hurried on. "Will you come with me and be the baby's nurse? We can offer you room and board and a salary, and everyone is quite kind in my father's house. You can stay till the babe is weaned, if not longer."

Mary Ann looked like she had been handed the moon. She was a young woman, not sixteen, a mother who had already lost a babe. At sixteen, Henrietta had been concluding her studies at Miss Gregoire's and writing Lady Mama instructions on how Jasper liked his household to run. She had never held a child of her own.

Until now.

"Will Lady Clarinda have it?" the matron asked.

"I hope she will." Henrietta looked at the baby's face, where a small bubble of milk blew and popped on the tiny Cupid's bow mouth. She was not doing this for Darien. She was obeying the surprising voice in her head that said "Mine." She felt the same inward sigh of happiness, of belonging, as when she met Clarinda and knew she had a mother again.

All the same, she felt like a thief when she emerged from the hospital holding the baby, with Mary Ann carrying a small bundle of clothes. James clucked at them.

"'Ey now, it's been 'ere all along? Right where ye wanted it! Whyn't leave it 'ere, then?"

"Drive us home, James," Henrietta said, handing the baby up to Mary Ann.

"A gentry throw!" James exclaimed. "And you want the squeaker in your nursery? What's 'er ladyship goin' to say?"

"You know she is mad about babies." Henrietta squeezed herself into the small seat beside the girl.

"Aye, but 'er own ones," James noted as he guided the Titans into the street.

Her family and friends wouldn't understand, even when she explained that she was relieving the strain on the Sisters of Benevolence to take the babe. And Darien would be furious. Henrietta hugged the baby tightly to her chest as the knowledge pierced her heart.

Whatever fragile rapport had sprung up between them

would be at an end now thanks to this supreme bit of meddling. She would miss him. He would never comprehend why she needed this.

She had not been able to save Fanny, or Elijah, or so many of the weak and deprived babes she saw in her charitable work. But this one, she could save.

CHAPTER SEVENTEEN

Henrietta approached the cheval glass in her chamber, regarding the stranger reflected there. The filmy white *chemise de le reine* that had felt scandalous in Alywen's dress shop swirled around her in a sensual whisper, hinting at grace, elegance, and freedom of movement—the ideals of the independent woman.

"For once I can agree to the bosom friends," Henrietta said, turning to study her profile. "All the same, I look undressed."

Duprix arranged the subtle flounces of the sleeves and the drape of the skirt. "I shall put a bandeau in your hair and leave it unpowdered, as M'sieur Daring prefers. He likes for you to look like one of those girls on the Greek vase."

"I am not dressing to please Darien," Henrietta said.

But was she dressing to please herself? She hardly knew this girl in the mirror. She was not the innocent Darien had guarded while she repaired her gown in the Chapel Royal of St. James. She was not the same woman he had dressed for dinner at home, blindly focused on her reforming causes.

She felt different. Awakened. His kiss had taught her something about herself.

She had a child to take care of now.

And Darien had not called since their falling out at the Bicclesfield ball. He was hardly likely to attend her debate. If Uncle Pelton could not aid him in his cause, what more could he want with Henrietta? He had drawn his masterful hands over her as if she were a musical instrument brought to life by his touch. And then he left.

Duprix unclenched crushed fabric from Henrietta's fists. "Is Ma'mselle nervous?"

"Incredibly, yes. I've participated in debates before, but tonight—it matters very much that people listen."

This debate meant more than a philosophical discussion, more than admittance into the Minerva Society. Her topic could influence the fate of the young girls above stairs, her beloved half-sisters, as well as the newest little one they had welcomed into their domain.

"Then it is well you look innocent and wise at the same time." Duprix focused on Henrietta's hair. "That is Lady Celeste's babe, yes?"

No reason to prevaricate; all the servants must know already. "Yes."

"What will M'sieur say when he knows you have taken her?"

What, indeed? She had sent a note informing him that she had located Celeste's daughter, that she was safe. She had heard nothing from him in response.

She knew how her actions would look to Miss Pennyroyal and others. Lacking the personal charms to attract Lord Daring, Henrietta had spirited away his child to gain his attention.

"A sash or zone for the bodice?" Henrietta suggested, feeling exposed.

Duprix shook her head. "You may take a shawl, but M'sieur Daring was right. Your décolletage is your best feature."

"And when I take an ague from the drafty lecture hall, you shall be called upon to nurse me. Cosmetics, Duprix?" She hesitated when the lady's maid picked up a small jar and a brush. "That is too fast even for me."

"If ma'mselle does not like it, I will wash it off," Duprix promised. With a few dabs, she darkened Henrietta's brown eyelashes to black, added a brush of rouge that made her cheekbones leap out from her face, and with a touch of paint made her lips fuller and more expressive. The maid stood back and surveyed her charge from head to toe. "*Voilà. C'est bon.*"

"Is that me?" Henrietta asked the mirror.

She didn't want her Season, or Darien, or the Minerva Society, or being a knight's daughter to take her away from what she knew and loved. She liked being plain Henrietta Wardley-Hines, discussing radical ideas at bluestocking salons, pushing for unpopular reforms, experimenting with innovations on her properties. She charted her path by the women she admired— her schoolteachers, Miss Gregoire. Her mother. Lady Bessington. Thinkers like Olympe de Gouges and Wollstonecraft. She would never give up the real pleasure and purpose of her life to be a toast at balls.

"What do you think of my topic?" Henrietta asked as Duprix dressed her hair with moonflowers and pearl pins. "Would it not be to the advantage of society to bestow education upon females as well as males?"

Duprix gave her Gallic shrug. "And what would it avail women, ma'mselle, to know what the men know? They will never respect us if we try to be little men, and we will lose the one advantage we have in being women."

Not for the first time, Henrietta wondered how old Duprix was, and why she had left France, and what had etched those hard lines onto her face. Who had she left behind?

"What sort of knowledge do you mean? I do not see that women have any advantage."

Duprix whistled softly. "If you do not know what I mean, ma'mselle, it is only because you have not been in the company of enough young men." Her lips turned up at one corner. "I think M'sieur Daring will be happy to teach you."

Darien wanted nothing more to do with her. He had knifed her in the heart, shaken her very understanding of the world. She had never questioned her father's decisions. He was a wise businessman and a kind employer, and his investments went to protect the peace and prosperity of the nation, to protect the world she knew.

A peace that came at the cost of lives, she now realized. British men had lost their lives in Mysore. And what of the people of Mysore, for that matter? How much of their blood had been shed to secure her peace and prosperity?

Her world felt riven to the core, the pieces drifting away from her, and she didn't know where she should jump for safety. Or what to do to make things right.

"Do you think it is right, Duprix? What is happening in France?"

Duprix pulled a shawl from the clothespress. "I think the citizens are right to demand change. There were too many with too little, too few with too much. But I do not wish for liberation bought by blood."

"Do you wish to go back?" The new French government had declared the émigrés traitors, their properties and assets forfeit.

"There is nothing in France for me to return to," Duprix said, "and that will not change no matter how many constitutions are passed."

Henrietta rose. The soft muslin fell about her like a cloud. One could nearly see the outlines of her figure, though she wore stays and a petticoat beneath. She felt scandalous. She felt ready to do something bold.

"I seem to have a knack for prying," she said. "No doubt Darien will have my head when he knows what I've done."

But she had done it anyway, just as she would go to this debate and argue her cause, just as she would keep knocking on doors to gather signatures and collect donations. Just as she would keep giving funds to the causes she believed in, but she would be more thoughtful, in future, about the consequences.

Another way Lord Darien Bales had changed her, like it or not.

Duprix smiled, her eyes soft with warmth. "There is no one quite like you, mademoiselle."

"That is what Charley says, though I do not think he means it kindly. Thank you, Duprix. I believe I am armed for the battle ahead."

She stood on the brink of an enormous change, and if she stepped out in this dress, there would be no returning to the girl she had been and the safe world that girl had known. Henrietta could only hope her brave words to Duprix were true.

THE MINERVA SOCIETY typically met in a member's home since women were not allowed in most coffee shops and clubs. But for their debates and other public lectures, Lady Bessington rented rooms at the London Tavern, and as James turned the pair into Bishopsgate Street, Henrietta noted considerable traffic. James squeezed her phaeton into a narrow space before the massive façade of the Tavern, and John the footman leapt down to make inquiries.

"The Corresponding Society is meetin' at the Black Lion

next door," he reported, his eyes alight with interest. "Quite a rabble in there, Miss Hetty!"

"I would like to attend one of their meetings," Henrietta said. "How vexing that they chose the same night as my debate."

"I think they're *at* your debate, miss." Peter, the second footman, helped her down from the vehicle, and both men shielded her from the jostling crowd as they made their way to the doors of the building.

"Present your ticket!" cried the usher. "Tickets sent to all subscribers! Tickets available for purchase here!"

Henrietta clutched her notes as the crowd pushed her forward. Her hands sweated inside her evening gloves. She was to stand in front of this great mass. When the usher accosted her, she stared at him with throat tight and mind blank.

"Ticket!" he snapped. "Ev'run has to have a ticket, e'en the doxies!" His scowl lifted into surprise. "Aye, is it you, Miss Wardley-Hines? Go on in, then." He blinked as he regarded her outfit. "Di'n recognize you in that rig, I grant you! Apologies! Go on in, now, they're waitin' for ye, miss." He shook his head, and Henrietta heard him mutter as she passed. "Looks like a Frenchie, to wit. Aye, now! Ticket from you, if you please."

"You needn't stay," she told her footmen. "In fact you might quite prefer going next door for a pint."

"We're stayin', Miss Hetty," John said. "You'll need a cool head about ye, from the looks o' this crowd."

"A pint sounds—" Peter began, and then started as if he'd been elbowed or kicked. He glared at his superior. "Aye, we'll be 'ere. And pints later, then."

The Tavern staff had arranged the Pillar Room to resemble the House of Commons, with benches lining the sides of the room beneath the Corinthian columns that gave the room its name. In the center stood a small raised platform with a lectern in the middle for the speaker, and on each side sat a table lined with chairs. A spectator's gallery occupied both ends of the room, the benches placed closely together, and these were already spilling over with people. Henrietta felt faint as she looked at the crush.

This was the largest meeting the Minerva Society had ever hosted. She saw several faces she recognized from the Biccles-field ball crowding the spectator's gallery. So Aunt Althea was right, and a good number of people had come for a peek at the bluestocking abolitionist who had routed Lord Daring. The eccentric reformer with the mouthful of a name, the girl with the wealth of her father's northern mills behind her. Drawing people to her debate had merely increased the number of gawkers ready to laugh at her freaks.

"Good heavens, Hetty, you look like Marie Antoinette! I adore the look on you. This is quite a change." Lady Bessington took her hands as Henrietta reached the dais and examined her from head to toe. "Marvelous," she said with a delighted laugh. "You look very innocent, sweet and uncomplicated. How clever."

Henrietta hoped that Pinochle's taunt about bringing down Lady Bess was no more than bluster. Lady Bessington was as immune to scandal as any woman could be. Her husband held one of the oldest earldoms in Scotland and a seat in the British House of Lords. Her family tree branched from royal stock. All four of her sons held positions of influence, and her daughters had married into high families across Europe. If her debate were a disaster, Henrietta would need Lady Bess for any last chance to join the Daughters of Minerva and honor her mother's memory.

She turned to the lectern and tripped when she saw the men seated at the small table on the pro side of the room. One of them had his striking visage plastered regularly across the

London newspapers, not to mention the several editions of his book.

"Bess." She gasped. "Did you know Mr. Oulidah Equiano is here?"

"I invited him, dear," Lady Bess answered, amused. "You do recall he signed our petition. Shall I introduce you?"

"Not now," Henrietta said. "I might have the vapors. Introduce me after, when I have my wits about me. Where did all these people come from?"

Lady Bess's eyes lit with the joy of battle. "The Corresponding Society sent a phalanx after they saw our advert in the paper. I suspect many other debate clubs came as well. They've been lying low, with Prime Minister Pitt so nervous after the burning breeches, but I shouldn't wonder if they're rousing for a fight. It's going to be quite an event, my dear, and you stirred the pot!"

"I don't wish to provoke a fight," Henrietta said. "I intend for us to have a polite, civil discussion about Miss Wollstonecraft's ideas."

"Well, you didn't mention Miss Wollstonecraft in the advert, which would have scared away a good number of those present," Bess said. "You said we would debate the responsibilities that men in power have toward their dependents, and that, my dear, smacks of French revolutionary sentiment."

Bess beamed as she surveyed their table of supporters. "You recognize who is seated next to Mr. Equiano, I hope? That's Charles James Fox, the firebrand, and next to him is Thomas Hardy, the shoemaker, the one who started the Corresponding Society. If we let either of them speak, there's bound to be a riot."

Her expression said she relished the prospect. "And just think what the papers will have to say about it tomorrow! We will have exposure for the Society and our aims, that much is for certain, and with all the attention, I can't but think you will be made a votary. Now go, dear, prepare yourself. Our fate is in your hands!"

Dragging her silk slippers, Henrietta approached the lectern and spread out her notes. Mr. Equiano winked as she glanced at his table, and she bit her lip in a smile. He was recently married, and she wondered about the type of woman who had the confidence to win and keep a man so known and much discussed, a man who could never go unnoticed, a man whom so many adored.

That brought her thoughts to Darien, and she would not think of Darien tonight. She would think of something calming —the garden at Hines House, the neat walk boxed with flowering herbs and colorful borders, the vegetables tangling around their stakes. Darien had kissed her in that garden, his mouth firm and masterful, cool and deliberate.

The kiss in his study had not been quite so calculated; she had felt something warm and urgent in him, something confusing and yet rousing as well. Oh, why was she thinking of Darien Bales when she must compose her thoughts and her speech?

She put herself back at Miss Gregoire's, in the small gazebo near a landscaped stream where she had spent hours curled up with her friends and a favorite book, dangling her feet in the water from the small ornamental bridge and feeding last week's bread to the swans. The patter of her heart slowed and eased. That gazebo at Miss Gregoire's was the one place on Earth where nothing was expected of her, nothing held in judgment, and nothing denied.

Though it was also the place where, as the end of every term drew near, she waited for a letter from her father admitting the house was bare and empty, that he needed her to come home and set all in order. That summons never came.

When Henrietta had at last been brought home, it was to be aid and support to Lady Mama. She'd been useful, finally; Lady Mama was ridiculously easy to please, everything Henrietta did charmed and delighted her. But she wasn't really needed. When she left to set up a household of her own, Lady Mama would express dismay at her loss but would not keep her from going.

She watched the crowd assemble with a growing sense of apprehension. Surely they could see through the fashionable gown to that lonely, grieving girl still inside her somewhere, the girl who had arrived at Miss Gregoire's orphaned, timid, and anxious to please. The men arraying themselves on the anti side, plump and self-important, with their equally plump and self-important daughters and wives behind them, had at the ready their biblical bromides and centuries-old convention to brandish as a club, beating her back into her place.

But she was not that hurt, unwanted girl any longer. She owned an estate and would soon own a mill of her own, where she would be needed, where she could set about proving that profits and industry did not have to cost human lives. She was a benefactor for five different institutions in Lancashire, Derbyshire, and London. She was not her mother, scorned for giving herself to a self-made man. She was not her stepmother, bargained away to repair the Warrefield fortunes.

She could be useful as part of the Minerva Society, upholding the truths that women like Miss Wollstonecraft were brave enough to make known. She could speak for every girl at Miss Gregoire's who had a keen mind and a sense of purpose, who knew she would have to fight to use her talents in this man-made world.

She drew a deep breath and glanced at Mr. Equiano. He had suffered far worse—physical affliction, hardship, and ill treatment from people who believed his race was not fully human. The same people who believed women could not be as strong or as intelligent or worth as much as men. It would always be a struggle to wring justice from the hands of those who had bent the world to suit themselves. But that did not mean they must not try.

"The ladies of the Minerva Society would like to thank you all for your presence this evening." Lady Bessington called the meeting to order with her clear, carrying voice. She stood like the figurehead of a ship on the dais, every line of her larger than life. "We are honored to have with us tonight so many distinguished guests." She gestured to the table of men on Henrietta's left, drawing all eyes. There were murmurs and some hisses. The fourth man was William Wilberforce, the MP from Hull who had put forward the bill in the House of Commons calling for abolition, and the fifth was William Godwin, a radical philosopher and ardent admirer of Miss Wollstonecraft.

Henrietta felt dizzy. The debates of the women's societies rarely drew attention. She had expected a sparse group of subscribers, their husbands and sons, and a few interested parties drawn by the advert she had dared to place despite the King's current feeling about debate societies. This burly, boisterous crowd from all walks of life was so far beyond her expectation that it almost seemed a dream.

Lady Bessington went on to briefly describe the Minerva Society, its history, its goals and aims, outlining some of its causes. Then she turned to Henrietta.

"Miss Henrietta Wardley-Hines," she said, and Henrietta stepped forward, feeling her delicate skirt swirl about her legs and her single, nearly sheer petticoat. She felt the penetrating stares of the crowd taking in her ruffled neckline, the loosely gathered sleeves, the pearl pins gleaming in her cinnamon hair.

"Miss Wardley-Hines is the daughter of Sir Jasper Wardley-Hines and sister to the 8th Baronet Wardley, Sir Charleton

Wardley-Hines, and owner of the estate of Birch Vale in Derbyshire. Tonight's topic of debate is as follows: What is the appropriate response of dependents when those charged to protect them fail in their duty? Miss Wardley-Hines," Bess said grandly, "the stage is yours."

Lady Bess fell away, but the gleeful, exultant look in her eye gave Henrietta heart. She might look like a rumpled kitten in this gown, come to put her milk teeth in the old argument that Mary Wollstonecraft had tried to reanimate. But she was a tiger, with fangs and claws, and she meant to leave a mark, if she could. She cleared her throat and began.

CHAPTER EIGHTEEN

"Most esteemed ladies, gentlemen, visitors, and friends." Henrietta's voice felt soft and cautious in her throat, not entirely hers. "Six thousand years ago, when the world was framed new, almighty God made a garden, and within it, as the crown of his creation, he made man. And beside him, from the same material and just as innocent, God made woman to be man's helpmeet, his companion, his wife. Milton, in his grand poem, describes paradise as a scene of perfect amity, of devotion and unity, of the most serene, wedded bliss."

Her ears pinkened as a couple of men shifted and cleared their throats. She was very conscious of the thin cotton fabric of her gown. It might have been wiser to wear one of Aunt Davinia's monstrosities with its layers of stays and petticoats and flounces as a shield from the probing eyes of her audience.

"But we fell," she went on, her voice gaining strength. "We fell from this original state, and the relations between men and women now are the result of sin and trespass." Except she had felt nothing sinful in her conversation with Darien over Etruscan artifacts, nothing of trespass in his solid strength beside her as they rode on their errands around town. And the heat that rose in her when he touched her, when he pulled her into his arms at the Bicclesfield ball—that was the problem with temptation, wasn't it? It felt delicious and thrilling and right.

She cleared her throat and continued. "It is therefore the result of grievous error that we have this system that has prevailed for thousands of years." She straightened her back and felt her lungs grow fuller, her voice larger. "It was the result of a curse that a woman should submit to a man, and he should rule over her, that she should have travail in childbirth. It was the serpent's doing that woman was made subservient, less than, dependent on man. Women's second-class, inferior status was not at all as God designed us to be."

She heard the rustles and murmurs, the encouraging sound of knuckles rapping on wood, saw the silent nods of feminine heads. She also heard grumbles of disapproval. This was not the quiet attention granted to the disciples of Minerva. One man shouted, in an irritated voice, "Adam's rib!"

Henrietta flinched and looked down at her notes. If she let the distractions rattle her, she would forget all her laboriously outlined points. But this debate she had argued many times, in Miss Gregoire's parlor and Lady Bess's salons, against everyone from her brother to the solicitor who insisted she could neither use her inheritance to buy a mill nor own it in her name.

"Our own King James Bible tells us, in its first account of creation," she said, "that man and woman were equivalent: 'man and woman he created them.' Chapter the second, verse seven-and-twenty," she added for the benefit of those whom she knew intended to quote the Bible back at her. "This is our proof that God intended, from the very beginning, for women to be fully human, equals and co-heirs to the perfection of His creation.

"We have seen well enough in our own time, without consulting the long scroll of history, to know what pain and sorrow this consequence of Eve's trespass has caused," she said.

"We see men made too weary by the world to show kindness and basic decency to their families. We see women cast out of their homes because the men upon whom they depend have failed them. Children starve in the streets without care or guidance, their innocence taken too soon. Men abandon their families for women not their wives, and women abandon their children. This is not at all what God intended."

There were more rustles and murmurs now, in higher registers as well as lower. She was attacking the one male prerogative that crossed class: his superiority to women. Henrietta raised her voice. "And in our very government, among the leaders who are appointed to guide and protect us, we see a shocking lack of attention to the plight of the many unfortunates who have been brought to their troubles by lack of male protection.

"This is the result of a belief that conceives of woman not as a person in her own right but as an appendage, a piece of movable goods to be sold or exchanged or thoughtlessly used. And it is wrong. This belief, that woman is inferior, worth less than a man," she said loudly, clearly, "is wrong. It is a curse. It is not as we were made to be.

"In this enlightened year of 1792, so close to the turn of a new century, when we see the light of liberty and equality flaming up around us"—there were many shocked gasps in response to this—"is it not time that we of England took our rightful place as the leaders of the world and the bearers of the light? Is it not time that we remake our society in the pattern in which God intended?

"Ladies and gentlemen, we have upheld for too long a law that does not benefit us. We have carried forth a belief that has done irreparable harm. It is time for a change. We need new beliefs and a new law that gives women the right to govern themselves with the same freedom and authority as men. And we need a system of education that gives women a grasp of knowledge and reason, for these are the foundations of virtue.

"I submit," she said, raising her voice to be heard over the rising din, "that all our injustices, and our fall from grace, can be remedied when we undo the curse that makes women weak and dependent, for true dignity and human happiness rest on strength of mind and body. Only when women are treated as equal heirs to reason can we have the world our Creator designed for us."

Her listeners could no longer remain silent. Among cries of "Justice!" and "Liberty!" and "England!" she heard "Abomination!" "Outrage!" "Heresy!" A few men spat on the floor.

"We shall now entertain counter remarks," Lady Bessington shouted, that battle gleam in her eye. She was enjoying the upheaval. The men in the front row of the spectator's gallery had notepads out, pencils furiously at work, and among them sat one lady journalist in a prim navy skirt and smart fitted jacket, the feather in her hat bobbing as she scribbled on her pad.

"Mr. Spickey," Bess said, acknowledging the portly gentleman who rose to his feet. "You have one minute, sir."

Henrietta quailed as she recognized the deacon of St. Marylebone Church. Mrs. Spickey sat behind him, red and rigid with outrage, and beside her sat Lord Pinochle, his eyes glittering with glee. Behind them, a wilting Constance avoided Henrietta's gaze.

Mr. Spickey pulled the lapels of his double-breasted coat over his large, corseted stomach. His periwig sat atop a broad, bulbous forehead shiny with perspiration. His breeches showed every bulge and bunch of the flesh beneath them, and the heels of his buckled shoes were dangerously high. His fashion was à la mode, but his ire was ancient.

"May I remind you," Mr. Spickey boomed, "that woman proved herself inferior when she defied the commandment of her Creator. God saw fit to give her a guide and governor to keep her from her erring ways. Eve cost us paradise!"

He had to shout over the roars of approval and endorsement, as well as the boos and hisses from the other side of the room. "Not a day goes by but that every man here, I don't doubt, has suffered female disobedience. Woman requires a ruler because she would create utter chaos—nay, she would bring on the end of the world if left to her own willful ways!"

He sat down to resounding applause and mopped his brow with a silk handkerchief. Pinochle handed him a silver box, and he promptly took snuff. Constance's eyes were as round as saucers.

"Rebuttal," said Lady Bessington, turning to Henrietta.

The crowd seemed larger, people still coming in the doors, yet a breathless silence fell. This was so much different, so much worse, than debating a point at the Minerva Society or over a beautifully laid dinner table at her uncle's house. How had she ever thought she could do this? She must look so foolish.

"If women must rely upon men," Henrietta said, "then their errors and foolishness must be attributed to a lack of proper guidance. Given that so many women do fall into error, shall we presume that the men in their lives have failed to properly protect, or instruct, or control them?

"And what is their recourse when they find themselves cast into the street, unprotected, left to make their own way, and reviled for it? Would it not be wiser to educate women, to cultivate reason and morality and a sound character? The honeysuckle twining about the oak may adorn it with beauty but may choke and kill its host. A woman taught the necessary skills of self-governance can survive when her support is taken from her, rather than be a burden on others."

Her own Reverend Dingley stood. She felt the scorn on his face like a slap.

"Woman," he thundered in a voice trained for the pulpit, "was not made the co-equal to man. Woman is made of softer matter for the purpose of providing companionship and a comfortable home, bearing children. Remember Milton's lines! 'For contemplation he and valour form'd, For softness she and sweet attractive grace.' Even Eve acknowledges this! 'God is thy law, thou mine,' she says to Adam. Woman was created to submit. It is her design."

"But Adam asks his Maker for an equal," Henrietta said. "'Among unequals what society can sort, what harmony or true delight?' It is fellowship he seeks, 'all rational delight.' An educated woman would make a better companion to a man, and a better guide for her children as well."

"Miss Wardley-Hines." Lord Pinochle stood, puffing out his chest. "Is this some personal grievance you bear? Are you attempting to bring your father, or someone else in your life, to a sense of the duty he has failed to execute?"

His malicious smile taunted her. He wanted everyone in the room to think she was accusing Darien, when Pinochle was responsible for worse.

"In no way does my point come from personal example," Henrietta replied with an angry flush. "I have benefitted from the protection and guidance of a most wonderful father. I hope every woman in this room has been equally fortunate in her protectors.

"But I am not speaking in the abstract, as you have guessed," she went on, projecting her voice above the titters and the whispers of "Daring!" "In the institutions that we of the Minerva Society support, I daily see women and children who are left destitute or worse by fathers, or brothers, or husbands who have failed to adhere to the responsibility that Mr. Spickey so clearly outlined for us. What choice do they have but to throw themselves upon the charity of others?

"If women are to be held responsible for the failures that leave them without protection, then the solution is to provide options for self-sufficiency. Education will teach them to choose well and to govern themselves. Any sensible woman would rather hold property than be property."

"Your attitudes will change, Miss Wardley-Hines, when you have children," Mrs. Spickey exclaimed, pressed beyond endurance. "Then you will know the real joys for which women have been created."

Henrietta thought of the small, dark-haired infant in her nursery, marked with the stain of illegitimacy from birth, being rocked to sleep in the arms of a girl whose own infant had been taken from her. Not even Mrs. Spickey could argue it was a woman's true purpose to be auctioned to her father's friend and thrown destitute in the street, then forced to bear a child from the injustice.

"If woman's sole purpose is to marry and mother, then why does God deny so many women this destiny?" Henrietta retorted. "And if marriage is sacred, then why do men abandon or ignore their vows? Or why, for that matter, are so many young women forced into unions they do not desire?"

She glared at Pinochle. Darien's carelessness with women was, partly, a ruse designed to stir conclusions from a few kisses. Pinochle had forced himself on his maid and planted her with a child he then instructed her to get rid of. She longed to denounce him before the crowd. His eyes dared her to make that mistake.

Henrietta took refuge in her argument, keeping her voice strong and clear. "We should require, first, that women be educated in virtue and reason, and then we must demand that men exercise virtue and reason as well."

"Woman is not made for self-sufficiency. Her frame is too weak and her faculties lacking. She is best suited to the keeping of home and rearing of children. She has not the strength of mind to participate in the public realm," someone shouted.

"The physical stature I will grant you, but what if her mind could be strengthened?" Henrietta countered.

"Woman is disobedient and immoral, ruled by her emotions, given to self-indulgence and lust!" Mr. Spickey roared. Mrs. Spickey's eyes bulged at this assertion, but she kept her mouth screwed shut.

"The same might be said of man," Henrietta retorted, glaring at Pinochle, who flushed.

"Woman is too pure to be sullied by public commerce and the base business of the world. She belongs in the home, where she may be protected and kept in comfort, tending to her children. Woman's more spiritual nature is meant to be a balm to the man who spends his days in labor. She would not be able to provide this solace, this inspiration, were she sullied with labor herself." This was delivered by a woman in sober black who was shaking her head.

"I am afraid I do not know how to reconcile these two," Henrietta said. "Is woman innately immoral and base, or is she innately noble and pure? In either case, what are the responsibilities of the men who are supposed to guide and protect her? And what is to be done with the women who lose their homes due to death or misfortune or, through the poor behavior of their menfolk, are deprived of the homes they had?"

"A woman who is wronged by her man ought to have some means of satisfaction," shouted a man clad in fustian, leaping to his feet. He had the darkened nails of a laborer, perhaps a blacksmith. "The law needs to be fair. And a government that gives more rights to some men while denying those of others ain't fair! The miss on the platform is right— the law needs to look the same on *all* God's creatures, even its women, even its other races, like that African there. King

George ain't being fair to us! We working men ought to have a voice!"

And that was the cue for any number of men, all throughout the room, to take to their feet and begin shouting in earnest. The noise echoed in the cavernous hall. Henrietta's debate about women's rights was over, and something else entirely was at play.

"Rabble!" Mr. Spickey shrieked, pointing at Thomas Hardy. "There's a reason you and your type oughtn't have a voice in government. Little better than animals, you are—no respect for decency!"

"We've plenty of respect for them as shows it to us!" Hardy roared back. "Who's made you so fat but the working man, I axe you? Who breaks his back so you can be so plump?"

"*Liberté!*" came the cry, along with a raised fist. "*Équalité! Fraternitié!*"

"Are women allowed to be part of the fraternity?" Henrietta shouted into the clamor. "Or is it only men who may be accorded the honor of equality?"

James appeared next to her, eyes bright, whip in hand. "Ey now, here's a hubble-bubble!" he crowed. "Best you make leg bail and clear the stage if these riffraff take over! There's a mobility at brew, and that Hardy's the bellwether."

"This is *my* debate, and I mean to restore order to it." Henrietta appealed to Lady Bessington, who adjusted her headdress as she waited out the melee, as serene as a ship in full sail. "Order!" Henrietta shouted. "I demand order."

James laughed at her. "As if they'll listen to a gentry mort! These'll listen to Queen Dick, an' that's all."

"It's time the King listened!" Hardy shouted, pounding his fist on the table. Fox and Wilberforce stepped away from him, taking refuge behind the spectator's gallery. Mr. Godwin gazed around in amazement, looking as if he wanted to throw himself into the fight but was uncertain where his opening lay. Mr. Equiano leaned on the table, smiling, watching the anger escalate. Passionate pleas for freedom were his métier.

"Our demands will be heard!" Hardy shouted. "We will not be denied!"

"Down with King George!" the call began, and at that, a crowd of blue-uniformed officers burst into the room.

Chaos erupted. Those who recognized the City Patrol bolted for the doors, creating a press of people who carried all before them. The volume in the room grew from a buzz to a roar, with shrieks punctuating the din as the officers laid about them with staves and cutlasses.

"Time to take French leave and disappear, Miss Hetty!" James raised his arm with the whip.

"James," Henrietta cried, "put that away. You'll hurt someone!"

And he did, several times, but he also kept the crowd off the dais as the government men surged into the room shouting, "In the King's name! Order in the name of King George!"

"Who's responsible fer this?" one of the officers bawled, glaring about him with a gimlet eye.

"I am!" bellowed Thomas Hardy, launching himself into the wall of men.

"Her! The one dressed like a French whore." Pinochle's cry rose above the din, his finger pointed at Henrietta. "She incited this mob."

"Touch 'er and I'll plump ye in the breadbasket, ye Moabites!" James roared, raising his whip as the officers advanced.

He delivered a few slashes before his height defeated him; a man behind him raised his staff and, with a cuff to the head, downed Henrietta's valiant protector. She screamed, her heart vaulting into her throat as rough hands caught her up.

"Don't leave him here!" She writhed in the hard grip of the man herding her toward the doorway, trying to tug her wrists free. All around her, men dressed like him, in the same blue uniform and hat, were pulling other protesters toward the exit. Many of them put up a worthy fight. "He's hurt."

"Leave the runt," the man holding her ordered, "an' lace 'im again if he gets cocky."

"He must come with me," Henrietta shouted, her voice hoarse with panic. "I am responsible for—"

Rough hands pushed her onto the sidewalk outside the Tavern, where a crowd thronged the street, held back by a string of men in uniform, cutlasses at the ready. From the blur of color rose the shocked, pale face of the second footman, Peter.

"Fetch Sir Jasper!" Henrietta cried. "He'll know what to do. John and James are still in there!"

While other men were hauled away by the watch, frog-marched down the street, the officer shoved Henrietta into a rickety coach pulled by a sway-backed nag with the emblem of the City Patrol on its harness. Her stomach twisted at the scent of several sweaty bodies, and her gown felt damp against her clammy skin.

Jasper wasn't here. Her father was on his way north with her man of business to see that Henrietta got her burnt-out mill. He had kissed her on the cheek and told her he was sorry he would miss her debate but that she was sure to be a sensation.

"I've no doubt I'll return to find the House passing a bill to do exactly what you propose," he'd said, his eyes bright with affection. "Now, no picking quarrels, minx."

Oh, she had started a quarrel all right. Her heart began a clawing descent down her windpipe, blocking her air.

"Where are they taking us?" she asked Thomas Hardy, who sat across from her, whistling despite one eye swelling shut.

"Watch house," he said cheerfully. "We'll make our bed in

the hole tonight an' be hauled afore the justice o' the peace in the mornin'. You'll be turned loose, miss, but it's the Old Bailey for me, I don't doubt. Hanged or transported, if Pitt has his way. He's been out for my hide for months."

Henrietta put a hand on her neck. "I am very sorry," she choked. Her stomach clenched at the thought of being brought up on charges. What would her father say? Or Charley? Aunt Althea would never allow a criminal in Marsibel's company. And she would certainly never be made a votary of the Minerva Society if she were sent to prison.

She felt cold all the way to her fingertips. Oh, what had she done?

At the end of a painful, bouncing journey, she and her fellow passengers stumbled out of the coach in front of the Bishopsgate watch house, a shabby building set amid a reeking fen. She smelled unwashed bodies and bad food, the lime thrown down to cover the rotting stench, the sooty smell of burning coal, and beyond that, the fetid reek of the river. A watchman herded her down a dark, damp hallway into a room equally close and rank-smelling.

"You'll get yer answers in the morn, when 'is worship speaks to ye," he snarled as he shoved her roughly through a wooden door. "Me, I'd leave ye 'ere to rot with the rest of the blowsabellas." And the door slammed shut in her face.

"Oi, brush off, ye clod'opper," a female voice screeched.

Henrietta turned and sneezed as the smoke from a rush light insulted her nose. An urge to cry tightened her throat, and she swallowed it. She'd argued that women needed to cultivate strength of mind and character. Well, here was her chance to prove her case.

Blinking her eyes to clear them of tears, she looked around the room and made out dim shapes. She stood in a long, narrow cell with a stone bench running along one side and a dark window letting in dim lamplight at one end. Several women looked her over from head to toe.

"This'un wears 'er bedgown to work," one snickered, fingering a ruffle on Henrietta's sleeve. "Rolled ye right out o' the sack, did 'e? What's a matter—didn't like the taste of 'is sugar stick?"

The lump in her throat turned to panic.

"'Igh-end wares," observed another, tugging at Henrietta's skirts. "Not Covent Garden, then, or I'd a seen ye! Where ye from, spooney? Cheapside? Drury Lane? Seven Dials?"

"Not the Dials," snorted a third. "Not a pox scar on 'er. That's a fine and fancy gown the Bartholomew doll 'as. I think me wants it." In the dim light, Henrietta saw the wicked gleam of the other woman's eyes through layers of heavy makeup. She took a step backward. In a moment, she saw, she was about to be swarmed by a horde of women, and if she didn't think quickly, she was going to end up naked and bleeding, with her eyes clawed out.

"I was...at the London Tavern," Henrietta said, trying to sound authoritative. As she edged backward, the stone seat hit the back of her knees, and she fell onto it. "I *thought* I was leading a debate on the rights of women. The recourse of dependents and why women should be educated." She surveyed the faces of the women around her, which ranged from scornful to disbelieving, and covered her mouth with her hand. "I had a very fine argument prepared as to why women should be allowed to govern themselves so they don't end up—"

"'Ere," said an older woman, the most well-dressed of the bunch. "'At's wot happens to those as shift for themselves." She kicked at the thin straw pallet lying on the floor, one bed to serve the entire group. "We end up 'ere, we do."

"Evidently," Henrietta said in a tiny voice.

These were the women she was arguing for. She oughtn't be

terrified of them. They were merely women bereft of protectors, left to live by their own wits and skills. Women who didn't give a fig for the Society she had tried so hard to enter because they had seen that society level its punishing hand against them, as it did to all women who would not keep to their place.

She had never felt so small or quite so helpless, not even when she was at Miss Gregoire's, waiting for her father to recall her. Who was going to help her now? Jasper was away, her uncle might not know for hours or days what had happened, and Charley—Charley might very well wash his hands of her. This debacle could sink her with her family for once and all.

She would have to get herself out. She rubbed her eyes, straightened her shoulders, and set aside the hand that was fingering the lace at her sleeve. Henrietta Wardley-Hines, bluestocking, reformer, and advocate of rights for women, did not slump in a filthy cell in the watchhouse and cry about her woes.

"Very well, then. Here we are, and here we cannot stay. What gets us out of here?"

"You do." The older woman bent at the waist and looked Henrietta in the eye. "You get us out of here, spooney, an' you'll get to keep your fancy frock, and your pretty little neck along with it."

CHAPTER NINETEEN

Henrietta was tired, she was hungry, and she had to relieve herself, but she was not yet in the extremes of agony that could compel her to use the chamber pot in the corner. A crowd of six women sat around her, suspicious, interested, or watching her with a veiled, quiet hope. The seventh, the older woman, lay on the pallet of dirty straw, snoring as ashen light poked its way through the window.

Shortly after Henrietta introduced herself, told in detail the enthralling story of how she landed in the watch house, and from there went on to answer their several questions about the life of a nob's daughter, Mame gave a snort, scratched beneath her stays, and lay down with a grumbling comment that Henrietta was no better than the rest of them, mark her words.

"And they let you learn anything ye want," one of the girls said. "At this Magdalen 'ouse o' yours. It ain't a pushin' school?"

"No, we set our girls to study proper subjects, if a tutor can be found," Henrietta said. "Miss Gregoire believes a young woman's interests ought to be cultivated, and her model is followed by the Sisters of Benevolence."

"School o' Venus," another snorted. "Alls we need is short

heels and great diddeys." She jiggled her bosoms as a third girl giggled.

"Don't you have a skill you would like to develop?" Henrietta asked. Despite the pressure on her bladder, her fear of these women had eased some hours ago, and she instead found herself interested in their stories. "Isn't there something you are quite good at?"

The woman laughed, but the sound was not one of mirth. "Aye, there's a thing or two I'm far good at, an' it's why the scouts snapped me, ain't it? While me randy swell bolts in t' other direction, cod piece aflap."

Henrietta refused to blush. Her companions had been making sport of her all night for her ignorance of their work. They were town women, to use the polite term, taken up by the watch for being loose and idle, or in Mame's case, disorderly, as she'd been hauled in for drunkenness and attacking her husband with a broom.

Later this morning, the justice of the peace would levy a fine, read them a sermon, and turn them back into the street. They were, to a girl, suspicious of Henrietta's claims. They considered London's Magdalen House the recourse for prostitutes who had grown too old or ill to work. The Sisters of Benevolence must be a trap, if not a brothel then the sort of establishment that catered to women who served the streets. They could not conceive of an institution interested in improving the health of their bodies and minds.

"I'm 'andy with a needle," said Alice, quiet and thin, who had watched Henrietta all evening without comment. She was new to street life and its punishments. She looked about the same age as Mary Ann.

If she were an aristocrat's sheltered daughter, with every comfort of life available to her, she would be dreaming of her debut and kisses on the hand from suitors eager to claim her dowry. Instead, she wore lines on her face from poverty, hard weather, and harder use. She could charge a higher price because she was young and comely and did not have the pox, though in her line of work, disease was a certainty.

"We have heaps of girls we've trained in stitchery," Henrietta said. "And we help them find employment. Many hire out as maids."

"Not in the gentry kens," scoffed the girl at her side. "No one as is decent wants a girl like us. Or if they gets us," she added with a curl of her lip, "you can bet there's a cove about thinks our past ain't all be'ind us, eh?"

Henrietta frowned. "We make every effort to ensure that our young women from the Benevolence Hospital go to respectable employers. Roslyn became a dresser to a countess, and Aylwen set up a shop of her own, taking many of the girls with her."

"I want to dance," said Belinda. "And no' in the chorus. I want to be a prima ballerina."

"Then I see no reason, with determination and good fortune, you should not be so." Henrietta gave her a warm smile.

"I want to sing," Lena announced.

Raucous laughter attended this remark, but when it quieted, Henrietta looked closely at the speaker. She had tight, frizzy curls, sloe-dark eyes, and warm brown skin unmarked yet by age or the scars of hardship. "Sing for us," Henrietta urged the girl.

Lena stood, folded her hands, put back her shoulders, and drew in a deep breath. She launched into "The Sweet Lass of Richmond Hill," and the room fell silent save for Mame's resonant snores. The girl's voice, though untrained, was piercingly beautiful.

"Lena," Henrietta said with tears in her eyes, "if you come to the Sisters of Benevolence, I will make sure there is money to pay for voice lessons."

The girl sat down, her face transfigured by wonder. An explosion of voices followed as every woman competed to name her talent and secure Henrietta's vow of support. Henrietta shamelessly promised everything she could, buoyed by the hope that each of these girls could earn her way into the life she should have had before misfortune and destitution or, in some cases, blatant trickery had brought her to where she was now.

If she meant to claim that education and opportunity could make women virtuous, contributing members of their society, then Henrietta would demonstrate with these candidates who had fallen into her lap, courtesy of the King's officers.

And if she were wrong—well, she was the daughter of Jasper Wardley-Hines and the late Apollonia Wardley-Hines. She would go down fighting.

Booted feet approached the door, and a key scratched the lock. Her companions scrambled to their feet, huddling around Mame's pallet like a flock of bedraggled birds. Henrietta stood, fatigue rattling her bones. She had been here for hours. Had someone come for her? Anyone?

The door opened, and she nearly fainted. Lord Darien Bales stood in the doorway, his eyes burning coals in his marble face.

She had feared she might never see him again. Never see his tall frame filling a doorway, his smile of amusement at her expense, those blue eyes alight with speculation or wariness or interest.

It took only the sight of him to know, with utter certainty, that she could not do without him in her life. She had been marked by their association, and she would never be able to let go of that.

The single rush light had burned to a stub, smarting her eyes through the darkened gloom. It must be the tail end of the evening. But Darien was the image of perfection with his hair neatly queued, his coat gleaming, his well-fitting breeches uncreased. His neckcloth lay in perfect folds, his shirt was the white of summer clouds, and his eyes were as dark as a storm over the sea.

"Ey now," one of the girls squealed. "This gorger's for me. 'Ere I am, chuck!"

Darien's eyes locked on Henrietta's, and she stood unmoving as his hostile gaze raked her to her feet, then back up. She must look like she'd been dragged through a hedge backward. Her lovely new gown was torn and soiled, the hem in tatters from having been stepped on by many feet besides hers, and she smelled of the several unwashed bodies in the room.

Her hair had come down during her arrest and hung in a long rope along her back. She looked like a wraith that might walk the moors, a specter conjured to haunt naughty children. Darien's lips tightened as he examined her face.

"This one," he said without emotion, with only a small, tight nod in her direction. "This is Miss Wardley-Hines. Sir Jasper's daughter," he stressed.

"Ooh, sir!" said a blend of female voices. "I'm with 'er, then."

"Take me too, 'andsome!"

"*I'm* the one as is Sir Jasper's daughter," Belinda lied outrageously. The girls vied to get closer, jostling Henrietta. Darien stepped into the room.

"Why, Lord Daring, as I live and breathe." Mame sat up, blinking in surprise. "And better-looking himself than those sketches in the papers have it. Scrapin' the bottom o' the barrel, ain't cher, a bang-up swell like yerself? Time was you could've 'ad any high-flyer, an' pay not a hap'ny for her neither!"

"I am retrieving a friend who seems to be here due to some egregious misunderstanding," Darien said tersely. "Tell him who you are, Henry."

"I am Henrietta Wardley-Hines," Henrietta squeaked. "And what are the charges against me, pray?"

"Rabble-rouser!" the warden exclaimed. "She was neck-deep with them good-for-nothing Corresponders, milord, for all that she's a woman and the Tavern ain't no place for 'er. Pitt meant to nab the lot of 'em, and that 'e did."

"Prime Minister Pitt will find, when he looks into the matter, that Miss Wardley-Hines had no part in instigating the riot you witnessed. Now let her go at once, or the Marquess of Langford will have a word or two for the King about how the City treats those it has detained."

Henrietta stared, goggle-eyed. *Darien* had come to her assistance, to deliver her from imprisonment. Darien!

"Aye, you, yer swell's 'ere to spring ye," the warden sneered, reaching for Henrietta. "Tried to tell 'im you belong 'ere, but wants you 'imself, he does. See that 'e delivers ye to yer father after, aye? For I've 'eard a word or two about this one, don't think I 'aven't!"

He froze at Darien's quiet voice. "Touch her and I'll lace your jacket, watchman."

"Insultin' a King's man!" the guard exclaimed. "Interferin' w' the King's peace!" But the arm fell away.

Henrietta stepped forward on legs that wobbled from a combination of nerves, thirst, and an oppressively full bladder. He had come for her.

"Have you found James? Is he here too?"

The women surged in one body behind her. "Take us! Take us all. Don't leave us 'ere, miss. You *promised*!"

Henrietta turned to face them, putting a hand over her heart. "Yes, I promised all of you aid. I must stop home to collect the coin to pay your fines, and then I will take each of you to the Sisters of Benevolence Hospital, or wherever you wish."

The warden snorted. "Ye cain't take 'em out. Ain't the rules."

"Oi, ye can spring us now, mum," several voices begged. A hand or two clutched a ruffle on her gown.

"Back, ye draggle-tails!" the warden shouted, fingering the club at his belt.

"Keep my card," Henrietta said, knowing most of them couldn't read the direction she had printed on the back. "If you are not here when I return, come to the Sisters as soon as you can. I promise—*oof*!"

A hard arm snaked around her waist and lifted her from the floor, pressing the air out of her lungs. "You are leaving *now*, Henry," Darien said, his voice full of wrath.

His body felt hard and at the same time supple, as if he were dangerous steel swathed in a few layers of protective fabric. A curl of pleasure curled through Henrietta's midsection at the contact of her body with his. She had the insane urge to curl into his arms in surrender, lay her head on his shoulder, and let him take her where he willed. Obstinately, she held stiff as the warden swung the barred door shut, shouting at the women still inside.

"I have to— You must put me down, Darien," Henrietta said, squirming.

"Not until you are delivered to the coach, baggage."

The scowl made him more handsome, not less. Henrietta felt a great wash of tenderness roll through her stomach, pressing on her bladder. He was still angry with her, but he was here.

She blinked, the grit of sleeplessness in her eyes. "Why did my uncle not come for me?"

"Pelton is in the carriage. He thought it best that he not be seen personally exonerating a person the Prime Minister ordered arrested."

Henrietta shrank against his shoulder. He was solid and unyielding. "If only you had seen it, Darien—they completely commandeered my debate! I doubt a single person will remember any of my points, and they were rather excellent. I would like a word with those Corresponders myself!"

Darien paused in the low, dark hall and stared at her. The rush light afforded ill light to see by, but she could read his disbelief.

"You spent the night in the watch house," he said deliberately, "and you are concerned that no one took your point in your debate."

"All night, was it? No wonder, then. Darien, I need to visit the necessary," she blurted, cheeks scorching.

"*Here?*"

"I'm afraid so." She nodded, squeezing her legs together.

The appalled look on his face as he regarded the enclosed yard behind the building would have made her giggle in other circumstances. It was clear he feared permanent damage to his gleaming top boots.

Setting his jaw, Lord Darien Bales carried Miss Henrietta Wardley-Hines to the clumsy wooden privy and then waited, knee-deep in muck and a combination of fog and morning dew, while she relieved herself. Oh, what the penny papers would have to say about *this* escapade did they learn of it, Henrietta thought as he scooped her up again and transported her to the hack waiting by the curb.

The hired coachman sat atop, his neck hunched, his collar turned up against the morning chill. "Uncle Pell." Henrietta sighed in relief as she climbed into the vehicle and discerned her uncle's anxious face in the gloom.

The sky held the yellow-gray tint of a smog-choked London morning, while the fetid odor of the river stung her eyes and nose. "Am I to go before the justice of the peace?"

"I took care of it," Pelton said. "Know the man well." With dismay, he took in her disheveled gown. "No harm befell you, puss?"

Darien slid his large frame onto the seat next to her, then reached to pull the shade over the window. He left his arm along the top of the seat as the coach jogged forward. She tried not to lean back into his solid heat. She was so tired, and he was angry over the inconvenience of having to spring her from the watch house. He had every right to be.

"I am unharmed," she assured her uncle. "I was put in the room with the...unfortunate women. Uncle, if you could have heard their stories—they exactly prove the points I was making at my debate, about what happens to women who are prepared for nothing but the keep of a man, then cast out when that man fails them." She lifted her head. "How did you find me?"

"Lord Darien," her uncle said. "I heard at the club that someone tipped Pitt off that the Corresponders meant to gather at your debate after being forbidden to meet on their own. Pitt called up the Bishopsgate watch, the City Patrol, the Marshals, and the new Middlesex Justices, too. He's been looking for a reason to come down on Hardy's group ever since that damnable closet fire. Confound it, Hetty, he wants Hardy charged for treason, and there you were, in the midst of it. A witness said he heard you claiming you were responsible for it all."

Henrietta laid her head on the cushioned back of the seat. "Lord Pinochle said that," she said with bitterness. "Lady Bess and I took away a maid he'd gotten with child, and he's searching for a way to punish me."

The cushion flexed, and Henrietta realized she had laid her head on Darien's arm. She straightened. "Am I to be charged with treason too?"

"I won't allow it," her uncle said swiftly.

"You can keep me from hanging, perhaps." Tears burned her gritty eyes. "But I could be transported, and the gossip—" She sagged on the rough, cracked seat of the hack, some nobleman's discarded vehicle. "Papa will bear it, and Lady Mama, but what will this do to Marsi's prospects?" A sob climbed her throat. "I shall never be made a votary of Minerva now. They are women of the highest character and ideals, unsullied in virtue."

"Lightskirts, was it?" The lump of cloth on the seat beside her uncle moved, and a familiar shock of pepper-brown hair emerged.

"James!" Henrietta cried in relief. "Were you hurt?"

"Only a dick to the knob, miss, and a few lumps to go with it. Wished I'd a seen the man what delivered it," James growled. "'E'd be missing his stumps about now."

"Who else was taken?"

"John took a knock when he tried to keep the pig from 'auling you off, and he's 'ome in the kitchen with a raw steak over 'is eye. That Lady Bess of yers is nimble on her feet, I tell you—scarpered 'erself out of the way in a trice. Was you alone, miss, up there on the platform in the thick of it. In with the Cyprians, were ye!" His laugh turned to a hacking cough.

Henrietta leaned away when a jostle of the carriage made her bump against Darien's shoulder. "I have not yet made out how Lord Darien knew to come find you, Uncle Pell."

"James came looking for Charley and found me at Brooks," Darien said.

James straightened. "Oh, did I?"

"However the way of it, the two of them found me at White's," her uncle said, his eyes flickering over Darien. "You're lucky they did, puss."

Darien was sitting very close. She fought the longing to curl against him. "You and my brother have become chums, then, if you've sponsored him into your club?"

"He has seen fit to lend a hand in a certain...affair of mine," Darien said. "So I thought I would return the favor and bail you out of gaol."

"Does this have anything to do with the opera dancer you were with before and he is with now?"

Darien's brows drew together. The growing light from outside made his eyes look blue-gray. "Does nothing shock you, Henry?"

She leaned her aching head against the seat. Tears of weariness and anger flooded her eyes. "Not after tonight. If you'd heard those women's stories— I don't suppose the marquess would use his name to grant them pardon too?"

"You might find it in you to be grateful to the marquess," Darien said. "With your father gone and Charley missing, it took his name to discharge you. And how will that reflect on Sir Pelton, going against Pitt's orders?"

He was angry with her. He was ever disapproving of her, Henrietta thought, and he had full call to be so. She had feathers in her head if she meant to send her heart after Lord Darien Bales. Everything with him was negotiation and wiles.

"And if Uncle Pell falls out of favor with Prime Minister Pitt, then he loses his influence in any suits and causes he has promised to aid," Henrietta retorted. "Yes, I see why you have so kindly interested yourself in my uncle's business. I do not know how to begin to thank you, Lord Darien. Or the marquess."

A dark look crossed his face. She was behaving badly, provoking him like this, and all because she wanted to lean on his shoulder and cry. These weak impulses were, no doubt, the effect of her sleepless night. She was glad to see the coach turn into Manchester Square.

"Almost home, James, and to our own beds," she said with

feigned cheer. "Poor Aunt Althea will never come down from the boughs, I suppose?"

James threw off the cloak. His smart livery was stained beyond repair, and his quick eyes darted between the two on the seat opposite him. "Ye've told 'im, aye? 'E deserves to know."

Henrietta's courage suddenly failed her. "Uncle, can you guess who was at my debate? Mr. Equiano himself. Lady Bess promised to introduce me, though of course that never happened. He signed our petition! The one I wrote!"

"Henry," Darien said, his voice low and quiet as the coach rattled to a stop. "You wrote that you had information for me. About...that matter of mine."

Yes, and he'd ignored her missive, it would appear. She studied him, savoring this last opportunity to be close. His hard look from earlier had turned into his habitual mask. He had come to rescue her from the watch house, of all places. Her heart swelled even as her stomach sank. If he had been angry with her before, he would want nothing to do with her now.

"Celeste sent the child to my keeping," she said in a quiet voice, gathering her tattered skirts. "She is here, at Hines House. You may send your solicitor to make arrangements with me."

And she plunged out of the coach so she could no longer see his face.

James hopped out behind them, and the cab rolled away. Henrietta leaned wearily on her uncle's arm. The night soil men went by with their wagon, and down the street, the dairy man set out the day's milk. At the house next door, a man in a jacket and trousers, dressed like a tradesman and leaning on the rail to the kitchen stairs, pulled a small notepad out of his pocket and studied the three of them.

She had been an oddity before; she was notorious now. The little scullery maid scrubbing the broad stair before Hines

House pulled her bucket of whitewash to the side, and Henrietta summoned a smile of thanks.

"You're very cool to a man who did you a service, Hetty," her uncle observed.

"He didn't help me for my own sake," Henrietta said. Darien's swift exit had torn something inside her, and she didn't care to examine it yet. She stumbled with weariness into the house as Dearbody opened the door. The butler's mouth dropped open in shock.

"He wanted to know where I'd hidden his child. We're at daggers drawn, Uncle, ever since he learned the King used Papa's loan to fund the wars in Mysore."

Her uncle's brow furrowed. "He lost his brother in Mysore, lass. Lord Lucien was sent there in the Second War and never heard from since the Treaty of Mangalore. The marquess wants him declared dead so Lord Darien can inherit and take his brother's estate in hand. Darien asked me how to defeat the suit."

"Oh no." Henrietta stopped short in the tiled foyer. "His brother? No wonder he gave me such a look—he must feel as if we murdered his family. And I was so beastly to him." She raised a hand to her mouth.

"Now, pet, you can mend your fences later," her uncle soothed, handing her over to her maid. Duprix choked back a cry at the state of Henrietta's gown and set her mouth like a fighter on the barricades.

"I can salvage it, ma'mselle, *bien sûr*," she clucked, guiding Henrietta to her room. "You were a triumph and all the men adored you, *oui?*"

Henrietta could not even recall her debate. The points blurred together in her mind, clouded by the fear and distress over her arrest. She was in disgrace and might be charged with treason. The cloud would cover her whole family, perhaps also the institutions she supported, and then what would she do? How would she care for the child she'd taken in?

She would never be admitted to the Minerva Society, never prove herself her mother's daughter. She'd be a stain on the Wardley name, a bigger scandal than Aunt Davinia. And if she were transported to the penal colonies as a traitor to the Crown, she would never see her family again. They would cast her out completely, with good reason.

At least it was early morning and she didn't have to face her family yet with the knowledge of how she'd disgraced them. She had a few hours to rest before the judge opened his office and she could claim her cellmates. Henrietta shoved her head beneath her goose-down pillow and sobbed until there was nothing left in her.

When sleep claimed her, it was fevered and fretful, haunted by the sight of James's bruises, the hard lines on the faces of the women in her cell as they shared their painful stories, the stricken expression of Constance Spickey as Henrietta spouted her heretical ideals.

And over and again, the face of a strange man, his mouth gushing blood as he fell toward her, mortally wounded, anguish and reproach in eyes the same shade as Darien's deepest blue.

CHAPTER TWENTY

After an hour or two of fitful sleep, Henrietta descended the stairs of Hines House with her old German riding habit and a mission.

Her debate had galloped away from her, and likely all hopes of being accepted into the Minerva Society, or indeed into any polite circles.

Darien had come for her, held her close, delivered her. Even though her father had sent his brother to his death in Mysore, paying for British wars. Though she had spirited away what might be his child. And she had lied to him, twice, and to herself as well, pretending his kiss had stirred nothing within her.

She felt something like relief at having everything broken. Her world was coming apart at the seams, but she saw her place in it. Plain old Henrietta Wardley-Hines, reformer, champion of the oppressed. Not fashionable. Not dashing. Not a girl who would interest Lord Daring. A person no one was likely to pay any attention to without her father's fortune at her back.

Plain Henrietta Wardley-Hines, under the possible taint of treason.

If she were to be taken up as a traitor to the Crown, there

were a few things she needed to settle first. James and the two footmen, bonded by their adventures of the evening, bore her back to the Bishopsgate watch house, where Henrietta dangled before the magistrate a purse large enough to cover the fines for all six of her younger cellmates. Mame had already paid her fine, recited the justice's piece for him, so well did she know it, and hurried back to her tavern before her husband could sell it away from her, as he'd threatened to do.

The Sisters of Benevolence Hospital was still bursting at the seams, but the matron welcomed the new girls with warm efficiency. Henrietta wondered how many of them would stay. Many times, those who sought refuge in the Hospital went back to their old circumstances, hoping to improve them. It was easier, sometimes, to return to a life with hardships one knew rather than make the difficult foray into the unknown.

As she had forayed into the beau monde *and* made an utter hash of it. No more. She knew her place.

Her family was assembled in the blue parlor when she returned, and Henrietta braced herself before she stepped through the door. This was what she had most feared: burdening her family with shame and disapprobation. They were all there: Lady Mama, Charley, Marsibel, and Aunt Althea. The people she would hurt most with her fall into disgrace.

She burst into tears when Lady Mama rose and enveloped her in a deep, long hug that smelled of talc and fresh baby.

"Hetty, dear, you mustn't cry. Haven't you seen the entrance hall? And Dearbody has worn himself out this morning trotting back and forth with our callers and their cards."

She showed Henrietta the piles of cards and flowers. The showiest arrangement was from Lady Bess, with a note declaring Henrietta's debate a smashing success. The Minerva

Society had been mentioned in every paper in London and would be talked of well outside Middlesex.

Marisbel, in a smart new walking gown and a jaunty hat, sat beside Henrietta as though she would personally protect her against accusations of treason did Prime Minister Pitt burst through the door. As the maids ferried in trays of refreshments, reporting the number of newsmen Dearbody had turned off the stoop, Charley paced the small parlor, hashing out the consequences of Henrietta's act.

"So we owe Daring for springing you from the watchhouse." Charley tugged at his cravat as if it were choking him. "Famous! And then he brought in Uncle Pell when I—er…"

"Retired to the arms of your light-o'-love. I suppose the King won't let me set foot in his library now." Henrietta tried to keep her voice light, but Charley's dismal outlook was depressing her spirits.

"The King is the least of it!" Charley exclaimed. "You'll be cut at all society functions, and likely I shall be too. And what of Marsi? Who's going to offer for the cousin of a criminal protester?"

"You mustn't rate her on my account," Marsibel said with a pretty color in her cheeks.

"Aunt Althea, I am sorry to be such a trial after all you have done for me," Henrietta said. "But you must not let Lord Pinochle court Marsi."

"I should say not," Aunt Althea said, her lip curling in disgust. "Lady Bessington informed us that he all but handed you over to Pitt's officers. I have no doubt your uncle shall have a thing or two to say to him."

Henrietta sat in amazed silence. Aunt Althea, on her side!

"What I cannot fathom," her aunt went on, "is how Lord Daring has come to interest himself so much in this family's affairs."

Henrietta pushed away the image of Darien's face, clouded with concern and righteous wrath, hovering so close as he carried her through the watchhouse. How she'd unthinkingly rested her head on his arm in the carriage.

"I had no idea how convenient it is to have a marquess one can conjure at any moment," Henrietta said. "It makes just anyone fall into line with one's wishes."

"Lord Darien," Lady Clarinda reflected, "would have no little influence of his own were he declared Langford's heir apparent."

And yet, if Henrietta understood, he didn't wish to inherit. What earthly reason could he have? It was the way of the world that lands and titles passed to the heirs male. There were plenty of peers about town who funded their dissolute lives with incomes they had inherited, not earned.

Charley gave his sister a shrewd stare. "I told you before, Hetty, he won't marry you."

Her cheeks tightened with a treacherous blush. "Lord Darien and I have agreed that we would not suit."

"I should say not," Aunt Althea exclaimed.

"Best you don't develop a tendre for him then, you goose," Charley said. "You're a millwright's daughter—"

"A knight's daughter," Clarinda reminded him gently.

"As if I would be such a ninnyhammer, Charley," Henrietta said.

"Many have been," Charley retorted. "Daughters of dukes."

"Sir Charleton is right, in this instance," Aunt Althea said. "It will be proper to send him a note of thanks, but that must make an end of it. It will not do to be seen too much in Lord Darien's pocket, Hetty."

Henrietta stood. It was time to make some things clear, especially to her foolish heart, which kept conjuring hazy recollections of Darien's strong arms about her, her body nestled against his. He did not belong to her, however much it felt like he did, or ought to.

"Lord Darien only ever concerned himself with me because he wanted to approach Uncle Pell for advice. In the interim, I involved myself in the affair of Lady Celeste's confinement, in which Darien has some interest. I expect he will send his solicitor to deal with me on the matter of the child, and that will be the conclusion of our acquaintance." How her heart ached at the thought.

Aunt Althea had already established her opinion on the wisdom of Henrietta's sheltering an illegitimate child, and she'd been subdued by Clarinda's quiet declaration that the child had a home at Hines House as long as Henrietta wished. Althea saw the wisdom of not pursuing this tack.

"All to the best that your association with him is over, Hetty," Aunt Althea said instead. "Mr. Rutherford Bales has invited Marsibel to view Hamilton's collection of Greek vases at the British Museum this afternoon. You might go with them as chaperone. It will be a respectable, quiet outing."

"Do you think I ought to show my face so soon?"

"Why not? You did nothing wrong save get caught up with the radical sentiments of Lady Bessington's little society and be betrayed by a lord who ought to have behaved like a gentleman. If you hide, it will appear you deserve to be disgraced."

"Very well." Henrietta nodded, though her chest hurt. It was good to have her family on her side. It was good to hope she still had a future. Even if it did not include Lord Darien Bales.

She looked into the nursery before she went to dress and found her half-sisters utterly absorbed with their new charge. Matilda, nine, instructed Henrietta on how to hold the baby while Amelia fussed with the embroidered blanket. Sophia leaned on Henrietta's knee and Charlotte on her shoulder as Henrietta sat in the wooden rocking chair. Fanny would have stood behind her, making faces at the child over her shoulder. Her absence was as sharp as a presence, but the great wave of grief pummeled less these days.

Henrietta's heart pinched as she stared into the foggy blue eyes of the infant, admired the peak of her nose, the folded-in mouth, the impossibly tiny eyelashes. The babe was a downy weight in her arms, a solid nugget swaddled in the softest Irish linen.

She couldn't allow herself to be charged with treason; she had a child to take care of.

Darien's child, possibly. It was a small part of him she could claim and love.

While Duprix fastened her into a Pierrot jacket of worked muslin over a double petticoat, Henrietta pondered her choices. She could withdraw to the north. Hodge might refuse to sell her his mill, but she still had Birch Vale. It wouldn't matter to her tenants whether she was a social success; the halls of St. James and the vast London houses were as remote as Persian palaces to most of them.

Once Jasper and Lady Mama returned north as well, Henrietta would have little reason to be in London. She had been foolish in her aspirations to the Minerva Society. How had she ever thought she might belong among those women of intellect and influence? She couldn't even lead a simple debate on the question of women's rights.

A worse thought struck her as Duprix dressed her hair with high, loose curls and added a light dusting of lavender powder. Pitt had already suppressed meetings of debating societies due to talk of treason and the unrest in France. He might shut down the Minerva Society entirely, and it would be all Henrietta's fault.

She felt as low as when her mother died when she descended to the formal parlor. Rutherford Bales sat there, wearing a small powdered periwig much like Sir Pelton's. His clothes were dark and severely cut, but his high, stiff cravat was perfectly tied.

"I am glad you still see fit to associate with us, Mr. Bales." Henrietta entered the room in the way Darien had taught her to walk, with gliding steps rather than her usual tromp. "I had hoped Marsi would not suffer a loss of friends because of me."

"I would never abandon her." Rutherford rose in a quick, clumsy bow. He had none of his cousin's elegant poise.

She seated herself, and Rutherford sat as well, his limbs gangly in the ill-fitting suit, his neck craned toward her. Darien had a strong, well-sculpted neck, as he had a strong and well-sculpted everything. Darien filled out his dinner jackets in a most fetching manner. Rutherford's coat hung on his lanky frame. How unjust of Lord Darien Bales to overshadow all other men.

"Mr. Bales." Henrietta turned her attention to him. Rufie's suit was worn, his shoes well-used. "Have you any hopes of a living? Or perhaps a position at university? It seems to me your talents ought not lie fallow." The parish that held Birch Vale had a rector, but perhaps she could find something nearby. Seeking to aid another was the surest way to lift herself out of the blue devils.

Darien would call it meddling. She pushed thoughts of Darien aside.

Rutherford cleared his throat. "I had hopes of the living on Horace's estate of Bellamy, but after Lucretius..." He trailed off, agonized. "And then, with Lucien missing..."

Henrietta nodded. Only the owner could assign a living on his estate. Darien must know that his cousin's fate hung in limbo while the oversight of Bellamy Hall was in question. Must know and yet refused to remedy it.

"Forgive me," she said, "but my father—as I think you know,

he had some part in funding the Third Mysore War." When Rufie gulped, his Adam's apple jouncing up and down, she hurried on. "I am terribly sorry if my family was in any way responsible for injuring yours. But I do not understand why Darien will not take over his brother's estate if Lord Lucien—" Had died at the hands of the Sultan's forces and, indirectly, those of Sir Jasper Wardley-Hines.

Rutherford stared at the patterned paper on the opposite wall. "Darien took his mother's death harder than any of the boys," he said at last. "They tried to shield him from it, but in retrospect, it made his grief worse. At the end, she went so quickly, and he was away at school—he didn't have the chance to say a proper farewell. Then, when Lucien bought his colors and left, Darien felt abandoned all over again. He and Lucien were very close."

"Lucifer and Daring," Henrietta murmured. "I've heard the stories."

"Not half of them, I'd wager." Rutherford splayed his hands over the knees of his dark breeches. "Horace always said Darien was going to give their father apoplexy if he didn't mend his ways, stop his carousing around town, ruining young women by the score. But it was Horse—Horace who had the apoplexy. And I think Darien feels he was the cause of it."

"He could not be responsible," Henrietta said.

Rufie shook his dark head. Not a hair shifted. "Not in the logical way of things. But grief has its own logic. Nell, their mother, was there to look after the children, but when Lucretius took ill, that dear boy—"

"A fever, I think?" Henrietta said gently when Rufie strangled into silence. She shared that agony; they'd lost Fanny to fever too.

"Darien was away on the Continent. He returned home only to bury him." Rufie swallowed hard. "He blames himself,

God knows why. I truly feared he wished to do himself in. Then Nell went away, leaving Horatia behind, and my brother, Rathbone, stepped in to take things in hand at Bellamy. My uncle the marquess thinks Darien will settle down if he has more responsibility. But Darien won't touch what he thinks belongs to his brother. He'll never agree to declaring Lucien dead. Never." He sent her an unhappy look.

"And his reputation leaves him with no credit," Henrietta said to herself. "No allies to protest the suit." No wonder he had pinned his hopes on Sir Pelton.

"His reputation. Yes." Rutherford cleared his throat, and Henrietta recalled with searing detail the kiss between her and Darien that Rutherford had witnessed. "I hope you will not hold it too much against him. How he has—er, behaved with other women. Including, um, Lady Celeste." He winced. "I am quite sure the right woman will be able to command his entire devotion."

Henrietta drew back. "But you must know…"

She let the protest dangle. Rutherford stared at her with appeal and a hint of worry. He had no notion that Darien's reputation was largely a ruse, a set of compromising situations staged to free trapped girls from unwanted unions.

The realization made her sway in her seat. Darien let his family, the people he loved most, believe him no better than what the gossip sheets portrayed. And yet he had trusted her with the truth.

Who else knew him as he truly was, a kind, sensitive man who could not walk past a person in need? He had sprung to her aid when he'd found her standing wretched and alone outside St. James, well before he knew she might be of use to him. He had helped her bring Mary Ann out of the workhouse and arrange Elijah's burial. He had gone to Colonel Pennyroyal to return the deed he'd won at cards. But no one knew any of this.

He was no paragon, certainly. Arrogant, commanding, high-handed, and far too absorbed with matters of style and dress. And dangerously sensual—that was true also. He had not tried to deny what happened with Celeste. Who, as far as Henrietta gathered, had used Darien to taunt the man she really wanted and been left with a babe in her belly for her tricks.

"Forgive me," Henrietta said again. "For inquiring into that which is none of my business."

"It is well within your rights to ask, since I hope very much to become an accepted member of your family," Rutherford said, color high in his cheeks.

Henrietta blinked and drew back. "You do?"

He had dark brown eyes, lovely, soulful, if far less striking than Darien's searing blue. Darien's eyes could ensorcel a woman—as so many had been ensnared before her, Henrietta reminded herself. She'd lied when she'd told Darien she wanted a staid, quiet man, a scholar or dreamy vicar. She wanted a man who sparked her mind and her blood.

Rufie gulped and nodded. "I am sure Lady Pomeroy has higher hopes, but I intend to convince her and Sir Pelton that no one shall love or provide for their daughter more devotedly than I can and will do."

"Marsibel?" Henrietta exclaimed. Her cousin appeared on the threshold, Darien beside her.

Darien. Here. Henrietta's mind ground to a halt as awareness of him washed through her in a tide of heat.

"Marsi, are you and Rufie—I mean, Mr. Bales—?"

Marsibel flushed a delicate rose-pink. "I must discuss it with my father and mother," she said. Her eyes lingered on Rufie with hope and softness. "But I hope we may persuade them of our suitability."

"I felt it incumbent upon me," Darien said coolly, "to inform Miss Pomeroy how very little my cousin has to offer her."

"Marsibel!" Henrietta repeated. "You're in love, and wish to marry, and you didn't tell me? How could I not have known?"

Fresh tears stung her eyes. Her cousin had finally grown up enough to be interesting, and now she would be lost to marriage, wifehood and motherhood, a realm Henrietta would never know. Marsibel flew into Henrietta's arms and the girls laughed and danced about together, then dried each other's tears, talking a mile a minute. Rutherford looked on with a fond smile, as calf-witted as any man in love.

Darien leaned against the door, affecting boredom. "Are you in transports to be part of the Bales family, Henry? I thought we were aggravating aristocrats."

He was so tall, so elegantly dressed, so overwhelmingly potent, and so dear. She felt struck like a bell, as she had upon seeing him at the door of her cell. Every nerve vibrated, every thought fell away as one clear truth washed through her, bright and obvious.

"Darien." She breathed his name, feeling her chest tighten. "I did not expect—" She had feared she would never see him again. Yet he was here.

He shrugged. "I felt I should look in on you all," he said. "See if—" But he bit off the words.

Henrietta rose and crossed the room, holding out her hands. As if he understood everything, he took her hands in his own, pressing her palms against his chest. His eyes burned bright blue.

"I did not know Lord Lucien was lost in Mysore. I am so very sorry to hear it. I don't know how you can bear to be around us."

He held perfectly still, yet she felt he leaned toward her, body and heart. "Your father is not to blame for what the King did with his money," he said gruffly. "And Lucien is not lost. He's alive. He's coming back."

Henrietta studied his face. In his eyes she saw the swirl of emotions, the bleakness, the longing, the fear. Her heart swelled. She longed to put her arms around him. She wanted to hold him and never let go.

"Then I look forward to meeting him," she said in a quiet voice, and the bleak look in his eyes eased. He pressed her palm to his cheek, his skin firm and warm and freshly shaven. The rancor between them was gone, dissolved in a moment, and in its place was a low harmonic hum, like a struck chord that resonated through both of them.

"So the child is here." His voice was a low rumble.

"Safe. Do you want to meet her?"

He hesitated, his eyes a cloudy violet hue. "No."

Henrietta nodded. If he wasn't ready, she wouldn't press him. And if he didn't see her, there was less chance he would try to take the babe away.

"I named her Celestina."

"Little heaven," he said softly, rubbing his jaw along her knuckles. The gesture seemed uncalculated, comforting, and yet it rattled her. "I will have my solicitor find a suitable family, perhaps someone on my estate. You may interview them if you like."

"I intend to keep her." Her lungs heaved for want of air, and she steeled herself against his response. But nothing could induce her to give up this child. Not even Darien.

He scowled. "An unmarried woman? You cannot. It would mean your ruin."

"I think you know I am already ruined. You recall where you found me this morning?"

She tried to tug her hands from his grip, but he refused to release her. He held to her as if she were the one thing keeping him tethered to Earth. He held her as if he could be her shield. And, in fact, she did not wish to let go of him either. That clear truth still flowed through her, dazzling, iridescent. Everything inside of her shifted to make room for it.

Darien held her arm when Dearbody announced the coach was ready. He sat beside her on the short ride to Great Russell Street and the British Museum, his thigh brushing her skirt, their shoulders touching. He held her hand on his arm as their group passed through the gateway and into the great, high-ceilinged hall of Montagu House, and she let herself fall into step with him. Nothing had been resolved, and yet they allowed the current to bear them together in its silent, inescapable pull.

At the top of an enormous staircase, they met Miss Forsythia Pennyroyal and her mother admiring the figures that were floating across the frescoed ceiling.

"So much bare skin," Mrs. Pennyroyal said with a sniff of disapproval. "One hardly knows where to set one's eyes."

"Oh dear. We cannot escape Miss Wardley-Hines anywhere we go." Forsythia turned from a line of broadsides tacked to one wall and wrinkled her nose as she saw Henrietta approaching. "We have heard of nothing but you all day, you and the Minerva Society. The *Times* estimated there were a thousand people come to hear your radical ideas." She avoided looking at Darien.

"Equality for women will not seem radical when it is an accepted truth," Henrietta said. She made no move to step away from Darien; if she was ruined already, why bother? "I wish you would attend a meeting of the Minerva Society, Miss Penny-royal. You might enjoy our discussions."

"It sounds far too fast a set for me," said Miss Pennyroyal. "I have my reputation to consider." She lugged her mother away, Mrs. Pennyroyal's nose in the air in an attitude identical to her daughter's.

Darien took down the broadsides, and Henrietta considered the cartoon. In it, she stood on the dais of the London Tavern, a flaming torch in one lifted hand, the red Phrygian cap of the French revolutionaries atop her curls. Her other hand was lifting a sheer skirt to show a set of men's pantaloons like those of the so-named sans-culottes, the Frenchmen who were agitating for liberty.

The ornate script of the caption read "Lady Revolution Lights the Way." Among the melee of fighting men, Thomas Hardy had his fist planted in the face of a King's officer, James was cracking his whip, and Mr. Equiano lofted a second torch inscribed "Abolition!"

Henrietta shook her head. "At least my gown is fetching in that one. Has it come out yet that I was taken up by the watch?"

"It will. Not even your uncle can hush the reporters. Pitt has certainly found he can't."

"How glad I am Marsibel's future is secure." She looked wistfully across the room to where Marsibel and Rutherford stood with their heads bent over a terra cotta vase, cooing like turtledoves. How sweet to see Marsibel so adored, but it made her feel melancholy too.

"There's a certain freedom to being ostracized," Darien remarked. "One may do as one likes."

She squeezed his arm, understanding. "I should find it terribly lonely, having only myself to please. I always appreciated my responsibilities. They suited my talents."

"Putting your nose into other people's business?"

"I believe you, sir, put your nose rather pointedly into my affairs this morning," she answered. "So I consider us square."

Lightly he brushed a finger over the tip of her nose. Everything inside Henrietta melted.

"You incited a riot in the London Tavern, spent the night in the watchhouse, and have taken in the illegitimate child of a duke's daughter. I look a paragon compared to you."

She gave a watery laugh, grateful for his levity. "Yes, I've tied my garter in public, to be sure. Perhaps you ought to take refuge with the Pennyroyals. Staid, respectable people who might reform you, as your friend Perry suggested. Not a sad rattle like me."

He steered her into a side gallery, empty of people, and paused beside a waist-high pedestal. The painted vase bore a muscled warrior wearing nothing but a short cloth about his hips, offering his helmet to a stately lady who held a shield and spear. Minerva again, accepting the homage due her as a powerful woman.

Henrietta would never be a Daughter of Minerva now.

"I haven't thanked you." Darien drew her closer to him, his smile full, his eyes gentle. "For charming my child from Celeste. She might have been lost were it not for you."

She thrilled as he stroked a thumb over the arm of her jacket. Oh, this man. She was lost to sense around him. "Do you forgive my meddling, then?"

"On the contrary, I am glad to know she is in good hands, in the event that—I mean, if anything were—"

Had the thought of fatherhood left him speechless? His baffled look made something light and airy bubble in her chest, dislodging the tight lump of loss.

Entirely against all strictures of propriety, as if he were hers that she might make such an intimate gesture, Henrietta placed her hands on either side of his face. She felt the warmth of his skin through her gloves.

"Lord Darien Bales," she whispered, falling into his violet eyes. "Lord Daring. If only the world knew the man I see."

She would remember later that she had been the one to lose her head. She would remember, later, how his gaze flicked past her powdered hair before he bent his head, meeting the lips she raised to his. At the moment, all she could do was quiver with relief.

She had wanted this since that morning, when he carried her through the watch house in his powerful arms. She had wanted this, truth be told, since the moment outside St. James Palace when she looked up from her torn skirts into his gentle, laughing eyes.

She tumbled headfirst into their first real kiss. He was not trying to scold her, or teach her a lesson, or master her. He desired her, took delight in her, and they stepped into that enchanted world together.

His thumbs brushed her ears as he cupped her cheeks, his fingers reaching into the soft hair pinned at her nape. It was a slow, hot, blossoming sort of kiss. His whole mouth was in play against hers—his firm lips, his nipping teeth, his exceedingly agile tongue. The rest of the world swirled away as if whisked behind a velvet curtain.

Her body came alive, heat and light traveling down the taut, alert cord forming at the center of her body. The kiss was a sweet dance, full of wonder and invitation, and she followed his lead as trustingly as she had followed him across the floor at the Bicclesfield ball.

After a long while they surfaced for air, and she found herself anchored by his hands around her face. Her own hands twined around his shoulders as if to pull herself up to meet him. Heat radiated off his body, and his scent, spicy and familiar, swamped all thought. His expression mirrored her own, warm, astonished.

Who knew a kiss could be like that? Playful, molten, intoxicating enough that she had forgotten who she was, that they were...in a broad museum gallery with any number of people in the next room, examining the Egyptian mummy.

A cold shock rushed to every part of her body, quenching the soft echo of his kiss. He looked around, and she forced her head to follow his gaze.

They were not alone in the room.

Marsibel wore a blank look, her mouth parted in shock. Rutherford looked nervous and appalled. At least half a dozen people stared with expressions that ranged from stupefaction to unholy glee, with murmurs, chuckles, here and there a hiss. Miss Forsythia Pennyroyal put a hand to her mouth with a cry.

"You!" she choked. "*You*! But you're—you're—" She turned and rushed from the room, her heels clacking on the floor.

"D-D-Darien?" Rutherford stuttered.

Darien smiled with triumph and determination and something else, something Henrietta might have called satisfaction if she were not still, stupidly, trying to conceive that she had just been caught with an infamous seducer in a very public kiss, a kiss that would leave her reputation thoroughly and utterly in tatters unless he—

"Rufie." Darien's arm curved possessively about her waist. She felt the heat and solidness of him through her stays. "Miss Pomeroy. You may be the first to congratulate us. Miss Wardley-Hines has consented to become my wife."

/ CHAPTER TWENTY-ONE

"Well, that tears it!" Charley smacked down the glass he'd just emptied of Darien's best whisky. "Mauling m'sister in full view of the Pennyroyals? It's the leg-shackle for you, that's certain!"

"Lower your voice," Darien said, arranging his cravat. "Your clabbering will wake Rufie."

"You didn't tell him?" Charley said in a stage whisper. "Don't you think you ought've?"

Darien shook his head. "I don't want him caught up in this mess. He's to be married."

"Well, so are you, from the sounds of things," Charley grouched.

They stood in Darien's library, which held the only mirror in the house, since his sorry excuse for a valet had still not installed a looking glass in Darien's dressing room. Charley poured another glass from the sideboard and threw it back in one swift gulp.

It was not yet daybreak, but Darien guessed that the young baronet had not wasted a night that could be spent gaming, drinking, and lingering in the arms of his mistress with activity as pedestrian as sleep. He would furthermore bet that more than once in the night, Sir Charleton had cursed the misfortune that made him the only man who'd stepped forward when a drunk, furious Freddy Highcastle stormed into the Bicclesfield card room demanding Daring produce a second.

Morning stubble shadowed Charley's jaw, and his eyes were bloodshot with weariness. Brash he might be, but he clearly had never before had the solemn duty of escorting a man to the field of honor.

Charley held up his coat and Darien squeezed into it. The younger man cleared his throat as Darien saw to the intricate row of buttons, then pulled the lace of his shirt sleeves free of the wide cuffs. "Did you leave letters?"

Darien suspected he, too, looked the worse for wear. He had at least lain down to rest, though sleep eluded him, not due to thoughts of pistols at dawn but to wondering how soon he might call on Henrietta. She'd gone stiff and cold after the discovery of their kiss in the British Museum, without a word to him thereafter.

All the maids Lord Daring had rejected, and Miss Wardley-Hines marched up the stairs of her father's house without even acknowledging his offer, much less swooning with acceptance. He would get through this part of the morning, and then he would address her.

"I left them in my study."

Atop his designs for a drainage pump for Henrietta's estate lay two vellum envelopes imprinted with his seal, one inscribed with his father's full titles and one that simply read "Henry." What a terrible and liberating exercise it was to tell someone you loved everything you most longed to tell them but for very good reasons would never utter without the threat of loss of life.

Not that he had any expectation of giving up his life in this venture. It was an annoyance, but it would be only an hour, maybe two, and then it would be over. He could close the chapter on Celeste and every bitter memory associated with her, and he would call upon his intended.

He wanted to marry Henrietta Wardley-Hines. Quite the surprise, that.

"I wish you would have let me tell her about the duel," Charley said.

Darien shook his head. "There's no reason she needs to know until after, if she needs to know at all. Did you find a sawbones?"

"He's outside. We picked him up on the way."

"We? You brought another witness?"

Darien saw for himself as they stepped out the door. In Charley's phaeton sat the surgeon who had attended his last duel with Havering. And, lounging against the tying post, James chewed a pie wrapped in grease-soaked paper. He scowled at Darien. Darien scowled back.

"He won't cry rope on us, but that's all I can say about him," Darien said.

"Did ye only offer for her as you meant to get yerself killed the next morn?" James barked.

"Stand down, halfling," Darien said. "No one is getting killed today."

"Wish ye'd brung the toledo instead o' the pops," James said, eying the pistol case Charley carried. "Swords is better."

"And the injuries potentially more lethal," Darien replied. "It was Freddy's challenge, so my choice of weapons. Freddy faints at the sight of blood. Has ever since Eton."

"Cove oughtn't be tilting if 'e can't stomach the claret," James scoffed. He held the horses while the men mounted, then tossed the ribbons to Darien with an agile flick. "Meself, I'd pink 'im, just to show 'im what's what."

"You will hold your peace," Darien said. "I'll delope, Freddy will miss, and we'll all go to the pub and have a pint. Saving for Charley, who will continue with whisky, or cast up his accounts all over his spanking new vehicle."

Two shadows stood in Hyde Park in the spot known as the Nursery. Above them draped a great willow that had witnessed many a senseless wounding and death in its long life, among various other follies of men. Freddy came first out of the mist.

"I thought Perry'd be with you."

"I thought he was with you," Darien answered. "You seemed rather thick a few months ago."

Freddy scowled. "Ain't seen him in days, and now Celeste is gone too."

"Gone where?"

"You tell me!" Freddy exploded. "Don't you have her pocketed somewhere?"

"I haven't seen your sister since we parted ways and she shattered a priceless Oriental vase to honor the occasion."

That gave Freddy pause. "So that's what happened to the Ming! She told Mother it was the dog." He frowned. "So she didn't send the brat to you, then follow behind?"

Darien shook his head. "She gave the child to a foundling hospital. Is she really fit for traveling so soon? Perhaps your parents sent her away."

"Mum's up in the boughs," Freddy reported. "No note, nothing."

Darien turned to the second man inspecting the pistols, a set custom-crafted by Wogdon, the craftsman known for making beautiful instruments of death. "Hullo, Havering. You look the worse for wear."

"Heard your news at Boodle's," Havering said. "Felicitations."

"Thank you," Darien replied.

Havering turned to his challenger. "See here, Freddy. If your sister's flown the coop, there's really no call to blow Daring's brains out, is there?"

Freddy's scowl deepened. "Felicitations for what?"

"Parson's mousetrap." Havering pointed. "Charley's bluestocking sister."

In the gray light, the rage that spread across Freddy's face was a dull brick red. "You'll marry his sister but not mine? I'll have your blood, Daring!" He roared and lunged for the pistols.

Fog skimmed the field as the men counted their paces. James, holding both teams in the narrow rut of the road, soothed the horses against the coming noise. The surgeon shook his head and retreated, his face showing what he thought of waiting for two perfectly healthy men to damage each other when so many ill people required his treatment. At least he stood to make ten times his customary fee.

Charley and Havering stood back, the viscount's son shoulder to shoulder with the tradesman's son, the accidental baronet. The duelists turned to face one another, two spare sons of the nobility who had been bred to no career, no vocation, no purpose in life but entertainment.

Darien had considered, in the small reaches of the night, what it would mean to his father if he lost his third son. Rathbone would become heir presumptive, and Rathbone was a man Darien couldn't like, no gentleman in any sense of the term.

A year ago—even a few months ago—the degenerate Lord Daring would have been relieved to punctuate his life with a bullet in the chest over a woman. He had been pursuing his own destruction, letting practiced hoydens like Celeste seduce him to their beds and canny innocents like Forsythia Pennyroyal drape themselves around his neck.

But now, though the morning seeped with fog and the early stink of this bustling city, his head was clear. He had, at the bottom of his cloudy darkness, glimpsed a pure light that pierced his gloom, a woman whose good sense and energy and spirit sliced through his self-pity and despair.

There was a child who, his get or not, he had promised to support. He had no notion what a future with Henrietta might look like, but he wanted to reach for it with both hands.

Havering dropped the handkerchief. Darien lifted his right arm and shot to the side, firing into the ground. The noise thudded through the clearing, the echo dampened by fog. The horses shook their heads and stamped.

"Damn you, Daring!" Freddy bellowed, aiming at his chest. "I want satisfaction."

"Then take your shot," Darien said. "I ruined your sister. I made it impossible that any decent man would have her, not even Havering. Whatever her other failings, I am responsible for Celeste's child." He dropped his arm, the spent pistol dangling from his hand. Honor demanded he stand his ground and let his challenger take aim. "Get it over with, Freddy."

Freddy's arm wavered as several expressions chased across his young face. Then, hissing a curse, he swung the barrel of his pistol and pulled the trigger at the same time.

Darien flinched. Every man on the field saw his body recoil, smelled the report, and heard the odd, particular sound of a lead bullet tearing through fabric and flesh. A hammer hit him in the chest. Even from twenty paces, Darien saw the whites of Freddy's astonished eyes.

"Ye plugged 'im!" James shrieked.

"Damn you all!" Freddy howled. "I meant to miss!" He threw the gun aside and started forward.

Darien's hand went cold and numb. His pistol thudded to the ground, and he thought hazily it would get dirt in the inlay or damage from the damp. Together, he and Freddy stared at his chest, the spatter of bright red across his crisp white neckcloth, the dark stain spreading across his exquisite plum coat. The polish on his buttons would never be the same. The thought came from somewhere outside him, as if his spirit had already unhooked from his body.

Freddy moved in slow motion toward him, his voice coming from underwater. "Devil take it, Daring, you're *bleeding*," he stammered. Then his eyes rolled back in his head, and the duke's son collapsed on the ground.

Havering saw to his man. Darien dropped to his knees, the cold damp seeping through his leather breeches. A dull pain started pulsing in his shoulder and chest. He wondered that it didn't hurt more—death, that is. Darkness crept around the edges of his vision.

He'd imagined it so many times, tormenting himself in the depths of night, when another faceless woman lay in his bed and his chest ached and his heart raced over the sound of his shallow breath. Horace had not suffered, Nell had said; he'd been dead before he'd reached the bottom of the stair. Lucretius's decline was slow and agonized, the fever racking him for days. He'd never know how Lucien died, swift and honorable and merciful, or tortured and slow and deranged by pain.

The pain, God, it was every kind of sensation, burning and stabbing and a wild ache at the same time. The darkness rolled in, and he turned toward it. He'd wanted it for so long. But as his vision narrowed he saw one face shining in his mind's eye—Henrietta, the way she had looked after he kissed her, warm and surprised and wondrous and desirous and his.

Henrietta could save him. He needed Henry. It was his last thought before he pitched forward into Charley's arms.

~

HENRIETTA WENT to bed thinking of Darien. That delicious kiss wove through her dreams, imprinted on her soul for eternity. When she opened her eyes, that startling moment slipped into her awareness with a glow of astonishment. That Darien should have the power to so entirely enthrall her! Darien, the man she had thought herself safe from.

As if she didn't know better. As if she didn't know she would end up like Forsythia Pennyroyal, another goose who had made a pitch for him and lost. Or worse, a soiled dove wrecked in his wake, whom no one else would touch.

She rose and washed, then sat at her dressing table to brush her hair. A quick twist and a few hairpins dispatched that chore. She shucked her bedgown and passed over the lovely morning gown that Duprix had laid out, choosing instead an ancient sepia-brown muslin with ink stains on the sleeves. It was her writing morning, and this was her writing dress.

The maid would bring tea and toast with preserves and her own butter to the sunny sitting room next to her bedchamber, and Lady Mama would leave her unmolested unless some urgent household matter arose. There were a great many things she had to organize before she could head north—various letters, columns, speeches, and petitions that she had promised to one cause or another. Then she would visit Mary Ann and the baby, join the family for lunch, and no doubt Aunt Althea would call to start preparations for the wedding. It was strange to think of Marsibel being married—it was almost like contemplating a marriage for Matilda, who was nine.

Of her own proposal, Henrietta refused to think. It was not

sincere—not real—and she refused to devote herself to fanciful imaginings.

She sharpened her quill, opened her inkpot, and was rereading her summary of Mary Wollstonecraft's arguments to be included in the next bulletin of the Minerva Society when, over the usual morning noise in the street, she heard male voices raised in a rowdy drinking song. It was not customary for their quiet square to be a route for drunk young gentlemen parading home from their night of debauchery, but one problem with drunk young gentlemen was that they never conformed to expectation.

"Voice, fiddle, and flute, no longer be mute," a male voice bellowed, off-key. It sounded like Charley. Henrietta shook her head. If Charley turned up here, drunk as a wheelbarrow, she would send him off with a flea in his ear. Miss Wollstonecraft said of women's education that—

"I'll lend you my name and inspire you to boot," caroled another male voice in a deeper register, one she didn't recognize. How exasperating of Charley to bring a friend. She would refuse to receive them. Wollstonecraft—

"And besides, I'll instruct you, like me, to entwine—"

This was a weaker voice, faltering, slurred. Still, she recognized it and rose from her desk. She opened the window and leaned out to catch all three men joining in the last line: "The myrtle of Venus with Bacchus's vine!"

"Soaked, at this hour! You should be ashamed of yourselves," Henrietta shouted. "Respectable people are still in their beds, you know."

"You ain't," said Charley, squinting up at her. "Come down, Hetty, and give a fellow a hand."

"He's awfully heavy," said the third man. She recognized Mr. Lionel Havering, whom she had danced with at the Bicclesfield ball. The man who had jilted Lady Celeste.

"Take him to his own bed," Henrietta said heartlessly. "I don't know why you think I would want him."

Darien's head slumped on his chest, his hair mussed and falling from its queue, his cravat dreadfully flattened, and a stained cloak thrown carelessly over his shoulder. His splendid boots dragged across the pavement as the other men hauled him along.

"Aw, Hetty, show a heart," Charley cried. "He's your intended."

He gave the last word a strange emphasis and shrugged the shoulder that bore half of Darien's weight. Darien's head rolled to the side, and he blinked up at her like a man blinded by the light. His face was as white as the part of his cravat that did not bear a dark muddy stain.

He wasn't drunk.

Henrietta clattered down the stairs ahead of Dearbody and pulled back the bolt. A quick glance at Charley's face showed his urgency.

"But to bring him here disguised!" she said loudly, seeing the heads turning on the street outside. Her voice sounded as strained and obvious as Charley's, barely audible over her suddenly pounding heart. "As if I want to see him in such a state."

"Hullo, Henry," Darien said, his head rolling forward again. He did appear drunk, when it came to that, his eyes heavy-lidded, his speech muffled. As his compatriots heaved him across the threshold, the cloak slipped and she saw the dark stain on his beautiful coat.

"How bad?" she whispered, staring at Havering's hand on Darien's waist. It was smeared with red.

"James is bringing the leech," Charley said grimly, and Henrietta's blood went cold.

"That's my girl," Darien announced.

"Not the parlor," Henrietta hissed, slamming the front door. "He'll upset Lady Mama and the girls. Take him upstairs to my sitting room."

The men dragged their burden up the stairs while James led another man in from the kitchen. Henrietta's heart stopped as she recognized the surgeon's bag. Darien's boots slipped and scuffed on the runner, as if his muscles did not obey his command.

"The swell's still in the rattler, dark in his daylights," James reported.

"Havering will take Freddy home," Charley said. "Best to pretend he's sodden too."

"Lord Alfred?" Henrietta gasped. "Darien, I told you to leave town! I *told* you."

Darien groaned as his friends lowered him to the settee. "Tole *you* Freddy was a terrible shot," he mumbled. "He missed."

"No, he didn't," Henrietta said, unfastening Darien's cravat with shaking hands while his friends held him upright. "But why the charade? Were you seen?"

"What do you think?" Charley snapped, all to pieces. "Daring insisted on an open carriage, so sure he'd walk away, and that imp of yours had to bring Freddy behind us as we can't leave him alone. The whole town will know what we're up to by noon."

"Imp, now?" James bridled. "Care I don't inform on ye for dueling!"

"Pitt's men are too busy tossing people in jail for expressing their opinions in public," Henrietta said, watching Havering and her brother wrestle Darien out of his coat. "I doubt he has time to arrest duelers. But to bring him here?"

"It was closest, I knew you'd be dressed, and he wanted to see you," Charley said.

Darien opened his eyes. "Henry," he slurred. "Kiss me ere I die."

"Oh, for heaven's sake." Henrietta put a hand to her chest, wishing it would cease its wild, erratic thumping. "Charley, you'd best fetch Jasper's brandy. We're going to need it."

"I'll see Freddy home, then call on you," Havering said, laying the soiled coat aside. "Devil take it, Daring, I wish I'd married the trull to save you this."

"Who knows where she is," Darien said. He let his head fall back on the couch. "Bon voyage to her. God, my arm! Someone needs to tell Rufie."

"I'll do it," Havering said. "And get out of Freddy where she went."

"Or where Perry went," Darien said. "Someone ought to find him too."

"Lady Celeste and Mr. Empson have gone where?" Henrietta asked, her eyes glued to the surgeon's shears as he began cutting Darien out of his waistcoat. She stepped forward to hold his injured arm as the doctor peeled away the thick silk.

"No, we meant—" Havering paused, incredulous. "Celeste and *Perry*? It can't be."

"I'd believe anything of her," Darien said. "See what Rufie knows. Henry, darling girl, where did you say that brandy was?"

"Charley's fetching it." She put a hand to his brow as the surgeon started on his shirt. "Darien, you impossible man, I told you he was going to shoot you."

Darien slid his good arm around her waist and leaned his head against her bosom. "Don't let me die, sawbones," he muttered. "I'm going to marry this girl."

"I haven't agreed to anything," Henrietta said, propping him up so the surgeon could finish removing his shirt. Darien had a chest like a classical Greek statue, strong, lean, every muscle gracefully defined. She couldn't bear to think of that beautiful form gone still and cold from one reckless moment.

"I shall live to convince you." Darien grasped her hand. "Henry, you sensible creature, make me the happiest of men."

"Let the surgeon do his work," Henrietta said, fighting to keep her voice calm. "Now, lie as still as you can. This is going to hurt like the devil."

Charley returned with the brandy and gave Darien a liberal portion. Henrietta raided the linen closet for bandages, filled a large ceramic bowl with hot water, and cast in a fistful of salt. Then she wrapped the bowl in towels and carried it upstairs. She could ask a maid for help, but it was best not to advertise to the entire household what they were up to. There was a chance the surgeon would patch up Darien and they could send him home with no one the wiser.

She took a deep breath outside the door of her sitting room. Lord, if that bullet had gone a few inches in another direction—he would have died without giving her a chance to say goodbye, to tell him anything. He would have died, and she would not have known till hours, perhaps days later. The thought made her lip tremble and her eyes sting.

She shook off the attack of sentiment.

"I am furious with you," she announced, setting the bowl on the table where the surgeon had unrolled his tools. Darien sat bare to the waist, his face clenched with pain. She threw a blanket over the low back of the couch, and he leaned against it while the surgeon probed his shoulder. His good hand fisted in one of the throw pillows, but surprise flickered in his eyes as he looked up.

She swept her hand to indicate the surgery in progress. "You agreed to a duel, you set the date, and you didn't tell me."

"Knew you'd fuss," he said through gritted teeth.

"I am fussing now. Behold."

"Hold him, please," the surgeon said with a frown as Darien flinched away from his probing instrument.

"Devil it, can't you go faster?" Darien snapped.

"Charley!" Henrietta called.

"Not for a monkey!" Charley called back. He sat in the empty bedroom on the other side of her sitting room, the connecting door open, the back of his chair facing the door. "I'm here as chaperone and witness. That's all the seconds needs to do. I don't have to hold his hand in his death throes."

"Death throes?" Henrietta stepped forward to push against Darien's chest. Good heavens, his torso was as hard as marble too. His skin felt clammy. His heart thudded against her fingertips. His gaze flew up to meet hers, and she couldn't look away.

"If I am able to extract the bullet, it is possible he may keep his arm," the surgeon said, peering into the wound. Henrietta had expected something more gaping, more horrifying than a neat circle with a black ring of singed flesh and powder. "The collarbone appears to be cracked, but the shoulder is attached. Most of the damage is in the muscle. I've seen men recover from wounds like these."

Hope entered Darien's eyes until the surgeon added, "Unless infection sets in, of course. There is always that."

Darien's heart skipped a beat beneath her fingertips, echoing the trip in her own chest. If the wound grew infected, she would have days with him, a week at most. She raised her other hand to his cheek and felt the tiny brush of stubble, his ridiculously soft skin, the firm, clean bone beneath. It would not be fair to discover him and not have time to learn more. It would be the world's cruelest joke.

And yet she knew as well as he that the world played cruel jokes daily.

"Ah, there you are," the surgeon announced, and Darien gave a long exhale. The doctor held up a leaden lump in the tiny claws of his instrument. "And intact, too. That's a help." He laid aside the instrument and took up his spool of thread. "Now to close the wound."

"You intend to clean it first," Henrietta reminded him.

The surgeon blinked. "To what purpose? All that is required is a few stitches."

"Forgive me," Henrietta said, reaching for her bowl. She was glad to have a task to keep her from collapsing in a heap of nerves. "But our nurse at school always insisted on a saline rinse for wounds."

"Don't kill 'im," Charley called from the next room. "He's heir to Langford."

"Lord Daring?" The surgeon paused, wide-eyed, scissors in the air.

Henrietta almost laughed, until she applied her sponge to Darien's shoulder and he tried to scramble away from the sting. "Damn it, Henry, that hurts worse than his poking!"

"Yes, the salt stings for a moment," she said. "Bear with me." When the surgeon wasn't looking, she dipped his needle in the hot water as she had seen the nurse do at Miss Gregoire's.

The surgeon set his stitches, and Charley scavenged a shirt of Sir Jasper's. The surgeon left with an additional fee in his pocket and instructions for the care of the patient. Henrietta brought Darien a glass of ale and a plate of bread and butter. He ate the bread and butter but traded the ale to Charley for the rest of the brandy. On the surgeon's advice, Henrietta moved him to the spare bedroom, the one Charley had perched in, so that he might rest.

"You didn't say yes," Darien said, watching as she bustled about the room, pulling draperies, arranging blankets.

"We'll discuss it later." Gently she tucked another pillow against his side to help him rest upright. His skin felt warm again, not clammy as he was before. The surgeon had fashioned a sling and insisted he move as little as possible until the collar-bone healed. Which meant she couldn't send him home.

She didn't want to. She wanted him right here where she could take care of him. She would persuade Lady Mama of the necessity. She hoped she would have the same luck persuading her father when he returned.

"You mean to say yes, don't you?" The hoarse note in his voice curled around her heart and tugged.

"Hush," Henrietta said, pouring a dose of laudanum. "Rest."

With his good hand, he grasped hers before she could slip away. "Henry. Everyone saw us."

"Yes, you made certain of that, didn't you?" His eyes had swept the room before he'd kissed her. He must have seen people drawing near. "I think you meant for us to be found."

He took the laudanum, watching her warily. His hand still clutched hers. "What I cannot conceive," she said, "is *why*."

"So you'd have to marry me, pea goose. I knew how it would go otherwise. You'd make me spend twelve months wooing you."

She scowled at him. "So you chose to make me a spectacle like you did all the others! One more silly damsel ruined by Lord Daring. When I'm already ruined for far different reasons."

"I couldn't wait twelve weeks," he muttered. "Twelve days." He pressed her hand to his chest, his eyes dark. "Don't leave me."

His husky plea riveted her as nothing else could have. That certainty ran through her again, cool and clear. She passed a hand over his brow. "I won't."

The anguish in his eyes clouded as the medication took effect. Gradually his eyelids closed, and sonorous snores told her he slept. For a long time, Henrietta sat with her hand against his heart, feeling the firm, steady beat.

Here he lay, the most beautiful, infuriating, haunted man she had ever met. She could count every beat of his heart, yet she had no notion what lay within those unknowable depths.

It was well she had not begun packing. His kiss she could shake off, a rote seduction she could laugh and shrug away. But he needed her, and she could not deny him.

She had known the man needed saving from himself. She had simply not expected he would be so literal about it.

CHAPTER TWENTY-TWO

"But you *do* mean to rivet 'im," Mary Ann said. "Don't ye?" She handed over Celestina. Henrietta tossed the cloth over her shoulder, elevated the infant, and rubbed her back. "Why should I?"

Clarinda looked up from her sewing. "Why not?" she asked curiously.

Lady Mama looked the picture of serene maternity as she sat embroidering a baby blanket of the softest, finest linen, with her beautiful girls dispersed about the family parlor at their favorite activities. Matilda stitched her sampler, Amelia sorted the silks in her mother's basket, and Sophia was busily winding thread as fast as Charlotte, who was chortling with glee, could unravel it.

Henrietta cradled the fussing babe. Darien's confession had rattled her almost as badly as his injury. That kiss had been divine, delicious, and a trap. Why should he want to marry her, plain Henrietta Wardley-Hines, when he could have any woman in London? In all of Britain. All the world. Did he think winning her in marriage would bring Uncle Pell to his side in the matter of his father's suit?

"Perhaps he was attempting to stir a different scandal, to lessen talk about my time in the watch house," Henrietta said. "Whatever he wants, I can't imagine it's *me*."

Don't leave me, he'd said, his eyes burning with anguish.

"'E's very 'andsome," Mary Ann said, wide-eyed. She'd peeked in when Henrietta checked that her patient was sleeping. Darien had been lying perfectly still, his mouth closed, his face turned up. Henrietta's heart ceased beating until she'd laid a hand on his chest and felt the gentle rise and fall. He also felt very warm, and she feared fever.

"Not a reason to wed," Henrietta said.

"But you did enjoy the kiss," Clarinda said.

"Still not sufficient reason."

She could not explain that odd, indelible pull that made her lose her head and kiss him. From the moment she'd peered into his eyes in the Ellesmere gallery, he had abandoned the mask with her. It was an intimacy all its own, seeing his true self—his grandiose dreams, his loyalty to his family, the grief and useless self-blame he wore like heavy chains.

He had entrusted her with his secret, and now he was entrusting her with his life. But what did he want from her? And could she afford the consequences if she trusted him in return?

Clarinda's soft mouth curved. "Give me that baby." She took the tiny bundle and, as if the infant were a bolt of cloth, flipped her on her belly and gave her a firm tap between the shoulder blades with the side of her hand. Celestina belched and sighed.

Henrietta collected her charge. "She'll sleep now for a while, Mary Ann. Go have a lie-down yourself. We'll find you when she's hungry."

"Aye, I could stand a few winks at that," said Mary Ann, wandering off with a yawn.

"Mary Ann looks much better," Clarinda said softly, watching her go. "You did the right thing, Hetty."

"Not by her son." Henrietta sat on the carpeted floor in a pool of skirts.

"That cannot be helped now, alas. But you did the right thing for Celestina too." Clarinda picked up her embroidery. "I think you may trust your instincts about Lord Darien as well."

Celestina dozed, her fists clutched to her cheeks, bow mouth still working. Henrietta lifted her tiny feet, each miniature toe with its diamond chip nail. The other girls gathered around.

"But look at what you had to endure, marrying beneath you," Henrietta said. "Worse for a man to so lower himself."

"It is no small thing to be the wife of a marquess's heir. Think of the influence you would have with your foundations. With your Society."

"A marquess's son," Henrietta corrected her. "His brother is still the heir."

"It would work in his interests, I should think," Clarinda said. "Everyone would suppose he has a claim to Jasper's wealth."

"He would be shunned for marrying beneath him," Henrietta said, "and I should look grasping and avaricious. And in addition to my estate and investments and my work for the Minerva Society, and Charley, who still needs looking after, I should have a husband who might very well racket his way about town spending my income. I hardly see the advantage to me."

"Conjugal felicity," Clarinda suggested.

Henrietta raised her brows, and Clarinda shrugged. "My darling girl. Do you really suppose I married your father for his money?"

"Of course not," Henrietta said, but out of loyalty more than belief. She lowered her eyes. "Darien has enjoyed felicity with a great many women," she said after a moment. "I shouldn't expect his interest in me to be real."

Clarinda watched her stepdaughter with an odd, soft smile on her face. "My dear, practical Hetty. How I admire your mind. But you may wish to rely on your heart in matters such as this."

Dearbody appeared at the door. "Lord Alfred Highcastle to see you, mum."

He glared at Henrietta. Her usurpation of his position that morning had made it necessary that he should learn of important goings-on in his own house from the scullery maid, the lowest among his domain.

"Show him in here, Dearbody," Clarinda replied.

Henrietta hovered over the child on the floor. "But the babies—?"

"He may see us at home," Clarinda said serenely. "And perhaps he has news of Lady Celeste." She gathered little Charlotte into her lap, Sophia beside her, while Matilda and Amelia took seats, agog at the prospect of a noble visitor.

Henrietta wavered. Part of her was furious with Lord Alfred for shooting Darien, intended or not, deserved or otherwise. But she was also holding his tiny niece.

Freddy stepped in the door. He had changed into riding dress. He looked handsome and miserable. His eyes went to Henrietta. "Is he—?"

"Sleeping, upstairs," Henrietta said tersely. "I really don't wish to disturb him."

Freddy twisted his hat in his hands, too distressed to notice Dearbody's attempts to take it. "Gad, what a fine hobble this is!" he exclaimed. "The duchess had her bristles up already with m'sister loping off. I never meant to wing him, I swear I didn't."

He looked so miserable, Henrietta took pity on him. "Oh, very well, sit. Lord Alfred, you know Lady Clarinda?"

"Lord Alfred," Clarinda greeted him. "The surgeon tells us Lord Darien will mend. What have you learned of Lady Celeste?"

"Cut sticks," Freddy said, taking a chair. "Gone to the Continent. The customs office stamped her papers to Calais."

"So soon after childbirth?" Clarinda murmured.

"Alone?" Henrietta asked.

"No." Freddy gave a short laugh. "With Perry."

"Mr. Empson?" Clarinda said. "Lord Darien's friend?"

"The third man," Henrietta surmised. Darien had said there was one.

How could any woman, once knowing Darien's embrace, want anyone else?

Freddy set his jaw. "Her maid 'fessed up once the duchess put the fear of God into her. Seems Celeste had been intriguing with Perry for months, but his uncle won't allow him to marry, so she—" His eyes lit on the young faces drinking in every word. "Er...she played her paw-paw tricks on Darien to bring Perry up to scratch. Never had a thought to marry Havering, for all that the settlements were drawn up."

"And I suppose your parents would not entertain Mr. Empson's suit," Clarinda guessed. "Given he has no rank, no fortune, and no commission."

"Gad!" Freddy yanked his hands through his hair. "I shot the wrong man! Perry's the one caused this bloody mess. I beg your pardon, Lady Clarinda," he said, appalled, as the girls grinned and giggled.

"But of course," Clarinda said. "And it is Lady Wardley-Hines now, as I am sure you are aware."

If Freddy thought it odd that her ladyship should prefer the lower address of a knight's wife to her born title as an earl's daughter, he didn't remark upon it.

"Nurse scolds us for playing paw-paw tricks," Matilda said,

to show she took no insult at the young lord's language. "Once, we put a mouse in her bed!"

"That's more or less what m'sister did to..." Freddy's eyes fell on the infant Henrietta held, and he stuttered into silence.

Henrietta rose with the babe, who grumbled and blew a spit bubble in her sleep. "I suppose James told you I took in your niece." She stepped close so Freddy could inspect the baby's face.

"But how—?" Freddy stammered, shying away.

"Lady Celeste sent her to the hospital I support, and I collected her. Of course I don't expect you to acknowledge her. I don't know if Darien will. But I have the care of her, at any rate."

"God's teeth, she looks like him," Freddy said in amazement.

Clarinda laughed. "Babies look like no one but themselves, Lord Alfred."

"No, she really does—especially that scowl." He raised his eyes to Henrietta's face. "Is it true you're to wed him?"

"He has done me the honor of making an offer," Henrietta said. She tamped down the butterflies at the thought of Darien as her husband. Hers in law if not in spirit. "I am not certain yet what will come of it."

"He's going to be furious that Perry served him such a turn," Freddy said. "I don't suppose—" He gave Henrietta a look of appeal, and despite herself, she laughed. It was easy to forget his high station given how young and brash he was.

"Yes, I can deliver that bad news, if I must."

"I don't doubt it'll fall on me to go after them," Freddy said, jamming his hat on his head. "I'll have a word or two for m'sister when I find them, you can be certain. And Perry, too."

"I cannot think they mean to stay in France," Henrietta said. "Things there are getting more dangerous by the day."

After Freddy had been shown out, still muttering to himself, Henrietta glanced at the mantle clock. "Aunt Althea and Marsibel will be here soon. Do you want me to take the girls upstairs?"

"No, leave them," Clarinda said. "Your aunt will go on as if Marsibel's wedding is the most important event of the Season, and I would like her to remember that we all have our own worlds." She looked at the bundle in Henrietta's arms. "Does she know yet?"

"Of my quondam marriage proposal, or Darien getting shot? I wonder which will give her more pleasure." Henrietta snuggled the sleeping baby upon her shoulder. "What a lecture she will read about me ruining myself with Lord Daring, when she can't say I wasn't warned."

THE ROOM WAS dim from the drawn curtains and the small fire banked in the hearth. Henrietta pushed the curtains wide and considered throwing up the sash, a habit the nurse at Miss Gregoire's approved despite the known dangers of bad air. In the bed, Darien moaned and thrashed.

"No," he muttered, and then, a hoarse shout of agony. "No! Open it!" he shouted again, raking his hands through the air. "Get him out of there, by God!"

"Darien." When her voice didn't rouse him, Henrietta leaned over and gently pressed his unhurt shoulder. "Darling! You must wake up."

His eyes flew open, and the horror in them pierced her gut. "He's—" He stopped when he recognized her and grasped her shoulders. "Henry. Was it a dream? Thank God. Lucien was locked in the tomb with Horace, but he was alive, and I couldn't get him out."

Her heart twisted. His grief haunted his dreams. She knew that feeling. "It was a nightmare. Your fears speaking to you."

The lines of pain around his mouth and eyes were not purely from his wound. But his color was healthy, and his smile brilliant.

"Did you call me darling?"

"Of course not. Part of your dream." She placed the bowl of warm water next to his bed. "I've come to minister to your wound and, if you feel able, bring you down to dinner."

"Only if I may sit next to you." He grimaced as he struggled to lift himself in the bed, and she leaned forward to pile the pillows behind his back. He wore a shadow of stubble along his face, his hair was mussed, his shirt rumpled, and he smelled of old sweat, a trace of blood, and the acrid whiff of gunpowder. Yet when he turned his face and his breath fell on her cheek, a warm, pleasurable bolt went through her middle. She turned to the bowl.

"Is it a great scandal that I am here? I don't want to trouble Clarinda."

"Pooh. She won't turn you out, unless Jasper insists on it. Aunt Althea raised a fine breeze, though."

She drew his shirt away from his shoulder, focusing on the bandaged wound instead of the broad, smooth expanse of skin revealed to her gaze. "But she railed at Charley for bringing you here drunk as an emperor, so I don't think you'll be arrested for dueling. Charley will say he brought you to sing under my window and you fell ill."

"A time-honored way of wooing," Darien said. "How clever of me."

She frowned as the bandage stuck to his skin. Gently, she dampened the cloth and then peeled the stained strips away. The wound gave her something to concentrate on besides his breadth, his nearness, his scent, his distracting heat.

"Lord Alfred called. He saw the baby."

Darien stilled. "And?"

"I gather that he will accept whatever decision you make about her. He's terribly embarrassed that he shot you after you deloped."

The dratted man grinned. "If you fall in love with me while nursing me back to health, I'll buy him his own set of dueling pistols for a reward." Then he winced as she sponged his wound. "Did he find out anything about Celeste?"

"She left for Calais on a packet late last evening." Henrietta paused. "With your friend Perry. The duke has already sent a man after them."

Darien's shoulders slumped. "Perry!" he swore. "He was the man? All this time?"

"Lord Alfred supposes Celeste seduced you to make Mr. Empson jealous."

"And I fell for it, like a great lumpen clod," Darien said. He looked up at the ceiling. "Could there be anything worse?"

"I'm afraid so," Henrietta said, kneading the sponge in her bowl of water. "Ruf—I mean, Mr. Bales called on Marsibel while she was here. It appears that Mr. Empson took with him some of your clothes, a great deal of your money, and a few of your sketches. Rufie suspects he means to pose as an engineer, or as you, to gain enough credit to live on."

"Damn his eyes," Darien said. "Doesn't he care that Celeste's babe could be his child?"

Henrietta's hands trembled as she sponged the dried blood from Darien's shoulder. "He could come back and claim paternity, couldn't he? It wouldn't matter that Celeste had given her up. The court would rule for the man."

"We'll make him sign something, and the duke as well," Darien promised. "If you want her, Henry. Though I can't think why you should."

"I just do," Henrietta said. "And not because of what happened to my sister, or Mary Ann's son. I—I simply know that she belongs to me."

Darien's eyes held steady on her face, though he winced. "Does it have to be salt water?"

"Nurse swore by it, and in all my days at Miss Gregoire's, I never saw a wound turn putrid."

Darien rested his head on the pillow and regarded the ceiling. "So that is how you find your strays," he said.

"I wish I could explain it." She caressed his bare shoulder with the sponge. "I suppose it is unfair when there are so many in need. But I—sometimes I meet someone, and it feels like they need me, in particular. That it's not simply aid they require, but what I can offer."

"Your dwarf," he said, his eyes dark and intent. "The girl from the workhouse. Celeste's daughter." He paused. "Me?"

She sat back self-consciously. "Turn so I might reach your back. Your cousin brought you a change of clothes."

Dear heaven, the man had a magnificent physique. She wanted to fit herself against that sculpted muscle, rub her cheek against the soft brown hair patching his chest and rib cage. No wonder so many women lost their heads over him.

"I hope Rufie brought something flattering," Darien said. "I wish to impress."

"Darien." She dunked the sponge and moved to the head of the bed, nestling herself behind him. "You do not have to pretend with me."

She moved her hand over the tops of his shoulders, skimming the ends of his hair, as soft as the baby's. The back of his neck was firm and smooth, and she wanted to press her lips there.

"You haven't said yes, Henry." She could feel as well as hear his voice, a low rumble in his chest.

"You dear oaf, I know very well you only kissed me because you feared you might die in a duel the next morning," she said lightly.

"I had no intention of dying," he retorted. "I *wanted* to kiss you."

"Yes, and you've kissed a great many girls you didn't marry. Aunt Althea is right, you know. The son of a marquess can't marry a tradesman's daughter. The latest cartoon claims you staged our little tableau because you want Sir Jasper to fund your inventions, which I think quite clever of you."

"Buffoons," Darien swore. "Did they give me fangs and claws this time?" The muscles in his neck grew taut. "Is a kiss no longer a time-honored way of wooing?"

"For anyone save Lord Daring, perhaps," Henrietta said. She realized the sponge lingered overlong on his lower back, on the sides of his abdomen with their visible bands of muscle. She found it hard to pull her hand away. "Charley says there is a bet in the book at Brooks that you will have a new interest within a fortnight."

"Then tell Charley to lay odds on you, and I'll make him wealthy." He lifted his head. "What do you want, Henry?"

She withdrew, and he turned with a swoop and pulled her down on the bed beside him.

"Your stitches!" she yelped, pressing the sponge to his shoulder.

"You can sew me up again." His gaze pinned her in place, dark and searching. She was in bed with a nearly naked man, and she felt warm and delighted and utterly safe. And something else, something that kindled and leapt through her innards as he reached up with his good hand and brushed his knuckles across her cheek.

"Henry." His voice grated, deep and low. "Do you know the one thing I regretted when I thought Freddy had killed me?"

"Not leading a more virtuous life?"

"Losing you," he whispered and dipped his head.

She met him eagerly, surrendering to an overpowering, incandescent kiss that lit her from the inside out. Excitement swept through her, strange and unfamiliar. His breath came short when he lifted his head, but so did hers.

"Your eyes," she said foolishly, drowning in his gaze. "They change color when you are—"

"Aroused by strong emotion?" He ran a slow, heavy hand from her shoulder to her hip. Molten heat splashed through her belly.

"Angry," she managed to say, "but also—"

"Desire, Henry," he purred. "And you feel it too." He brushed a thumb over her collarbone, cupping her breast with his hand. She whimpered as another wave of heat splashed in her belly. He kissed her deeply and thoroughly, pulling her so she lay half across his body, and she moaned and moved closer.

He tore his mouth from hers and clamped strong hands to her hips so she couldn't move further. "Henry," he choked. "Will you believe now that I *want* to marry you?"

She was beginning to hate the name less. Coming as a hoarse whisper, with his face inflamed with passion, it seemed an endearment, a declaration.

"I thought you did not despoil virgins," she said, sliding off his body.

His slow, delighted smile melted every part of her that wasn't already pudding. He anchored an arm about her to hold her close. "And so I shall not. We will marry in proper fashion, you shall pledge to be buxom at bed and board, and we shall have a wedding night and a honeymoon away from all the world." He pressed a kiss to her forehead. "I see now the appeal of these time-honored traditions."

"No doubt, as they traditionally benefit the male." She pushed off the bed. "You needs must dress for dinner."

Her legs wobbled as she stood. She was ruined in truth, spoiled for any other man. No other would bring leaping to life in her what she felt for Darien Bales.

He had felt this, though. Many, many times before. Men did. They were permitted their passions—encouraged, actually—while women, who were not supposed to harbor passions, paid a high price.

His hot hand roamed up her side, staking a claim already. "I would have waited had I known *you* were coming to me, Henry," he said softly. It was as though he read her thoughts. "But I didn't know."

She turned away, reaching for the fresh bandage. "Mary Wollstonecraft does not approve of marrying for love alone."

"What possible reason could she give for such lunacy?" His hand fell away.

"She says love should not dethrone superior powers. And fondness is a poor substitute for friendship."

His brows snapped together. "Is Miss Wollstonecraft married?"

"She is not. But she says that caresses cannot satisfy a noble mind that longs for respect." He held silent as she began wrapping his shoulder. "I feel in very distinguished company, you know. The women whom Lord Daring has ruined. A duke's daughter, then me. All this effort merely to spite your father."

He flinched. "That was never the plan. Never."

"Oh, your plan was to use Marsibel to gain influence with Sir Pelton? But I kept getting in the way, didn't I." Henrietta tucked in the ends of the bandage.

"Sad to say, your friend Perry has planted the rumor, and people like Miss Pennyroyal believe it. Regardless of what the gossips say, you have achieved your aim—my uncle is in your debt. There is no reason to carry on the charade, Darien. Havering will talk to his father, Freddy will influence his, and Lady Mama will speak to the Earl of Warrefield. You will have lords enough to stand against your father's suit. You need not antagonize him by pretending you mean to throw away your name and legacy on a mill owner's daughter."

His hand closed over hers as she picked up his shirt. "Why can you not believe I wish to marry you?"

Because the very notion was inconceivable. She might prove the curiosity of a moment, but she was not of his world. A Henrietta Wardley-Hines had nothing to offer a Lord Darien Bales, son of a marquess.

"A Long Meg and an antidote, with questionable political beliefs? You ought to fear I would sully the family name, especially now."

A muscle flickered along his jaw. "Pitt won't dare look cross at you if you're betrothed to me."

Henrietta concentrated on tying the strings of his shirt. That was true. The prime minister would not antagonize a powerful lord. She would not be accused of treason or transported. She would not sink her family, stain the Wardley name. She would step into the ranks of the nobility, have the protection of the Bales name, and gain a husband who—

As she reached for his waistcoat, Darien lifted his hand and deliberately placed it on her hip. Her mind blanked as liquid warmth washed through her.

He smiled, his eyes heavy lidded. "I want you, Henry," he said, watching her face. "And you want me. I think those grounds enough for marriage."

He knew the weakness she felt at his touch, the desire to press as close to his body as possible. And she saw he would use his advantage. He was not the same breed as Lord Pinochle, true. But he was a man all the same, lured by the pleasures of the flesh.

Passing, unstable pleasures when compared to the delights of a sturdy, well-stocked mind. Darien might believe that romantic fancies could overcome the vast difference in their stations, but those illusions would dissolve when the real challenges emerged.

"This is exactly why Miss Wollstonecraft disapproves," Henrietta said, stripping his hand from her hip and striving to gather her wits. "That a woman should give over her future, her property, her security, and her livelihood, all for passion, which can change from one day to the next. I confess I feel there should be a more equal exchange, in the general way of things. Now, put on this coat and come to dinner. And no more seductive looks from you, Lord *Daring*, or Charley shall turn you into the street."

She buttoned him into his coat and made herself a promise. Her future was already in peril, depending on what Prime Minister Pitt decided about her case. She would not lose her mind over this man.

She had already lost her heart, but that was an unreliable organ anyway. She could survive without it.

CHAPTER TWENTY-THREE

A marquess's son upstairs, a duke's son in the parlor, a viscount's heir leaving his card; Lady Mama made no secret of her delight at the quality of persons circulating through her home. But she was just as surprised as Henrietta when the Earl of Warrefield knocked on the door of Hines House.

"Papa!" Clarinda said, ringing for tea. "I didn't know you were in town."

"Need to be in my seat if there's talk of war." The earl handed Dearbody his hat and walking stick. "Havey-cavey business coming down the line. What on earth are they thinking across the Channel? Bunch of boisterous frogs."

"I believe the Jacobins have many valid complaints," Henrietta said, sorting the stack of correspondence. "Representation in government, for one, which was exactly what the American colonists quarreled with us about."

"Hetty, you featherbrain," Warrefield exclaimed. "Is it true Pitt's bringing a suit against you for disturbing the King's peace?"

Henrietta dropped a letter through nerveless fingers. "Lady Bess warned me there might be a complaint. She thinks it a strong advert for the Minerva Society, but I cannot say I like the idea."

"I should say not! Ain't her neck if you get tossed in the watch house again."

"You heard about that?" Henrietta asked in a faint voice. "Lady Bess thinks the attention will be good for our causes, and now that the National Assembly in France has abolished slavery, she thinks our petition—"

"Oh, *hang* your petition," Warrefield exclaimed. "You'll never get the Lords to go for it, and that's that. But you will season a fine stew for your father if your name gets drawn through the muck, and he's responsible for you, you know! What if they seize his assets and have him declared traitor to the Crown? Pitt's mad enough about this French business to do it."

Henrietta sat down next to Lady Clarinda. So this was the heart of the earl's concern. The Wardley-Hines fortune, after the union of their families, had refortified the Warrefield name and dignity by replenishing its coffers, and his successful son-in-law continued to quietly subsidize many of the earl's favorite pursuits that his estates, large and profitable as they were, could not support in the manner he desired.

"What do you suggest, Papa?" Clarinda inquired.

"Well, hanged if I know," her father snapped. "Where's Pell Mell when you need him? He ought to come up with some defense. A Whig if I ever saw one, but he's a head on his shoulders for all that."

"I did mean to go north," Henrietta said. "Look in on some of Papa's mills, then Birch Vale. Though I should hate to leave—"

"Clary?" The earl frowned and shot a look at his daughter. "She can't travel now. Too close to her time, and too fat to fit in a carriage besides."

"Yes, Lady Mama will stay here until after her confinement," Henrietta answered. "But I have other...obligations." Her thoughts went to the man upstairs, who was tossing in a feverish sleep, and higher still, where a new infant had command of the nursery.

"Well, we must get you out of the scrape somehow," the earl groused. "My countess will plague me until you do. Already afraid she can't hold her head up, what with you running around with this Daring."

"And why should she be concerned if I have been seen once or twice with Lord Darien?" Henrietta asked, indignant.

The earl stared. "Tare an' hounds! You think we want our name on the list of families he's ruined? Highcastle's already getting laughed out of White's, can't find his daughter or her lover or her throw. The countess will have my hide if we get grouped in with them. I like Langford, but I must say, he got a rotten deal with his sons. Lost his first heir, can't find his second, and can't bring to heel the third. Makes me glad I had daughters, trouble though they be."

"To have Papa in town!" Clarinda murmured after her sire took his leave. "I suppose I shall have to call on the countess, though perhaps you oughtn't come with me, Hetty. At the very least we must invite her to dine."

"I knew I should have left town," Henrietta muttered. "A suit against me! For treason, or something else? Lady Mama, I never meant to bring down such trouble on your and Papa's heads."

"Jasper will sort everything," Clarinda said. "Did Lady Bessington promise to call today? My word, there has been quite a parade of nobility in these rooms. Dearbody is beside himself with joy."

But even Clarinda was astonished by their next visitor.

"The Marquess of Langford, mum." Dearbody hovered in

the doorway of Darien's chamber, gazing with wonder upon the card he held.

Henrietta sat on Darien's bed, repairing his shoulder after he'd torn out the surgeon's stitches with another nightmare. Clarinda sat in a low chair against the wall, embroidering baby linens. Darien scowled like a man who had been shot and was not taking pleasure in his recovery.

"Devil take it. Rufie will have told him something that put a bee in his bonnet, I don't doubt. Lady Clarinda, I apologize profoundly."

"I haven't seen your father in an age," Clarinda murmured. "Bring him down, Hetty, when he's dressed?"

But the marquess wasn't content to wait. Henrietta heard a deep male voice in the hall when Clarinda stepped out. "Lady Clarinda, you will forgive the intrusion, but I must see my son."

"Milord Langford. You might have heard that I have the honor to be addressed as Lady Wardley-Hines now. Lord Darien will join us as soon as he is able."

"I must see him immediately. I have several appointments today, and I'm afraid they cannot wait."

"I see," said Clarinda. "How distressing to learn your son was injured in a matter of honor."

"What, the duel? Not surprised at all he got into a mill. Rather expecting it. No, I am here to stop this marriage!"

"Oh?" A long pause ensued. "Oh. Then by all means, milord."

A tall, broad man strode into the room. He was built on Darien's lines but heavier, with a powdered white wig and Darien's piercing blue eyes. Henrietta froze with her needle in the air. The marquess froze as his eyes followed the line of thread to his son's bare chest, taking in Darien sitting on the bed clad in nothing but his stockings and breeches. His lordship paled.

"If it isn't my worthy sire," Darien drawled. "Come to read me another juniper lecture?"

"Scandal enough you've engaged in another duel, puppy," the marquess barked. "What's this Rufie says about you getting married?"

"Henrietta, dear," Clarinda said, reseating herself with her embroidery, "the Marquess of Langford. My lord, this is Henrietta Wardley-Hines, daughter of Sir Jasper Wardley-Hines."

The marquess glared at Henrietta. "I mean no insult, Clarinda," he growled, "but my son cannot marry your daughter."

"Finally!" Henrietta exclaimed. "Someone who can talk some sense into him. I've had no success in the matter."

This gave the marquess pause. His pointed gaze swung to his son. "You'll want to excuse the ladies while we discuss the matter. This is between us."

"As you can see, I am presently occupied." Darien winced as Henrietta threaded the needle through his flesh. "As you intruded upon us, we might as well have it out here, and Henry can bring up any reasons you've forgotten. She's already gone through most of the arguments why I can't marry her."

"Listen to your father, Darien," Henrietta scolded, keeping her eyes on her task. She'd donned her old muslin gown that morning and pinned her hair up in a floppy lace cap. Perhaps her looking like a scullery maid might add weight to his lordship's argument. His was likely the only voice his son would heed.

"Well, you can't," the marquess said. "When I told you to get married, pup, I didn't mean cast yourself away on anyone. A tradesman's daughter, of all things!"

"Although you will have heard, I am sure, that Jasper was recently made Knight Bachelor," Clarinda murmured from her seat. "And Hetty's brother, Sir Charleton, is the 8th Baronet

Wardley. So her family is not exactly low. The Wardleys have been long established in Cheshire."

"Not as long as the Bales have been in Langford," the marquess snapped. "A woman may marry below her rank, but not a man, and not my heir."

"That is precisely what I told him," Henrietta said, setting another stitch in Darien's skin. "The Hines are tradesmen and farmers' sons. I doubt any of your friends would receive me. Go on, sir. Objection one—the class difference is too large, and not at all to his credit. Objection two?"

"Money," the marquess said instantly. "We're nowhere near dun territory, but you cannot afford to marry where you wish, pup. You'll need a bride with a handsome dowry."

"You heard him," Darien said to Henrietta, watching her fingers with the needle and thread. "Your paltry interest in your father's mills at Salford will not do, though Sir Jasper tells me you enjoy a profit of several thousand pounds a year."

"Three, maybe five thousand at most," Henrietta said. "And the bulk of it is reinvested or goes to saving for mills of my own. Hold still."

"Wool?" the marquess asked, momentarily diverted.

"No, cotton, most of which comes from India and Belgium since I object to the way that cotton is raised in the Americas. Jasper is known for his innovations," Henrietta said with pride. "And I mean to engage your son to engineer a drainage system for my farm. He is a very talented draughtsman, you know."

"Idle sketches," the marquess said. "Fine for a lesser gentleman to be a hobbyist, but not the son of a marquess."

"Did you wed me, you would have my engineering services for free," Darien said to Henrietta. "Otherwise you will be obliged to pay me substantial fees for my time."

"Will you please hold still." Henrietta bit her lip and leaned closer. "I think one or two more stitches will do it."

"You have forgotten Birch Vale, Hetty," Clarinda said in her musical voice. "I know it is very little, only what—three thousand acres?"

"Three thousand acres?" the marquess said. "Three thousand pounds a year?"

"With a good harvest, though the place is in need of improvements. I would like to see what Lord Darien has done with The Revels. He tells me he designed a canal for Bellamy. I have considered one for shipping our butter."

"You do have the most excellent butter," Clarinda said. "I shall call for tea and some bread. I think Lord Langford would like a taste." She rang a small bell and spoke in a quiet undertone to the maid who appeared.

"Something in the water, do you suppose?" Darien asked, watching Henrietta set another neat, careful stitch.

"No, I think it is the feed. Our milk is very sweet." She tugged slightly at the thread, and he grimaced. She sponged away the drop of blood with her saline rinse. The marquess watched her, an alert, calculating expression in his eyes.

"Objection three," Henrietta said. "Darien needs a fashionable wife. I would be a terrible hostess. I have very radical opinions."

"Henry has a deplorable sense of style," Darien told his father. "She won't spend a sovereign more than she must to clothe herself, and she'll let anyone dress her. She'll never bankrupt her husband with gowns and fripperies."

"I have Duprix to dress me, thank you," Henrietta said. She tied off the thread, then leaned forward and bit through it. "Have you told your father I was taken up by the watch?"

"Put in the bridewell?" The marquess recoiled.

"Yes, political dissenter," Darien said solemnly. "Had to go myself and bail her out, with the help of her uncle—you know Sir Pelton, I'm sure. Pitt's cracking down on public debates, and

Henry got herself caught up with the London Corresponding Society. Put Pitt's nose quite out of joint."

"He could use it," the marquess said. "Can't say I hold with Fox and all his pot-stirring, but Pitt's a mushroom trying to get out of his father's shade. Do him good to have some air let out." He regarded Henrietta with narrowed eyes. "Bluestocking, are you?"

"It is my dearest hope to be made a votary of the Minerva Society," she confirmed. "Lady Bessington has been a mentor and a great inspiration to me."

"Ah, Bess," the marquess said, and his face softened with a memory that lit his eyes and made his mouth curve in a smile. "There's not many a dame like her anymore. She reminds me a good deal of my marchioness."

"I do wish I could have met Lady Langford," Clarinda murmured. "I'm told she was a great one for causes, and very clever besides."

"Translated Italian poetry," the marquess said with a proud smile. "Work of some Renaissance poet. Febea, I think."

Henrietta put down her sponge. "Febea!" she exclaimed. "The Earl of Warrefield has a copy of her *Orlando Furioso*. It was a very small printing, and I've never found a copy of my own."

"Well, I can give you one," the marquess said grandly. "And perhaps let you look at a few of her old papers besides."

"I'd be very much obliged to you," Henrietta said, dazzled.

"But perhaps not until after you've had your tour of the King's collection," Darien said. "His Majesty envies Warrefield his catalogue so much that he's considering hiring Henry to make one for him."

"A commission from King George?" The marquess blinked. Not even he, with his rank, ran tame through Buckingham

House, where the royal family liked to withdraw from the public halls of St. James.

"We are losing sight of our objectives," Henrietta scolded as Darien picked up his discarded shirt. "No, you needn't wear that old thing. I've a fresh one for you."

"I beg your pardon for my state, Clarinda," Darien said, glancing at his hostess.

"No need," Clarinda said with calm composure. "I am an old and happily married lady. Though Hetty is not."

"He is my patient," Henrietta said. Being this close to a nearly naked Darien made her stomach turn like churned butter, but it would gain her nothing to let the others see her in such a state. "Besides, it's nothing I haven't seen before. He looks just like Lord Ellesmere's Apollo."

Darien gave her a wicked smile as he handed her his rumpled shirt. "Are you comparing me to a Greek god?"

Vain, irritating man. Henrietta waved a hand toward his chest. "You must be aware of your...attributes."

"I am," Darien said smugly as he held out his arms. "But I didn't think *you* were."

Henrietta glanced at the marquess as Darien's head disappeared into his shirt. His lordship's ire had been replaced with a hungry, frightened look that she felt embarrassed to witness. Lord Langford had seen how close he'd come to losing son number three.

"So, class," Darien said, his voice muffled as he emerged from the voluminous shirt. "Unfashionable dress, unfashionable opinions, and not enough money. Henry, I think you told me you have not much of a settlement."

"True," Henrietta agreed, arranging the ruffles of his shirt-front. She had the distracting urge to kiss his skin before it disappeared beneath his clothing. "I use my income from

Jasper's mills to improve Birch Vale, and Papa has settled most everything on Lady Mama and the babies, as he ought."

"Ten thousand pounds for your dowry, Hetty," Clarinda said mildly. "And the inheritance from your mother when you turn five and twenty?"

"Oh. I'd forgotten about my dowry. And I plan on using Mama's inheritance to rebuild my mill, if Hodge sells to me. So that ten thousand is already spoken for." Henrietta buttoned Darien's waistcoat. Her stomach shifted again when she looked up to find everyone watching her. "What?"

"She comes with an estate, an interest in her father's mills, and twenty thousand pounds?" The marquess wheeled on Clarinda. "How is it she is not married already?"

Clarinda shrugged. "Henrietta has only just been presented, and she has been too busy to entertain suitors."

"She has some philosophical objections to marriage," Darien said. "The law's attitude toward women's property, or some such."

"The law's habit of regarding women *as* property," Henrietta reminded him. This conversation was veering from the course she'd plotted for it. "Whatever I bring to my marriage will become my husband's, his to use and dispose of as he may please. I have no wish to find myself in the position of Mrs. Pennyroyal. Now, tell me how I am to tie this impossible cravat."

The marquess watched as Darien held a hand mirror in his good hand and directed this next and most important step in his toilette. Henrietta did the best she could, slapping his hand away when he tried interfering. But when she looked up, she found Darien watching her with an impossible affection in his eyes.

Her breath dissolved into a tight, warm glow in her chest.

"A bluestocking for my son?" The marquess lifted a brow.

"Another Wollstonecraft in the making," Darien confirmed.

His lordship shuddered. "Bah. Well, anything can be got 'round with the right settlements. I could give her another ten thousand for her jointure, if she makes a respectable man of you, and five thousand apiece for your children."

Henrietta paused with her hands at Darien's throat, feeling the heat wafting from him to her fingertips. "You cannot be suggesting what it seems you are suggesting, sir."

"Oh, look, here's tea," Clarinda announced as a maid opened the connecting door to Henrietta's sitting room. "Shall we go through? Hetty's parlor has the loveliest light, and Langford, I should like to offer you bread and some of this excellent butter."

She processed into the sitting room, and the marquess followed. Henrietta made a hurried adjustment to Darien's coat and tugged him to his feet.

"Your father—" she began.

But as Darien stepped into her parlor, he froze. The opposite door to her sleeping chamber stood open and Mary Ann leaned over the bed, cooing as she unwrapped a tiny infant, who stared at her with a newborn's total concentration.

"Oh, Hetty," Clarinda said from behind the tea service. "Mary Ann asked if she might bring up the baby. Is this a bad time?"

Darien didn't move, his gaze fixed on the other room and the occupant of the broad four-poster bed. Henrietta stopped breathing as she watched the expressions move over his face.

The marquess frowned and looked at Clarinda. "I thought you were—?" He tried and failed not to look at her enlarged waistline.

"Henrietta has taken in a ward," Clarinda said. "Lady Celeste's daughter."

"Where did she come by that whelp?"

"Found it in a parsley bed, of course," Henrietta said, moving toward the bedchamber.

The marquess's horrified tone was a bracing slap to attention. Darien had warned her that Polite Society wouldn't accept her as a mother. But thanks to her spectacular display at her debate, she no longer had reason to think society's approval within her reach anyway.

She cared what Darien thought, though.

"I am told Lady Celeste was called away to the Continent," Clarinda said. "Hetty was so good as to give the child a home."

The marquess, too, stared through the door at the baby. "Baseborn brat," he said under his breath. "The only thing my son has ever produced. And in your house, Clarinda? I am surprised you allow it."

Clarinda paused with her hand over the teapot. "My lord, every child's life is precious. You know that as much as I."

The hurt stood out in his lordship's face, the same pain Henrietta had seen in Darien's eyes. All four of them paused for a moment in tableau, bound by their shared knowledge of loss.

"If you will excuse me," Henrietta said. "I want to see Celestina while she is awake. Newborns sleep all the time, did you know that?"

"You may...bring her in here," Darien said, pausing near a chair. "My father can leave if he does not wish to see his grandchild."

"That is not my grandchild," the marquess said swiftly.

"Then that leaves you with Horatia," Darien said. "Unless Lucien has some family we don't know about."

"Damn you," the marquess choked, glaring at his son. "Do you think it amusing to taunt me? You won't find a wife who will take your by-blow."

"Henry already has," Darien said and followed her into the room.

~

"SHE'S SO TINY," Darien whispered, overcome with awe.

Henrietta sat on the bed like a cozy Madonna, the baby nestled in her lap. Her hair was coming loose from her cap, and her eyes, which had been a stormy gray all through the interview with his father, had subsided to their customary gray green.

She sent the wet nurse away, and Darien swallowed the strange urge to thank the girl for caring for his daughter. One did not thank the servants, who were paid to dispatch their business, but he wondered how she must feel, watching another child thrive in her care when she had not been able to nourish her own.

In the next room, Clarinda sat with his father, sipping tea and no doubt discussing marriage settlements. Lady Clarinda was as canny as her husband when it came to business dealings. She had dangled Henrietta—or rather, her properties—like a piece of choice meat before a famished dog.

"Look at her fingers," Darien said, moved.

Henrietta held a tiny digit. "Look at her toes. Every nail is perfect."

"And her eyebrows."

"She scrunches her brow in a very fierce way sometimes. It reminds me of you."

"Her eyes are so blue. Just like mine."

Henrietta leaned closer and peered at the baby, who peered back. "But hers don't have that ring of violet around the iris. I suspect she will be beautiful, much like her mother." She laughed. "I shall not know how to teach her to deal with men. But Lady Mama can."

Darien watched Henrietta, not the child. His Henry continued to surprise him. Sitting here like this, she was the most beautiful woman he had ever met, with her elegant shoulders and regal neck, her determined jaw and fierce chin, those eyes as mysterious and inviting as the depths of a forest.

Impossible for her to pretend she did not want him. He knew she did.

"My solicitor wrote that he has found a family for her," he said cautiously. "A church sexton and his wife, with three children of their own."

She stilled, her finger caught in the baby's small fist. Her cinnamon curls fell over her face, hiding her profile.

"They cannot give her what I can."

"Henry, you saw my father's reaction. You will hear the same from all sides. A young unmarried woman cannot adopt a baseborn brat."

"You asked me to marry you. You could adopt her. Make her yours in truth."

Men of his rank rarely acknowledged their bastards. But the thought that the child might truly be his stirred a wasp's nest of emotion in Darien's chest. Amidst the turmoil he felt an aching wish to sit with Henrietta just like this, picking out their individual features in a child of their own, one they made together.

"An illegitimate child in the nursery with our trueborn children? It isn't done."

She bit out a laugh. "It is done all the time. Lady Melbourne has several cuckoos in her nest, and they say the Duchess of Devonshire plans to bring home her...indiscretion."

Darien saw her rigid back and shoulders. "I am thinking of you, Henry. Each time you look at her, especially if she resembles Celeste, you'll be forced to recall—" He swallowed. It wasn't infidelity. He couldn't imagine wanting any other woman now. No other woman could fascinate him as she did. "My past."

She raised her eyes in that curious, direct manner of hers.

"When I look at Celestina, I will simply see *her*," she said. "The same way I simply see you."

Darien's throat went dry. The soft down of the bed felt like knives under his thigh. Impossible that she could see him, all of him, and love him. Not after all he had done.

"Are you accepting my hand?" he managed.

She swaddled the baby and held her out. "Do you wish to hold her?"

"I might drop her," Darien said, alarmed.

"It is not that difficult." Henrietta rose, smiling. "You make a basket with your arms and hold her in it." She demonstrated.

"Henry." He cleared his throat, and she paused before the connecting door. "I think my father was in earnest, that he will settle something on you if you marry me."

Her eyes grew stormy. "He came here expressly to forbid you to marry me!"

Darien laughed at her expression, though it made his shoulder hurt. "I suspect you won him over. He never could resist a strong, managing, housewifely sort of woman."

"Housewifely! I am an activist and a reformer. I told him that."

Darien nodded. "So was my mother. A firebrand and a scholar, involved in more charities than we could count. It made her an excellent wife and mother, and an even better marchioness."

Henrietta shook her head with a little *tsk*. "I find it hard to believe that my paltry ten thousand would sway your father in my favor."

"If he has tasted your butter," Darien said, "he might offer for you himself."

"Don't be absurd." She opened the door and went still as stone.

"And here she is," Clarinda said. "Duchess, may I present

my daughter, Henrietta. Hetty, dear, I believe you've met the Duchess of Highcastle? Lord Langford and I were so cozy, I hope you don't mind that I received her here."

The duchess glared at Henrietta. She was magnificent and awful in an ornate *polonaise* robe, her powdered hair built into a towering edifice atop which perched a picture hat piled with feathers. Her features gathered into a mask of fury as Darien stepped to Henrietta's side.

"You!" she said, the word an epithet. "You...defiler of women!"

"Careful, Medora," said the marquess, settled into a Hepplewhite chair with a plate full of buttered bread. "He's not the one who twirled her off to the Continent."

"He might have married her," the duchess spat. "Instead of throwing her over like a hothouse strumpet."

"I am very sorry, madam," Darien said, "but I do not think your daughter wished me for a husband."

"The heir to Langford?" the duchess said. "We could have paid off Havering! We had to anyway."

"My father has an heir," Darien said, his eyes traveling across the room. "My brother Lucien."

"We'll not discuss it here," the marquess warned.

The duchess regarded the bundle in Henrietta's arms. "Freddy said it was here," she said with great scorn. "I suppose you're pleased, since you came banging on the door to get it. The front door, of all things. So the entire square might see a tradesman's daughter on my stoop."

"A knight's daughter, Medora." The marquess sipped his tea.

The duchess's eagle eyes turned to Henrietta. "What is its name, then?"

"Celestina, Your Grace."

The duchess snorted. "To remind us ever of our shame. How lovely."

Darien slipped his good arm around Henrietta's waist, lending her silent support. His Henry felt calm and warm and strong.

"The duke won't own it," the duchess warned.

"I do not require him to," Darien said evenly. "I shall be the child's guardian. Celeste surrendered her rights when she sent the child to Henrietta."

Henrietta's shoulders stiffened, and he squeezed her lightly. She must know they had to provide a united front, or the duchess would scent blood and pounce.

"She'll be knocking up my door again, I don't doubt, the next time she wants something," the duchess said. Her eyes dipped to the infant, who stared unblinking at the feathers of her hat. The duchess looked away.

"I won't ask a thing from you or the duke," Henrietta promised. "Darien is having papers drawn up by his solicitors. She will be my daughter."

There was no talking her out of it now, he saw. He'd been hoisted by his own petard.

"And what will you do with her?" the duchess snapped. "Bring her up to trade?"

"I have an estate she may inherit," Henrietta said. "And who knows but that she will be interested in running my mills."

"If you don't find yourself in prison or transported. Don't you know Pitt means to bring a suit against you?"

The color left Henrietta's face. "Suit?" Darien asked.

"There won't be a suit once their betrothal is announced. Pitt won't dare reach for such high fruit. I'll squash him like the toad-eater he is," the marquess said.

"Pitt called up every police force in the city to monitor our debate," Henrietta said hollowly. "I don't doubt he means to make an example of me."

"You forget that Sir Pelton will speak to Mr. Pitt," Clarinda murmured, "and Sir Jasper will have some influence. Your Grace, another dish of tea?"

Darien could tell Henrietta was not reassured by these promises. Determined always to stand on her own two feet, she never believed anyone would rescue her. He gave her another squeeze. He had to find a way to make her believe he would shield her, no matter what. He had to convince her to trust him with her fortune, her future, her assorted wards and charges.

He had to prove himself worthy of her trust.

The duchess turned her stony glare on Darien. "Freddy said you meant to marry her. A bit ridiculous, Daring, all the girls you've compromised, to throw yourself over for a bluestocking."

"That's my new daughter, Medora," the marquess said, "and my granddaughter, too. Hold that viperous tongue, if you don't mind."

"You'd best watch your step, Cassius," the duchess replied. "Highcastle knows about the suit you mean to bring in Lords, and he's not inclined to favor it, given the reputation of your erstwhile *heir*."

"The inheritance must be settled," the marquess retorted, "and Highcastle knows that as well as I do. He'd best hope he won't be fighting his own suit. Your son challenged mine to a duel, remember."

Her Grace's eyebrows, artificially dark, snapped together in a marvelous scowl. "You wouldn't dare!"

"I won't cry rope on Freddy," Darien said, shifting on his feet. He ached to sit down, but the duchess would take it as a sign of weakness.

"Well, *I* might," the marquess said and sank his teeth into a piece of bread and butter.

The duchess held perfectly still, only the ostrich features on her outrageous hat trembling from the force of her wrath. "What do you want?" she said to Darien in a strained voice.

"Nothing from you," Darien replied. "Freddy and I have settled the matter of the family's honor." He moved his arm slightly in its sling.

He willed Henrietta not to make one of her remarks. She had a neck-or-nothing brother; she must know it was customary for men of their rank to shoot at each other in the morning, then have a drink and cards together that night.

Clarinda spoke. "It might do to arrange something for the child."

"What? Dower her? Unacceptable," the duchess said through gritted teeth.

Henrietta lifted her chin. "I would consider a trust for Celestina's education," she said. "There is a school in Bath, Miss Gregoire's Academy for Girls, where I spent many happy years. I hope to send Celestina there, if Darien approves."

"I expect I will," Darien said. "The more I hear of this Miss Gregoire, the more I like her."

Finally—finally—she looked up at him and smiled. She hadn't believed he was on her side. Well, she would find out. He meant to stay at her side as long as she would have him.

"There you have it, Medora," the marquess said. "Set up a trust for the child's schooling. She'll learn how to support herself in the world, and she'll never come with hand out to you for money."

"She'll have me—" Darien began, but Henrietta, without appearing to move, elbowed him in the ribs on his uninjured side.

"Oh, very well," the duchess said with ill grace. "If you promise not to prosecute Freddy for shooting you, and if you give me your word this child will never trouble me nor the duke for acknowledgement. You may have your solicitors get in touch with Highcastle's."

"Thank you, Your Grace," Henrietta said, holding the child close.

The duchess turned, her plumed hat nodding. "Well, Clarinda, you must be very pleased with yourself! We all thought you'd lowered yourself abominably when you married, but here you are with your husband made knight, and now his daughter is going to marry into a marquessate."

"I have indeed been very fortunate," Clarinda answered, one hand on her middle. "In most everything."

"I hope *your* daughters never shame you as mine has," the duchess said, pulling on her gloves. She advanced to the door and glared as the marquess drew to his feet. "If you see Highcastle at the club, have a drink with him, will you? He's dreadfully cut up by all this."

"I'll make a point of it," the marquess agreed.

"Well, good day, then," the duchess said. "Clarinda, I'll send a footman round to you later. I want to know where you get that butter."

"And just like that," Henrietta said after the duchess departed, "you're all friends again, and will chum together at the clubs, even though you ruined her daughter and her son shot you."

"Well, of course," the marquess said. "There ain't that many of us at this rank, gel. We may fight like the sons of Atreus, but we have to stick together in the end."

"You'll get used to it," Darien said.

"She is learning," Clarinda said kindly. "And now her daughter is provided for. Well done, Hetty."

"That's one solved," the marquess said with a nod. "Once Jasper is home, we'll draw up settlements, so that's another." He set his plate aside.

"I haven't agreed to anything," Henrietta reminded them all, but no one was listening. The marquess regarded his son.

"There's one more matter we need to settle, puppy," he said.

CHAPTER TWENTY-FOUR

Darien heard the stir below when Sir Jasper returned that afternoon, shaking off the dust of the Great North Road. There followed the sound of quick, booted steps on the stairs first to the family parlor, then the nursery as Jasper threw himself into the embrace of his loving wife and daughters. Darien wondered what explanation was being given for his presence, and what Jasper would have to say about it.

Jasper was quite a different father than the marquess had been, taking a keener interest in his children's daily lives. Darien knew which pattern he would follow if Henrietta ever granted him the great good fortune of setting up a household with him.

He set aside his book when Henrietta came in later, her face drawn and white, to report that a summons had come from a footman in royal livery, scheduling an audience with His Majesty the King at the request of Prime Minister Pitt. Clarinda convened a war council, calling it dinner, and the marquess consented to attend.

Darien intercepted his father when he arrived at Hines House. He needed to warn him, in private, of the role Wardley-Hines funds had played in the wars in Mysore. The marquess might change his mind about Henrietta, though Darien would not.

"His money supported General Cornwallis's troops?" The marquess stood at the window of the blue parlor, looking over the square, his fists clenched over the skirts of his dress coat. Darien thought again of those white streaks beneath his wig.

"For the Third War, as I understand it," Darien answered.

The marquess sighed heavily and turned. "That wasn't the battle that took Lucien anyway. He disappeared after the Treaty of Mangalore, after the Second War. I wish to God I knew where he is." He met his son's eyes, his expression bleak. "Kings will have their way with us, lad. 'Tis how the world turns."

Not in the American colonies, Darien thought, and it seemed not in France either. His father belonged to an old order, as did the Wardleys. But the Hines were of a new order, one that prided industry over birth and name. Darien offered her an alliance with one of Britain's oldest peerages, and Henrietta Wardley-Hines was the only woman in the realm who did not spring at the title.

He wondered what it would take to persuade her. What he could possibly offer that would make her want to bind herself to him.

"Hello, Uncle Daring," said a timid voice, and Darien turned with disbelief as a young woman entered the room. She was a slim young thing of fourteen, with yards of midnight hair and the Bales blue eyes.

"Horatia? Why on earth did he drag you down from Bellamy Hall?"

"Grandfather thought I might like to see London."

Darien guessed that producing his niece was a last, desperate gambit in his father's campaign to guilt Darien into taking charge of Horace's estate. The girl did not appear to be thriving in his cousin Rathbone's care; she was rail-thin and dressed in a childish white frock that accented her pallor. The knowledge was a fresh lash in an open wound. Darien had failed Lucretius, and he was failing Horatia too.

Henrietta took the girl in hand before introductions were completed. "You lovely thing! Come meet my sisters and the baby," and she whisked Horatia to the nursery, no doubt to regale his impressionable niece with tales of reform societies, charitable works, and Wollstonecraft. By the time they sat to table, Henrietta had brought another stray to her bosom and Horatia was in thrall.

Darien could not say he was surprised. Who would not want to be in Henrietta's orbit? Who would not want to dwell in that pure, sane, steady light?

It occurred to him that he might use Horatia to ally Henrietta to his cause, then realized over dinner that his father intended to use the same tactic. The marquess responded to Sir Jasper's friendly questions about Bellamy with a grim picture of an estate left in limbo after Lucretius died. With the legal guardian absent, Rathbone could spend the estate's income as he wished but saw no reason to invest in the land or Horatia's care.

Construction on the canal Darien designed had stalled, and after a bad harvest, the tenants had ground the year's seed corn to get them through the winter. Hoof-rot had decimated the sheepfold, and there were more women and children in the workhouse than the parish had ever seen. Rathbone raised rents and yet claimed there was no money for improvements, while he and his wife attended the races, hunting parties, and assembly balls.

Henrietta's eyes lit with a fire Darien recognized as the marquess described a forsaken people who, while not yet in starvation, were watching it limp down the road toward them.

"All this because Lord Lucien was lost in Mysore." Sir Jasper put down his knife. "You must know the King used a loan of mine to fund the last war."

"I do not hold you responsible." The marquess's gaze held steady, as did his voice.

"I do." Quite against convention, Jasper stood and walked down the table to where the marquess sat in the place of honor next to Clarinda. "My condolences, Langford. And my apologies as well."

He extended his hand, and the marquess rose and gravely shook it. Charley raised his glass to Darien, a silent offering, and Darien drank with him. Charley had brought him to Henry and thereby saved him. One Bales life for another.

"Hetty rang a peal over my head, if you must know," Jasper said as he seated himself. "She won't have our family support war, and I agree."

"Will my son be a hen-pecked husband?" the marquess asked.

Jasper laughed. "They'll need breeches of two sizes in that house, for certain." He smiled down the table at his daughter, who sat beside Darien, cutting his food into tiny pieces.

"To peace!" Sir Pelton proclaimed, lifting his wine in a toast. The footmen rushed forward to fill glasses.

"And what arrangement has been made for your schooling, Miss Bales?" Henrietta asked. She heaped spinach pudding onto the girl's plate after spooning a healthy portion for Darien. "At Miss Gregoire's Academy in Bath, we were allowed to study anything we liked. Miss Gregoire does not hold that female education should be restricted to music and dancing and art."

"I am not allowed dancing," said Horatia. "Aunt Perdita says it would be improper to have a young man teach me. I am only to practice with my friends, but I don't have any friends."

"Doesn't she—" Darien began, but Henrietta cut him off.

"Art and music, then?"

Horatia shook her head. "Too frivolous. She will have tutors for her girls, and I may learn from them when they are older. I am allowed to study French and a little history."

"Astronomy?" Henrietta said. "Mathematics? The natural sciences? Miss Gregoire says philosophy is the foundation of any education."

Horatia accepted a generous helping of beef ragout. "How I should adore a place like Miss Gregoire's."

"You will fit right in. All the girls there are very lively and smart."

"I am not at all à la mode," Horatia said, comparing her plain frock to Henrietta's elegant open robe of green satin, which brought out the green in her eyes. She looked with envy at the embroidered coral stomacher and the graceful fall of the sleeves. "Aunt has dresses made for her daughters, but—"

"I daresay your aunt could feed you better," Henrietta went on, serving the younger girl another helping of mushroom fricassee. Horatia ate not as one starved, so long deprived as to be ill or without appetite, but as a healthy and growing girl whose diet was restricted more than was good for her. "I perceive your aunt favors the welfare of her own children above yours."

Her mild tone held no accusation, but Rutherford looked stricken. Darien suffered another lashing of guilt.

Horatia focused on her plate. "My aunt and uncle have been most generous," she said carefully. "My aunt has been good enough to see to my keeping, even though I have a mother who—" Her voice broke, but she recovered and plunged through. "A mother who ought to take charge of my care and conduct, instead of racketing through Europe with her cicisbeo." Her tone quavered on the last words. "It is not easy to have a cuckoo in one's nest."

"Horatia," Henrietta said gently, "your aunt and uncle are

living in your family home, supporting themselves and their children in fine style on the income that should be going toward your future."

"Henry," Darien said in warning. She didn't need to air his family ills before the Pomeroys. Nor rake him over the coals in public. He had his father for that.

"Your son will have told you I am a tragic meddler," Henrietta said to the marquess. "But if Mr. Bales is to marry my cousin, I think it fair we inquire after his prospects. The living at Bellamy cannot be awarded until Lord Lucien returns, can it?"

"It cannot, indeed," the marquess agreed. Darien stared at his plate.

"Well, then, let us have some cheerful news," Henrietta said. "Papa! May I?"

Darien sat at attention, panicking. He did not have a betrothal ring. He'd meant to ask his father about his mother's jewels.

"What, tell us that you're to be hauled before the King like common rabble?" Jasper teased, helping himself to a dish of artichokes.

"My other news." Henrietta looked around the table with solemn glee. "I," she announced, "am owner of the old corn mill at Bamford! Hodge accepted my terms—I think Jasper had something to do with that, thank you, Papa—and my solicitor is drawing up the papers as we speak. I"— she lifted her glass triumphantly—"shall be in *trade*! Though I do not expect it will prohibit me from being transported, if Prime Minister Pitt has determined on it."

An awful pause followed. Darien gripped his glass till he feared it would shatter. So Henry had her mill, her plans and her causes and her future. Did she mean to include him in any of these? He had no indication that she did.

"To Hetty and her mill!" Marsibel raised her glass, and Darien forced himself to join another toast.

The marquess turned to Jasper. "Do you know, I've been considering building a factory on the Trent, but I'm not sure there's a high enough drop to power a water wheel."

"It's steam you want, in that case," Jasper returned. "I'm building my next mill with Watt's atmospheric engine. Uses half the coal of Newcomen's, and you needn't be near a river at all."

The marquess insisted that Darien return to Langford House to complete his recovery, and Lady Clarinda made no protest to keep him. Henrietta offered no demurral either. She whisked Horatia away shortly after tea, and Darien found them packing his things in the bedchamber he had occupied.

Henry was blithely sending him on his way, and he had no declaration from her, no promise, not even a few silly, tender words. She could not simply walk away from him. She could *not*.

"—besotted," Horatia was saying. "Lucretius and I used to laugh at the way girls cast lures at Daring and Lucifer. But the way he looks at you..."

"As if I were a thorn in his side?" Henrietta answered.

"As if you were food and drink together, all that could sustain him." Horatia's voice turned wistful. "I should like someone to look at me like that, someday."

Henrietta shook out one of his shirts. "Miss Wollstonecraft believes it is better to inspire admiration for one's wit and sense rather than passion for one's person," she said. "All the same, I hope you know your uncle is not the sad rattle he is made out to be."

"Such talk is not meant for her ears," Darien snapped. "I'll do that."

Henrietta lifted her eyebrow. "And how are you to manage with one arm? Horatia cannot; she is holding the baby."

"Here, you angel," Horatia cooed, rocking Celestina in her arms.

Darien growled and rubbed his shoulder, which ached like the devil. "We could have made our announcement tonight, Henry. Your father and mine are downstairs haggling over our marriage settlements as we speak."

"Neither of them has thought to consult me on the matter," she said, folding the shirt.

"Devil take it! Why won't you marry me?"

She flared her eyes at him. "You kissed me in the Egyptian gallery for all to see. I can only assume you meant to draw attention away from my other scandalous behavior, which the broadsides have taken due note of, thank you. But everyone knows Lord Daring doesn't marry on a kiss, and besides that, my reputation has already been damaged beyond repair. Ergo, you are under no obligation to extend your hand, nor I to accept it."

Darien sent his niece a glare, encouraging her to retreat. She did, withdrawing with the baby to the sitting room where, with one hand, she turned over the haphazard stack of books on Henrietta's desk.

He lowered his voice. "You kissed me back, Henry."

She tucked the shirt into the valise Rutherford had provided. "A few kisses are hardly grounds for marriage."

He stepped close, looming over her. Where was the luscious woman who had melted in his arms among the ancient artifacts? "There is more than kissing involved in a marriage." He traced a finger along the alluring neckline of her gown. "I shall be happy to demonstrate."

Her resistance baffled him. Lord knew he'd never denied himself gratification with anything. He didn't understand what she wanted, and if he didn't understand, how could he offer it and secure her to his side? Make her want no man but him?

She snatched up a cravat and flapped the cloth at him, forcing him to step back. "I would insist on certain conditions. You will not like them."

"How many conditions?" he asked warily.

"Two come immediately to mind."

Horatia moved past the doorway, humming to the baby, and her happiness was an accusation. In his own grief and blind obstinacy, he had allowed Ratty to drive his brother's legacy to rack and ruin, just as his father said. Worse, he had neglected his niece, Horace's remaining child. There was a liveliness in Horatia's step and a glow on her cheek that had not been there when she'd arrived. She had flowered instantly under Henrietta's attention. And the fault was his that Horatia had been deprived at all.

"I presume I am looking at your conditions," Darien grated out.

"Horatia and Celestina comprise the first." Henrietta folded his cravat with precision and tucked it into the valise beside his shirts.

"And the second?"

She faced him. "Your father's suit," she said in a quiet voice.

Darien stiffened, a cold despair washing through him. She, his hoped-for wife, was supposed to take *his* side.

"You want me to do as he demands? Take away Lucien's birthright, when it was never meant for—" Couldn't she see how wrong it was? In his nightmares, he moved through Bellamy's rooms as if he were the master of Horace's domain, while Lucien bellowed from the family tomb in the graveyard. And Darien had put him there.

He had to make her see how impossible this demand was. He couldn't meet it. She couldn't ask it of him. "You wish to become a countess by courtesy, is that it? You'd be near the equal of Clarinda or Lady Bess. I am surprised a title could tempt you," Darien snarled.

Henrietta didn't rile at his insults. She stepped forward and placed her hands alongside his face, her gaze meeting his directly. He hated how vulnerable her touch made him feel, how much he craved her strength.

"You heard what your father said," she said. "And Horatia. I have an estate of my own and I am responsible for the souls upon it. I could not be married to you and watch nothing be done to save Bellamy."

"It is Lucien's place to oversee Bellamy," Darien said hoarsely. "Lucien is the heir. I cannot take what is his. It is theft, and it is murder. If I become Earl of Aldthorpe...there's nothing for him to come back for." He closed his eyes in pain.

"Oh, my darling," Henrietta whispered. She stroked his cheek, and he leaned into her steady, solid comfort. He hated that she should have such power over him. A man ought to be his own master.

"You need not take the title, if that is the rub," she said. "You need only consent to a legal act that will nominate you as your father's heir, and Horace's, so you may make decisions for the estate. You would make a better steward than your cousin, from the sound of things."

"I shall not have him declared dead," Darien rasped. "I shall not behave as if he is." He pulled his face away from her hand. "I'll— I can go to Bellamy and make Ratty behave."

She picked up another cravat. "I wish you well in the attempt. I hope you will leave Horatia here while you are away."

Darien caught her hand as his composure cracked. He was doing it again. Ridden by grief, by shame at his own failures, he turned into a howling and desperate animal striking out at whoever was near, clawing everything around him to destruction. He let his hands curl into fists so he could not touch her. He could not hurt Henry, his valiant, determined, magnificent Henry. He could not haul her down into his despair. He needed her to save him from it.

"I'll go to India. I'll find Lucien. I'll bring him back."

"Very well." Henrietta bit her lip and nodded. "I will look after the girls while you are gone."

Guilt goaded him past his patience. "They are my wards," he growled. "I will provide for them." Did she think him incapable? "I asked you to marry me. Not take charge of my family affairs."

"Oh, you *asked* me to marry you. Why was that again?"

Her face shuttered, settling into cool, firm lines that told him he had pushed too far. He didn't have an answer to that. He had found her outside the palace of St. James, cursing her gown, and he had not walked past her, though he might have. Others had.

And when she kissed him in her family garden, practice for imaginary future suitors, then strolled away untouched, he'd known—he decided in that moment—he would find a way to bind her to him and she would never walk away from him again.

Sheer impulse, the way he had always operated. The blind, groping need that had led him into destruction, and now he thought could lead him out.

"I thought so." Henrietta snapped the valise shut and pushed it into his good hand. "If you see Lady Celeste on the Continent, tell her I have her daughter."

"You're supposed to be ruined," Darien demanded, outraged that she was doing it again, walking away. That was how his world operated. A kiss was as binding as a vow. It could make marriages, and it could break them. What more would it *take* with this woman?

She turned toward him at the door. "I have a mill to build

and an estate to oversee, and I hope someday to rebuild my credit enough to be accepted into the Minerva Society," she said with a brittle composure that told him she was furious. "Nothing about me is ruined. As to the matter of marriage, I have outlined my terms."

He ground his teeth together. She asked him to deny Lucien, his other half, his best self. To accept that he would not come back, with his cocksure swagger and laughing blue eyes and bold grin. She was asking him to say aloud that Lucien no longer lived.

"I cannot accept your conditions." The words squeezed the air out of his lungs. They clawed up his chest, shredding him from the inside.

She straightened her shoulders, those elegant square shoulders that bore so much. "Perhaps that is for the best," she said before she exited. "It would not do for Prime Minister Pitt to haul away your would-be wife in chains."

CHAPTER TWENTY-FIVE

The Hines carriage arrived in style at St. James Palace on the day that Henrietta's fate would be decided. As the Pomeroy coach drew up behind them, packed with her relatives, Henrietta descended the steps with Charley's aid and recalled with a melancholy fondness the last time she set foot on these cobblestones. Then, the turreted brick gatehouse had simply felt like the entrance to another world. Now, it was the path to her doom.

Another coach drew up behind the Pomeroy vehicle, with a team of six matched blacks and the Bales arms picked out on the door. Henrietta watched in amazement as Rutherford scrambled out and moved toward Marsibel like a bee to honey. The Marquess of Langford, in full court dress, assisted Horatia from the coach. Then Darien, stepping down last, looked around and met her eyes.

The others faded into the background as her whole world tilted on its axis and reoriented toward him.

She suspected he would always do that to her. Become the center of her world each time he stepped into it.

He no longer wore the sling. His back was straight, his hair clipped and queued, and like everything else she had laid eyes on that day, he was unbearably beautiful. Her heart expanded, reaching toward him.

"Lord Darien," she murmured as he came to her like a compass needle pointing north. She felt her insides shift and settle. A thrill shot through her body as he bowed over her hand. "I recall we met here before."

"Your dress has considerably improved."

He appraised her from head to slipper. Duprix had rebuilt her court gown completely, shearing away the excess ruffles and shirring the stomacher and underskirt with neat rows of tiny pink ribbons. The brushed green silk made Henrietta's eyes gleam a deep emerald, matching the jeweled collar at her throat. Instead of ostrich feathers, a set of tall, soft plumes nodded like angelic thoughts above her head.

Her panniers swayed elegantly as he led her through the gate and a phalanx of red-coated yeoman guards conducted them through the long hallways of St. James. She clutched his arm, her face pale.

"I expect that Lord Pinochle has been bending the Prime Minister's ear about me," she said in a subdued tone. "I don't expect Mr. Pitt to approve of my stealing his maid away when good servants are so hard to keep. Likely there is a crime in it somewhere."

"Pinochle is in no position to harass anyone at the moment," Darien said. "It seems his debts have caught up with him and he has withdrawn to the Continent. His servants were offered board wages, but not a one of them wanted to stay in that house."

Henrietta's heart fluttered in her chest. Nancy was safe. She need never fear Pinochle might try to find her or her child. "You did this?" she whispered.

His mouth twisted in a wry grin. "My father. You are right that a marquess is a handy threat to wave about." He covered her hand with his, squeezing her gloved fingers. "I won't let them take you, Henry."

Her throat was too tight to speak. The threat of transportation did seem remote, especially when men like Jasper filled the King's war chest. But a worse result seemed far more likely—she would be squashed, silenced, dismissed. Her argument about justice and reform and proper rights for women would be flicked from the monarch's sleeve like a flower bug, while men like Pitt kept the wheel of government turning, crushing the lesser in body and soul.

"Perhaps I shall flee to the Continent too," she said. "Flanders has always interested me. There is a long history of fabric production."

She wished, for a wild moment, that they could run away together. Leave everything that was unsettled, everyone they owed behind.

Horatia's innocent remarks over the past few days had drawn a picture for Henrietta of the Bales family and Darien's place within it. The spirited youngest, indulged and protected by his brothers. As his family members left him, one by one, he'd found refuge in larking about the Continent, escape in turning his reputation for wildness to some use.

But she better understood his outrage at the unfairness of the world, that the two men destined to inherit the Langford patrimony should not be here to take it up.

"I'll run away with you if you wed me first." The sculpted planes of his face were severe, but so dear as he stared down at her. She wanted to trace those fine, beautiful lips with her fingers.

"I thought you had withdrawn your offer," she said. "We

have not seen you at Hines House since—" Since their last, terrible parting.

"I've been attending to business. Henry, you goose." His face filled her vision, her heart, her world. "My offer stands until you finally accept. You won't be rid of me. Not ever."

She nodded as tears rose to her eyes. Somehow she, the most unlikely of women, had won this most winsome of men. She was the most unsuitable woman he could possibly have chosen, and he had come, with his father, to support her as she went on trial before the King.

"Could get you a special license," the marquess rumbled from behind them. "The Archbishop of York is my cousin."

"You talk to her, then," Darien said as they lined up outside the King's presence chamber. "I would swear she loves me, but I can't persuade her to take on the leg-shackle."

"Thought it was all they were out for, women," the marquess remarked.

"Not this one," Darien said.

Henrietta clenched her hand on her arm, wondering if she were being foolish. She had been convinced that love alone was slender ground on which to marry when there was so much else to consider. But her objections were harder and harder to call to mind. With Darien at her side, all she could think about was how magnificent he was. How deep and good he ran, true to the bone.

She would deal with that discovery later. She had to survive this interview first.

"The Most Honorable Marquess of Langford," the herald intoned as they filed by rank into the King's presence chamber. The marquess had left off his coronet, but his dress sword banged against his boot, a mark of respect.

"Langford!" King George sat up in his chair. The red velvet upholstery matched the patterned red canopy suspended from the ceiling. Henrietta glanced at the sculpted head of a woman looming above the fireplace and hoped it was Minerva. She could use some of her strength today.

"Heard you were in town, old man," the King said. "But Pitt's taking up my afternoon. Some chit he wants to put through the wringer."

"The chit," said the marquess, "is to be my daughter. So naturally I interest myself in her future." He made a deep leg to Queen Charlotte. "Your Majesty."

"Hello, Cassius," the Queen said with a small smile.

"Haha! Hear that, Pittsy?" the King bellowed across the room. "Daring's getting shackled to the bluestocking! You owe me a pony."

"You may add it to the great list of debts I owe you, sir," came the reply.

"Lord Darien Bales, son of the Marquess of Langford, and Miss Henrietta Wardley-Hines, daughter of Sir Jasper Wardley-Hines," the herald droned, and Darien swept Henrietta into the room.

"Riveted him after all, did you?" the King said with glee. "Well done, minx! You just won me five hundred pounds off Pittsy. Much obliged."

In fact, the King's was not the only bet lodged on the chances of Miss Wardley-Hines succeeding where so many had failed, and many a gentleman forced to settle a debt entered into the book at White's laid a curse on her head and on those of her progeny down five generations.

"Your Majesties." Henrietta made her curtsies to the King and Queen.

"Daring," the Queen observed, "I counseled you, when you were last here, to find yourself a bride. But I did not expect you to be so obliging."

Darien swept into his bow, and the Queen's eyes lingered

on the striking figure he cut. It was more than his height, the saber swinging against his legs, the chest and shoulders filling out his tailed coat that gave him presence. There was a new sureness to Lord Daring these days. As if he had settled something within himself. He still had that alert, watchful air, but he looked less desperate. Perhaps it was the birth of his daughter, or being reconciled with his father, or his brush with mortality that made self-destruction look less appealing.

It never occurred to Henrietta that she might be the reason for Darien's new dignity, and she would have scoffed at the idea. But the Queen watched her with a considering look while Sir Jasper and his wife, Sir Pelton and his lady, and Marsibel and Rutherford, bringing up the rear, all made their bows.

"Brought the whole family to a private audience, Pell?" said the King with a touch of spleen. "Pittsy has a piece to say, but I've a few questions of my own first. Langford, what is the trouble with your son's estate? Pitt tells me there's a pile of suits backed up. It's going to be a devil of a headache for the assizes."

"Since we've had no word from Lucien since the Treaty of Mangalore," the marquess said in a level tone, "I think it time to settle things on Darien. The King's Bench has advised me to bring a suit before the Lords."

"Cursed Mysore," the King barked. "We'll settle it this time. We're taking the sultan's sons hostage and bringing them to England to civilize them. Man's on his way now." He glared at Darien. "Well, boy? Time to cast off the life of dissipation and take up your duties, ain't it? Set an example for Prinny."

"If Your Majesty so advises," Darien said in a neutral tone.

"Take it," the King grumbled. "The world's going arse up, first those blasted Colonies and now France. We must keep a steady hand on the reins."

Henrietta squeezed Darien's arm in sympathy. He must have known it would end here, with king and father and country all backing him into a corner. He had fought valiantly to preserve Lucien's inheritance, but he was a man of honor in the end. He had proven it with the Pennyroyals, with Celeste, and with her. And if he consented to her conditions—

Her heart thumped against the tight press of the stomacher. Could he really wish to marry her, this complicated, infuriating man?

If he were forced to yield to his father's suit, he would no longer need her uncle's influence. And she would not need his name to save her reputation if she might, by some act of divine mercy, survive this afternoon intact.

The herald appeared at the door. "Their Graces the Duke and Duchess of Highcastle. The Honorable Lord Alfred Highcastle. The Honorable Lionel Havering, son of the Viscount Bourchier."

"Don't recall asking for any of you," the King riled. "Highcastle, what's the meaning of this?"

"Told Langford I'd look in," Highcastle said carelessly. "Though I've a mind to let Pitt string the bluestocking up by her thumbs. Daughters fleeing to the Continent." He glanced at the marquess. "Kittens with claws."

The marquess rolled his eyes and nodded.

"Is there any word on Lady Celeste?" murmured the Queen.

"They married in St. Denis, but I fear it's none too safe for them in France," said the duchess. "We hope to bring them home soon. Langford has promised to buy Mr. Empson a commission."

"So long as he returns my sketches," Darien whispered in Henrietta's ear. "And repays my loan."

She stifled a gurgle, clutching his arm. With the influx of people, she was beginning to guess what his business of the past few days had been.

"And you?" The King eyed Havering. "Planning a breach of promise suit?"

Havering shrugged. "Daring did me a service, sir. I'm here on his behalf."

The King turned his protuberant stare to Sir Pelton. "And you're giving your daughter to a Bales as well. Glad you shook off Pinochle! That 'un spent far too much time with my wastrel son."

Lady Pomeroy's nostrils flared, but she pinched her lips shut.

"All right, Pittsy," His Majesty announced, reveling in his role as puppeteer. "Time to state what claim you've got against the future countess of Aldthorpe. Can't wait to hear this, I must say."

Henrietta struggled for breath as the prime minister stepped forward. Duprix had laced her stomacher too tightly. She was going to faint from nerves, just like the fragile ladies Miss Wollstonecraft deplored.

She could grovel and be spared, she saw that at once. But for a full pardon, the prime minister would require her to repudiate her beliefs, to deny the women she had modeled herself on, Lady Bess and Miss Gregoire. She worried the necklace at her throat. What would her mother have advised her to do?

Her fingers stilled, the answer obvious. Apollonia Wardley had defied convention, propriety, and censure to marry where she willed and support the causes she believed in. Her mother would have been standing next to her, insisting upon a woman's right to have a choice. Henrietta drew a deep breath.

"This is not a trial, sire," said Pitt, pointing his nose skyward. "I only wish to discuss a few questionable remarks that were made on a certain evening under the aegis of the Minerva Society. I have, to that end, invited some witnesses who can attest to the best of their recollection what transpired."

The herald went to work again. Lady Bessington sailed into the room, an owlish Lord Bessington blinking in her wake.

"Bess? And you brought your leg-shackle!" The King laughed. "Like to know how you got him away from the card table."

"Your Majesties." Lady Bessington swept into a curtsy. "We shall retire to Cresswell Castle for the summer and would be honored if Your Majesty would care to come for some shooting."

"Fox, you scoundrel," the King shouted as Charles James Fox made his leg. "No blood in my drawing room, hear? The Queen won't have it."

"I would not dream of subjecting Her Majesty to such a scene," said the politician. "I hope Minister Pitt feels the same."

A somber-looking, elegant man entered behind Fox and made his bow. Henrietta reached out a hand.

"Mr. Equiano. I am *most* pleased to make your acquaintance."

His eyes twinkled as he bowed to her. "I believe we share some common interests, Miss Wardley-Hines. Lady Bess told me of your work for the settlers in Sierra Leone. The Sons of Africa approve."

"My daughter is also a benefactor of the Sisters of Benevolence Hospital for Foundlings and Women in Distressed Circumstances," Clarinda put in. She stood composed and graceful on her husband's arm, yet somehow drew every eye in the room to her and the rounded swell of her middle. "She and Sir Jasper support several workhouses and hospitals throughout Lancashire, Cheshire, and Derbyshire as well."

This proud litany, a pointed reminder to Pitt, who was looking more irritated by the moment, gave way to surprise when the herald opened the door to announce the Earl of Warrefield.

"Why, Papa!" Clarinda murmured. "What a pleasure to see you."

"Eh? You invited me," said Warrefield, making his bow to Their Majesties. "Is my granddaughter up to more mischief? Can't say I'm surprised." His eyes raked Darien. "Though if she's game to take on this one, she's primed for anything, I'd guess." He blinked at the marquess. "God's teeth, Langford! Down from the wild reaches of the north?"

"Warrefield!" The marquess grinned. "New wife keeping you in trim?"

"More lords here than in session," the earl exclaimed. "Highcastle! What in blazes?" He greeted his crony with a hearty clasp on the back. "Not down in the mouth about that worthless gel of yours, I hope?"

"How sharper than a serpent's tooth," the duchess murmured.

Henrietta looked around to find that more people had filed into the room. Several of them ranged behind Pitt. Fox and Equiano stood against the far wall, opposite the monarchs' thrones, forming an impromptu spectator's gallery. Many more moved behind Henrietta—her family, the Bales men, the Bessingtons. As Pitt cleared his throat and began a brief and highly biased summary of the events of the evening that led to her arrest, Henrietta noticed that Havering, Warrefield, and the ducal family, while appearing to promenade slowly about the chamber, ended by arranging themselves among her supporters.

She had supporters. Darien stood at ease beside her, leaning on his back leg, his hand on his sword. He looked elegant and careless and in complete command. Her eyes stung with tears.

Once again, he had come to her rescue, and he had brought a small army with him. She wanted to weep with joy, save that looking like a witless pea goose would undermine her claims completely.

He met her eyes with an amused smile. "I invited the Spick-eys, but they, for some reason, declined to support your cause."

Henrietta sniffled. "How did you know they were in attendance?"

"Because I was there also, seated on the pro side, I'll have you know. If I hadn't paused to untangle James, we'd have seen where you were taken." He squeezed her hand with his warm larger one. "James knew where to find your uncle, if not Charley, and he knew every holding cell in the city. It was sheer misfortune we came to the Bishopsgate watch house dead last."

Darien looked up and addressed the King. "I should like it known, Your Majesty, that in his haste to judge her a traitor, Mr. Pitt's men placed my betrothed, a gentleman's daughter, in a cell with...common women."

"Six of whom she persuaded," added Lady Bess, "to seek refuge at the Sisters of Benevolence Hospital, which is run by the Minerva Society."

"Seven," Henrietta said, on the verge of tears and exasperated with herself for it. "Mame came to the Sisters after she was beaten and turned out by her husband because she refused to sell her alehouse to settle his debts. Her children have been taken from her, and she nearly lost her life. He sold it, of course, without her consent."

She looked over the small crowd, then to the prime minister. "I am grateful to you, Mr. Pitt, for the women I met that night. Their stories were illuminating. Do you wish to hear them?"

She went on despite his gesture of dissent. "Alice's brother sold her to a friend to settle a gaming debt. Belinda's mother thought she was apprenticing her daughter to a seamstress; it was a brothel. Lena's father refuses to acknowledge her because her mother was enslaved. Phoebe sells herself because her father spends the family's income on gin. Tabitha and Cecilia have no father at all."

She lifted her chin. "Their stories, Mr. Pitt, prove the points I put forward at my debate. I do not believe it is treason to acknowledge what happens to the vulnerable in this society we have built. Not just women and children but the lame, the ill, the elderly—what happens when they have no one to protect them and no means to see to their own welfare?"

"You propose that they revolt against their guardians," Pitt said sternly. "To cast down the rules they believe have failed them."

"Not at all," Henrietta replied. "I propose—"

"To rebel," Pitt emphasized, gliding forward. "Against the King, our protector and provider under the law."

"To reform the law," Henrietta said stubbornly, "so that it benefits *all* the King's subjects."

"You call to bring down the monarchy, a noble structure sanctioned by God," Pitt thundered. "To tear apart the fabric of a society that has nurtured the greatest fruits of civilization. Scientific progress. Unrivaled literature. You would undo the achievements of centuries." He paused. "Like the French, among whom Miss Wollstonecraft has spent a great deal of time. I understand you borrow very much from her."

Henrietta put back her shoulders, feeling air leave the room. She saw his strategy. Pitt meant to align her with the Jacobins and revolutionaries and declare her a traitor, like Thomas Paine. Charley had warned her the King's temper was fragile, and possibly his mental stability. The strain on the Queen was terrible. If she angered the monarchs, she could suffer worse than jail.

But neither could she lie. "I agree with many of Miss Wollestonecraft's ideals. That is true."

Pitt produced a slim volume Henrietta recognized. "Let us see what Miss Wollstonecraft has to say." He opened to a marked page. "'The rich are idle, vain, and helpless.'" He glanced at the Highcastles, who huffed in indignation. "'A man of rank and fortune has nothing to do but pursue some extravagant freak.'" The Earl of Warrefield shifted on his feet.

"And this: 'He who will pass life away in bounding from one pleasure to another must not complain if he acquires neither wisdom nor respectability of character.'" Pitt lowered the book. "So far, Miss Wollstonecraft seems to be remarking on Miss Wardley-Hines's betrothed."

Several titters met this remark, but Darien kept his face impassive. Letting her fight her own battle but ready to leap to her aid. Henrietta's heart swelled.

"It is Miss Wollstonecraft's comments on women that concern me, sir," Henrietta said.

"Ah, yes. Let us consider these lines: 'They are made to be loved, and must not aim at respect.' Or this? 'She was created to be the toy of man, his rattle, and it must jingle in his ears whenever he chooses to be amused.' Indeed. 'Genteel women are slaves to their bodies, and glory in their subjection.'" He raised a brow. "Slaves, Miss Wardley-Hines?"

Mr. Equiano stood, quiet and attentive, near Lady Bess. Henrietta swallowed.

"I would not presume that my experiences as a woman share anything with the horrors endured by those subjected to the detestable institution of slavery," she said. Equiano gave her a slight nod of acknowledgement. She turned to face not Pitt but the monarchs on their thrones.

Charlotte's face was carefully bland. The Queen was uniquely situated to understand her points, Henrietta realized. Her African blood was general knowledge, passed to her through descent from the Portuguese royal house. And as she was the highest woman in the realm, her life was the most regimented, the most examined, the most proscribed.

"When a woman is born, even into fortunate circumstances

like mine," Henrietta said, "her education is at the discretion of her parents. If she has an enlightened parent, as I did, she is educated well." Queen Charlotte gave a stiff tilt of her head; she was known for having granted a high-quality education to the princesses.

"Likewise, a girl is subject to the marriage her parents choose for her," Henrietta went on.

The Queen did not respond to this. Her marriage to a man she had never met, through a contract signed by her brother and a ceremony that took place within six hours of her landing on English soil, was already popular legend.

Henrietta looked at Clarinda. "And when she is married, to a man selected for the good of the family, she is transported to a strange place, where she must serve and please someone who may be unfamiliar to her. Her possessions, her income, her very person belong to him. The law grants him authority over her affairs and her children and allows him the greatest intimacies with her body. She becomes his property, to direct and dispose of as he wishes."

She swallowed the tight knot in her throat. This was not the time to think of marital intimacies with Darien. If she couldn't convince the monarchs her goals were not treasonous, she'd become the property of the Crown and be disposed of in far worse ways than marriage.

"These are the laws of God and nature," Pitt pointed out, "as well as those passed by our Parliament, upheld by the King's justices."

"But these laws are not protecting those most in need." Henrietta curled her hands into fists. This was worse than having dozens of strangers come peer at her at her debate. Her voice echoed in the ornate chamber, every word falling harsh and clear.

"My point, sir, is that a woman is subject to her protector

and his whims, denied any ability to earn her own wage, govern her children, or govern herself except by his authority. But when a woman is left with no guardian, or one who inadequately provides for or injures her, what recourse does she have?"

"To foment rebellion?" Pitt said silkily. "Miss Wollstonecraft rails much against tyranny, does she not? 'It is the pestiferous purple which renders the progress of civilization a curse'—I am afraid I cannot agree with her there. And here: 'men who are slaves to their mistress tyrannize over their sisters, wives, and daughters.' You share her claims of tyranny, Miss Wardley-Hines?"

"My claim is what Miss Wollstonecraft says next," Henrietta said. "'Strengthen the female mind by enlarging it, and there will be an end to blind obedience.'"

Pitt returned to the book. "'But as blind obedience is ever sought for by power, tyrants and sensualists are in the right when they endeavor to keep women in the dark,'" he quoted back. "'The sensualist, indeed, is the most dangerous of tyrants, and women have been duped by their lovers, as princes by their ministers, whilst dreaming that they reigned over them.' There are several accusations here, Miss Wardley-Hines, and none speak well of the present company."

Darien stood unflinching as Pitt's gaze speared him. His reputation as a sensualist held him open, as always, to ridicule. The minister would indict her on a minor point and miss the larger if she let him. And if it were thought treasonous for women to complain of ill treatment, their claims dismissed as mere rebellion, how much more suffering would follow? Henrietta's temper rose.

"The tyranny of which she speaks is that exercised by women who are taught only habits of self-beautification and indolence," she said, "and thus attempt to rule men through their passions, rather than engaging with them as equals in reason, intelligence, and morality, as they ought." She avoided looking at the Highcastles. Celeste was ample illustration of this point.

"Are you quite sure that is her argument? For Miss Wollstonecraft asks here 'Where shall we find men who will stand forth to assert the rights of man?'" Henrietta winced. That indeed smacked of Thomas Paine. "And here, she insists that slavery to 'tyrannic kings and venal ministers' should be abolished, 'as their deadly grasp stops the progress of the human mind.' My, but that does seem a call for the overturn of the natural order."

"'If they really be capable of acting like rational creatures, let them not be treated like slaves, but given the chance to attain strength of mind, perseverance, and fortitude.'" Henrietta fought to keep her voice steady. "'The order of society would not be inverted, for woman would then only have the rank that reason assigned her, and arts could not be practiced to bring the balance even, much less turn it.' Liberating the mind of woman, Mr. Pitt, would likewise free men from women's cunning, which is exercised only to overcome their disadvantages."

Pitt's brows lifted. "Emancipation, then—but from what, exactly?"

"From—" Henrietta bit her lip. She could not find words that would not brand her a traitor for certain. She groped about, at a loss, while every eye in the room burned into her, waiting. She felt the tide of helplessness rising to pull her under. Pull down her, the Wardley name, and every hope of her future with it.

"Well, I never," cracked a voice from the door. "Charley, your sister is a legal scholar now, debating at the bar? I always said she was my favorite."

"Miss Davinia Wardley," the herald offered belatedly as a

stately matron processed into the room, her ebony walking stick rapping on the wooden floor.

Henrietta's jaw dropped. "Aunt Davinia! What are you doing here?"

"Charlotte, my dear, what is the meaning of this?" Aunt Davinia addressed the Queen, who gazed upon her with open delight. "Bess writes me that your minister"—she glared at this offending personage—"wants to put my grand-niece in jail? That takes a nerve! Some people don't know their place."

"We are endeavoring to ascertain," Pitt said crisply, "whether the points made by Miss Wardley-Hines on behalf of the Minerva Society were slanders or claims of treason against His Majesty the King."

"Fustian," Davinia barked, banging her stick on the floor. "No Wardley was ever a traitor. We've been Royalists since the time of Charles I. By my eyes." She lifted a pair of spectacles attached to her bodice by a golden chain, and her stern, strong-featured face softened as she considered Henrietta from head to toe. "She looks our Polly to the life, don't she, Jasper?"

Jasper cleared his throat. "Yes," he said stiffly, and his wife laid a hand on his arm. "Yes, she resembles her mother very much."

"Clarinda, you ought to sit or that child is going to fall right out of you," Davinia said. "Warrefield, your new wife too good for taking the waters with the rest of us?" She glared at the earl, who glowered back. "Now, which of my grand-nieces is Mr. Pitt pestering? Both of them? Come here, you pretty thing," she said to Marsibel, who curtsied and blushed. "I approve of Mr. Bales for you. Pinochle would never have done, as I told you, Althea."

Lady Pomeroy clenched her jaw. Her elder sister Apollonia had outshone her in everything, including their aunt's affections, and now her daughter was marrying higher than Althea had ever hoped for Marsibel. It must be galling, Henrietta thought.

"Medora!" Davinia addressed the Duchess of Highcastle. "You're in straits, darling. We need to have a good long coze, you and Charlotte and I."

The duchess nodded, looking near tears.

"Miss Wardley," Pitt began.

"You may address me as the Dowager Duchess of Cumberland if you're going to read me a lecture too." Davinia leaned on Charley's arm as he led her to where the monarchs presided.

"You dare! In this chamber," the King roared, sitting up.

"It was a marriage, whether you recognize it or not, George," Davinia said tartly. She gave the sovereigns a curtsy as majestic as it was correct, then plumped herself down in a chair that a guard scrambled to put beside the Queen. There she sat as if she were accustomed to the honor, which, as a former favorite lady-in-waiting, she was.

"Now, then. Langford!" Davinia barked, and the marquess snapped to attention, his eyes wide with alarm. "What did you dangle before Jasper to get Hetty for your hey-go-mad son?"

"Twenty thousand pounds on her, and ten for each of their children," the marquess confessed.

Davinia hooted with laughter, her stout frame vibrating from the feathers in her remarkable headdress to the flounces at the hem of her elaborate overskirt. "Hoy, Jasper, you are a shrewd negotiator! Told George it was time you got some honors, though I suggested a barony. Knew you were worthy of our name."

"Thank you, Aunt Davinia," Sir Jasper said.

"And you." Her eyes scanned Darien. "We'll see some better behavior from you in future?"

Darien swept her a deep bow. "I understand where you learned your managing ways," he murmured to Henrietta.

She smiled at him. "Aunt Davinia raised me, along with Miss Gregoire. I owe my good fortune to my father, but I owe everything I am to the example these women set for me."

And now, Aunt Davinia had bestirred herself from Bath on Henrietta's behalf. Or perhaps she had come instead to protect the Wardley name. Like Thomas Hardy at her debate, her aunt's powerful personality would dominate the room, and Henrietta would be pushed into the scenery once again.

Davinia held out a hand to Sir Pelton, who bowed over it. "Pell, I don't know what you're about here, but let's tie it up, shall we? I want to see the gardens that my dear Charlotte is planning." She patted her old friend on the knee.

The Queen's eyes lit with enthusiasm. "Yes, indeed! We're almost done here, aren't we, milord?"

The King stared at Davinia as if she were a beautiful and poisonous snake. Davinia eyed the prime minister as one would a weevil in the kitchen flour. "Tell me, sir, what madness is your Pittsy about now?"

The chamber echoed with an appalled silence around that forbidden word "mad."

Pitt drew himself up. He had not become the youngest prime minister in the history of Great Britain for lack of wisdom or merit. "Miss Wardley-Hines," he said doggedly, "it seems to me that you and Miss Wollstonecraft are calling for outright revolution. Is this true?"

Henrietta straightened her back as every eye in the room skewered her. "Yes," she said.

A gasp ran around the chamber. Several people stepped back as if officers would descend on Henrietta at once and whisk her away. Aunt Davinia folded her hands on her cane with a small, curious smile.

Henrietta caught the expression, and a thrill of surprise ran through her. Aunt Davinia had not come to preempt her interview but to insist that she was given a fair hearing.

The knowledge gave her the courage to speak into the affronted silence.

"Miss Wollstonecraft insists that if women are inferior, it is expectation and lack of education that have made them so. But these are defects that can and ought to be remedied. If you continue from the passage you last quoted, Mr. Pitt, I believe you will find she says this: 'It is time to effect a revolution in female manners—time to restore them to their lost dignity, make them part of the human species, and by laboring to reform themselves, reform the world.'"

Pitt fumbled with the pages, frowning. The long silence that ensued was broken by the whack of Aunt Davinia's cane on the floor.

"Well! My Hetty, the reformer. No wonder Pitt threw you in the watch house for speaking your mind. He'd understand women better did he ever go near one." She turned to the King. "What, may I ask, is treasonous about treating half of the population as if they possess a mind and a soul?"

Pitt ground his teeth. "This debate and those like it, sir, represent a real threat to your authority and the order upon which this kingdom stands. We understand that Miss Wardley-Hines was responsible for the near riot in the London Tavern, at which were made several seditious remarks."

"You must realize, Mr. Pitt, that there were many in attendance that evening who are not regular members of the Minerva Society," Lady Bessington said. "I'm afraid we cannot claim responsibility for their views. I can assure you, Your Majesty, that the Minerva Society only admits loyal subjects. Davinia, wouldn't you agree?"

"The topic concerned what remedy is available when those

in power fail in their duty," Pitt sputtered. "The remedy which Miss Wollstonecraft suggests is to remove tyrants from power."

"If Miss Wollstonecraft requires examination," Henrietta said, "then I beg you will call upon her to account for her works. My remedy, which bears repeating, is improved education for women that fits them for employment and pursuits beyond adornment of their persons, and a law which regards them as subjects able to govern themselves and their own property. Women are rational beings, sir. They must be taught proper conduct, their minds formed to dignity and reason and then held accountable for its exercise. That, Your Majesties, is the revolution I desire. To make women not the dependents but the equals, partners, and worthy companions of men."

She dug her nails into her palms to quell their trembling. There, she had said it, if not to, then before Darien. What she expected from a marriage. What she needed him to understand, and agree to, before she could accept his hand. If it were sedition to ask to be treated as his equal in intelligence, capability, and sense—and to demand a voice in the decisions that would govern her future—then she was guilty beyond a doubt.

"Pittsy?" The King, never one for subtleties, glared at his minister. "Don't see what any of this has to do with us."

Lady Bessington dropped a stately curtsy. "If you require no further information regarding the Minerva Society, sir, I beg that his lordship and I be excused. We are planning a ball for this evening to which Your Majesties are, of course, invited."

Bess and Aunt Davinia had neatly turned the tables, giving the Prime Minister no purchase. He watched Henrietta shrewdly, but when the King sighed and rolled his eyes toward the ceiling, Pitt gave a small, stiff bow. "If His Majesty is satisfied on this matter, then so am I. For the moment."

Queen Charlotte laid a hand on her husband's arm as his

protuberant gaze ranged around the room. "Shall we see to our tea, milord?"

The audience, taking this as dismissal, filed out backward. Mr. Equiano bowed over Henrietta's hand.

"I would be honored, Miss Wardley-Hines, to assist when you present the Minerva Society's petition for full abolition to Parliament," he said.

"Oh!" Henrietta stared at him, astounded. "Oh, indeed, yes!"

"While I would never dream of concerning myself with matters of state," Aunt Davinia said loudly, "one might think Mr. Pitt ought to convene a committee to investigate means for improving the lot of women. My niece makes many excellent points. No more than what I've been saying for years, of course."

"A committee to consider the rights of women." The King rubbed his nose. "See to it, Pittsy." He eyed Henrietta. "Put this one and Lady Bess in charge."

Henrietta sank into a deep curtsy. "Your Majesty. I would be *most* honored to accept such a commission."

King George snorted. "Don't imagine it will go anywhere, but we must keep the ladies content."

Queen Charlotte rose and gave her husband a fond smile, holding out her arm so her companion might appear to be escorting her while she helped him to his feet. "As ever, milord, you are the wisest and most generous of men."

The monarchs departed, and Henrietta stood in the cleared space, looking about her. She felt exhilarated and deflated at the same time. "I am not to be transported? Pilloried? Fined?"

Aunt Davinia rose and shook out her massive skirts. "Pitt can't arrest everyone who speaks their mind. He'd have half the kingdom in prison." She chucked Henrietta beneath her chin, a tender gesture she recalled from her youth. "You did well speaking *your* mind, Hetty. It's time someone did."

Henrietta's eyes filled with tears of relief. "I'm afraid I've brought a shadow on the name. I'm not certain Aunt Althea will ever forgive me."

"Althea worries about the wrong things," Davinia replied. She turned to Darien. "Lord Daring, greater than life, and far more dashing than the broadsheets depict. Yes, we've seen them, even in Bath." She held out her hand for him to take.

Darien sketched a bow, still stiff from his injury. "I hope you will believe Henrietta has had a steadying influence on me."

Davinia gave a scratchy laugh. "I hope you were listening. If you're to join the family, boy, it's not Jasper's approval you'll be needing. It's mine."

CHAPTER TWENTY-SIX

Most of the party gathered again at Lady Bessington's that evening. Henrietta allowed Duprix to dress her in her most daring gown yet, a style that a few fashionable ladies were wearing in France. It was modeled after the robes of Greek statuary and consisted of a small bodice, with a few drapes and tucks to resemble a tunic, and skirts that fell in straight, graceful lines to the floor. The style suited Henrietta's shape exactly.

"You will start a new rage, ma'mselle," Duprix murmured, studding Henrietta's unpowdered hair with pearls. "The dashing young countess. Everyone will notice." She paused. "You will require a proper lady's maid, of course."

If she married the son and heir of a marquess, she would have the power to shape public opinion, Henrietta knew. She could set fashions and insist on standards, like a certain respect accorded to women and support for their education. Her opinion would be sought and her voice heeded. She need only bow to those who outranked her, and they would be few.

His rank was dead last on the list of reasons she wanted to marry Darien.

Dancing was in progress at Lady Bess's, but Henrietta went

to Aunt Davinia, who had settled into a rout chair on one side of the elegant ballroom.

"Thank you for coming all this way for me. I am very glad you're here."

"Oh, my Hetty." Davinia put her spectacles to use. "You're your mother returned to us. She would have cheered at the way you stood up to Pitt."

Henrietta swallowed back a great lump in her throat. "Would she?"

The frosted gray curls of her wig never moved as Davinia shook her head. "I don't agree with your methods, of course. You don't make a fuss about it, gel. You look as they want you to, follow their rules, win their admiration, and then"—she snapped her fingers—"you do as you wish."

"Miss Wollstonecraft deplores that strategy," Henrietta replied. "It might benefit individual women, but it does not change the law to benefit all."

Davinia chuckled. "La, I've missed you." She watched as Henrietta's eyes drifted across the room. "You chose a good match, you know."

"Darien?" Henrietta startled. "I did not exactly *choose* him."

Her aunt snorted. "What does that matter? He's a head on his shoulders. Won't let you lead him about by the nose." Her eyes gleamed as they followed Darien's well-knit form dancing a galop with Forsythia Pennyroyal. "But knows his way around the bedroom, I'll wager."

"I have not made that a consideration," Henrietta said, reddening.

"Well, you should. Cumberland was a bull 'twixt the sheets, for all that they called him the Butcher." Her aunt's mouth softened in a fond reminisce. "Still, Daring's not a dirty dish. His mother's boy underneath it all. Always supposed he needed a proper woman to manage him, and I was right. As usual."

"Darien only offered for me to salvage my reputation."

Aunt Davinia's spectacles enlarged her eyes to surprised green orbs. "Hetty, have you feathers in your head? That man would swim to the moon if you asked him. He's calf-sick with love."

Henrietta watched Miss Pennyroyal blush and giggle as Darien spoke. Of course any woman would melt in his arms. Most women, and some men, would always respond to him thus. That would not change.

He met Henrietta's gaze and smiled. It was an eloquent smile, full of promise, the kind of communication a man exchanged with the woman to whom he belonged.

She did not require him to change. He was perfect as he was.

Davinia waved her cane in summons. Darien bowed to Forsythia and gave her hand to Charley. Charley, dancing? Henrietta stared, an odd lump rising to her throat.

Charley did not need her, not really. He would manage on his own. So would Lady Mama and Jasper and the girls. They would miss her—and she them—but they would carry on. Perhaps she had needed to look after them more than they needed her.

Then Darien was before her, his gaze sweeping her attire and lingering with appreciation on her throat.

"Dance with your lady," Davinia ordered. "And make her a declaration, you half-wit. She thinks you offered for her out of duty."

"My aunt is accustomed to having her way," Henrietta apologized as Davinia called to the musicians to strike up an allemande. Darien swept her into an indecently close hold, and her heart smiled and hummed at his nearness.

"Your aunt would be a royal duchess if George had acknowledged the union," Darien said. "It's fair to say she outranks my marquess by leagues. I don't know why you don't trot her out everywhere."

He held up her arm as she turned about. To keep her balance, she had to step toward him, and his thigh brushed hers through the thin gown. Her insides melted like chocolate.

"It appears, however, that I might in time make you a marchioness."

"You have settled things with your father?" She searched his face. "The King gave you little choice."

"You were right. The estate must be taken in hand." He shrugged, as if evading a cold touch of superstition. "And Horatia must be removed from that house. I could strangle my cousin Rathbone for the muddle he made of things."

"We could take her to Italy to see her mother," Henrietta suggested.

"You know, Henry, it is very bad *ton* to induce a man to marry you by taking his wards hostage." She moved the wrong way in the figure, and he pulled her close, guiding her into the correct steps. "Fortunately, my reputation will be upheld by how toothsome you look tonight. I never supposed, when I set out to reform you, that you would turn into such a striking beauty."

"Pish," Henrietta said.

"I mean it. No man here can take his eyes off you."

"Because of the gossip. Everyone is wondering why I wasn't thrown in Old Bailey."

"Everyone is wondering," he said, guiding her through another turn, "why I should be so lucky, having done nothing at all to deserve you."

His hands clasping hers were warm and full of delicious promise. "I expect you would be receiving condolences," she said. "Lord Daring, who walked away from the most beautiful maids in the kingdom, and he finally kissed the wrong woman."

"No," Darien said, watching her with that violet glow in his eyes, "I finally kissed the *right* woman."

Lost in his gaze, she floated across the floor. "Celestina?"

"Will take my name and be a lovely big sister to our own babes."

"And Horatia?"

He nodded, looking pained. "Need never see Ratty and that viperous wife of his again. Though I am not entirely persuaded," he added, "that this bluestocking school of yours is the place for a Bales. We are a conservative lineage, High Tories from the cradle, and you, my dear"—he leaned in to sniff her neck—"have a rather radical odor about you."

"Miss Gregoire does not indoctrinate in politics or anything else. She encourages girls to think for themselves." He used their crossed arms to pull her toward him again, and she conceded, squeezing his fingers. They moved about the floor in perfect harmony.

"I will not put aside my ideals for your Tory friends," she warned. "I won't give up my hospitals or causes. I want to run my farm, and my mills, and put some of my improving ideas into practice. And I am afraid..."

She trailed off, dreading what she needed to say. Darien twirled her again, his hand rising to grip her waist.

"When we are married," she forced herself to say, "I beg you will be discreet about your *affaires*. I am sure your friends will ever be laughing behind my back. I ask only that you not give them reason to laugh in my face."

His eyes tightened at the corners, but he kissed her fingers. "If I make you a promise to forsake all others, Henry, then I will. And it will be no loss."

She shook her head. "Please be honest with me. I am aware of your history, and the way things are. I only ask not to know if you—when you—"

He scowled. "You plan to be faithful to me, do you not?"

"Of course!" she said, scandalized.

"Then if you expect to be faithful to me, why should you not expect fidelity as well?" He continued, overriding her protest. "You plan to honor your other vows, do you not—to love, honor, and obey?"

"Yes, but—"

His eyebrows rose. "Obey? Truly?"

"To the best of my ability," she said indignantly.

"To honor?" he pressed on.

"Of course."

"To love?"

She looked into his eyes and saw the doubt, the vulnerability. She stopped in her turn, struck by realization. Lord Daring, the town's most notorious rake, had been linked with dozens of women, but none had cherished him. Loved him completely, unstintingly, simply for who he was.

He doubted, with all his guilt and self-recrimination, that anyone could. He didn't fully believe her yet.

"Oh, Darien," she whispered.

He dropped to one knee, bringing her hands to his heart. She felt the bandage beneath his coat, a reminder of the scars he bore.

"Henrietta, you magnificent goose. I am mad about you. I adore you entirely. You are my Beatrice. Yes, I know you dislike her, but you are the light that steadies my course. I knew when I found you cursing outside St. James Palace that you were put there for me. Marry me, you reckless, willful, wonderful girl. You've ruined me for anyone else."

He brought her clasped hands to his lips, feathering her gloved knuckles with kisses. The dancers about them stared. Neither cared.

"St. James?" she said, her voice wavering. "Even then?"

"Yes," he said simply.

She sniffled. "All right, then."

"Truly?" His voice caught.

She nodded, letting the tears well. "Yes. I will love you always. For our whole lives." She laughed at the look of relief, astonishment, and lingering doubt in his eyes. "Forever," she said firmly. "I will prove it."

He rose and gave her a resounding kiss, one that made the rest of the room swirl away. She surfaced to a circle of applause.

Darien bowed and moved them smoothly back into the dance, bringing his emotions under control. "Now," he said, and she felt the low scratch of his voice in her chest, "do you still believe that foolishness of Miss Wollstonecraft's that men and women should not base their marriage on passion?"

Henrietta felt she moved over clouds. She belonged here with this man, beside him, in his arms. He was the thing she'd been missing.

"Pooh," she said. "Let Miss Wollstonecraft set the terms for her own marriage, and we shall set the terms for ours. I want love, and passion, and respect, and amiability. And your engineering services. And conversation. And art, and travel, and—"

"And fidelity," he said. "And a house full of children. And a wife who will always remain her sensible self, and pull her own weight, rather than depending on me for everything, including her pin money."

"Oh, I see," she said with a grin. "Using my own philosophy against me."

He gave her a look of amusement, delight, and, yes, love. He was not a man given to declarations, and yet he had made one for her, beautifully. He would demonstrate his devotion to her daily, in ways large and small. In the steady hand at her back shielding her against the disparagement of others. In the sacrifices to make her happy, like acknowledging a bastard child, taking in her wards and his, allowing his wife to run her mills and poke about his building projects and traipse their lands in muddy boots, baby on her hip. That was how he would show his love.

"Miss Wardley-Hines." Forsythia Pennyroyal approached later as Henrietta stood with Lady Bess at the side of the room. "May I offer felicitations on your upcoming marriage."

"Thank you," said Henrietta. "I hope you and your family are well?"

"Yes, thank you." She avoided looking at Darien, whose face had gone carefully blank. "Lady Bessington says if I wish to join the Minerva Society, I require the sponsorship of a votary."

Henrietta's stomach tightened. Foolish to despair of the one thing she did not have when she had been given so much, and forgiven much. "I am sure someone will be willing to stand your sponsor, Miss Pennyroyal. The votaries are the most elect, most elite of the Society, the women who have done the most to enhance its mission and dignify its name. They—"

"I will put your name forward at the next conclave," Lady Bess said, "and your aunt will second. I expect the vote will be unanimous, Hetty, dear."

"Oh, Bess," Henrietta whispered, putting her hands to her mouth.

"Ha!" Bess crowed. "Daring proposes to you in a ballroom, but *I* wring tears when I tell you that you will be a Daughter of Minerva. Do you know, another young girl asked me how to join the Society after she saw you at your debate. A Miss Spickey, I believe."

"Constance?" Henrietta grinned. "But that is wonderful! She truly needs us."

Lady Bess turned to Darien with a smile. "She will make it fashionable for young women to join the Minerva Society. And I suspect she will set the fashion in other ways as well."

"I am beginning to think," Darien said, "that the benefits of this union accrue mostly to me." She leaned in for his kiss.

"Get you a special license already!" Aunt Davinia barked, pounding her cane on the floor. "Happens I know the Archbishop of Canterbury. Could get you one in a trice."

LORD DARIEN BALES and Miss Henrietta Wardley-Hines did not, after all, marry by special license. In fact, considering the scandalous reputation of both parties, the broadsides found little to lampoon about their rather conventional wedding. The banns were published for the required three weeks in the parish of Marylebone, and they wed, of all places, in the chapel of the parish workhouse which, though new, was not particularly grand.

Henrietta, who had eyes only for her groom, was informed later that the ceremony was crowded with titled families, high-ranking cabinet members, the widow and orphans of a famous war hero, and the celebrated Mr. Ouladah Equiano and his bride. Prime Minister Pitt declined his invitation with regrets. His presence was not missed.

The wedding breakfast, which seated three hundred, was held at Hines House and presided over by Davinia Wardley, common-law wife to the late Duke of Cumberland. The gossip columns reported that a prodigious amount of champagne was consumed. They reported also that the bride insisted the vibrant blue-violet color of her gown was made to match the color of the bridegroom's eyes. Yet the lady reporter who penned the column could confirm that Lord Darien's eyes were in fact the striking shade of lapis lazuli, like an illuminated manuscript of medieval times.

Comments were stirred by the cut and style of the bride's

gown, draped like a classical chiton. Sliver sandals laced over her feet, Roman-style, and the high sash added a military flair. A silver leaf woven into her unpowdered coiffure gave, from the back and side, the look of a helmet. The reporter had it on good authority that the costume was a tribute to Minerva, and the same matching silver leaf could be seen in the hair of an entire table of dignified female guests. One of them, the writer noted, was an elegant, soft-spoken schoolmistress who had come from Bath and went by the name of Miss Gregoire, and who spent some time in private conversation with the groom's ward, Miss Horatia Bales.

The bride's stepmother made no attempt to hide her enceinte shape and, it was said by some, rather looked as if she were flaunting it. The bride's father wore the cross of his order pinned to his coat, but this ornament was no more conspicuous than any of the other insignia decorating the varied guests.

After an endless round of toasts initiated by the Marquess of Langford, who was garrulous and clearly overproud of a son who really had not done much to recommend him, the gossip columns reported that the wedded couple departed to the bride's estate with the unromantic intention of installing a new drainage system for her fields. Firm promises were made about returning for the wedding of the bride's cousin to the groom's cousin, and the mother of the next bride was heard to say, in an aside to a friend, that Miss Pomeroy's ceremony should be done with a little more style and, Lady Pomeroy hoped, at least as many important guests.

At the close of Parliament a few weeks later, the new Lady Darien Bales found herself sitting in the spectator's gallery of the chamber of the King's Bench, screened from the rest of Westminster's great hall while the court resolved a short but sad suit. Mr. Rathbone Bales and his wife, Perdita, were absent, but Miss Horatia Bales clung quietly to Henrietta's hand.

Lord Darien, heir presumptive, sat at a table as witness. The end of it was that Lord Lucien Bales was declared dead in absentia and Lord Darien Bales recognized as heir apparent to the Marquess of Langford and legal guardian to his niece, though he declined the courtesy title Earl of Aldthorpe. The matter entered into the Official Rolls, the suit concluded and the family exited, the new heir somber about his elevation and his lady clutching her handkerchief.

In her new role as hostess, Henrietta organized the family dinner at Langford House that evening, which included the Pomeroys and the Wardley-Hines. The first piece of business, after a toast was drunk to the absent Lord Lucien, wherever he might be, was to settle the living of St. Alcelda on Mr. Rutherford Bales.

The second was to send word to Bellamy Hall that Mr. Rathbone Bales and his wife should prepare to return to the life and lodging of a solicitor's family, a remove from which several unpleasant scenes were expected to ensue.

The newlyweds departed from Portsmouth the next morning on a wedding trip to the Austrian Netherlands. Despite the fact that France had recently declared war on Austria, Henrietta chose Flanders as their honeymoon destination. With them went the groom's father, who had not been abroad in an age; Miss Bales, for whom it was thought travel would be very educational; and Miss Celestina, whose parents did not wish to be parted from her.

The Marquess of Langford strolled the gently rolling deck and considered the odd company in which he found himself. Near the mast sat his new daughter's cocky groom, throwing the bones and telling Banbury stories to the sailors, who laughed uproariously as each tale grew wilder than the last. At the stern clustered the women, the baby's wet nurse and the two maids scooped from some place called the Benevolence Hospital.

He'd heard Hetty had sent others from the same place to her estate. It must be some sort of placement agency. A pretty picture they made: the fair nurse who was rocking a drowsy Celestina, the dark-haired one who was singing in a voice fit for the stage, and the redhead teaching dance steps to Horatia, who laughed as he hadn't heard her laugh in years.

Strolling the deck in the opposite direction was the woman who had brought all this into his life, leaning on the arm of her husband as they cooed in lover's language to one another. Every so often, a sweet nothing drifted to the marquess's ear.

"—invented an automated loom using punch cards that weaves patterns directly onto the silk, called *jacquard*—"

"—improved on Newcomen's engine, but it requires a great deal of coal to create the steam."

"—Hopton Wood Stone for the inside. He said the Duchess of Devonshire has it all over Chatsworth—"

The marquess smiled. This was the best sort of lover's talk, the kind to rivet his son to his wife's side. No sensible man would risk the love and loyalty of such an intelligent, warm-hearted woman as Henrietta, and his youngest and wildest boy, it seemed, had finally come to his senses.

They reminded him of another pair of lovers who had once crossed the English Channel, a raven-haired southern princess who recited Italian poetry to her young British lord until his heart had swelled and burst out of his chest. God, he missed Pip. He missed all of them—Horace, Lucien, Lucretius, even Nell. The ache was enormous. And yet he was happy.

HENRIETTA FELL SILENT, watching the English coast fade into the gray sea. Darien rested his chin on her head.

"Do you wish you were a countess?" he asked.

"No." She squeezed his hand. "You will keep Bellamy in trust for Horatia, and Lucien still bears the title. And we will continue to pray for his safe return."

"You are like no other woman on Earth, Henrietta Bales."

She laughed. "I am often told that. Though I do wonder if a countess would have better luck securing subscriptions for her charitable homes and signatures for her petitions. Ah, well, Bess will see to it."

"Is there a place for the husbands, do you think? The"—he searched for a word—"Gentlemen of Minerva. The Hounds of Actaeon."

He pressed a kiss to her ear when she laughed again. "Neither sounds flattering. Perhaps you can form a society of your own."

"For the reformation of rakes." She stilled, and he noticed. "Still you do not believe me?"

Henrietta pressed a small kiss to his neck, that firm, strong, splendid stretch of skin. She had ample evidence of her husband's devotion; their conjugal relations were *most* satisfactory. "I will concede the point in two score years, when I may say you have never looked at another woman."

He chuckled, and she felt the flutter in her chest. "Minx." He nuzzled her hair, then fell quiet. "You've never said why you chose me. I know very well it wasn't because I kissed you at the museum."

She leaned her head on his shoulder. "Apollo."

"You adore me for my physique? I should have known."

She shook her head, glancing up at him. "Lord Ellesmere's. I turned, and there you were. Looking—" So wary, so guarded, with such desperate appeal in his eyes. As if she, and she alone, held out the hope that could save him. "I'd been told to have nothing to do with you, because of your reputation. And then you handed me that ostrich feather, and I knew I had to take you in."

His lips moved through her hair, his arms tight about her. "I hear Queen Charlotte has banned ostrich feathers from her drawing rooms. Too many of them tickling her nose."

"I cannot blame her. I have banished all avian elements from my wardrobe. No more birds."

"We shall name our firstborn Apollo Horatius Wardley Bales," he said.

"I like Lucretia Frances. Or Apollonia."

"We shall keep producing children until we run out of names. My scandalous bluestocking."

"Lord Daring," she said affectionately. "My rake."

"Reformed rake, my Lady Daring," he reminded her, and she turned her face up for his kiss.

Shortly after the ship bearing the Marquess of Langford and the household of his newlywed son departed Portsmouth, a new vessel nosed into port bearing cotton, spices, and tea from India. From it descended a tall, black-haired officer with a rugged look to him that could not be traced to any dishevelment of his person.

His uniform was neat, his boots polished, his face closely shaved, his sleek black hair pulled back in a queue. But his luggage was exceedingly light for a man who laid claim to being a gentleman, and there was no overabundance of coin in his pocket, save those that had been given him to transport and guard the Indian boys in his care, the sons of Tipu Sultan and their servants, hostages and surety that the King of Mysore would adhere to the recent treaty.

The soldier's bright blue eyes, a distinct color shared by certain members of his family, were shadowed with a careful blankness as of veiled secrets. The sallow undertone of his complexion suggested that, for all that he had been in tropical climes, he had not been exposed to much sunlight of late. He paused on the wharf and turned his face to the sky, as if he had not set foot in his homeland for some time.

His name met with surprise from the official holding the shipping manifest, who divulged that a family with that name had sailed just that morning.

"I shall be sorry to miss them, if that's the case," said the stranger.

"Ye know 'em, major?" the officer asked, noting his officer's insignia.

"After a fashion," the major replied.

Major Lord Lucien Bales, Earl of Aldthorpe, would be surprised to discover he was a dead man.

His family would be more surprised that he wasn't.

ABOUT THE AUTHOR

Misty Urban fell in love with stories at an early age and has spent her life among books as a teacher, scholar, editor, writer, and bookseller. Her favorite stories take you new places, teach you new things, and end with a win. She especially likes romances about unconventional heroines who defy the odds and the unexpected heroes who woo them, so that's mostly what she writes. When she puts down the book she likes to take long walks, drag her family to new places, or hang out around water, dreaming up new stories.

Visit her at mistyurban.com
Join author's newsletter

ALSO BY MISTY URBAN

Ladies Least Likely

Viscount Overboard

The Forger and the Duke

The Painter Takes an Earl

The Mad Baron's Bride

Marry Me, Marquess

My Lady Melisende

The Knight Falls First

Lady Daring

Tell Me Sweet

Contemporary Novels

My Day As Regan Forrester

My Thing with Timothy Kay

A small press bound by the belief that every voice matters.

Sign up for our newsletter to learn about new releases and more.
https://oliver-heberbooks.com/subscribe/

Follow us on social media:

facebook.com/oliverheberbooks

instagram.com/oliverheberbooks

amazon.com/oliverheberbooks

youtube.com/@OliverHeberBooksPublisher

www.ingramcontent.com/pod-product-compliance
Lightning Source LLC
Chambersburg PA
CBHW020351010826
48973CB00005B/1360